S0-BYN-669

SAILING TO UTOPIA

MICHAEL MOORCOCK

Sailing To Utopia
by Michael Moorcock

Cover Illustration by Rick Berry
Interior Illustrations by Rick Berry
Jacket and Book Design by **Michelle Prahler**
3D Jacket Background by Henry Gordon Higgenbothem
Art Direction by **Richard Thomas**

Published by:
White Wolf Inc.
735 Park North Blvd. Suite 128
Clarkston, Georgia 30021

www.white-wolf.com

BY THE SAME AUTHOR

THE TALE OF THE ETERNAL CHAMPION
Special Editor: John Davey
New Omnibus Editions, revised and with new introductions by the author

1. The Eternal Champion
2. Von Bek
3. Hawkmoon
4. A Nomad of the Time Streams
5. Elric: Song of the Black Sword
6. The Roads Between the Worlds
7. Corum: The Coming of Chaos

8. Sailing to Utopia
9. Kane of Old Mars
10. The Dancers at the End of Time
11. Elric: The Stealer of Souls
12. The Prince with the Silver Hand
13. Legends from the End of Time
14. Earl Aubec
15. Count Brass

Other novels

Gloriana; or, The Unfulfill'd Queen
The Brothel in Rosenstrasse
Mother London
Blood (Morrow)
Fabulous Harbours (forthcoming, Morrow)
The War Amongst the Angels (forthcoming, Morrow)
Karl Glogauer novels
Behold the Man
The Vengeance of Rome (in preparation)

Breakfast in the Ruins
Cornelius novels
The Cornelius Chronicles (Avon)
A Cornelius Calendar
Colonel Pyat novels
Byzantium Endures
The Laughter of Carthage
Jerusalem Commands

Short stories and graphic novels

Casablanca
Lunching with the Antichrist (Mark Ziesing)
The Swords of Heaven, The Flowers of Hell (with Howard V. Chaykin)

The Crystal and the Amulet (with James Cawthorn)
Stormbringer (with P. Craig Russell, Topps, forthcoming)
etc.

Nonfiction

The Retreat from Liberty
Letters from Hollywood (illus. M. Foreman)

Wizardry and Wild Romance
Death Is No Obstacle (with Colin Greenland)
etc.

Editor

New Worlds
The Traps of Time
The Best of New Worlds
Best SF Stories from New Worlds

New Worlds: An Anthology
Before Armageddon
England Invaded
The Inner Landscape
The New Nature of the Catastrophe

Records

With THE DEEP FIX:
The New Worlds Fair (Griffin Records)
Dodgem Dude
The Brothel in Rosenstrasse etc.

With HAWKWIND:
Warrior on the Edge of Time
Sonic Attack
Zones
Out and Intake
Live Chronicles (Griffin Records, USA) etc.

Also work with Blue Oyster Cult,
Robert Calvert, etc.

SAILING TO UTOPIA

C O N T E N T S

INTRODUCTION

Dear Reader,

With the exception of *The Ice Schooner*, all the stories here are a result of a collaboration of some kind and are, indeed, amongst the few collaborations I have produced. *The Black Corridor* used material supplied by Hilary Bailey, *Flux* was written with Barrington Bayley and *The Distant Suns* with Jim Cawthorn. All the stories owe their existence to the editors who commissioned them — to Keith Roberts, editor of SCIENCE FANTASY magazine, for *The Ice Schooner*, to Terry Carr, editor of the Ace "Specials", for *The Black Corridor*, to the late E. J. Carnell, editor of NEW WORLDS, for *Flux*, and to the ex-editor of THE ILLUSTRATED WEEKLY OF INDIA for *The Distant Suns*.

If they have anything in common it is, I suppose, that they show how ecological issues were as important to the writers of the 1960s as they are to today's public. Most of the terms developed to describe these issues entered our vocabularies via SF magazines, either in fiction or non-fiction. Since the 1950s British SF in particular, exemplified by Brian W. Aldiss and J.G. Ballard, has been obsessed with environmental change and in examining the moral and physical implications of our affect on the planet.

While I make no claims at all for any kind of mediumship, it is remarkable how science fiction — especially the literary SF identified with the so-called New Wave — has been able to predict and examine crucial issues long before they become the stuff of newspaper articles and TV features. Indeed it can be argued that the writers most successfully identifying our current problems are those who weren't interested in the kind of prediction offered by "hard" SF but whose attention was largely given to environmental, social and psychological issues. The work of Philip K. Dick, for instance, seems increasingly to describe our present world, while the world of Heinlein becomes more than ever divorced from contemporary realities.

One of the most observant and witty writers of SF since the 1950s is Robert Sheckley who, with the likes of Dick and Alfred Bester, gave us some of the very best SF to come out of America and who continue to inspire new generations. Growing up in the 1950s, not very familiar with Murdoch, Lessing or Angus Wilson and not much interested in the personal discomforts of the Angry Young Men who, while they failed entirely to confront any of the issues they raised, succeeded dramatically in lowering the tone and the aspirations of the modern novel, I was extremely grateful to the likes of Dick, Bester and Sheckley. They had more relevance to my experience, more energy, imagination and intelligence and were better at their craft than any three dozen of the self-involved chaps whose petulant portraits turned up so regularly in the morning Press. Baffled by what literary editors seemed to consider excellence, I was an impatient and eclectic reader looking for fiction that reflected something other than the personal concerns with sex and power of a group of xenophobic and disturbed young Englishmen. Dick, Bester and Sheckley wrote about sex and power, among other things, but not their own parochial concerns. Without seeming old-fashioned they gave me much of the substance I had learned to demand from the Victorian novel.

Dick and Bester died too soon. Happily Sheckley is still very much with us and remains one of the subtlest of SF ironists. So, with apologies for the quality (but just look at the width!) and with thanks for our years of friendship in which we discovered that we love the world and despair of it in pretty much the same way, I dedicate this book to Bob Sheckley, who helped me out of a gutter.

Yours,
Michael Moorcock

THE ICE SCHOONER

For Keith Roberts — master steersman

SAILING TO UTOPIA

CHAPTER ONE

KONRAD ARFLANE

When Konrad Arflane found himself without an ice ship to command, he left the city-crevasse of Brershill and set off on skis across the great ice plateau; he went with the intention of deciding whether he should live or die.

In order to allow himself no compromise, he took a small supply of food and equipment, reckoning that if he had not made up his mind within eight days he would die anyway of starvation and exposure.

As he saw it, his reason for doing this was a good one. Although only thirty-five and one of the best-known skippers on the plateau, he had little chance of obtaining a new captaincy in Brershill and refused to consider serving as a first or second officer under another master even if it were possible to get such a berth. Only fifteen years before, Brershill had had a fleet of over fifty ships. Now she had twenty-three. While he was not a morbid man, Arflane had decided that there was only one alternative to taking a command with some foreign city, and that was to die.

So he set off, heading south across the plateau. There would be few ships in that direction and little to disturb him.

Arflane was a tall, heavy man with a full, red beard that sparkled with rime. He was dressed in the black fur of the seal and the white fur of the bear. To protect his head from the cut of the cold wind he wore a thick bearskin hood; to protect his eyes from the reflected glare of the sun on the ice, he wore a visor of thin cloth stretched on a sealbone frame. At his hip he had a short cutlass in a sealskin scabbard, and in either hand he held eight-foot harpoons, which served him both as weapons and as ski-poles. His skis were long strips cut from the bone of the great land whale. On these he was able to make good speed and soon found himself well beyond the normal shipping routes.

As his distant ancestors had been men of the sea, Konrad Arflane was a man of the ice. He had the same solitary habits, the same air of self-sufficiency, the same distant expression in his grey eyes. The only great difference between Arflane and his ancestors was that they had been forced at times to desert the sea, whereas he was never away from the ice; for in these days it encircled the world.

As Arflane knew, at all points of the compass lay ice of one sort or another; cliffs of ice, plains of ice, valleys of ice and even, though he had only heard of them, whole cities of ice. Ice that constantly changed its colour as the sky changed colour; ice of pale blue, purple and ultramarine, ice of crimson, of yellow and emerald green. In summer crevasses, glaciers and grottoes were made even more beautiful by the deep, rich, glittering shades they reflected, and in winter the bleak ice mountains and plateaux possessed overpowering grandeur as they rose white, grey and black beneath the grim, snow-filled skies. At all seasons there was no scenery that was not ice in its many varieties and colourings and Arflane was deeply aware that the landscape would never change. There would be ice for eternity.

The great ice plateau, which was the territory best known to Arflane, occupied and entirely covered the part of the world once known as the Matto Grosso. The original mountains and valleys had long since been engulfed and the present plateau was several hundred miles in diameter, gradually sloping at its furthest points and joining with the rougher ice surrounding it. Arflane knew the plateau better than most men, for he had first sailed it with his father before his second birthday and had been master of a staysail schooner before he was twenty-one. His father had been called Konrad Arflane, as had all in the male line for hundreds of years, and they had been masters of ships. Only a few generations back, members of the Arflane family had owned several vessels.

The ice ships — trading vessels and hunting craft for th
— were sailing ships mounted on runners like giant skis v
them across the ice at speed. Centuries old, the ships were th
source of communication, sustenance and trade for the inh
the Eight Cities of the plateau. These settlements, situated i
below the level of the ice, owned sailing craft and their powe
on the size and quality of their fleets.

Arflane's home city, Brershill, had once been the most j
them all, but her fleet was diminishing rapidly and there
more masters than ships; for Friesgalt, always Brershill's gre
had risen to become the pre-eminent city of the plateau, di
terms of trade, monopolizing the hunting grounds, and buyi
Arflane's barquentine, ships from the men of other cities
unable to compete.

When he was six days out of Brershill and still undecide
fate, Konrad Arflane saw a dark object moving slowly towarc
the frozen white plain. He stopped and stared ahead,
distinguish the nature of the object. There was nothing b\
could judge its size. It could be anything from a wounded l
dragging itself on its huge, muscular flippers, to a wild dc
lost its way far from the warm ponds where it preyed on the

Arflane's normal expression was remote and insouciant,
moment there was a hint of curiosity in his eyes as he stoo
the object's slow progress. He considered what he should dc

Moody skies, immense, grey, and heavy with snow, rc
his head, blotting out the sun. Lifting his visor, Arflane pe
moving thing, wondering if he should approach it or ignore
not come out onto the ice to hunt, but if the thing were a
he could finish it and cut his mark on it he would become cor
rich and his future would be that much easier to decide.

Frowning, he dug his harpoons into the ice and pusl
forward on his skis. His muscles rolled beneath his fur jacl
pack on his back was jostled as he went skimming swiftly t
thing. His movements were economical, almost nervous.
forward on the skis, riding the ice with ease.

For a moment the red sun broke through the layers of

nd ice sparkled like diamonds from horizon to horizon. Arflane saw
hat it was a man who lay on the ice. Then the sun was obscured again.

Arflane felt resentful. A whale, or even a seal, could have been
illed and put to good use, but a man was of no use at all. What was
ven more annoying was that he had deliberately chosen this way so
hat he would avoid contact with men or ships.

Even as he sped across the silent ice towards the man, Arflane
onsidered ignoring him. The ethics of the icelands put him under no
bligation to help; he would feel no pang of conscience if he left the
nan to die. For some reason, though he was taciturn by nature, Arflane
ound himself continuing to approach. It was difficult to arouse his
uriosity, but, once aroused, it had to be satisfied. The presence of men
vas very rare in this region.

When he was close enough to be able to make out details of the
igure on the ice, he brought himself to a gradual halt and watched.

There was certainly little life left in the man. The exposed face,
eet and hands were purple with cold and covered with frostbite
wellings. Blood had frozen on the head and arms. One leg was
ompletely useless, either broken or numb. Inadequate tatters of rich
urs were tied around the body with strips of gut and leather; the head
vas bare and the grey hair shone with frost. This was an old man, but
he body, though wasted, was big, and the shoulders were wide. The
nan continued to crawl with extraordinary animal tenacity. The red,
half-blind eyes stared ahead; the great, gaunt skull, with its blue lips
rozen in a grin, rolled as the figure moved on elbows and belly over
he frozen plain. Arflane was unnoticed.

Konrad Arflane stared moodily at the figure for a moment, then
ne turned to go back. He felt an obscure admiration for the dying old
nan. He thought that it would be wrong to intrude on such a private
ordeal. He poised his harpoons, ready to push himself across the ice in
the direction from which he had come, but, hearing a sound behind
him, he glanced back and saw that the creature had collapsed and now
ay completely still on the white ice. It would not be long before he
lied.

On impulse, Arflane pushed himself around again and slid forward
on the skis until he was able to crouch beside the body. Laying down a
harpoon and steadying himself with the other, he grasped one of the

shoulders in his thickly gloved hand. The grip was gentle, vi
caress. "You are a determined old man," he murmured.

The great head moved so that Arflane could now see th
face beneath the ice-matted mane of hair. The eyes opened slov
were full of an introverted madness. The blue, swollen lips pa
a guttural sound came from the throat. Arflane looked broodir
the insane eyes for a moment; then he unslung his bulky p
opened it, taking out a flask of spirit. He clumsily removed
from the flask and put the neck to the puffy, twisted mouth, p
little of the spirit between the lips. The old man swallowed, c
and gasped, then, quite levelly, he said: "I feel as if I burn, y
impossible. Before you go, sir, tell me if it is far to Friesgalt…"

The eyes closed and the head dropped. Arflane looked
indecisively. He could tell, both from the remains of the cloth
from the accent, that the dying man was a Friesgaltian aristocr
had he come to be alone on the ice without retainers? Onc
Arflane considered leaving him to die. He had nothing to ga
trying to save him, he was as good as dead. Arflane had only cc
and hatred for the grand lords of Friesgalt, whose tall ice sc
these days dominated the frozen plains. Compared to the men
cities the Friesgaltian nobility was soft-living and godless. It
mocked the doctrine of the Ice Mother; it heated its houses to
it was often thriftless. It refused to make its women do the
manual work; it even gave some of them equality with men.

Arflane sighed and then frowned again, looking down at
aristocrat, judging him. He balanced his own prejudice and h
of self-preservation against his grudging admiration for th
tenacity and courage. If he were the survivor of a shipwre
plainly he had crawled many miles to get this far. A wreck c
the only explanation for his presence on the ice. Arflane mad
mind. He took a fur-lined sleeping sack from his pack, unrolle
spread it out. Walking clumsily on his skis, he went to the m
and got them into the neck of the sack and began to wrestle th
the body down into it until he could tie the sack's hood tightl
the man's head, leaving only the smallest aperture through w
could breathe. Then he shifted his pack so that it hung forwar
chest by its straps and hauled the sleeping sack onto his back t
muffled face was just above the level of his own broad shoulde

a pouch at his belt, he took two lengths of leather and strapped the fur-swathed old man in place. Then, with difficulty even for someone of his strength, he heaved on his harpoons and began the long ski trek to Friesgalt.

The wind was rising at his back. Above him it had cut the clouds into swirling grey streamers and revealed the sun, which threw the shadows of the clouds onto the ice. The ice seemed alive, like a racing tide, black in the shadow and red in the sunlight, sparkling like clear water. The plateau seemed infinite, having no projections, no landmarks, no indication of horizon save for the clouds which appeared to touch the ice far away. The sun was setting and he had only two hours or so in which to travel, for it was unwise to travel at night. He was heading towards the west, towards Friesgalt, chasing the great red globe as it sank. Light snow and tiny pieces of ice whirled over the plateau, moved, as he was moved, by the cold wind. Arflane's powerful arms pumped the tall harpoons up and down as he leaned forward, partly for speed, partly because of the burden on his back, his legs spread slightly on the tough whalebone skis.

He sped on, until the dusk faded into the darkness of night and the moon and stars could occasionally be seen through the thickening clouds. Then he slowed himself and stopped. The wind was falling, its sound now like a distant sigh; even that faded as Arflane removed the body from his back and the pack from his chest and pitched his tent, driving in the bone spikes at an angle to the ice.

When the tent was ready he got the old man inside it and started his heating unit; a precious possession but one which he mistrusted almost as much as naked fire, which he had seen only twice in his life. The unit was powered by small solar batteries, and Arflane, like everyone else, did not understand how it worked. Even the explanations in the old books meant nothing to him. The batteries were supposed to be almost everlasting, but good ones were becoming scarcer.

He prepared broth for them both, and with some more spirit from his flask revived the old man, loosening the thongs around the sack's neck.

The moon shone through the worn fabric of the tent and gave Arflane just enough light to work by.

The Friesgaltian coughed and groaned. Arflane felt him shudder.

"Do you want some broth?" Arflane asked him.

"A little, if you can spare it." The exhausted voice, still cont.
the traces of an earlier strength, had a puzzled note.

Arflane put a beaker of warm broth to the broken lips.
Friesgaltian swallowed and grunted. "Enough for the meantime; I tl
you." Arflane replaced the beaker on the heater and squatted in sile
for a while. It was the Friesgaltian who spoke first.

"How far are we from Friesgalt?"

"Not far. Perhaps ten hours' journey on skis. We could move ‹
while the moon is up, but I'm not following a properly mapped route.
shan't risk traveling until dawn."

"Of course. I had thought it was closer, but…" The old man coughec
again, weakly, and a thin sigh followed. "One misjudges distances easily.
I was lucky. You saved me. I am grateful. You are from Brershill, I can
tell by your accent. Why…?"

"I don't know," said Arflane.

Silence followed and Arflane prepared to lie down on the
groundsheet. The old man had his sleeping sack but it would not be
too cold if, against his normal instincts, he left the heating unit on.
The weak voice spoke again. "It is unusual for a man to travel the
unmapped ice alone, even in summer."

"True," Arflane replied.

After a pause, the Friesgaltian said hoarsely, evidently tiring: "I am
the Lord Pyotr Rorsefne. Most men would have left me to die on the
ice — even the men of my own city."

Arflane grunted impatiently.

"You are a generous man," added the principal Ship Lord of Friesgalt
before he slept at last.

"Possibly just a fool," said Arflane, shaking his head. He lay back
on the groundsheet, his hands behind his head. He pursed his lips for
a moment, frowning lightly. Then he smiled a little ironically. The smile
faded as he, too, fell asleep.

CHAPTER TWO

ULSENN'S WIFE

Scarcely more than eight hours after dawn Konrad Arflane sighted Friesgalt. Like all the Eight Cities it lay beneath the surface of the ice, carved into the faces of a wide natural crevasse almost a mile deep. Its main chambers and passages were hollowed from the rock that began several hundred feet below, though many of its storehouses and upper chambers had been cut from the ice itself. Little of Friesgalt was visible above the surface; the only feature to be seen clearly was the wall of ice blocks that surrounded the crevasse and protected the entrance to the city both from the elements and from human enemies.

It was, however, the field of high ships' masts that really indicated the city's location. At first sight it seemed that a forest sprouted from the ice, with every tree symmetrical and every branch straight and horizontal; a dense, still, even menacing forest that defied nature and seemed like an ancient geometrician's dream of ideally ordered landscape.

When he was close enough to make out more detail, Arflane saw that fifty or sixty good-sized ice ships lay anchored to the ice by means of mooring lines attached to bone spikes hammered into the hard surface. Their weathered fibreglass hulls were scarred by centuries of use and most of their accessories were not the original parts, but copies made from natural materials. Belaying pins had been carved from walrus ivory, booms had been fashioned of whalebone, and the rigging was a mixture of precious nylon, gut and strips of sealskin. Many of their runners were also fashioned of whalebone, as were the spars that joined them to the hulls.

The sails, like the hulls, were of the original synthetic material. There were great stocks of nylon sailcloth in every city; indeed, their very economy was heavily based on the amount of fabric existing in their storechambers. Every ship but one, which was preparing to get under way, had its sails tightly furled.

Twenty ships long and three deep, Friesgalt's docks were impressive. There were no new ships here. There was no means, in Arflane's world, of building new ones. All the ships were worn by age, but were nonetheless sturdy and powerful; and every ship had an individual line, partly due to the various embellishments made by generations of crews and skippers, partly because of the cuts of rigging favoured by different captains and owners.

The yards of the masts, the riggings, the decks and the surrounding ice were thick with working, fur-clad sailors, their breath white in the cold air. They were loading and unloading the vessels, making repairs and putting their craft in order. Stacks of baled pelts, barrels and boxes stood near the ships. Cargo booms jutted over the sides of the vessels, being used to winch the goods up to deck level and then swing over the hatches where they dropped the bales and barrels into the waiting hands of the men whose job it was to stow the cargo. Other cargoes were being piled on sledges that were either pulled by dogs or dragged by hand towards the city.

Beneath the lowering sky, from which a little light snow fluttered, dogs barked, men shouted, and the indefinable smell of shipping mingled with the more easily distinguished smells of oil and skins and whale flesh.

Some distance off along the line a whaler was crewing up. The whaling men generally kept themselves apart from other sailors, disdaining their company, and the crews of the trading vessels were relieved that they did so; for both the North Ice and the South Ice whalers were more than boisterous in their methods of entertaining themselves. They were nearly all large men, swaggering along with their ten-foot harpoons on their shoulders, careless of where they swung them. They wore full, thick beards; their hair was also thick and much longer than the norm. It was often, like their beards, plaited, fashioned into strange barbaric styles, and held in place by whale grease. Their furs were rich, of a kind normally worn only by aristocrats, for whale men could afford anything they pleased to purchase if they were successful; but the furs were stained and worn casually. Arflane had been a whaling skipper through much of his career, and felt a comradeship for these coarse-voiced North Ice whaling men as they swung aboard their ship.

Aside from the few whalers, which were mainly three-masted barques or barquentines, there were all kinds of boats and ships on the oil-slippery ice. There were the little yachts and ketches used for work around the dock, and brigs, brigantines, two-mast two-topsail schooners, cutters and sloops. Most of the trading ships were three-mast square-rigged ships, but there was a fair scattering of two-mast brigs and two-mast schooners. Their colours for the most part were dull weather-beaten browns, blacks, greens.

The hunting ships of the whaling men were invariably black-hulled, stained by the blood of generations of slaughtered land whales.

Arflane could now make out the names of the nearer craft. He recognized most of them without needing to read the characters carved into their sides. A heavy three-master, the *Land Whale*, was nearest him; it was from the city of Djobhabn, southernmost of the Eight, and had a strong resemblance to the one-time sea mammal which, many centuries earlier, had left the oceans as the ice had gradually covered them, returning once again to the land it had left in favour of the sea. The *Land Whale* was heavy and powerful, with a broad prow that tapered gradually towards the stern. Her runners were short and she squatted on them, close to the ice.

A two-masted brig, the *Heurfrast*, named for the Ice Mother's mythical son, lay nearby, unloading a cargo of sealskins and bear pelts, evidently just back from a successful hunting expedition. Another two-master — a brigantine — was taking on tubs of whale oil, preparatory, Arflane guessed, to making a trading voyage among the other cities; this was the *Good Wind*, christened in the hope that the name would bring luck to the ship. Arflane knew her for an unreliable vessel, ironically subject to getting herself becalmed at crucial times; she had had many owners. Other two-masted brigs and two- or three-masted schooners, as well as barques, were there, and Arflane knew every ship by its name; he could see the barquentine *Katarina Ulsenn* and its sister ships, the *Nastasya Ulsenn* and the *Ingrid Ulsenn*, all owned by the powerful Ulsenn family of Friesgalt and named after Ulsenn matrons. There was the Brershillian square-rigger, the *Leaper*, and another three-master from Brershill, the slender hunting barque *Bear Scenter*. Two trading brigs, small and bulky, were from Chaddersgalt, the city closest to Brershill, and others were from Djobhabn, Abersgalt, Fyorsgep and Keltshill, the rest of the Eight Cities.

The whale-hunting craft lay away from the main gathering of ships. They were battered-looking vessels, with a spirit of pride and defiance about them. Traditionally, whaling ships were called by paradoxical names, and Arflane recognized whalers called *Sweet Girl*, *Truelove*, *Smiling Lady*, *Gentle Touch*, *Soft Heart*, *Kindness* and similar names, while others were called *Good Fortune*, *Hopeful*, *Lucky Lance* and the like. From them came the reek of their trade: blood and animal flesh.

Also to one side, but at the other end of the line to the whaling ships, stood the ice clippers, their masts towering well above those of all the surrounding craft, their whole appearance one of cruel arrogance. These were the fast-running, slim-prowed and stately queens of the plateau that, at their best, could travel at more than twice the speed of any other ship. Their hulls, supported on slender runners, dwarfed everything nearby, and from their decks one could look down on the poop of any other ship.

Tallest and most graceful of all these four-masted clippers was the principal ship of the Friesgaltian fleet, the *Ice Spirit*, with her sails trimly furled and every inch of her gleaming with polished bone, fibreglass, soft gold, silver, copper and even iron. An elegant craft, with very clean lines, she would have surprised her ancient designer if he could have seen her now, for she bore embellishments.

Her bow, bowsprit and forecastle were decorated with the huge elongated skulls of the adapted sperm whale. The beaklike mouths bristled with savage teeth, grinning out disdainfully on the other shipping, witnesses to the skill, bravery and power of the ship's owners, the Rorsefne family. Though she was known as a schooner, the *Ice Spirit* was really a square-rigged barque in the old terminology of the sea. Originally all the big clippers had been fore-and-aft schooner-rigged, but this rig had been proven impracticable soon after ice navigation had become fully understood and square rig had been substituted; but the old name of schooner had stuck. The Rorsefne flag flew from above her royals; all four flags were large. Painted in black, white, gold and red by some half-barbaric artist, the Rorsefne standard showed the symbolic white hands of the Ice Mother, flanked by a bear and a whale, symbols of courage and vitality, while cupped in the hands was an ice ship. A grandiose flag, thought Arflane, hefting his near-dead burden on his back and skimming closer to the great concourse of craft.

As Arflane approached the ships, the schooner he had noticed preparing to leave let go its moorings and its huge sails bulged as the wind filled them. Only the mainsail and two forestay sails had been unfurled, enough to take the ship out slowly until it was clear of the others.

It turned into the wind and slid gracefully towards him on its great runners. He stopped and saluted cheerfully as the ship sailed by. It was the *Snow Girl* out of Brershill. The runners squealed on the smooth ice as the helmsman swung his wheel and steered a course between the few irregularities worn by the constant passage of ships. One or two of the sailors recognized him and waved back from where they hung in the rigging, but most were busy with the sails. Through the clear, freezing air, Arflane heard the voice of the skipper shouting his orders into a megaphone. Then the ship had passed him, letting down more sail and gathering speed.

Arflane felt a pang as he turned and watched the ship skim over the ice towards the east. It was a good craft, one he would be pleased to command. The wind caught more sail and the *Snow Girl* leaped suddenly, like an animal. Startled by the sudden burst of speed, the black and white snow-kites that had been circling above her squawked wildly and flapped upwards, before diving back to the main gathering of ships to drift expectantly above them or perch in the top trees in the hope of snatching titbits of whale meat or seal blubber from the carcasses being unloaded.

Arflane dug his lances deep into the ice and pushed his overloaded skis forward, sliding now between the lines and hulls of the ships, avoiding the curious sailors who glanced at him as they worked, and making his way towards the high wall of ice blocks sheltering the city-crevasse of Friesgalt.

At the main gate, which was barely large enough to let through a sledge, a guard stood squarely in the entrance, an arrow nocked to his ivory bow. The guard was a fair-haired youngster with his fur hood flung back from his head and an anxious expression on his face which made Arflane believe that the lad had only recently been appointed to guard the gate.

"You are not of Friesgalt and you are plainly not a trader from the ships," said the youth. "What do you want?"

"I carry your Lord Rorsefne on my back," said Arflane. "Where shall I take him?"

"The Lord Rorsefne!" The guard stepped forward, lowering his bow and pulling back the headpiece of the sleeping sack so that he could make out the face of Arflane's burden. "Are there no others? Is he dead?"

"Almost."

"They left months ago — on a secret expedition. Where did you find him?"

"A day's journey or so east of here." Arflane loosened the straps and began lowering the old man to the ice. "I'll leave him with you."

The young man looked hesitant and then said: "No — stay until my relief arrives. He is due now. You must tell all you know. They might want to send out a rescue party."

"I can't help them," Arflane said impatiently.

"Please stay — just to tell them exactly how you found him. It will be easier for me."

Arflane shrugged. "There is nothing to tell." He bent and began dragging the body inside the gate. "But I'll wait, if you like, until they give me back my sleeping sack."

Beyond the gate was a second wall of ice blocks, at chest height. Peering over it, Arflane saw the steep path that led down to the first level of the city. There were other levels at intervals, going down as far as the eye could see. On the far side of the crevasse Arflane made out some of the doorways and windows of the residential levels. Many of them were embellished with ornate carvings and bas-reliefs chiseled from the living rock. More elaborate than any cave-dwellings of millennia ago, these troglodytic chambers had from the outside much of the appearance of the first permanent shelters mankind's ancestors had possessed. The reversion to this mode of existence had been made necessary centuries earlier when it had become impossible to build surface houses as the temperature decreased and the level of the ice rose. The first crevasse-dwellers had shown forethought in anticipating the conditions to come and had built their living quarters as far below ground as possible in order to retain as much heat as they could. These same men had built the ice ships, knowing that, with the impossibility of sustaining supplies of fuel, these were the most practical form of transportation.

Arflane could now see the young guard's relief on the nearside ramp leading to the second level to the top. He was dressed in white bearskins and armed with a bow and a quiver of arrows. He toiled up the slope in the spiked boots that it was best to wear when ascending or descending the levels, for there was only a single leather rope to stop a man from falling off the comparatively narrow ramp into the gorge.

When the relief came the young guard explained what had happened. The relief, an old man with an expressionless face, nodded and went to take up his position on the gate.

Arflane squatted and unlaced his skis while the young guard fetched him a pair of spiked boots. When Arflane had got these on, they lifted the faintly stirring bundle between them and began carefully to descend the ramp.

The light from the surface grew fainter as they descended, passing a number of men and women busy with trade goods being taken to the surface and supplies of food and hides being brought down. Some of the people realized the identity of the Lord Rorsefne. Arflane and the guard refused to answer their incredulous and anxious questions but stumbled on into the ever-increasing darkness.

It took a long time to get the Lord Rorsefne to a level lying midway on the face of the crevasse. The level was lighted dimly by bulbs powered by the same source that heated the residential sections of the cavern city. This source lay at the very bottom of the crevasse and was regarded, even by the myth-mocking Friesgaltian aristocracy, with superstition. To the ice-dwellers, cold was the natural condition of everything and heat was an evil necessity for their survival, but it did not make it any the less unnatural. In the Ice Mother's land there was no heat and none was needed to sustain the eternal life of all those who joined Her when they died and became cold. Heat could destroy the ice, and this was sure proof of its evil. Down at the bottom of the crevasse, the heat, it was rumoured, reached an impossible temperature and it was here that those who had offended the Ice Mother went in spirit after they had died.

The Lord Rorsefne's family inhabited a whole level of the city on both sides of the crevasse. A bridge spanned the gorge and the two men had to cross it to reach the main chambers of the Rorsefne household. The bridge, made of hide, swayed and sagged as they crossed. Waiting for them on the other side was a square-faced middle-aged man in the yellow indoor livery of the Rorsefnes.

"What have you got there?" he asked impatiently, thinking that Arflane and the guard were traders trying to sell something.

"Your master," Arflane said with a slight smile. He had the satisfaction of seeing the servant's face fall as he recognized the half-hidden features of the man in the sleeping sack.

Hurriedly, the servant helped them through a low door which had the Rorsefne arms carved into the rock above it. They went through two more doors before reaching the entrance hall.

The big hall was well lit by light tubes embedded in the wall. It was overheated also, and Arflane began to sweat in mental and physical discomfort. He pushed back his hood and loosened the thongs of his coat. The hall was richly furnished; Arflane had seen nothing like it. Painted hangings of the softest leather covered the rock walls; and even here, in the entrance hall, there were chairs made of wood, some with upholstery of real cloth. Arflane had only seen sailcloth and one wooden artifact in his life. Leather, no matter how finely it could be tanned, was never so delicate as the silk and linen he looked at now. It was hundreds of years old, preserved in the cold of the storechambers, no doubt, and must date back to a time before his ancestors had come to live in the ravines of the south, when there was still vegetation on the land and not just in the warm ponds and the ocean of blasphemous legend. Arflane knew that the world, like the stars and the moon, was comprised almost wholly of ice and that one day at the will of the Ice Mother even the warm ponds and the rock-caverns that sustained animal and human life would be turned into the ice which was the natural state of all matter.

The yellow-clad servant had disappeared but now returned with a man almost as tall as Arflane. He was thin-faced, with pursed lips and pale blue eyes. His skin was white, as if it had never been exposed above ground, and he wore a wine-red jacket and tight black trousers of soft leather. His clothing seemed effete to Arflane.

He stopped near the unconscious body of Rorsefne and looked down at it thoughtfully; and then he raised his head and glanced distastefully at Arflane and the guard.

"Very well," he said. "You may go."

The man could not help his voice — perhaps not his tone either — but both irritated Arflane. He turned to leave. He had expected, without desiring it, at least some formal statement of thanks.

"Not you, stranger," said the tall man. "I meant the guard."

The guard left and Arflane watched the servants carry the old man away. He said: "I'd like my sleeping sack back later," then looked into the face of the tall man.

"How is the Lord Rorsefne?" said the other distantly.

"Dying, perhaps. Another would be — but he could live. He'll lose some fingers and toes at the very least."

Expressionlessly, the other man nodded. "I am Janek Ulsenn," he said, "the Lord Rorsefne's son-in-law. Naturally we are grateful to you. How did you find the lord?"

Arflane explained briefly.

Ulsenn frowned. "He told you nothing else?"

"It's a marvel he had the strength to tell me as much." Arflane could have liked the old man, but he knew he could never like Ulsenn.

"Indeed?" Ulsenn thought for a moment. "Well, I will see you have your reward. A thousand good bearskins should satisfy you, eh?"

It was a fortune.

"I helped the old man because I admired his courage," Arflane said brusquely. "I do not want your skins."

Ulsenn seemed momentarily surprised. "What *do* you want? I see you're," he paused, "from another city. You are not a nobleman. What...?" He was plainly puzzled. "It is unheard of that a man — without a code — would bother to do what you did. Even one of us would hesitate to save a stranger." His final sentence held a note of belligerence, as if he resented the idea of a foreigner and commoner making the gesture Arflane had made, as if selfless action were the prerogative of the rich and powerful.

Arflane shrugged. "I liked the old man's courage." He made to leave, but as he did so a door opened on his right and a black-haired woman wearing a heavy dress of fawn and blue entered the hall. Her pale face was long and firm-jawed, and she walked with natural grace. Her hair flowed over her shoulders, and she had gold-flecked brown eyes. She glanced at Ulsenn with a slight interrogatory frown.

Arflane inclined his head slightly and reached for the door handle.

The woman's voice was soft, perhaps a trifle hesitant. "Are you the man who saved my father's life?"

Unwillingly, Arflane turned back and stood facing her with his legs spread apart as if on the deck of a ship. "I am, madam — if he survives," he said shortly.

"This is my wife," said Ulsenn with equally poor grace. "The Lady Ulrica."

She smiled pleasantly. "He wanted me to thank you and wants to express his gratitude himself when he feels stronger. He would like you to stay here until then — as his guest."

Arflane had not looked directly at her until now and when he raised his head to stare for a moment into her golden eyes she appeared to give a faint start, but at once was composed again.

"Thank you," he said, looking with some amusement in Ulsenn's direction, "but your husband might not feel so hospitable."

Ulsenn's wife gave her husband a glance of vexed surprise. Either she was genuinely upset by Ulsenn's treatment of Arflane, or she was acting for Arflane's benefit. If she were acting, Arflane was still at a loss to understand her motives; for all he knew, she was merely using this opportunity to embarrass her husband in front of a stranger of lower rank than himself.

Ulsenn sighed. "Nonsense. He must stay if your father desires it. The Lord Rorsefne, after all, is head of the house. I'll have Onvald bring him something."

"Perhaps our guest would prefer to eat with us," she said sharply. There was definitely animosity between the two.

"Ah, yes," muttered Ulsenn bleakly.

Wearying of this, Arflane said with as much politeness as he could muster: "With your permission I'll eat at a traders' lodging and rest there, too. I have heard you have a good travelers' hostel on the sixteenth level." The guard had told him that as they had passed the place earlier.

She said quietly, "Please stay with us. After what —"

Arflane bowed and again looked directly at her, trying to judge her sincerity. This woman was not of the same stuff as her husband, he decided. She resembled her father in features to some extent and he thought he saw the qualities in her that he had admired in the old man; but he would not stay now.

She avoided his glance. "Very well. What name shall be asked at the travelers' lodging?"

"Captain Konrad Arflane," he said gruffly, as if reluctantly confiding a secret, "of Brershill. Ice Mother protect you."

Then, with a curt nod to them both, he left the hall, passing through the triple doors and slamming the last heavily and fiercely behind him.

CHAPTER THREE

THE ICE SPIRIT

Against his normal instincts, Konrad Arflane decided to wait in Friesgalt until the old man could talk to him. He was not sure why he waited; if asked, he would have said it was because he did not want to lose a good sleeping sack and besides, he had nothing better to do. He would not have admitted that it was Ulrica Ulsenn who kept him in the city.

He spent most of his time wandering around on the surface among the big ships. He deliberately did not call at the Rorsefne household, being too stubborn. He waited for them to contact him.

In spite of his strong dislike of the man, Arflane thought he understood Janek Ulsenn better than other Friesgaltians he had encountered. Ulsenn was not typical of the modern aristocracy of Friesgalt, who belittled the rigid and haughty code of their ancestors. In the other poorer cities the old traditions were still respected, though the merchant princes there had never had the power of families like the Rorsefnes and Ulsenns. Arflane could admire Ulsenn at least for refusing to soften his attitudes. In that respect he and Ulsenn had something in common. Arflane hated the signs of gradual change in his environment that he had half-consciously noted. Thinking was looser; the softening of the harsh but sensible laws of survival in the icelands was even illustrated by his own recent action in helping the old man. Only disaster could come of this trend towards decadence and more like Ulsenn were needed in positions of influence where they could stop the gradual rejection of traditional social behaviour, traditional religion and traditional thinking. There was no other way to ensure their ability to stay alive in an environment where animal life was not meant to exist. Let the rot set in, Arflane thought, and the Ice Mother would lose no time in sweeping away the last surviving members of the race.

It was a sign of the times that Arflane had become something of a hero in the city. A century earlier they would have sneered at his weakness. Now they congratulated him and he in turn despised them, understanding that they patronized him as they might have honoured a brave animal, that they had contempt for his values and, indeed, his very poverty. He wandered alone, his face stern, his manner surly, avoiding everyone and knowing without caring that he was reinforcing their opinion that all not of Friesgalt were uncouth and barbaric.

On the third day of his stay he went to look, with grudging admiration, at the *Ice Spirit*.

As he came up to the ship, ducking under her taut mooring lines, someone shouted down at him.

"Captain Arflane!"

He looked up reluctantly. A fair, bearded face peered over the rail. "Would you like to come aboard and look around the ship, sir?"

Arflane shook his head; but a leather ladder was already bouncing down the side, its bottom striking the ice near his feet. He frowned, desiring no unnecessary involvement with the Friesgaltians, but deeply curious to set foot on the deck of a vessel that was almost a myth in the icelands.

He made up his mind quickly, grasped the ladder and began to climb towards the ivory-inlaid rail far above.

Swinging his leg over the rail, he was greeted with a smile by the bearded man, dressed in a rich jerkin of white bear cub's fur and tight, grey sealskin trousers, almost a uniform among Friesgaltian ships' officers.

"I thought you might like to inspect the ship, captain, as a fellow sailor." The man's smile was frank and his tone did not have the hint of condescension Arflane half expected. "My name's Petchnyoff, second officer of the *Ice Spirit*." He was a comparatively young man for a second officer. His beard and hair were soft and blond, tending to give him a foolish look, but his voice was strong and steady. "Can I show you around?"

"Thanks," said Arflane. "Shouldn't you ask your captain first?" He, when commanding his own ship, was firm about such courtesies.

Petchnyoff smiled. "The *Ice Spirit* has no captain, as such. She's captained by the Lord Rorsefne under normal conditions, or by someone he has appointed when he's unable to be aboard. In your case, I'm sure he'd want me to show you over the ship."

Arflane disapproved of this system, which he had heard about; in his opinion a ship should have a permanent captain, a man who spent most of his life aboard her. It was the only way to get the full feel of a ship and learn what she could do and what she could not.

The ship had three decks, main, middle and poop, each of diminishing area, with the two upper decks aft of them as they stood there. The decks were of pitted fibreglass, like the hull, and spread with ground-up bone to give the feet better purchase. Most of the ship's superstructure was of the same fibreglass, worn, scratched and battered from countless voyages over countless years. Some doors and hatch-covers had been replaced by facsimiles fashioned of large pieces of ivory glued together and carved elaborately in contrast to the unadorned fibreglass. The ivory was yellowed and old in many places and looked almost as ancient as the originals. Lines — a mixture of nylon, gut and leather — stretched from the rails into the top trees.

Arflane looked up, getting the best impression of the ship's size he had had yet. The masts were so high they seemed almost to disappear from sight. The ship was well kept, he noted, with every yard and inch of rigging so straight and true that he would not have been surprised to have seen men crawling about in the top trees, measuring the angle of the gaffs. The sails were furled tight, with every fold of identical depth; and Arflane saw that the ivory booms, too, were carved with intricate pictorial designs. This was a show ship and he was filled with resentment that she was so rarely sailed on a working trip.

Petchnyoff stood patiently at his side, looking up also. The light had turned grey and cold, giving an unreal quality to the day.

"It'll snow soon," said the second officer.

Arflane nodded. He liked nothing better than a snowstorm. "She's very tidily kept," he said.

Petchnyoff noted his tone and grinned. "Too tidy, you think. You could be right. We have to keep the crew occupied. We get precious little chance of sailing her, particularly since the Lord Rorsefne's been away." He led Arflane towards an ivory door let into the side of the middle deck. "I'll show you below first."

The cabin they entered held two bunks and was more luxuriously furnished than any cabin Arflane had seen. There were heavy chests, furs, a table of whalebone and chairs of skins slung on bone frames. A door led off this into a narrow companionway.

"These are the cabins of the captain and any guests he happens to have with him," Petchnyoff explained, pointing out doors as they passed them. "The cabin we came through was mine. I share it with the third officer, Kristoff Hinsen. He's on duty, but he wants to meet you."

Petchnyoff showed Arflane the vast holds of the ship. They seemed to go on forever. Arflane began to think that he was lost in a maze the size of a city, the ship was so big. The crew's quarters were clean and spacious. They were under-occupied since only a skeleton crew was aboard, primarily to keep the ship looking at her best and ready to sail at the whim of her owner-captain. Most of the ship's ports were of the original thick, unbreakable glass. As he went by one, Arflane noticed that it was darker outside and that snow was falling in great sheets onto the ice, limiting visibility to a few yards.

Arflane could not help being impressed by the capacity of the ship and envied Petchnyoff his command. If Brershill had one vessel like this, he thought, the city would work her to good advantage and soon regain her status. Perhaps he should be thankful that the Friesgaltians did not make better use of her, otherwise they might have captured an even bigger portion of the trade.

They climbed up eventually to the poop deck. It was occupied by an old man who appeared not to notice them. He was staring intently at the dimly seen wheel positioned below on the middle deck. It had been lashed fast so that the runners which it steered would not shift and strain the ship's moorings. Though the old man's eyes were focused on the wheel he seemed to be contemplating some inner thought. He

SAILING TO UTOPIA

turned as they joined him at the rail. His beard was white and he wore his coarse fur hood up, shadowing his eyes. He had his jerkin tightly laced and there were mittens on his hands. Snow had settled on his shoulders; the snow was still heavy, darkening the air and drifting through the rigging to heap itself on the decks. Arflane heard it pattering on the canvas high above.

"This is our third officer, Kristoff Hinsen," Petchnyoff said, slapping the old man's arm. "Meet the Lord Rorsefne's saviour, Kristoff."

Kristoff regarded Arflane thoughtfully. He had a face like an old snow-kite, with knowing beady black eyes and a hooked nose.

"You're Captain Arflane. You commanded the *North Wind*, eh?"

"I'm surprised you should know about that," Arflane replied. "I left her five years ago."

"Aye. Remember a ship you nosed into an ice break south of here? The *Tanya Ulsenn*?"

Arflane laughed. "I do. We were racing for a whale herd that had been sighted. The others dropped out until there was only us and the *Tanya*. It was a profitable trip once we'd put the *Tanya* into the ice break. Were you aboard her?"

"I was the captain. I lost my commission through your trick."

Arflane had acted according to the accepted code of the ice sailors, but he studied Kristoff's face for signs of resentment. There seemed to be none.

"They were better times for me," said Arflane.

"And for me," Kristoff said. He chuckled. "So our victories and defeats come to the same thing in the end. You've no ship to captain now — and I'm third officer aboard a fancy hussy who lies in bed all day."

"She should sail," Arflane said, looking around him. "She's worth ten of any other ship."

"The day this old whore sails on a working trip — that's the day the world will end!" Kristoff kicked at the deck in disgust. "I tried your tactic once, you know, Captain Arflane, when I was second officer aboard the *Heurfrast*. The captain was hurt — tangled up in a harpoon line of all things — and I was in command. You know that old hunter, the *Heurfrast*?"

Arflane nodded.

"Well, she's hard to handle until you get the feel of her and then she's easy. It was a year or so later when we were racing two brigs from Abersgalt. One overturned in our path and we had to go round her, which gave the other a good start on us. We managed to get up behind her and then we saw this ice break ahead. I decided to try nosing her in."

"What happened?" Arflane asked, smiling.

"We *both* went in — I didn't have your sense of timing. For that, they pensioned me off on this petrified cow-whale. I realize now that your trick was harder than I thought."

"I was lucky," Arflane said.

"But you'd used that tactic before — and since. You were a good captain. We Friesgaltians don't usually admit there are any better sailors than our own."

"Thanks," said Arflane, unable to resist the old man's flattery and beginning to feel more comfortable now that he was in the company of men of his own trade. "You nearly pulled yourself out of my trap, I remember."

"Nearly," Hinsen sighed. "The sailing isn't what it was, Captain Arflane."

Arflane grunted agreement.

Petchnyoff smiled and pulled up his hood against the weather. The snow fell so thickly that it was impossible to make out more than the faint outlines of the nearer ships.

Standing there in relaxed silence, Arflane fancied that they could be the only three men in all the world; for everything was still beneath the falling snow that muffled any sound.

"We'll see less of this weather as time goes on," said Petchnyoff thankfully. "Snow comes only once in ten or fifteen days now. My father remembers it falling so often it seemed to last the whole summer. And the winds were harsher in the winter too."

Hinsen dusted snow off his jerkin. "You're right, lad. The world has changed since I was young — she's warming up. In a few generations we'll be skipping about on the surface naked." He laughed at his own joke.

Arflane felt uneasy. He did not want to spoil the pleasant mood, but he had to speak. "Not talk the Ice Mother should hear, friends," he said awkwardly. "Besides, what you say is untrue. The climate alters a little one way or another from year to year, but over a lifetime it grows steadily colder. That must be so. The world is dying."

"So our ancestors thought, and symbolized their ideas in the creed of the Ice Mother," Petchnyoff said, smiling. "But what if there were no Ice Mother? Suppose the sun were getting hotter and the world changing back to what it was before the ice came? What if the idea were true that this is only one of several ages when the ice has covered the world? Certain old books say as much, captain."

"I would call that blasphemous nonsense," Arflane said sharply. "You know yourself that those books contain many strange notions which we know to be false. The only book I believe is the Book of the Ice Mother. She came from the centre of the universe, bringing cleansing ice; one day Her purpose will be fulfilled and all will be ice, all will be purified. Read what you will into that, say that the Ice Mother does not exist — that Her story only represents the truth — but you must admit that even some of the old books said the same, that all heat must disappear."

Hinsen glanced at him sardonically. "There are signs that the old ideas are false," he murmured. "Followers of the Ice Mother say 'All must grow cold'; but you know that we have scholars in Friesgalt who make it their business to measure the weather. We got our power through their knowledge. The scholars say the level of the ice has dropped a few degrees in the last two or three years, and one day the sun will burn yellow-hot again and it will melt the ice away. They say that the sun is hotter already and the beasts move south, anticipating the change. They smell a new sort of life, Arflane. Life like the weed-plants we find in the warm ponds, but growing on land out of stuff that is like little bits of crumbled rock — out of earth. They believe that these must already exist somewhere — that they have always existed, perhaps on islands in the sea…"

"There is no *sea*!"

"The scholars think we could not have survived if there were not a sea somewhere, and these plants growing on islands."

"No!" Arflane turned his back on Hinsen.

"You say not? But reason says it is the truth."

"Reason?" Arflane sneered. "Or some twist of mind that passes for reason? There's no true logic in what you say. You only prattle a warped idea you would *rather* believe. Your kind of thinking will bring disaster to us all!"

Hinsen shook his head. "I see this as a fact, Captain Arflane — the ice is softening as we grow soft. Just as the beasts scent the new life, so do we — that is why our ideas are changing. I *desire* no change. I am only sorry, for I could love no other world than the one I know. I'll die in my own world, but what will our descendants miss? The wind, the snow, and the swift ice — the sight of a herd of whales speeding in flight before your fleet, the harpoon's leap, the fight under a red, round sun hanging frozen in the blue sky; the spout of black whale blood, brave as the men who let it... Where will all that be when the icelands become dirty, unfirm earth and brittle green? What will men become? All we love and admire will be belittled and then forgotten in that clogged, hot, unhealthy place. What a tangled, untidy world it will be. But it *will* be!"

Arflane slapped the rail, scattering the snow. "You are insane! How can all this change?"

"You could be right," Hinsen replied softly. "But what I see, sane or not, is what I see, straight and definite — inevitable."

"You'd deny every rule of nature?" Arflane asked mockingly. "Even a fool must admit that nothing becomes hot of its own accord after it has become cold. See what is about you, not what you *think* is here! I understand your reasoning. But it is soft reasoning, wishful reasoning. Death, Kristoff Hinsen, *death* is all that is inevitable! Once there was this dirt, this green, this life — I accept that. But it died. Does a man die, become cold, and then suddenly grow warm again, springing up saying 'I died, but now I live!'? Can't you see how your logic deceives you? Whether the Ice Mother is real or only a symbol of what is real, She must be honoured. Lose sight of that, as you in Friesgalt have done, and our people will die sooner than they need. You think me a superstitious barbarian, I know, for holding the views I hold — but there is good sense in what I say."

"I envy you for being able to stay so certain," Kristoff Hinsen said calmly.

"And I pity you for your unnecessary sorrow!"

Embarrassed, Petchnyoff took Arflane's arm. "Can I show you the rest of the ship, captain?"

"Thank you," said Arflane brusquely, "but I have seen all I want. She is a good ship. Don't let her rot, also."

His face troubled, Hinsen started to say something, but Arflane turned away. He left the poop and descended to the lower deck, clambered over the side, climbed down the ladder and marched back towards the underground city, his boots crunching in the snow.

CHAPTER FOUR

THE SHIPSMASHER HOSTEL

After his visit to the ice schooner Konrad Arflane became increasingly impatient with his wait in Friesgalt. He had still had no word from the Ulsenns about the old man's condition and he was disturbed by the atmosphere he found in the city. He had come to no decision regarding his own affairs; but he resolved to try to get a berth, even as a petty officer for the time being, on the next Brershill ship that came in.

He took to haunting the fringes of the great dock, avoiding contact with all the ships and in particular the *Ice Spirit*, and looking out for a Brershill craft.

On the fourth morning of his wait a three-masted barque was sighted. She was gliding in under full sail, flying a Brershill flag and traveling faster than was wise for a vessel so close to the dock. Arflane smiled as she came nearer, recognizing her as the *Tender Maiden*, a whaler skippered by his old friend Captain Jarhan Brenn. She seemed to be sailing straight for the part of the dock where ships were thickest, and the men working there began to scatter in panic, doubtless fearing that she was out of control. When she was only a short distance from the dock she turned smoothly and rapidly in a narrow arc, reefed sails and slid towards the far end of the line where other whaling vessels were already moored. Arflane began to run across the ice, his ridged boots giving him good purchase.

Panting, he reached the *Tender Maiden* just as she was throwing down her anchor ropes to the mooring hands who stood by with their spikes and mallets.

Arflane grinned a little as he seized the bone spikes and heavy iron mallet from a surprised mooring hand and began driving a spike into the ice. He reached out for a nearby line and tautened it, lashing it fast to the spike. The ship stirred for a moment, resisting the lines, and then was still.

From above him on the deck he heard someone laughing. Looking up, he saw that the ship's captain, Jarhan Brenn, was standing at the rail.

"Arflane! Are you down to working as a mooring hand? Where's your ship?"

Arflane shrugged and spread his hands ironically, then grabbed hold of the mooring line and began to swing himself up it until he was able to grasp the rail and climb over it to stand beside his old friend.

"No ship," he told Brenn. "She was given up to honour a bad debt of the owner's. Sold to a Friesgalt merchant."

Brenn nodded sympathetically. "Not the last, I'd guess. You should have stayed at the whaling. There's always work for us whalers, whatever happens. And you didn't even marry the woman in the end." He chuckled.

Brenn was referring to a time, six years since, when Arflane had taken a trading command as a favour to a girl he had wished to marry. It was only after he had done this that he had realized that he wanted no part of a girl who could demand such terms. By then it had been too late to get back his command of the whaler.

He smiled ruefully at Brenn and shrugged again. "With my poor luck, Brenn, I doubt I'd have sighted a whale in all these six years."

His friend was a short, stocky man, with a round, ruddy face and a fringe beard. He was dressed in heavy black fur, but his head and hands were bare. His greying hair was cropped close, for a whaler, but his rough, strong hands showed the calluses that only a harpoon could make. Brenn was respected as a skipper in both the South Ice and North

Ice hunting fields. Currently, by the look of his rig, he was hunting the North Ice.

"Poor luck isn't yours alone," Brenn grunted in disgust. "Our holds are just about empty. Two calves and an old cow are all we have aboard. We ran out of provisions and plan to trade our cargo for more supplies, then we'll try the South Ice and hope the hunting's better. Whales are getting hard to find in the north."

Brenn was unusual in that he hunted both south and north. Most whaling men preferred one type of field or the other (for their characteristics were very different) but Brenn did not mind.

"Aren't all the hunting fields poor this season?" Arflane asked. "I heard that even seal and bear are scarcer, and no walrus have been seen for two seasons."

Brenn pursed his lips. "The patch will pass, with the Ice Mother's help." He slapped Arflane's arm and began to move down the deck to supervise the unloading of the cargo from the central hold. The ship stank of whale blood and blubber. "Look at our catch," he said, as Arflane followed him. "There was no need for flenching. We just hauled 'em in and stowed 'em whole." Flenching was the whaling man's term for cutting up the whale. This was normally done on the ice, and then the pieces were winched aboard for stowing. If there had been no need to do this, then the catch must be small indeed.

Balancing himself by gripping a ratline, Arflane peered into the hold. It was dark, but he could make out the stiff bodies of two small calves and a cow-whale which did not look much bigger. He shook his head in sympathy. There was hardly enough there to re-provision the ship for the long haul to the South Ice. Brenn must be in a gloomier mood than he seemed.

Brenn shouted orders and his hands began to lower themselves into the hold as derricks were swung across and tackles dropped. The whaling men worked slowly and were plainly depressed. They had every reason to be in poor spirits, since the proceeds of a catch were always divided up at the end of a hunting voyage, and every man's share depended on the number and size of the whales caught. Brenn must have asked his crew to forgo its share in this small catch in the hope that the South Ice would yield a better one. Whaling men normally came into a dock with plenty of credit and they liked to spend it. Whalers with no credit were surly and quick-tempered. Arflane realized that Brenn would be aware of this and must be worrying how he would be able to control his crew during their stay in Friesgalt.

"Where are you berthing?" he asked quietly, watching as the first of the calves was swung up out of the hold. The dead calf had the marks of four or five harpoons in its hide. Its four great flippers, front and back, waved as it turned in the tackle. Like all young land whales, there was only sparse hair on its body. Land whales normally grew their full covering of wiry hair at maturity, after three years. As it was, this calf was twelve feet long and must have weighed only a few tons.

Brenn sighed. "Well, I've good credit at the Shipsmasher hostel. I always pay in a certain amount of my profit there every time we dock in Friesgalt. My men will be looked after all right, for a few days at least, and by that time we should be ready to sail again. It depends on the sort of bargain I can make with the merchants — and how soon I can make it. I'll be out looking for the best offer tomorrow."

The Shipsmasher, named, like all whaling men's hostels, after a famous whale, was not the best hostel in Friesgalt. It had claims, in fact, for being the worst. It was a "top-deck" hostel on the third level from the top, cut from ice and not from rock. Arflane realized that this was a bad time to ask his friend for a berth. Brenn must be cutting all possible corners to provision and re-equip his ship on the gamble that the South Ice would yield a better catch.

The derricks creaked as the calf was swung towards the side.

"We're getting 'em out as soon as possible," Brenn said. "There's a chance that someone will want the catch right away. The faster the better."

Brenn shouted to his first officer, a tall, thin man by the name of Olaf Bergsenn. "Take over, Olaf, I'm going to the Shipsmasher. Bring the men there when you're finished. You know who to put on watch."

Bergsenn's lugubrious face did not change expression as he nodded once and moved along the stained deck to supervise the unloading.

A gangplank had been lowered and Arflane and Brenn walked down it in short, jerky steps, watched by a knot of gloomy harpooners who lounged, harpoons across their shoulders, near the mainmast. It was a tradition that only the captain could leave the ship before the cargo had been unloaded.

When they got to the city wall, the guard recognized Arflane and let him and Brenn through. They began to descend the ramp. The ice of the ramp and the wall beside it was ingrained with powdered rock that had itself worn so it now resembled stone. The rope rail on the other side of the ramp also showed signs of constant wear. On the far wall of the crevasse, for some distance down, Arflane could see people moving up and down the ramps, or working on the ledges. At almost every level the chasm was criss-crossed by rope bridges, and some way up the crevasse, above their heads now, was the single permanent bridge, which was only used when especially needed.

As they stumbled down the ramps towards the third level Brenn smiled once or twice at Arflane, but was silent. Arflane wondered if he were intruding and asked his friend if he would like him to leave him at the Shipsmasher, but Brenn shook his head.

"I wouldn't miss a chance of seeing you, Arflane. Let me talk to Flatch, then we'll have a barrel of beer and I'll tell you all my troubles and listen to yours."

There were three whaling hostels on the third level. They walked past the first two — the King Herdarda and the Killer Pers — and came to the Shipsmasher. Like the other two, the Shipsmasher had a huge whale jawbone for a doorway and a small whale skull hanging as a sign outside.

They opened the battered door and walked straight into the hostel's main room.

It was dark, large and high-roofed, though it gave the impression of being cramped. Its walls were covered with crudely tanned whale hides. Faulty lighting strips flickered at odd places on ceiling and walls and the place smelled strongly of ale, whale meat and human sweat. Crude pictures of whales, whaling men and whaling ships were hung on the hides, as were harpoons, lances and the three-foot broadbladed cutlasses, similar to the one Arflane wore, that were used mainly for flenching. Some of the harpoons had been twisted into fantastic shapes, telling of the death-struggles of particular whales. None of these whaling tools was crossed, for the whale men regarded it as unlucky to cross harpoons or flenching cutlasses.

Groups of whaling men lounged at the closely packed tables, sitting on hard benches and drinking a beer that was brewed from one of the many kinds of weed found in the warm ponds. This ale was extremely bitter and few but whaling men would drink it.

Arflane and Brenn walked through the clusters of tables up to the small counter. Behind it, in a cubbyhole, sat a shadowy figure who rose as they approached.

Flatch, the owner of the Shipsmasher, had been a whaling man years before. He was taller than Arflane but almost unbelievably obese, with a great belly and enormously fat arm and leg. He had only one eye, one ear, one arm and one leg, as if a huge knife had been used to sheer off everything down one side of him. He had lost these various organs and limbs in an encounter with the whale called Shipsmasher, a huge bull that he had been the first to harpoon. The whale had been killed, but Flatch had been unable to carry on whaling and had bought the hostel out of his share of the proceeds. As a tribute to his kill he had named the hostel after it. As recompense he had used the whale's ivory to replace his arm and leg, and a triangle of its hide was used as a patch for his missing eye.

Flatch's remaining eye peered through the layers of fat surrounding it and he raised his whalebone arm in greeting.

"Captain Arflane. Captain Brenn." His voice was high and unpleasant, but at the same time barely audible, as if it was forced to travel up through all the fat around his throat. His many chins moved slightly as he spoke, but it was impossible to tell if he greeted them with any particular feeling.

"Good morning, Flatch," Brenn said cordially. "You'll remember the beer and provisions I've supplied you with all these past seasons?"

"I do, Captain Brenn."

"I've need of the credit for a few days. My men must be fed, boozed and whored here until I'm ready to sail for the South Ice. I've had bad luck in the north. I ask you only fair return for what I've invested, no more."

Flatch parted his fat lips and his jowls moved up and down. "You'll get it, Captain Brenn. Your help saw me through a bad time for two seasons. Your men will be looked after."

Brenn grinned, as if in relief. He seemed to have been expecting an argument. "I'll want a room for myself," he said. He turned to Arflane. "Where are you staying, Arflane?"

"I have a room in a hostel some levels down," Konrad Arflane told him.

"How many in your crew, captain?" Flatch asked.

Brenn told him, and answered the few other questions Flatch asked him. He began to relax more, glancing around the hostel's main room, looking at some of the pictures on the walls.

As he was finishing with Flatch a man got up from a nearby table and took several steps towards them before stopping and confronting them.

He cradled a long, heavy harpoon in one massive arm and the other hand was on his hip. His face, even in the poor, flickering light, could be seen to be red, mottled and ravaged by wind, sun and frostbite. It was a near-fleshless head and the bones jutted like the ribs of a ship. His nose was long and narrow, like the inverted prow of a clipper, and there was a deep scar under his right eye and another on his left cheek. His hair was black, piled and plaited on his head in a kind of coiled pyramid that broke at the top into two stiff pieces resembling the fins of a whale or a seal. This strange hairstyle was held in place by clotted blubber and its smell was strong. His furs were of fine quality, but matted with whale blood and blubber, smelling rancid; the jacket was open to the neck, revealing a whale-tooth necklace. From both earlobes were suspended pieces of flat, carved ivory. He wore boots of soft leather, drawn up to the knee and fastened against his fur breeches by means of bone pins. Around his waist was a broad belt, from which hung a scabbarded cutlass and a large pouch. He seemed a savage, even among whaling men, but he had a powerful presence, partially due to his narrow eyes, which were cold, glinting blue.

"You're sailing to the South Ice, did I hear you say, skipper?" His voice was deep and harsh. "To the south?"

"Aye." Brenn looked the man up and down. "And I'm fully crewed — or as fully crewed as I can afford."

The huge man nodded and moved his tongue inside his mouth before spitting into a spittoon near the counter.

The spittoon had been made from a whale's cranium. "I'm not asking for a berth, skipper. I'm my own man. Captains ask me to sail with them, not the other way about. I'm Urquart."

Arflane had already recognized the man, but Brenn by some fluke could never have seen him. Brenn's expression changed. "Urquart — Long Lance Urquart. I'm honoured to meet you." Urquart was known as the greatest harpooner in the history of the icelands. He was rumoured to have killed more than twenty bull-whales single-handed.

Urquart moved his head slightly, as if acknowledging Brenn's compliment. "Aye." He spat again and looked broodingly at the cranium spittoon. "I'm a South Ice man myself. You hunt the North Ice mainly, I hear."

"Mainly," Brenn agreed, "but I know the South Ice well enough." His tone was puzzled, though he was too polite, or too overawed, to ask Urquart directly why he had addressed him.

Urquart leaned on his harpoon, clutching it with both big, bony hands and sucking in his lips. The harpoon was ten feet long, and its many barbs were six inches or more across, curving down for nearly two feet of its length, with a big metal ring fixed beneath them where tackle was tied.

"There's a great many North Ice men have turned to the South Ice this season as well as last," said Urquart. "They've found few fish, Captain Brenn."

Whaling men — particularly harpooners — invariably called whales "fish" in a spirit of studied disdain for the huge mammals.

"You mean the hunting's poor there, too." Brenn's face clouded.

"Not so poor as on the North Ice from what I hear," Urquart said slowly. "But I only tell you because you seem about to take a risk. I've seen many skippers — good ones like yourself — do the same. I speak friendly, Captain Brenn. The luck is bad, both north and south. A decent herd's not been sighted all season. The fish are moving south, beyond our range. Our ships follow them further and further. Soon it'll not be possible to provision for long enough voyages." Urquart paused, and then he added, "The fish are leaving."

"Why tell me this?" Brenn said, half angry with Urquart in his disappointment.

"Because you're Konrad Arflane's friend," Urquart said without looking at Arflane, who had never met him in his life before, had only seen him at a distance.

Arflane was astonished. "You don't know me, man…"

"I know your actions," Urquart murmured, then drew in a deep breath as if talking had winded him. He turned slowly on his heel and walked with a long, loping stride towards the door, ducked his head beneath the top of the frame and was gone.

Brenn snorted and shifted his feet. He slapped his leg several times and then frowned at Arflane. "What was he talking about?"

Arflane leaned back against the counter. "I don't know, Brenn. But if Urquart warned you that the fishing is poor on the South Ice, you should heed that."

Brenn laughed briefly and bitterly. "I can't afford to heed it, Arflane. I'll just pray all night to the Ice Mother and hope She gives me better luck. It's all I can do, man!" His voice had risen almost to a shout.

Flatch had reseated himself in his cubbyhole behind the counter, but he rose, looking like some monstrous beast himself, and glanced enquiringly with his single eye as Brenn faced him again and ordered whale steaks with seka weed and a barrel of beer to be brought to them at their table.

Later, after Brenn's men had come in and been cheered by the discovery that Flatch was willing to provide them with everything they needed, Arflane and Brenn sat opposite each other at a side table with the beer barrel against the wall. Every so often they would turn the spigot and replenish their cups. The cups were unbreakable, fashioned of some ancient plastic substance. The beer did not, as they had hoped, improve their spirits, although Brenn managed to look confident enough whenever any of his men addressed him through the shadowy gloom of the hostel room.

The beer had in fact succeeded in turning Brenn in on himself and he was uncommunicative, constantly twisting his head around to look at the door, which had now been closed. Arflane knew that Brenn was expecting no-one.

At last he leaned over the table and said, "Urquart seemed a gloomy individual, Brenn — perhaps even mad. He sees the bad luck of everything. I've been here for some days, and I've seen the catches unloaded. They're smaller than usual, certainly, but not that small. We've both had as poor catches and they've done us no harm in the long term. It happened to me for several seasons running and then I had plenty of luck for another three. The owners were worried, but…"

Brenn looked up from his cup. "There you have it, Arflane. I'm my own master now. The *Tender Maiden's* mine. I bought her two seasons back." Again he laughed bitterly. "I thought I was doing a sensible thing, seeing that so many of us have had our ships sold over our heads in past years. It looks as if I'll be selling my own craft over my own head at this rate, or hiring out to some Friesgaltian merchant. I'll have no choice. And there's my crew — willing to gamble with me. Do I tell them Urquart's news? They've wives and children, as I have. Shall I tell them?"

"It would do no good," Arflane said quietly.

"And where are the fish going?" Brenn continued. He put his cup down heavily. "What's happening to the herds?"

"Urquart said they're going south. Perhaps the clever man will be the one who learns how to follow them — how to live off what provisions he can find on the ice. There are more warm ponds to the south — possibly a means of tracking the herds could be devised…"

"Will that help me this season?"

"I don't know," Arflane admitted. He was thinking now about his conversation aboard the *Ice Spirit* and he began to feel even more depressed.

Flatch's whores came down to the main room of the hostel. Flatch had done nothing by halves. There was a girl for every man, including Arflane and Brenn. Katarina, Flatch's youngest daughter, a girl of eighteen, approached them, holding the hand of another girl who was as dark and pretty as Flatch's daughter was fair and plain. Katarina introduced the other girl as Maji.

Arflane attempted to sound jovial. "Here," he said to Brenn, "here's someone to cheer you up."

Leaning back, with the drunken, dark-haired girl Maji cuddled against his chest, Brenn roared with laughter at his own joke. The girl giggled. On the other side of the table Arflane smiled and stroked Katarina's hair. She was a warm-hearted girl and able instinctively to make men relax. Maji winked up at Brenn. The women had succeeded, where Arflane had failed, in restoring Brenn's natural optimism.

It was very late. The air was stale and hot and the hostel room was noisy with the drunken voices of the whalers. Through the poor, flickering light Arflane could see their fur-clad silhouettes reeling from table to table or sitting slumped on the benches. Brenn's crew was not the only one in the Shipsmasher. There were men from two other ships there, a Friesgaltian North Ice whaler and another North Icer from Abersgalt. If South Ice men had been there there might have been trouble, but these crews seemed to be mingling well with Brenn's men. Out of the press of bulky bodies rose the long lances of the harpooners, swaying like slender masts in a high wind, their barbed tips casting distorted shadows in the shuddering light from the faulty strips. There were thumps as men fell or knocked over barrels. There was the smell of spilled bitter beer which ran over the tables and swamped the floor. Arflane heard the giggles of the girls and the harsh laughter of the men and, though the temperature was too warm for his own comfort, he felt himself begin to relax now that he was in the company of men whom he understood. Off-ship, crews had more or less equal status with the officers, and this contributed to the free and easy atmosphere in the Shipsmasher.

Arflane poured himself another cup of beer as Brenn began a fresh story.

The outer door opened suddenly and cold air blew in, making Arflane shiver, though he was grateful for it. Silence fell as the men turned. The door slammed shut and a man of medium height, swathed in a heavy sealskin cloak, began to walk between the tables.

He was not a whaling man.

That could be judged from the cut of his cloak, the way he walked, the texture of his skin. His hair was short and dark, cut in a fringe over his eyes and scarcely reaching to the nape of his neck. There was a gold bracelet curving up his right forearm and a silver ring on the second finger of his right hand. He moved casually, but somewhat deliberately, and had a slight, ironic smile on his lips. He was handsome and fairly young. He nodded a greeting to the men, who still stared at him suspiciously.

One heavily built harpooner opened his mouth and laughed at the young man, and others began to laugh too. The young man raised his eyebrows and put his head to one side, looking at them coolly.

"I am seeking Captain Arflane." His voice was melodious and aristocratic, with a Friesgalt accent. "I heard he was here."

"I'm Arflane. What do you want?" Konrad Arflane looked with some hostility at the young man.

"I'm Manfred Rorsefne. May I join you?"

Arflane shrugged and Rorsefne came and sat on the bench next to Katarina Flatch.

"Have a drink," said Arflane, pushing his full cup toward Rorsefne. He realized, as he made the movement, that he was quite drunk. This realization caused him to pause and rub his forehead. When he looked up at Manfred Rorsefne, he was glowering.

Rorsefne shook his head. "No, thank you, captain. I'm not in a drinking mood. I wanted to speak with you alone if that is possible."

Suddenly petulant, Arflane said, "It is not. I'm enjoying the company of my friends. What is a Rorsefne doing in a top-deck hostel anyway?"

"Looking for you, obviously." Manfred Rorsefne sighed theatrically. "And looking for you at this hour because it is important. However," he began to rise, "I will come to your hostel in the morning. I am sorry for intruding, captain." He glanced at Katarina Flatch a trifle cynically.

As Rorsefne made his way towards the door, one of the men thrust a harpoon shaft in front of his legs and he tripped and stumbled. He tried to recover his balance, but another shaft took him in the back and sent him sprawling. He fell as the whalers laughed raucously.

Arflane watched expressionlessly. Even an aristocrat was not safe in a whaling hostel if he had no connection with whaling. Manfred Rorsefne was simply paying for his folly.

The big harpooner who had first laughed at Rorsefne now stood up and grabbed the young man by the collar of his cloak. The cloak came away and the harpooner staggered back, laughing drunkenly. Another joined him, a stocky, red-headed man, and reached down to grab Rorsefne's jacket. But Rorsefne rolled over to face the man, his smile still ironic, and tried to get to his feet.

Brenn leaned forward to see what was going on. He glanced at Arflane. "D'you want me to stop them?"

Arflane shook his head. "It's his own fault. He's a fool for coming here."

"I've never heard of an intrusion like it," Brenn agreed, settling back.

Rorsefne was now on his feet, reaching past the red-headed whale man towards the sealskin cloak held by the big harpooner. "I'll thank you for my cloak," he said, his tone light, but shaking slightly.

"That's our payment for your entertainment," grinned the harpooner. "You can go now."

Rorsefne's eyes were hooded as he folded his arms across his chest. Arflane admired him for taking a stand.

"It would seem," said Rorsefne quietly, "that I have given you more entertainment than you have given me." His voice was now firm.

Arflane got up on impulse and squeezed past Flatch's daughter to stand to the left of the harpooner. Arflane was so drunk that he had to lean for a moment against the edge of a table.

"Give him the cloak, lad," he said, his voice slurring. "And let's get on with our drinking. The boy's not worth our trouble."

The big harpooner ignored Arflane and continued to grin at the young aristocrat, dangling the rich cloak in one hand, teasing him. Arflane lurched forward and grabbed the cloak out of the man's hand. The harpooner turned, grunting, and hit Arflane across the face. Brenn stood up from his corner, shouting at his man, but the harpooner ignored him and bent to pick up the cloak from where it had fallen. Perhaps encouraged by Arflane's action, Manfred Rorsefne also stooped forward towards the cloak. The red-headed whale man hit him. Rorsefne reeled and then struck back.

Arflane, sobered somewhat by the blow, took hold of the harpooner by the shoulder, swung him round, and punched him in the face. Brenn came scrambling over the table, shouting incoherently and trying to stop the fight before it went too far. He attempted to pull Arflane and the harpooner apart.

The Friesgalt whale men were now yelling angrily, siding, perhaps for the sake of the fight, with Manfred Rorsefne, who was wrestling with the red-headed whaler.

The fight became confused. Screaming girls gathered their skirts about them and made for the back room of the hostel. Harpoons were used like quarter-staves to batter at heads and bodies.

Arflane saw Brenn go down with a blow on the head and tried to reach his friend. Every whale man in the hostel seemed to be against him. He struck out in all directions but was soon overcome by their numbers. Even as he fell to the floor, still fighting, he felt the cold air come through the door again and wondered who had entered.

Then a great roaring voice, like the noise of the north wind at its height, sounded over the din of the fight. Arflane felt the whale man's hands leave him and got up, wiping blood from his eyes. His ears were ringing as the voice he had heard roared again.

"Fish, you cave-bound fools! Fish, I tell you! Fish, you dog-hunters! Fish, you beer-swillers! Fish to take the rust off your lances! A herd of a hundred or more, not fifty miles distant at sou'-sou'-west!"

Blinking through the blood, which came from a shallow cut on his forehead, Arflane saw that the speaker was the man he and Brenn had encountered earlier — Long Lance Urquart.

Urquart had one arm curled around his great harpoon and the other around the shoulders of a half-grown boy who looked both excited and embarrassed. The lad wore a single plait, coated with whale grease, and a white bearskin coat that showed by its richness that he was a whaling hand, probably a cabin boy.

"Tell them, Stefan," Urquart said, more softly now that he could be heard.

The boy spoke in a stutter, pointing back through the still open doorway into the light. "Our ship passed them coming in at dusk. We were loaded up and could not stop, for we had to make Friesgalt by nightfall. But we saw them. Heading from north to south, on a line roughly twenty degrees west. A big herd. My father — our skipper — says there hasn't been a bigger herd in twenty seasons."

Arflane bent to help Brenn who was staggering to his feet, clutching his head.

"Did you hear that, Brenn?"

"I did." Brenn smiled in spite of his bruised, swollen lips. "The Ice Mother's good to us."

"There's enough out there for every ship in the dock," Urquart continued, "and more besides. They're traveling fast, from what the lad's father says, but good sailing should catch 'em."

Arflane looked around the room, trying to find Manfred Rorsefne. He saw him leaning against a wall, a flenching cutlass, that had obviously been one of the wall's ornaments, clutched in his right hand. He still wore his ironic smile. Arflane looked at him thoughtfully.

Urquart also turned his attention from the men and seemed surprised when he saw Rorsefne there. The expression passed quickly and his gaunt features became frozen again. He took his arm from the boy's shoulders and shifted his harpoon to cradle it in his other arm. He walked towards Manfred Rorsefne and took the cutlass from him.

"Thanks," said Rorsefne, grinning, "it was becoming heavy."

"What were you doing in this place?" Urquart asked brusquely. Arflane was surprised by his familiarity with the youth.

Rorsefne nodded his head in Arflane's direction. "I came to give a message to Captain Arflane, but he was busy with his friends. Some others decided I should provide entertainment since I was here. Captain Arflane and I seemed agreed that they had had enough…"

Urquart's narrow, blue eyes turned to look carefully at Arflane. "You helped him, captain?"

Arflane let his face show his disgust. "He was a fool to come alone to a place like this. If you know him take him home, Urquart."

The men were beginning to leave the hostel, pulling their hoods about their heads, picking up their harpoons as they hurried back to their ships, knowing that their skippers would want to sail with the first light.

Brenn clapped Arflane on the shoulder. "I must go. We've enough provisions for a short haul. It was good to see you, Arflane."

In the company of two of his harpooners, Brenn left the hostel. Save for Urquart, Rorsefne and Arflane, the place was now empty.

Flatch came stumping down between the overturned tables, his gross body swaying from side to side. He was followed by three of his daughters who began to clean up the mess. They appeared to take it for granted. Flatch watched them work and did not approach the three men.

Urquart's strangely arranged hair threw a huge shadow on the far wall, by the door. Arflane had not noticed before how closely it resembled the tail of a land whale.

"So you helped another Rorsefne," Urquart murmured, "though once again you had no need to."

Arflane rubbed his damaged forehead. "I was drunk. I didn't interfere for his sake."

"It was a good fight, however," Manfred Rorsefne said lightly. "I did not realize I could fight so well."

"They were playing." Arflane's tone was weary and contemptuous.

Gravely, Urquart nodded in agreement. He shifted his grip on his harpoon and looked directly at Rorsefne. "They were playing with you," he repeated.

"Then it was a good game, cousin," Rorsefne said, looking up into Urquart's bleak eyes. "Eh?" The Long Lance's tall, gaunt figure was immobile, the features composed. His eyes looked towards the door. Arflane wondered why Rorsefne called Urquart "cousin", for it was unlikely that there was a true blood link between the aristocrat and the savage harpooner.

"I will escort you both back to the deeper levels," said Urquart slowly.

"What's the danger now?" Manfred Rorsefne asked him. "None. We'll go alone, cousin, and then perhaps I'll be able to deliver my message to Captain Arflane after all."

Urquart shrugged, turned and left the hostel without a word.

Manfred grinned at Arflane who merely scowled in return. "A moody man, cousin Long Lance. Now, captain, would you be willing to listen while I tell you what I came to say?"

Arflane spat into the whale cranium nearby. "It can do no harm," he said.

As they walked carefully down the sloping ramps to the lower levels, avoiding the drunken whalers who staggered past them on their way up, Manfred Rorsefne said nothing and Arflane was too bored and tired to ask him directly what his message was. The effects of the beer had worn off, and the pains in his bruised body were beginning to make themselves felt. The shadowy figures of the whalers, hurrying back to their ships through the dim light, could be seen in front of them and behind them. Occasionally a man shouted, but for the most part the whalers moved in comparative silence, though the constant shuffle of their ridged boots on the causeways echoed around the crevasse. Here and there a man clung to the swaying guard ropes, having staggered too close to the edge. It was not unusual for drunken sailors to lose their footing and fall to the mysterious bottom of the gorge.

Only when Arflane stopped at the entrance to his hostel and the last of the whalers had gone by did Rorsefne speak.

"My uncle's better. He seems eager to see you."

"Your uncle?"

"Pyotr Rorsefne. He is better."

"When does he want to see me?"

"Now, if it is convenient."

"I'm too tired. Your fight..."

"I apologize, but I had no intention of involving you..."

"You should not have gone to the Shipsmasher. You knew that."

"True. The mistake was mine, captain. In fact, if cousin Long Lance had not brought his good news, I could have your death on my conscience now..."

"Don't be stupid," Arflane said disdainfully. "Why d'you call Urquart your cousin?"

"It embarrasses him. It's a family secret. I'm not supposed to tell anyone that Urquart is my uncle's natural son. Are you coming to our quarters? You could sleep there, if you're so tired, and see my uncle first thing in the morning."

Arflane shrugged and followed Manfred Rorsefne down the ramp. He was half asleep and half drunk and the memory which kept recurring as he walked was not that of Pyotr Rorsefne, but of his daughter.

CHAPTER FIVE

THE RORSEFNE HOUSEHOLD

Waking in a bed that was too soft and too hot, Konrad Arflane looked dazedly about the small room. It was lined with rich wall hangings of painted canvas depicting famous Rorsefne ships on their voyages and hunts. Here a four-masted schooner was attacked by gigantic land whales, there a whale was slain by a captain with poised harpoon; elsewhere ships floundered in ice breaks or approached cities across the panorama of the ice; old wars were fought, old victories glorified; valiant Rorsefne men were at all times in the forefront, usually managing to bear the Rorsefne flag. Action and violence were on all sides.

There was a trace of humour in Arflane's expression as he stared round at the paintings. He sat up, pushing the furs away from his naked body. His clothes lay on a bench against the wall nearest the door. He swung his legs to the floor and stood up, walking across the carpet of fur to where a wash-stand had been prepared for him. As he washed, dousing himself in cold water, he realized that his memory of how he had arrived here was vague. He must have been very drunk to have agreed to Manfred Rorsefne's suggestion that he stay the night. He could not understand how he had come to accept the invitation. As he dressed, pulling on the tight undergarments of soft leather and struggling into his jacket and trousers, he wondered if he would see Ulrica Ulsenn that day.

Someone knocked and then Manfred Rorsefne entered, wearing a fur cloak dyed in red and blue squares. He smiled quizzically at Arflane.

"Well, captain? Are you feeling any ill effects?"

"I was drunk, I suppose," Arflane said resentfully, as if blaming the young man. "Do we see old Rorsefne now?"

"Breakfast first, I think." Manfred led him into a wide passage also covered in dark, painted wall hangings. They passed through a door at the end and entered a large room in the centre of which was a square table made of beautifully carved whale ivory. On the table were several loaves of a kind of bread made from warm-pond weed, dishes of whale, seal and bear meat, a full tureen containing a stew, and a large jug of *hess*, which had a taste similar to tea.

Already seated at the table was Ulrica Ulsenn, wearing a simple dress of black and red leather. She glanced up as Arflane entered, gave him a shy smile and looked down at her plate.

"Good morning," Arflane said gruffly.

"Good morning." Her voice was almost inaudible. Manfred Rorsefne pulled back the chair next to hers.

"Would you care to sit here, captain?"

Uneasily, Arflane went to sit down. As he pulled his chair in to the table, his knee brushed hers. They both recoiled at once. On the opposite side of the table Manfred Rorsefne was helping himself to seal meat and bread. He glanced humorously at his cousin and Arflane. Two female servants came into the room. They were dressed in long brown dresses, with Rorsefne insignia on the sleeves.

One of them remained in the background; the other stepped forward and curtsied. Ulrica Ulsenn smiled at her. "Some more *hess*, please, Mirayn."

The girl took the half-empty jug from the table. "Is everything else in order, my lady?"

"Yes, thank you." Ulrica glanced at Arflane. "Is there anything you lack, captain?"

Arflane shook his head.

As the servants were leaving, Janek Ulsenn pushed in past them.

He saw Arflane beside his wife and nodded brusquely, then sat down and began to serve himself from the dishes.

There was an unmistakable atmosphere of tension in the room. Arflane and Ulrica Ulsenn avoided looking at one another. Janek Ulsenn glowered, but did not lift his eyes from his food; Manfred Rorsefne looked amusedly at all of them, adding, it would seem deliberately, to their discomfort.

"I hear a big herd's been sighted," Janek Ulsenn said at last, addressing Manfred and ignoring his wife and Arflane.

"I was one of the first to hear the news," Manfred smiled. "Wasn't I, Captain Arflane?"

Arflane made a noise through his nose and continued to eat. He was embarrassingly aware of Ulrica Ulsenn's presence so close to him.

"Are we sending a ship?" Manfred asked Janek Ulsenn. "We ought to. There's plenty of fish for all, by the sound of it. We ought to go ourselves — we could take the two-mast schooner and enjoy the hunt for as long as it lasted."

Ulrica seemed to welcome the suggestion. "A splendid idea, Manfred. Father's better, so he won't need me. I'll come too." Her eyes sparkled. "I haven't seen a hunt for three seasons!"

Janek Ulsenn rubbed his nose and frowned. "I've no time to spare for a foolhardy pleasure voyage."

"We could be back within a day." Manfred's tone was eager. "We'll go, Ulrica, if Janek hasn't the spirit for it. Captain Arflane can take command…"

Arflane scowled. "Lord Ulsenn chose the right word — foolhardy. A yacht — with a woman on board — whale hunting! I'd take no such responsibility. I'd advise you to forget the idea. All it would need would be for one bull to turn and your boat would be smashed in seconds."

"Don't be dull, captain," Manfred admonished. "Ulrica will come anyway. Won't you, Ulrica?"

Ulrica Ulsenn shrugged slightly. "If Janek has no objection."

"I have," Ulsenn muttered.

"You are right to advise her against a trip like that," Arflane said. He was unwilling to join forces with Ulsenn, but in this case he knew it was his duty. There was a good chance that a yacht would be destroyed in the hunt.

Ulsenn straightened up, his eyes resentful. "But if you wish to go, Ulrica," he said firmly, staring hard at Arflane, "you may do so."

Arflane shifted his own gaze so that he looked directly into Ulsenn's eyes. "In which case, I feel that you must have an experienced man in command. I'll skipper the craft."

"You must come too, cousin Janek," Manfred put in banteringly. "You have a duty to our people. They will respect you the more if they see that you are willing to face danger."

"I do not care what they think," Ulsenn said, glaring at Manfred Rorsefne. "I am not afraid of danger. I am busy. Someone has to run your father's affairs while he is ill!"

"One day is all you would lose." Manfred was plainly taunting the man.

Ulsenn paused, evidently torn between decisions. He got up from the table, his breakfast unfinished.

"I'll consider it," he said as he left the room.

Ulrica Ulsenn rose.

"You deliberately upset him, Manfred. You have offended him and embarrassed Captain Arflane. You must apologize."

Manfred made a mock bow to Arflane. "I am sorry, captain."

Arflane looked thoughtfully up into Ulrica Ulsenn's beautiful face. She flushed and left the room in the direction her husband had taken.

As the door closed, Manfred burst into laughter. "Forgive me, captain. Janek is so pompous and Ulrica hates him as much as I do. But Ulrica is so *loyal*!"

"A rare quality," Arflane said dryly.

"Oh, indeed!" Manfred got up from the table. "Now. We'll go to see the only one of them who is worth any loyalty."

Heads of bear, walrus, whale and wolf decorated the skin-covered walls of the large bedroom. At the far end was the high, wide bed and in it, propped against folded furs, lay Pyotr Rorsefne. His bandaged hands lay on the bed covers; apart from some faint scars on his face, these were the only sign that he had been so close to death. His face was red

SAILING TO UTOPIA

and healthy, his eyes bright, and his movements alert as he turned his head to look towards Arflane and Manfred Rorsefne. His great mane of grey hair was combed and fell to his shoulders. He now had a heavy moustache and beard; both were nearly snow white. His body, what Arflane could see of it, had filled out and it was hard to believe that such a recovery could have been possible. Arflane credited the miracle to the old man's natural vitality and love of life, rather than to any care he had received. Momentarily, he wondered why Rorsefne was still in bed.

"Hello, Arflane. I recognize you, you see!" His voice was rich and vibrant, with all trace of weakness gone. "I'm well again — or as well as I'll ever be. Forgive this manner of meeting, but those milksops think I won't be able to get my balance. Lost the feet — but the rest I kept."

Arflane nodded, responding against his will to the old man's friendliness.

Manfred brought up a chair from a corner of the room.

"Sit down," Pyotr Rorsefne said. "We'll talk. You can leave us now, Manfred."

Arflane seated himself beside the bed and Manfred, reluctantly it seemed, left the room.

"You and I thwarted the Ice Mother," Rorsefne smiled, looking closely at Arflane. "What do you feel about that, captain?"

"A man has a right to try to preserve his life for as long as possible," Arflane replied. "The Ice Mother surely does not resent having to wait a little longer."

"It used to be thought that no man should interfere in another man's life — or his death. It used to be said that if a man was about to be taken by the Ice Mother then it was no-one's right to thwart her. That was the old philosophy."

"I know. Perhaps I'm as soft as some of the others I've condemned while I've been here."

"You've condemned us, have you?"

"I see a turning away from the Ice Mother. I see disaster resulting from that, sir."

"You hold with the old ideas, not the new ones. You do not believe the ice is melting?"

"I do not, sir."

A small table stood beside the bed. On it was a large chart box, writing materials, a jug of *hess* and a cup. Pyotr Rorsefne reached towards the cup. Arflane forestalled him, poured some *hess* from the jug, and handed him the drink. Rorsefne grunted his thanks. His expression was thoughtful and calculating as he looked into Arflane's face.

Konrad Arflane stared back, boldly enough. This man was one he believed he could understand. Unlike the rest of his family, he did not make Arflane feel uncomfortable.

"I own many ships," Rorsefne murmured.

"I know. Many more than actually sail."

"Something else you disapprove of, captain? The big clippers not at work. Yet you're aware, I'm sure, that if I set them to hunting and trading, we should reduce all the other cities to poverty within a decade."

"You're generous." Arflane found it surprising that Rorsefne should boast about his charity; it did not seem to fit with the rest of his character.

"I'm wise." Rorsefne gesticulated with one bandaged hand. "Friesgalt needs the competition as much as your city and its like need the trade. Already we're too fat, soft, complacent. You agree, I think."

Arflane nodded.

"It's the way of things," Rorsefne sighed. "Once a city becomes so powerful, it begins to decline. It lacks stimulus. We are reaching the point, here on the plateau of the Eight Cities, where we have nothing left to spur us on. What's more, the game is leaving. I see death for all in not too short a time, Arflane."

Arflane shrugged. "It's the Ice Mother's will. It must happen sooner or later. I'm not sure that I follow all your reasoning, but I do know that the softer people become, the less chance they have of survival..."

"If the natural conditions are softer, then the people can afford to become so," Rorsefne said quietly. "And our scientists tell us that the level of the ice is dropping, that the weather is improving, season by season."

"I once saw a great line of ice cliffs on the horizon," Arflane interrupted. "I was astonished. There'd never been cliffs there before — particularly ones that stood on their peaks, with their bases in the clouds. I began to doubt all I knew about the world. I went home and told them what I had seen. They laughed at me. They said that what I had seen was an illusion — something to do with light — and that if I went to look the next day the cliffs would be gone. I went the next day. The cliffs were gone. I knew then that I could not always trust my senses, but that I could trust what I knew to be right within me. I know that the ice is not melting. I know that your scientists have been deceived, as I was, by illusions."

Rorsefne sighed. "I would like to agree with you, Arflane…"

"But you do not. I have had this argument already."

"No, I meant it. I want to agree with you. It is simply that I need proof, one way or the other."

"Proof surrounds you. The natural course is towards utter coldness and death. The sun must die and the wind must blow us into the night."

"I've read that there were other ages when ice covered the world and then disappeared." Rorsefne straightened his back and leaned forward. "What of those?"

"They were only the beginning. Two or three times, the Ice Mother was driven back. But She was stronger, and had patience. You know the answers. They are in the creed."

"The scientists say that again Her power is waning."

"That cannot be. Her total domination of all matter is inevitable."

"You quote the creed. Have you no doubts?"

Arflane got up from his seat. "None."

"I envy you."

"That, too, has already been said to me. There is nothing to envy. Perhaps it is better to believe in an illusion."

"I cannot believe in it, Arflane." Rorsefne leaned forward, his bandaged hands reaching for Arflane's arm. "Wait. I told you I needed proof. I know, I think, where that proof may be found."

"Where?"

"Where I went with my ship and my crew. Where I returned from. A city — many months travel from here, to the distant north. New York. Have you heard of it?"

Arflane laughed. "A myth. I spoke of illusions…"

"I've seen it — from a distance, true, but there was no doubting its existence. My men saw it. We were short of provisions and under attack from barbarians. We were forced to turn before we could get closer. I planned to go back with a fleet. I saw New York, where the Ice Ghosts have their court. The city of the Ice Mother. A city of marvels. I saw its buildings rising tier upon tier into the sky."

"I know the tale. The city was drowned by water and then frozen, preserved complete beneath the ice. An impossible legend. I may believe in the doctrines of the Ice Mother, my lord, but I am not so superstitious…"

"It is true. I have seen New York. Its towers thrust upwards from a gleaming field of smooth ice. There is no telling how deep they go. Perhaps the Ice Mother's court is there, perhaps that part is a myth… But if the city has been preserved, then its knowledge has been preserved too. One way or the other, Arflane, the proof I spoke of is in New York."

Arflane was perplexed, wondering if the old man's fever was still with him.

Rorsefne seemed to guess his thoughts. He laughed, tapping the chart box. "I'm sane, captain. Everything is in here. With a good ship — better than the one I took — New York can be reached and the truth discovered."

Arflane sat down again. "How was the first ship wrecked?"

Rorsefne sighed. "A series of misfortunes — ice breaks, shifting cliffs, land whale attacks, the attacks of the barbarians. Finally, ascending to the plateau up the Great North Course, the ship could stand no more and fell apart, killing most of us. The rest set off to walk to Friesgalt, the boats being crushed, hoping we should meet a ship. We did not. Soon, only I remained alive."

"So bad luck was the cause of the wreck?"

"Essentially. A better ship would not suffer such luck."

"You know this city's location?"

"More — I have the whole course plotted."

"How did you know where to go?"

"It wasn't difficult. I read the old books, compared the locations they gave."

"And now you want to take a fleet there?"

"No." Rorsefne sank back on the furs. "I would be a hindrance on such a voyage. I went secretly the first time, because I wanted no rumours spreading to disturb the people. At a time of stress, such news could destroy the stability of our entire society. I think it best to keep the city a secret until one ship has been to New York and discovered what knowledge the city actually does hold. I intend to send the *Ice Spirit*."

"She's the best ship in the Eight Cities."

"They say a ship's as good as her master," Rorsefne murmured. His strength was beginning to fail him. "I know of no better master than yourself, Captain Arflane. I trust you — and your reputation is good."

Arflane did not refuse immediately, as he had expected he would. He had half anticipated the old man's suggestion, but he was not sure that Rorsefne was completely sane. Perhaps he, too, had seen a mirage of some kind, or a line of mountains that had looked like a city from a distance. Yet the idea of New York, the thought of discovering the mythical palace of the Ice Mother and of verifying his own instinctive knowledge of the inevitability of the ice's rule, appealed to him and excited his imagination. He had, after all, nothing to keep him on the plateau; the quest was a noble one, almost a holy one. To go north towards the home of the Ice Mother, to sail, like the mariners of ancient times, on a great voyage of many months, seeking knowledge that might change the world, suited his essentially romantic nature. What was more, he would command the finest ship in the world, sailing across unknown seas of ice, discovering new races of men if Rorsefne's talk of barbarians were true. New York, the fabled city, whose tall towers jutted from a plain of smooth ice… What if after all it did not exist? He would sail on and on, farther and farther north, while everything else traveled south.

Rorsefne's eyes were half closed now. His appearance of health had been deceptive; he had exhausted himself.

Arflane got up for the second time.

"I have agreed — against my better judgment — to captain a yacht in which your family intend to follow a whale hunt today."

Rorsefne smiled weakly. "Ulrica's idea?"

"Manfred's. He has somehow committed Lord Janek Ulsenn, your daughter and myself to the scheme. Your daughter supported Manfred. As head of the family you should…"

"It is not your affair, captain. I know you speak from good will, but Manfred and Ulrica know what is right for them. Rorsefne stock breeds best encountering danger — it needs to seek it out." Rorsefne paused, studying Arflane's face again, frowning a little curiously. "I should not have thought it like you to offer unasked-for advice, captain..."

"It is not my way, normally." Arflane himself was now perplexed. "I don't know why I mentioned this. I apologize." He was not acting in a normal fashion at all, he realized. What was causing the change?

For a moment he saw the whole Rorsefne family as representing danger for him, but the danger was nebulous. He felt a faint stirring of panic and rubbed his bearded chin rapidly. Looking down into Rorsefne's face, he saw that the man was smiling very slightly. The smile seemed sympathetic.

"Is Janek going, did you say?" Rorsefne asked suddenly, breaking the mood.

"It seems so."

Rorsefne laughed quietly. "I wonder how he was convinced. No matter. With luck he'll be the one killed and she'll find herself a man to marry, though they're scarce enough. You'll skipper the yacht?"

"I said I would, though I don't know why. I am doing many things I would not do elsewhere. I am in something of a quandary, Lord Rorsefne."

"Don't worry," Rorsefne chuckled. "You're simply not adjusted to our way of doing things."

"Your nephew puzzles me. Somehow he managed to talk me into agreeing with him, when everything I feel disagrees with him. He is a subtle young man."

"He has his own kind of strength," Rorsefne said affectionately. "Do not underestimate Manfred, captain. He appears weak, both in character and in physique, but he likes to give that appearance."

"You make him seem very mysterious," Arflane said half jokingly.

"He is more complicated than us, I think," Rorsefne replied. "He represents something new — possibly just a new generation. You dislike him, I can see. You may come to like him as much as you like my daughter."

"Now you are being mysterious, sir. I expressed no liking for anyone in particular."

Rorsefne ignored this remark. "See me after the hunt," he said in his failing voice. "I'll show you the charts. You can tell me then if you accept the commission."

"Very well. Good-bye, sir."

Leaving the room, Arflane realized that he had been drawn irrevocably into the affairs of the Rorsefne household and that, ever since he had saved the man's life, his fate had been linked with theirs. They had somehow seduced him, made him their man. He knew that he would take the command offered by Pyotr Rorsefne just as he had taken the command of the yacht offered by Manfred Rorsefne. Without appearing to have lost any of his integrity, he was no longer his own master. Pyotr Rorsefne's strength of character, Ulrica Ulsenn's beauty and grace, Manfred Rorsefne's subtlety, even Janek Ulsenn's belligerence, had combined to trap him. Disturbed, Arflane walked back towards the breakfast room.

CHAPTER FIVE

THE WHALE HUNT

Divided from the main fleet by a low wall of ice blocks, the yacht, slim-prowed and handsome, lay in her anchor lines in the private Rorsefne yard.

Tramping across the ice in the cold morning, with the sky a smoky yellow, broken by streaks of orange and a dark pink that the ice reflected, Arflane followed Manfred Rorsefne as he made his way towards the yacht through the still-soft layers of snow. Behind Arflane came Janek and Ulrica Ulsenn, sitting on a small, ornate sleigh drawn by servants. Man and wife sat side by side, swathed in rich furs, their hands buried in huge muffs, their faces almost wholly hidden by their hoods.

The yacht had already been crewed, and the men were preparing to sail. A bulky, spring-operated harpoon gun, rather like a giant crossbow, had been loaded and set up in the bow. The big harpoon with its half-score of tapering barbs jutted out over the bowsprit, a savage phallus.

Arflane smiled as he looked at the heavy harpoon. It seemed too big for the slender yacht that carried it. It dominated the boat — a fore-and-aft-rigged schooner — it drew all attention to itself. It was a fine, cruel harpoon.

He followed Manfred up the gangplank and was surprised to see Urquart standing there, watching them from sharp, sardonic eyes, his own harpoon cradled as always in his left arm, his gaunt features and tall body immobile until he turned his back on them suddenly and walked aft up the deck towards the wheelhouse.

Janek Ulsenn, his lips pursed and his expression one of thinly disguised anxiety, was helping his wife on board. Arflane thought that perhaps she should be helping her husband.

A ship's officer in white and grey fur came along the deck towards the new arrivals. He spoke to Manfred Rorsefne, though protocol demanded that he address the senior member of the family, Janek Ulsenn.

"We're ready to sail, sir. Will you be taking command?"

Manfred shook his head slowly and smiled, stepping aside so that he no longer stood between Arflane and the officer.

"This is Captain Arflane. He will be master on this trip. He has all powers of captain."

The officer, a stocky man in his thirties with a black, rimed beard, nodded to Arflane in recognition. "I know of you, sir. Proud to sail with you. Can I show you the ship before we loose lines?"

"Thanks." Arflane left the rest of the party and accompanied the officer towards the wheelhouse. "What's your name?"

"Haeber, sir. First officer. We have a second officer, a bosun and the usual small complement. Not a bad crew, sir."

"Used to whale hunting?"

A shadow passed across Haeber's face. He said quietly: "No, sir."

"Any of the men whaling hands?"

"Very few, sir. We have Mr Urquart aboard, as you know, but he's a harpooner of course."

"Then your men will have to learn quickly, won't they?"

"I suppose so, sir." Haeber's tone was carefully noncommittal. For a moment it was in Arflane's mind to echo Haeber's doubt; then he spoke briskly.

"If your crew's as good as you say, Mr Haeber, then we'll have no trouble on the hunt. I know whales. Make sure you listen carefully to every order I give and there'll be no great problems."

"Aye, aye, sir." Haeber's voice became more confident.

The yacht was small and neat. She was a fine craft of her class, but Arflane could see at once that his suspicions as to her usefulness as a whaler were justified. She would be fast — faster than the ordinary whaling vessels — but she had no strength to her. She was a brittle boat. Her runners and struts were too thin for heavy work and her hull was liable to crack on collision with an outcrop of ice, another ship, or a fully grown whale.

Arflane decided he would take the wheel himself. This would give the crew confidence, for his helmsmanship was well known and highly regarded. But first he would let one of the officers take the ship onto the open ice while he got the feel of her. Her sails were ready for letting out and men stood by the anchor capstans along both sides of the deck.

After testing the wheel, Arflane took the megaphone Haeber handed him and climbed the companionway to the bridge above the wheelhouse.

Ahead he could see the distant outlines of ships sailing under full canvas towards the South Ice. The professional whalers were well ahead and Arflane was satisfied that at least the yacht would not get in their way before the main hunting began and the whale herd scattered. It was always at this time that the greatest confusion arose, with danger of collision as the ships set off after their individual prey. The yacht should come in after the whalers had divided and be able to select a small whale to chase — preferably some half-grown calf. Arflane sighed, annoyed at having to hunt such unmanly prey just for the sport of the aristocrats who were now traipsing along the deck towards the bridge. They were evidently planning to join him and, since the craft was theirs, they had a right to be on the bridge so long as they did not interfere with the captain's efficient command of the ship.

Arflane lifted the megaphone.

"All hands to their posts!"

The few crewmen who were not at their posts hastened to them. The others tensed, ready to obey Arflane's orders.

"Cast off anchors!"

As one, the anchor men let go the anchor lines and the ship began to slide towards the gap in the ice wall. Her runners scraped and bumped rhythmically as she gained speed down the slight incline and passed between the blocks, making for the open ice.

"Ready the mains'l!"

The men in the yards of the mainmast placed their hands on their halyards.

"Let go the mains'l!"

The sail cracked open, its boom swinging as it filled out. The boat's speed doubled almost at once. At regular intervals Arflane ordered more sail on and soon the yacht was gliding over the ice under full canvas. Air slapped Arflane's face, making it tingle with cold. He breathed in deeply, savouring the sharp chill of it in his nostrils and lungs, clearing the stale city air from his system. He gripped the bridge rail as the boat rode the faint undulations of the ice, carving her way through the thin layer of snow, crossing the black scars left by the runners of the ships who had gone ahead of her.

The sun was almost at zenith, a dull, deep red in the torn sky. Clouds swept before them, their colours changing gradually from pale yellow to white against the clear blue; the colour of the ice changed to match the clouds, now pure white and sparkling. The other ships were hull-down below the distant horizon. Save for the slight sounds that the ship made, the creak of yards and the bump of the runners, there was silence.

Tossed by the tearing skids, a fine spray of snow rose on both sides of the boat as she plunged towards the South Ice.

Arflane was conscious of the three members of the Friesgalt ruling family standing behind him. He did not turn. Instead he looked curiously at the figure who could be seen leaning in the bow by the harpoon gun, his gloved fingers gripping a line, his bizarre, strangely dressed hair streaming behind him, his lance cradled in the crook of his arm. Urquart, either from pride or from a wish for privacy, had spoken to no-one since he had come aboard. Indeed, he had boarded the craft of his own accord and his right to be there had not been questioned.

"Will we catch the whalers, captain?" Manfred Rorsefne spoke as quietly as ever; there was no need to raise his voice in the near-tangible silence of the icelands.

Arflane shook his head. "No."

He knew in fact there was every chance of catching the professional whalers; but he had no intention of doing so and fouling their hunting.

As soon as they were well under way, he planned to take in sail on some pretext and cut his speed.

An hour later the excuse occurred to him. They were leaving the clean ice and entering a region sparsely occupied by ridges of ice standing alone and fashioned into strange shapes by the action of the wind. He deliberately allowed the boat to pass close by one of these, to emphasize the danger of hitting it.

When they were past the spur, he half-turned to Rorsefne, who was standing behind him. "I'm cutting speed until we're through the ridges. If I don't, there's every chance of our hitting one and breaking up — then we'll never see the whale herd."

Rorsefne gave him a cynical smile, doubtless guessing the real reason for the decision, but made no comment.

Sail was taken in, under Arflane's instructions, and the boat's speed decreased by almost half. The atmosphere on board became less tense. Urquart, still in his self-appointed place in the bow, turned to glance up at the bridge. Then as if he had satisfied himself on some point, he shrugged slightly and turned back to look out towards the horizon.

The Ulsenns were sitting on a bench under the awning behind Arflane. Manfred Rorsefne leaned on the rail, staring up at the streamers of clouds above them.

The ridges they were now passing were carved into impossible shapes by the elements.

Some were like half-finished bridges, curving over the ice and ending suddenly in jagged outline. Others were squat, a mixture of rounded surfaces and sharp angles; and still others were tall and slender, like gigantic harpoons stuck butt-foremost into the ice. Most of them were in clumps set far enough apart to afford easy passage for the yacht as she glided on her course, but every so often Haeber, at the wheel, would steer a turn or two to one side or another to avoid a ridge.

The ice under the runners was rougher than it had been, for this ground was not traveled as much as the smoother terrain surrounding the cities. The boat's motion was still easy, but the undulation was more marked than before.

In spite of the lack of canvas, the yacht continued to make good speed, sails swelling with the steady following wind.

Knowing there was as yet little for him to do, Arflane agreed to Rorsefne's suggestion that they go below and eat. He left Haeber in charge of the bridge and the bosun at the wheel.

The cabins below were surprisingly large, since no space was used for carrying cargo of any kind other than ordinary supplies. The main cabin was as luxuriously furnished, by Arflane's standards, as the *Ice Spirit's* had been, with chairs of canvas stretched on bone frames, an ivory table and ivory shelves and lockers lining the bulkhead. The floor was carpeted in the tawny summer coat of the wolf (a beast becoming increasingly rare) and the ports were large, letting in a great deal more light than was usual in a boat of her size.

The four of them sat around the carved ivory table while the cook served their midday meal of broth made from the meat of the snow-kite, seal steaks and a mess of the lichen that grew on the surface of the ice in certain parts of the plateau. There was hardly any conversation during the meal, which suited Arflane. He sat at one end of the table, while Ulrica Ulsenn sat at the other. Janek Ulsenn and Manfred Rorsefne sat on his right and left. Occasionally Arflane would look up from his food at the same time as Ulrica Ulsenn and their eyes would meet. For him, it was another uncomfortable meal.

By the early afternoon the boat was nearing the region where the whales had been sighted. Arflane, glad to be away from the company of the Ulsenns and Manfred Rorsefne, took over the wheel from the bosun.

The masts of some of the whalers were now visible in the distance. The whaling fleet had not, it appeared, divided yet. All the ships seemed to be following much the same course, which meant that the whales were still out of sight.

As they drew nearer, Arflane saw the masts of the ships begin to separate; it could only mean that the herd had been sighted. The whalers were spreading out, each ship chasing its individual quarry.

Arflane blew into the bridge speaking tube. Manfred Rorsefne answered.

"The herd's been spotted," Arflane told him. "It's splitting up. Th' big ones will be what the whalers are after. I suppose we'll find a litt' whale for ourselves."

"How long to go, captain?" Rorsefne's voice now held a trace of excitement.

"About an hour," Arflane answered tersely, and replaced the stopper of the speaking tube.

On the horizon to starboard was a great cliff of ice rising hundreds of feet into the deep purple of the sky. To port were small sharp ridges of ice running parallel to the cliffs. The yacht was sailing between them now towards the slaughtering grounds where ships could be discerned already engaged in hunting down and killing the great beasts.

Standing on the bridge, Arflane prepared to go down and take the wheel again as he saw the prey that the yacht would hunt: a few bewildered calves about half a mile ahead of them, almost directly in line with the boat's present course. Rorsefne and the Ulsenns came up to the rail, craning their necks as they stared at the quarry.

They were soon passing close enough to be able to see individual ships at work.

With both hands firmly on the wheel and Haeber beside him with his megaphone ready to relay orders, Arflane guided the boat surely on her course, often steering in a wide arc to avoid the working ships.

Dark red whale blood ran over the churned whiteness of the ice; small boats, with harpooners ready in their bows, sped after the huge mammals or elsewhere were hauled at breakneck pace in the wake of skewered leviathans, towed by taut harpoon lines wound around the small capstans in the bows. One boat passed quite close, seeming hardly to touch the ground as it bounced over the ice, drawn by a pain-enraged cow who was four times the length and twice the height of the boat itself. She was opening and shutting her massive, tooth-filled jaws as she moved, using front and back flippers to push herself at almost unbelievable speed away from the source of her agony. The boat's runners, sprung on a matrix of bone, came close to breaking as she was hurled into the air and crashed down again. Her crew were sweating and clinging grimly to her sides to avoid being flung out; those who could doused the running lines with water to stop them burning. The cow's hide, scarred, ripped and bleeding from the wounds of a dozen harpoons, was a brown-grey colour and covered in wiry hair. Like most of her kind, it did not occur to her to turn on the boat which she could have snapped in two in an instant with her fifteen-foot jaws.

She was soon past, and beginning to falter as Arflane watched.

In another place a bull had been turned over onto his back and was waving his massive flippers feebly in his death throes. Around him, several boatloads of hunters had disembarked onto the ice and were warily approaching with lances and flenching cutlasses at the ready. The men were dwarfed by the monster who lay dying on his back, his mouth opening and shutting, gasping for breath.

Beyond, Arflane saw a cow writhing and shuddering as her blood spouted from a score of wounds.

The yacht was almost on the calves now.

Arflane's eyes were attracted by a movement to starboard. A huge bull-whale was rushing across the ice directly in the path of the yacht, towing a longboat behind him. A collision was imminent.

Desperately, he swung his wheel hard over. The yacht's runners squealed as she began to turn, narrowly missing the snorting whale, but still in danger of fouling the boat's lines and wrecking them both. Arflane leaned with all his strength on the wheel and barely succeeded in steering the yacht onto a parallel course. Now he could see the occupants of the boat. Standing by the prow, a harpoon ready in one hand, the other gripping the side, was Captain Brenn. His face was twisted in hatred for the beast as it dragged his longboat after it. The whale, startled by the sudden appearance of the yacht, now turned round until its tiny eyes glimpsed Brenn's boat. Instantly it rushed down on Brenn and his crew. Arflane heard the captain scream as the huge jaws opened to their full extent and crunched over the longboat.

A great cry went up from the whalers as the bull shook the broken boat. Arflane saw his friend flung to the ice and attempt to crawl away, but now the whale saw him and its jaws opened again, closing on Brenn's body.

For a moment the whaling captain's legs kicked, then they too disappeared. Arflane had automatically turned the wheel again, to go to the rescue of his friend, but it was too late.

As they bore down on the towering bulk of the bull, he saw that Urquart was no longer at the bow. Manfred Rorsefne stood in his place, swinging the great harpoon gun into line.

Arflane grabbed his megaphone and yelled through it.

"Rorsefne! Fool! Don't shoot it!"

The other evidently heard him, waved a one-handed acknowledgment, then bent back over the gun.

Arflane tried to turn the boat's runners in time, but it was too late. There was a thudding concussion that ran all along the boat as the massive harpoon left the gun and, its line racing behind it, buried itself deep in the whale's side.

The monster rose on its hind flippers, its front limbs waving. A high screaming sound came from its open jaws and its shadow completely covered the yacht. The boat lurched forward, dragged by the harpoon line, its forward runners rising off the ice. Then the line came free. Rorsefne had not secured it properly. The boat thudded down.

The bull lowered his bulk to the ice and began to move rapidly towards the yacht, its jaws snapping. Arflane managed to turn again; the jaws missed the prow, but the gigantic body smashed against the starboard side. The yacht rocked, nearly toppled, then righted herself.

Manfred Rorsefne was fumbling with the gun, trying to load another harpoon. Then the starboard runners, strained beyond endurance by the jolt they had taken, cracked and broke. The yacht collapsed onto her starboard side, the deck sloping at a steep angle. Arflane was sent flying against the bulkhead as the yacht skidded sideways across the ice, colliding with the rear quarters of the whale as it turned to attack.

Arflane reached out and grabbed the rail of the companionway. He began with great difficulty to crawl up to the bridge. His only thoughts now were for the safety of Ulrica Ulsenn.

As he clambered up, he stared into the terrified face of Janek Ulsenn. He swung aside to let the man push past him. When he reached the bridge, he saw Ulrica lying crumpled against the rail.

Arflane slithered across the sloping deck, and crouched to turn her over. She was not dead, but there was a livid bruise on her forehead.

Arflane paused, staring at the beautiful face; then he swung her across his shoulder and began to fight his way back to the companionway as the whale bellowed and returned to the attack.

When he reached the deck the crewmen were clambering desperately over the port rail, dropping to the ice and running for their lives. Manfred Rorsefne, Urquart and Haeber were nowhere to be seen; but Arflane made out the figure of Janek Ulsenn being helped away from the wrecked boat by two of the crew.

Climbing across the sloping deck by means of the tangle of rigging, Arflane had almost reached the rail when the whale crashed down on the boat's bow. He fell backwards against the wheelhouse, seeing the vast bulk of the creature's head a few feet away from him.

He lost his hold on Ulrica and she rolled away from him towards the stern. He crawled after her, grabbing at the trailing fabric of her long skirt. Again the boat listed, this time towards the bow; he barely managed to stop himself from being catapulted into the gaping jaws by clinging to the mainmast shrouds. Supporting the woman with one arm, he glanced around for a means of escape.

As the whale's head turned, the cold, pain-glazed eyes of the monster regarding him, he grabbed the starboard rail and flung himself and the girl towards and over it, careless of any consideration other than escaping the beast for a few moments.

They fell heavily to the snow. He dragged himself upright, once again got Ulrica Ulsenn over his shoulder and began to stumble away, his boots sliding on the ice beneath the thin covering of snow. Ahead of him lay a harpoon that must have been shaken from the ship. He paused to pick it up, then staggered on. Behind him the whale snorted; he heard the thump of its flippers, felt them shaking the ground as the beast lumbered in pursuit.

He turned, saw the creature bearing down on him, threw Ulrica's body as far away from him as possible and poised the harpoon. His only chance was to strike one of the eyes and pierce the brain, killing the beast before it killed him; then he might save Ulrica.

He flung the harpoon at the whale's glaring right eye. The barbs struck true, pierced, but did not reach the brain. The whale stopped in its tracks, turning as it attempted to shake the lance from its blinded eye.

The left eye saw Arflane.

The creature paused, snorting and squealing in a curiously high-pitched tone.

Then, before it could come at him again, Arflane glimpsed a movement to his right. The whale also saw the movement and it lifted its head, opening its jaws.

Urquart, with his huge harpoon held in one hand, came running at the beast, hurled himself without stopping at its body, his fingers grasping its hair.

The whale reared again, but could not dislodge the harpooner. Urquart began relentlessly to climb up onto its back. The whale, instinctively aware that once it rolled over and exposed its belly it would be lost, bucked and threshed, but could not rid itself of the small creature that had now reached its back and, on hands and knees, was moving up to its head.

The whale saw Arflane again and snorted.

Cautiously, it pushed itself forward on its flippers, forgetting its burden. Arflane was transfixed, watching in fascination as Urquart slowly rose to a standing position, planting his feet firmly on the whale's back and raising his harpoon in both hands.

The whale quivered, as if anticipating its death. Then Urquart's muscles strained as, with all his strength, he drove the mighty harpoon deep into the creature's vertebrae, dragged it clear and plunged it in again.

A great column of blood gouted from the whale's back obscuring all sight of Urquart and spattering down on Arflane. He turned towards Ulrica Ulsenn as she stirred and moaned.

The hot black blood rained down on her too, drenching them both.

She stood up dazedly and opened her arms, her golden eyes looking into Arflane's.

He stepped forward and embraced her, holding her tightly against his blood-slippery body while behind them the monster screamed, shuddered and died. For minutes its pungent, salty blood gushed out in huge spurts, drenching them, but they were hardly aware of it.

Arflane held the woman to him. Her hands clutched at his back as she shivered and whimpered. She had begun to weep.

He stood there holding her for several minutes at the very least, his own eyes tightly shut, before he became aware of the presence of others.

He opened his eyes and looked about him.

Urquart lounged nearby, his body relaxed, his eyes hooded, his face as sternly set as ever. Near him was Manfred Rorsefne. The young man's left arm hung limply at his side and his face was white with pain, but when he spoke it was in the same light, insouciant tone he always used.

"Forgive me this interruption, captain. But I think we are about to see the noble Lord Janek…"

Reluctantly Arflane released Ulrica; she wiped blood from her face and looked about her vaguely. For a second she held his arm, then released it as she recognized her cousin.

Arflane turned and saw the dead bulk of the monster towering over them only a few feet away. Rounding it, aided by two of his men, came Janek Ulsenn. He had broken at least one leg, probably both.

"Haeber is dead," Manfred said. "And half the crew."

"We all deserve to be dead," grunted Arflane. "I knew that boat was too brittle — and you were a fool to use the harpoon. It might have avoided us if you hadn't provoked it."

"And then we should have missed the excitement!" Rorsefne exclaimed. "Don't be ungrateful, captain."

Janek Ulsenn looked at his wife and saw something in her expression which made him frown. He glanced at Arflane questioningly. Manfred Rorsefne stepped forward and gave Ulsenn a mock salute.

"Your wife is still in one piece, Janek, if that's what concerns you. Doubtless you're curious as to her fate after you left her on the bridge…"

Arflane looked at Rorsefne. "How did you know he did that?"

Manfred smiled. "I, captain, climbed the rigging. I had a splendid view. I saw everything. No-one saw me." He turned his attention back to Janek Ulsenn. "Ulrica's life was saved by Captain Arflane and later, when he killed the whale, by cousin Urquart. Will you thank them, my lord?"

Janek Ulsenn said: "I have broken both my legs."

Ulrica Ulsenn spoke for the first time. Her voice was as vibrant as ever, though a little distant, as if she had not entirely recovered from her shock.

"Thank you, Captain Arflane. I am very grateful. You seem to make it your business saving Rorsefnes." She smiled weakly and looked round at Urquart. "Thank you, Long Lance. You are a brave man. You are both brave."

The glance she then turned on her husband was one of pure contempt. His own expression, already drawn by the pain from his broken legs, became increasingly tense. He spoke sharply. "There is a ship which will take us back." He motioned with his head. "It is over there. We will go to it, Ulrica."

When Ulrica obediently followed her departing husband as he was helped away by his men, Arflane made to step forward; but Manfred Rorsefne's hand gripped his shoulder.

"She is his wife," Manfred said softly and quite seriously.

Arflane tried to shake off the young man's grip. In a lighter tone Manfred added: "Surely you, of all people, respect our old laws and customs most, Captain Arflane?"

Arflane spat on the ice.

CHAPTER SEVEN

THE FUNERAL ON THE ICE

Lord Pyotr Rorsefne had died in their absence; two days later his funeral took place.

Also to be buried that day were Brenn of the *Tender Maiden* and Haeber, first officer of the ice yacht. There were three separate funerals being held beyond the city, but only Rorsefne's was splendid.

Looking across the white ice, with its surface snow whipped into eddying movement by the frigid wind, Arflane could see all three burial parties. He reflected that it was the Rorsefnes who had killed his old friend Brenn, and Haeber too; their jaunt to the whaling grounds had caused both deaths. But he could not feel much bitterness.

On his distant left and right were black sledges bearing the plain coffins of Brenn and Haeber, while ahead of him moved the funeral procession of Pyotr Rorsefne, of which he was part, coming behind the relatives and before the servants and other mourners. His face was solemn but Arflane felt very little emotion at all, although initially he had been shocked to learn of Rorsefne's death.

Wearing the black sealskin mourning cloak stitched with the red insignia of the Rorsefne clan, Arflane sat in a sleigh drawn by wolves with black-dyed coats. He held the reins himself. Also in heavy black cloaks, Manfred Rorsefne and the dead man's daughter, Ulrica, sat together on another sleigh drawn by black wolves, and behind them were miscellaneous members of the Rorsefne and Ulsenn families. Janek Ulsenn was too ill to attend. At the head of the procession, moving slowly, was the black funeral sleigh, with its high prow and stern, bearing the ornate ivory coffin in which lay the dead Lord Rorsefne.

Ponderously, the dark procession crossed the ice. Above it, heavy white clouds gathered and the sun was obscured. Light snow was falling.

At length the burial pit came into sight. It had been carved from the ice and gleaming blocks of ice stood piled to one side. Near this pile stood a large loading boom which had been used to haul up the blocks. The boom with its struts and hanging tackle resembled a gallows, silhouetted against the cold sky.

The air was very quiet, save for the slow scrape of the runners and the faint moan of the wind.

A motionless figure stood near the piled ice blocks. It was Urquart, face frozen as usual, bearing his long lance as usual, come to witness his father's burial. Snow had settled on his piled hair and his shoulders, increasing his resemblance to a member of the Ice Mother's hierarchy.

They came nearer and Arflane was able to hear the creak of the loading beam as it swung in the wind; he saw that Urquart's face was not quite without expression. There was a peculiar look of disappointment there, as well as a trace of anger.

The procession gradually came to a halt near the black hole in the ice. Snow pattered on the coffin and the wind caught their cloaks and ripped the hood from Ulrica Ulsenn's head. Arflane glimpsed her tear-streaked face as she pulled the fabric back into place. Manfred Rorsefne, his broken arm in a sling beneath his cloak, turned to nod at Arflane. They got down from their sleighs and, with four of the male relatives, approached the coffin.

Manfred, helped by a boy of about fifteen, cut loose the black wolves and handed their harness to two servants who stood ready. Then, three men on either side, they pushed the heavy sleigh to the pit.

It balanced on the edge for a moment, as if in reluctance, then slid over and fell into the darkness. They heard it crash at the bottom; then they walked to the pile of ice blocks to throw them into the pit and seal it. But Urquart had already taken the first block in both hands, his harpoon for once lying on the ice where he had placed it. He lifted the block high and flung it down with great force, his lips drawn back from his teeth, his eyes full of fire. He paused, looking into the pit, wiping his hands on his greasy coat, then, picking up his harpoon, he walked away as Arflane and the others began to push the rest of the blocks towards the edge.

It took an hour to fill the pit and erect the flag bearing the Rorsefne arms. The flag fluttered in the wind. Gathered around it now were the mourners, their heads bowed as Manfred Rorsefne used his good hand to climb clumsily to the top of the heaped ice to begin the funeral oration.

"The Ice Mother's son returns to her cold womb," he began in the traditional way. "As She gave him life, She takes it; but he will exist now for eternity in the halls of ice where the Mother holds court. Imperishable, She rules the world. Imperishable are those who join Her now. Imperishable, She will make the world one thing, without age or movement; without desire or frustration; without anger or joy; perfect and whole and silent. Let us join Her soon."

He had spoken well and clearly, with some emotion.

Arflane dropped to one knee and repeated the final sentence. "Let us join Her soon."

Behind him, responding with less fervour, the others followed his example, muttering the words where he had spoken them boldly.

CHAPTER EIGHT

RORSEFNE'S WILL

Arflane, possibly more than anyone, sensed the guilt Ulrica Ulsenn felt over her father's death. Very little guilt, or indeed grief now, showed on her features, but her manner was at once remote and tense. It was at her instigation, as well as Manfred's, that the disastrous expedition had set off on the very day her father had died.

Arflane realized that she was not to blame for thinking him almost completely recovered; in fact there seemed no logical reason why he should have weakened so rapidly. It appeared that his heart, always considered healthy, had given out soon after he had dictated a will which was to be read later that afternoon to Arflane and the close relatives. Pyotr Rorsefne had died at about the same time the whale had attacked and destroyed the yacht, a few hours after he had spoken to Arflane of New York.

Sitting stiffly upright in a chair, hands clasped in her lap, Ulrica Ulsenn waited with Arflane, Manfred Rorsefne and her husband, who lay on a raised stretcher, in the ante-room adjoining what had been her father's study. The room was small, its walls crowded with hunting trophies from Pyotr Rorsefne's youth. Arflane found unpleasant the musty smell that came from the heads of the beasts.

The door of the study opened and Strom, the wizened old man

who had been Pyotr Rorsefne's general retainer, beckoned them wordlessly into the room.

Arflane and Manfred Rorsefne stooped to pick up Ulsenn's stretcher and followed Ulrica Ulsenn into the study.

The study was reminiscent of a ship's cabin, though the light came from dim lighting strips instead of portholes. Its walls were lined from floor to ceiling with lockers. A large desk of yellow ivory stood in the centre; on it rested a single sheet of thin plastic. The sheet was large and covered in brown writing, as if it had been inscribed in blood. It curled at the ends; evidently it had been unrolled only recently.

The old man took Manfred Rorsefne to the desk and sat him down in front of the paper; then he left the room.

Manfred sighed and tapped his fingers on the desk as he read the will. Normally Janek Ulsenn should have fulfilled this function, but the fever which had followed his accident had left him weak and only now was he pushing himself into a sitting position so that he could look over the top of the desk and regard his wife's cousin through baleful, disturbed eyes.

"What does it say?" he asked, weakly but impatiently.

"Little that we did not expect," Manfred told him, still reading. There was a slight smile on his lips now.

"Why is this man here?" Ulsenn motioned with his hand toward Arflane.

"He is mentioned in the will, cousin."

Arflane glanced over Ulsenn's head at Ulrica, but she refused to look in his direction.

"Read it out," said Ulsenn, sinking back onto one arm. "Read it out, Manfred."

Manfred shrugged and began to read.

"'The Will of Pyotr Rorsefne, Chief Ship Lord of Friesgalt'," he began. "'The Rorsefne is dead. The Ulsenn rules.'" He glanced sardonically at the reclining figure. "'Save all my fortune and estates and ships, which I hereby will to be divided equally between my daughter and my nephew, I hereby present the command of my schooner the *Ice Spirit* to Captain Konrad Arflane of Brershill, so that he may take her to New York on the course charted on the maps I also leave to him. If Captain Arflane should find the city of New York and live to return to Friesgalt, he shall become whole owner of the *Ice Spirit*, and any cargo she may then carry. To benefit from my will, my daughter Ulrica and my nephew Manfred must accompany Captain Arflane upon his voyage. Captain Arflane shall have complete power over all who sail with him. Pyotr Rorsefne of Friesgalt.'"

Ulsenn was raising himself to a sitting position again. He glowered at Arflane. "The old man was full of fever. He was insane. Forget this condition. Dismiss Captain Arflane, divide the property as the will stipulates. Would you embark upon another crazy voyage so soon after the first? Be warned; the first voyage anticipates the second, should you take it!"

"By the Ice Mother, cousin, how superstitious you have become," Manfred Rorsefne murmured. "You know very well that should we ignore one part of the will, then the other becomes invalid. And think how you would benefit if we did perish! Your wife's share and mine would make you the most powerful man to have ruled in all the Eight Cities."

"I care nothing for the wealth. I am wealthy enough. It is my wife I wish to protect!"

Again Manfred Rorsefne smiled sardonically, recalling Ulsenn's desertion of his wife aboard the yacht. Ulsenn scowled at him, then relapsed, gasping, onto his pillows.

Stony-faced, Ulrica rose. "He had best be taken to his bed," she said.

Arflane and Manfred picked up the stretcher between them, and Ulrica led the way through dark passages to Ulsenn's bedroom, where servants took him and helped him into the large bed. His face was white with pain and he was almost fainting, but he continued to mutter about the stupidity of the old man's will.

"I wonder if he will decide to accompany us when we sail," Manfred said as they left. He smiled ironically. "Probably he will find that his health and his duties as the new lord will keep him in the crevasse."

The three of them walked back to one of the main living rooms. It was furnished with brightly painted wall hangings and chairs and couches of wood and fibreglass frames padded and covered in animal skins. Arflane threw himself onto one of the couches and Ulrica sat opposite him, her eyes downcast. Only her long-fingered hands moved slightly in her lap.

Manfred did not sit.

"I must go to proclaim my uncle's will — or rather most of it," he said. He had to go to the top of the crevasse-city and use a megaphone to repeat the words of the will to all the citizens. Friesgalt was acknowledging Pyotr Rorsefne's death in the traditional way. All work had ceased and the citizens had retired to their cavern homes for the three days of mourning.

When Manfred left Ulrica did not, as Arflane had expected, make some excuse to follow. Instead she ordered a servant to bring them some hot *hess*. "You will have some, captain?" she asked faintly.

Arflane nodded, looking at her curiously. She got up and moved about the room for a moment, pretending to inspect scenes on the wall hangings; they must have been more than familiar to her.

Arflane said at length, "You should not feel that you did any wrong, Lady Ulsenn."

She turned, raising her eyebrows. "Wrong? What do you mean?"

"You did not desert your father. We all thought he was completely recovered. He said so himself. You are not guilty."

"Thank you," she said. She bowed her head, a trace of irony in her tone. "I was not aware that I felt guilt."

"I'm sorry that I should have thought so," he said.

When she next looked at him, it was with a more candid expression as she studied his face. Gradually despair and quiet agony came into her eyes.

He rose awkwardly and went towards her, taking her hands in his, holding them firmly.

"You are strong, Captain Arflane," she murmured. "I am weak."

"Not so," he said heavily. "Not so, ma'am."

She gently removed her hands from his and went to sit on a couch. The servant returned, placed the *hess* on a small table near the couch and left again. She reached forward and poured a goblet of the stuff, handing it up to him. He took it, standing over her with his legs slightly apart, looking down at her sympathetically.

"I was thinking that there is much of your father in you," he said. "The strength is there."

"You did not know my father well," she reminded him quietly.

"Well enough, I think. You forget that I saw him when he thought he was alone and dying. It was what I felt was in him, then, that I see in you now. I would not have saved his life if I had not seen that quality."

She gave a great sigh and her golden eyes glistened with tears. "Perhaps you were wrong," she said.

He sat beside her on the couch, shaking his head. "All the strength of the family went into you for this generation. Your weakness is probably his, too."

"What weakness?"

"A wild imagination. It took him to New York — or so he said — and it took you on the whale hunt."

She smiled gratefully, her features softening as she looked directly at him. "If you are trying to comfort me, captain, I think you are succeeding."

"I'd comfort you more if —" He had not meant to speak. He had not meant to take her hands again as he did; but she did not resist and though her expression became serious and thoughtful, she did not seem offended.

Now Arflane breathed rapidly, remembering when he had embraced her on the ice. She flushed, but still she let him grip her hands.

"I love you," said Arflane, almost miserably.

Then she burst into tears, took her hands away, and flung herself against him. He held her tightly while she wept, stroking her long, fine hair, kissing her forehead, caressing her shoulders. He felt the tears in his own eyes as he responded to her grief. Only barely aware of what he did next, he picked her up in his arms and carried her from the room. The passages were deserted as he took her towards her bedroom, where he still believed he intended to lay her on the bed and let her sleep. He kicked open the door — it was across the corridor from Ulsenn's — and kicked it shut behind him when he had entered.

The room was furnished with chairs, lockers and a dressing table of softly tinted ivory. White furs were heaped on the wide bed and also lined the walls.

He stopped and placed her on the bed, but he did not straighten up.

Now he knew that, in spite of the dreadful guilt he felt, he could do nothing to control his actions. He kissed her mouth. Her arms went around his neck as she responded, and he lowered his massive body onto hers, feeling the warmth and the contours of her flesh through the fabric of the dress, feeling her writhe and tremble beneath him like a frightened bird.

She shuddered under his touch and told him that she was a virgin, that she had never allowed Janek to consummate their marriage. Then she reached over to him and kissed him.

CHAPTER NINE

ULRICA ULSENN'S CONSCIENCE

Early in the morning, looking down on her as she slept with her face just visible above the furs and her black hair spread out on the pillow, Arflane felt remorse. No remorse, he knew, would be sufficient to make him part with Ulrica now, but he had broken the law he respected; the law he regarded as just and vital to the existence of his world. This morning he saw himself as a hypocrite, as a deceiver, and as a thief. While he was reconciled to these new rôles, the fact that he had assumed them depressed him; and he was further depressed by the knowledge that he had taken advantage of the woman's vulnerability at a time when her own guilt and grief had combined to weaken her moral strength.

Arflane did not regret his actions. He considered regret a useless emotion. What was done was done, and now he must decide what to do next.

He sighed as he clothed himself, unwilling to leave her but aware of what the law would do to her if she were discovered as an adulteress. At worst, she would be exposed on the ice to die. At the very least both he and she would be ostracized in all the Eight Cities; this in itself was effectually a lingering death sentence.

She opened her eyes and smiled at him sweetly; then the smile faltered.

"I'm leaving," he whispered. "We'll talk later."

She sat up in the bed, the furs falling away from her breasts. He bent forward to kiss her, gently pulling her arms from his neck as she tried to embrace him.

"What are you going to do?" she asked.

"I don't know. I'd thought of going away — to Brershill."

"Janek would break your city apart to find us. Many would die."

"I know. Would he divorce you?"

"He owns me because I have the highest rank of any woman in Friesgalt; because I am beautiful and well mannered and rich." She shrugged. "He is not particularly interested in demanding his rights. He would divorce me because I refused to entertain his guests, not because I refused to make love to him."

"Then what can we do? I shall deceive him only while I must protect you. I doubt in any case if I would be able to deceive him for long."

She nodded. "I doubt it, also." She smiled up at him again. "But if you took me away, where could we go?"

He shook his head. "I don't know. To New York, perhaps. Remember the will?"

"Yes — New York."

"We will talk later today, when we have an opportunity," he said. "I must go before the servants come."

It had not occurred to either of them to question the fact that she was Janek Ulsenn's property, no matter how little he deserved her; but now, as he made to leave, she grasped his arm and spoke earnestly.

"I am yours," she said. "I am rightfully yours, despite my marriage vows. Remember that."

He muttered something and went to the door, opening it cautiously and slipping into the corridor.

From Ulsenn's room, as Arflane passed it, there came a groan of pain as the new Lord of Friesgalt turned in his bed and twisted his useless legs.

At breakfast they were as shy as ever of exchanging glances. They sat at opposite ends of the table, with Manfred Rorsefne between them. His arm was still strapped in splints to his chest, but he appeared to be in as lighthearted a mood as ever.

"I gather my uncle had already told you he wanted you to command the *Ice Spirit* and take her to New York?" he said to Arflane.

Arflane nodded.

"And did you agree?" Manfred asked.

"I half agreed," Arflane replied, pretending a greater interest in his meal than he felt, resentful of Manfred's presence in the room.

"What do you say now?"

"I'll skipper the ship," Arflane said. "She'll take time to crew and provision. She may need to be refitted. Also I'll want a careful look at those charts."

"I'll get them for you," Manfred promised. He glanced sideways at Ulrica. "How do you feel about the proposed voyage, cousin?"

She flushed. "It was my father's wish," she said flatly.

"Good." Manfred sat back in his chair, evidently in no hurry to leave. Arflane resisted the temptation to frown.

He tried to prolong the meal, hoping that Manfred would lose patience, but finally he was forced to let the servants take away his plate. Manfred made light conversation, seemingly oblivious of Arflane's reluctance to talk to him. At length, evidently unable to bear this, Ulrica got up from the table and left the room. Arflane controlled his desire to follow her immediately.

Almost as soon as she had gone, Manfred Rorsefne pushed back his chair and stood up. "Wait here, captain. I'll bring the charts."

Arflane wondered if Manfred guessed anything of what had happened during the night. He was almost sure that, if he did guess, the young man would say nothing to Janek Ulsenn, whom he despised. Yet three days before, on the ice, Manfred had restrained him from following Ulrica and had seemed resolved to make sure that Arflane would not interfere between Ulsenn and his wife. Arflane found the young man an enigma. At some times he seemed cynical and contemptuous of tradition; at others he seemed anxious to preserve it.

Rorsefne returned with the maps tucked under his good arm. Arflane took them from him and spread them out on the table that had been cleared of the remains of the meal.

The largest chart was drawn to the smallest scale, showing an area of several thousand miles. Superimposed on it in outline were what Arflane recognized as the buried continents of North and South America. Old Pyotr Rorsefne must have gone to considerable trouble with his charts, if this were his work. Clearly marked was the plateau occupying what had once been the Matto Grosso territory and where the Eight Cities now lay; also clearly marked, about two-thirds up the eastern coastline of the northern continent, was New York. From the Matto Grosso to New York a line had been drawn. In Rorsefne's handwriting were the words "Direct Course (Impossible)". A dotted line showed another route that roughly followed the ancient land masses, angling approximately north-west by north before swinging gradually to east by north. This was marked "Likely Course". Here and there it had been corrected in a different coloured ink; it was obvious that these were the changes made on the actual voyage, but there were only a few scribbled indications of what the ship had been avoiding. There were several references to ice breaks, mountains, barbarian camps, but no details of their precise positions.

"These charts were amended from memory," Manfred said. "The log and the original charts were lost in the wreck."

"Couldn't we look for the wreck?" Arflane asked.

"We could — but it would hardly be worth it. The ship broke up completely. Anything like the log or the charts would have been destroyed or buried by now."

Arflane spread the other charts out. They were of little help, merely giving a clearer idea of the region a few hundred miles beyond the plateau.

Arflane spoke rather petulantly. "All we know is where to look when we get there," he said. "And we know that it's possible to get there. We can follow this course and hope for the best — but I'd expected more detailed information. I wonder if the old man really did find New York."

"We'll know in a few months, with any luck." Manfred smiled.

"I'm still unhappy with the maps." Arflane began to roll up the big chart.

"We'll have a better ship, a better crew — and a better captain than my uncle took." Manfred spoke reassuringly.

Arflane tidied the other charts. "I'll pick every member of my crew myself. I'll check every inch of rigging and every ounce of provisions we take aboard. It will be at least two weeks before we're ready to sail."

Manfred was about to speak when the door opened. Four servants walked in, carrying Janek Ulsenn's stretcher. The new ruler of Friesgalt seemed in better health than he had the previous evening. He sat up in the stretcher.

"There you are, Manfred. Have you seen Strom this morning?"

Manfred shook his head. "I was in my uncle's quarters earlier. I didn't see him."

Ulsenn signaled abruptly for the servants to lower the stretcher to the floor. They did so carefully.

"Why were you in those quarters? They are mine now, you know." Ulsenn's haughty voice rose.

Manfred indicated the rolled charts on the table.

"I had to get these to show Captain Arflane. They are the charts we need to plan the *Ice Spirit's* voyage."

"You mean to follow the letter of the will, then?" Janek Ulsenn said acidly. "I still object to the venture. Pyotr Rorsefne was mad when he wrote it. He has made a common foreign sailor one of his heirs! He might just as well have left his wealth to Urquart, who is, after all, his kin. I could declare the will void…"

Manfred pursed his lips and shook his head slowly. "You could not, cousin. Not the will of the old lord. I have declared it publicly. Everyone will know if you do not adhere to its instructions…"

A thought occurred to Arflane. "You told the whole crevasse about New York? The old man didn't want the knowledge made general —"

"I didn't mention New York by name, but only as a 'distant city below the plateau'," Manfred assured him.

Ulsenn smiled. "Then there you are. You merely said to the most distant of the Eight Cities…"

Manfred sneered very slightly. "Below the plateau? Besides, if it were one of the Eight that the will referred to, then it would have been making what was virtually a declaration of war. Your pain clouds your intelligence, cousin."

Ulsenn coughed and glared up at Manfred. "You are impertinent, Manfred. I am Lord now. I could order you both put to death..."

"With no trial? These are empty threats, cousin. Would the people accept such an action?"

In spite of the great personal authority of the Chief Ship Lord, the real power still rested in the hands of the mass of citizens, who had been known in the past to depose an unwelcome or tyrannical owner of the title. Ulsenn could not afford to take drastic action against any member of the much-respected Rorsefne family. As it was, his own standing in the city was comparatively slight. He had risen to the title by marriage, not by direct blood line or by any other means. If he were to imprison Manfred or someone whom Manfred protected, Ulsenn might easily find himself with a civil war on his hands, and he knew what the result of such a war would be.

Ulsenn, therefore, remained silent.

"It is Pyotr Rorsefne's *will*, cousin," Manfred reminded him firmly. "Whatever you may feel about it, Captain Arflane commands the *Ice Spirit*. Don't worry. Ulrica and I will go along to represent the family."

Ulsenn darted a sharp, enigmatic look at Arflane. He signaled for his servants to pick up the stretcher. "If Ulrica goes — I will go!" The servants carried him from the room.

Arflane realized that Manfred Rorsefne was looking with amused interest at his face. The young man must have read the expression there. Arflane had not been prepared for this declaration. He had been confident that Ulsenn would have been too involved with his new power, too ill and too cowardly to join the expedition. He had been confident in his anticipation of Ulrica's company on the proposed voyage. Now he could anticipate nothing.

Manfred laughed.

"Cheer up, captain. Janek won't bother us on the voyage. He's an accountant, a stay-at-home merchant who knows nothing of sailing. He could not interfere if he wished to. He won't help us find the Ice Mother's lair — but he won't hinder us, either."

Although Manfred's reassurance seemed genuine, Arflane still could not tell if the young man had actually guessed the real reason for his disappointment. For that matter, he wondered if Janek Ulsenn had guessed what had happened in his wife's bedroom that night. The look he had given Arflane seemed to indicate that he suspected something, though it seemed impossible that he could know what had actually taken place.

Arflane was disturbed by the turn of events. He wanted to see Ulrica at once and talk to her about what had happened. He had a sudden feeling of deep apprehension.

"When will you begin inspecting the ship and picking the crew, captain?" Manfred was asking.

"Tomorrow," Arflane told him ungraciously. "I'll see you before I get out there."

He made a curt farewell gesture with his hand and left the room. He began to walk through the low corridors, searching for Ulrica.

He found her in the main living room where, on the previous night, he had first caressed her. She rose hurriedly when he entered. She was pale; she held her body rigidly, her hands gripped tightly together at her waist. She had bound up her hair, drawing it back tightly from her face. She was wearing the black dress of fine sealskin which she had worn the day before at the funeral. Arflane closed the door, but she moved towards it, attempting to pass him. He barred the way with one arm and tried to look into her eyes, but she averted her head.

"Ulrica, what is it?" The sense of foreboding was now even stronger. "What is it? Did you hear that your husband intends to come with us on the voyage? Is that why...?"

She looked at him coolly and he dropped his arm away from the door.

"I am sorry, Captain Arflane," she said formally. "But it would be best if you forgot what passed between us. We were both in unusual states of mind. I realize now that it is my duty to remain faithful to my —"

Her whole manner was artificially polite.

"Ulrica!" He gripped her shoulders tightly. "Did he tell you to say this? Has he threatened you...?"

She shook her head. "Let me go, captain."

"Ulrica..." His voice had broken. He spoke weakly, dropping his hands from her shoulders. "Ulrica, why...?"

"I seem to remember you speaking quite passionately in favour of the old traditions," she said. "More than once I've heard you say that to let slip our code will mean our perishing as a people. You mentioned that you admired my father's strength of mind and that you saw the same quality in me. Perhaps you did, captain. I intend to stay faithful to my husband."

"You aren't saying what you mean. I can tell that. You love me. This mood is just a reaction — because things seem too complicated now. You told me that you were rightfully mine. You *meant* what you said this morning." He hated the tone of desperation in his own voice, but he could not control it.

"I mean what I am saying now, captain; and if you respect the old way of life, then you will respect my request that you see as little of me as possible from now on."

"No!" He roared in anger and lurched towards her. She stepped back, face frozen and eyes cold. He reached out to touch her and then slowly withdrew his hands and stepped aside to let her pass.

She opened the door. He understood now that no outside event had caused this change in her. The cause was her own conscience. He could not argue with her decision. Morally, it was right. There was nothing he could do; there was no hope he could hold. He watched her walk slowly away from him down the corridor. Then he slammed the door, his face twisted in an expression of agonized despair. There was a snapping sound and the door swung back. He had broken its lock. It would no longer close properly.

He hurried to his room and began to bundle his belongings together. He would make sure that he obeyed her request. He would not see her again, at least until the ship was ready to sail. He would go out to the *Ice Spirit* at once and begin his work.

He slung the sack over his shoulder and hurried through the winding corridors to the outer entrance. Bloody thoughts were in his mind and he wanted to get into the open, hoping that the clean air of the surface would blow them away.

As he reached the outer door, he met Manfred Rorsefne in the hall. The young man looked amused.

"Where are you off to, captain?"

Arflane glared at him, wanting to strangle the supercilious expression from Rorsefne's face.

"I see you're leaving, captain. Off to the *Ice Spirit* so soon? I thought you were going tomorrow…"

"Today," Arflane growled. He recovered some of his self-assurance. "Today. I'll get started at once. I'll sleep on board until we sail. It will be best…"

"Perhaps it will," Rorsefne agreed, speaking half to himself as he watched the big, red-bearded sailor stride rapidly from the house.

CHAPTER TEN

KONRAD ARFLANE'S MOOD

Of the newly discovered facts about his own character that obsessed Konrad Arflane, the most startling was that he had never suspected himself capable of renouncing all his principles in order to possess another man's wife. He also found it difficult to equate with his own idea of himself the knowledge that, having been stopped from seeing the woman, he should not become reconciled, or indeed grateful.

He was far from being either. He slept badly, his attention turned constantly to thoughts of Ulrica Ulsenn. He waited without hope for her to come to him and when she did not he was angry. He stalked about the big ship, bawling out the men over quibbling details, dismissing hands he had hired the day before, muttering offensively to his officers in front of the men, demanding that he should be made aware of all problems aboard, then swearing furiously when some unnecessary matter was brought to him.

He had had the reputation of being a particularly good skipper; stern and remote, but fair. The whaling hands, whom he preferred for his crewmen, had been eager to sign with the *Ice Spirit*, in spite of the mysterious voyage she was to make. Now many were regretting it.

Arflane had appointed three officers — or rather he had let two appointments stand and had signed on Long Lance Urquart as third officer, below Petchnyoff and old Kristoff Hinsen. Urquart seemed oblivious to Arflane's irrational moods, but the two other men were puzzled and upset by the change in their new skipper. Whenever Urquart was not in their quarters — which was often — they would take the opportunity to discuss the problem. Both had liked Arflane when they had first met him. Petchnyoff had had a high regard for his integrity and strength of will; Kristoff Hinsen felt a more intimate relationship with him, based on memories of the days when they had been rival skippers. Neither was capable of analyzing the cause of the change in Arflane's temperament; yet so much did they trust their earlier impressions of him that they were prepared for a while to put up with his moods in the hope that, once under way, he would become the man they had first encountered. Petchnyoff's patience as the days passed was increasingly strained and he began to think of resigning his command, but Hinsen persuaded him to wait a little longer.

The huge vessel was being fitted with completely new canvas and rigging. Arflane personally inspected every pin, every knot, and every line. He climbed over the ship inch by inch, checking the set of the yards, the tension of the rigging, the snugness of the hatch-covers, the feel of the bulkheads, until he was satisfied. He tested the wheel time after time, turning the runners this way and that to get to know their exact responses. Normally the steering runners and their turntable were immovably locked in relation with each other. On the foredeck, though, immediately above the great gland of the steering pin, was housed the emergency bolt, with a heavy mallet secured beside it. Dropping the bolt would release the skids, allowing them to turn in towards each other creating in effect a huge ploughshare that dug into the ice, bringing the vessel to a squealing and frequently destructive halt. Arflane tested this apparatus for hours. He also dropped the heavy anchors once or twice. These were on either side of the ship, beneath her bilges. They consisted of two great blades. Above them, through guides let into the hull, rods reached to the upper deck. Pins driven through the rods kept the blades clear of ice; beside each stanchion, mallets were kept ready to knock the pegs clear in case of danger or emergency. The heavy anchors were seldom used, and never by a good skipper; contact with racing ice would wear them rapidly away, and replacements were now nearly unobtainable.

At first men and officers had called out cheerfully to him as he went about the ship; but they soon learned to avoid him, and the superstitious whaling hands began to speak of curses and of a foredoomed voyage; yet very few disembarked of their own accord.

Arflane would watch moodily from the bridge as bale after bale and barrel after barrel of provisions was swung aboard, packing every inch of available space. With each fresh ton that was taken into the holds, he would again test the wheel and the heavy anchors to see how the *Ice Spirit* responded.

One day on deck Arflane saw Petchnyoff inspecting the work of a sailor who had been one of a party securing the mainmast ratlines. He strode up to the pair and pulled at the lines, checking the knots. One of them was not as firm as it could be.

"Call that a knot, do you, Mr Petchnyoff?" he said offensively. "I thought you were supposed to be inspecting this work!"

"I am, sir."

"I'd like to be able to trust my officers," Arflane said with a sneer. "Try to see that I can in future."

He marched off along the deck. Petchnyoff slammed a belaying pin he had been holding down onto the deck, narrowly missing the surprised hand.

That evening, Petchnyoff had got half his kit packed before Hinsen could convince him to stay on board.

The weeks went by. There were four floggings for minor offenses. It was as if Arflane were deliberately trying to get his crew to leave him before the ship set sail. Yet many of the men were fascinated by him, and the fact that Urquart had thrown in his lot with Arflane must have had something to do with the whaling hands staying.

Manfred Rorsefne would occasionally come aboard to confer with Arflane. Originally Arflane had said that it would take a fortnight to ready the ship, but he had put off the sailing date further and further on one excuse and another, telling Rorsefne that he was still not happy that everything had been done that could be done, reminding him that a voyage of this kind demanded a ship that was as perfect as possible.

"True, but we'll miss the summer at this rate," Manfred Rorsefne reminded him gently. Arflane scowled in reply, saying he could sail in any weather. His carefulness on one hand, and his apparent recklessness on the other, did little to reassure Rorsefne; but he said nothing.

Finally there was absolutely no more to be done aboard the ice schooner. She was in superb trim; all her ivory was polished and shining, her decks were scrubbed and freshly boned. Her four masts gleamed with white, furled canvas; her rigging was straight and taut; the boats, swinging in davits fashioned from the jawbones of whales, hung true and firm; every pin was in place and every piece of gear was where it should be. The barbaric whale skulls at her prow glared towards the north as if defying all the dangers that might be awaiting them. The *Ice Spirit* was ready to sail.

Still reluctant to send for his passengers, Arflane stood in silence on the bridge and looked at the ship. For a moment it occurred to him that he could take her out now, leaving the Ulsenns and Manfred Rorsefne behind. The ice ahead was obscured by clouds of snow that were lifted by the wind and sent drifting across the bow; the sky was grey and heavy. Gripping the rail in his gauntleted hands, Arflane knew it would not be difficult to slip out to the open ice in weather like this.

He sighed and turned to Kristoff Hinsen who stood beside him.

"Send a man to the Rorsefne place, Mr Hinsen. Tell them if the wind holds we'll sail tomorrow morning."

"Aye, aye, sir." Hinsen paused, his weatherbeaten features creased in doubt. "Tomorrow morning, sir?"

Arflane turned his brooding eyes on Hinsen. "I said tomorrow. That's the message, Mr Hinsen."

"Aye, aye, sir." Hinsen left the bridge hurriedly.

Arflane knew why Hinsen queried his orders. The weather was bad and obviously getting worse. By morning they would have a heavy snowstorm; visibility would be poor, and the men would find it difficult to set the canvas. But Arflane had made up his mind; he looked away, back towards the bow.

Two hours later he saw a covered sleigh being drawn across the ice from the city. Tawny wolves pulled it, their paws slipping on the ice.

A strong gust of wind blew suddenly from the west and buffeted the side of the ship so that it moved slightly to starboard in its mooring cables. Arflane did not need to order the cables checked. Several hands instantly ran to see to them. It was a larger crew than he normally liked to handle, but he had to admit, even in his poor temper, that their discipline was very good.

The wolves came to an untidy stop close to the ship's side. Arflane cursed and swung down from the bridge, moving to the rail and leaning over it. The driver had brought the carriage in too close for his own safety.

"Get that thing back!" Arflane yelled. "Get beyond the mooring pegs. Don't you know better than to come so close to a ship of this size while there's a heavy wind blowing? If we slip one cable you'll be crushed."

A muffled head poked itself from the carriage window. "We are here, Captain Arflane. Manfred Rorsefne and the Ulsenns."

"Tell your driver to get back! He ought to —" A fresh gust of wind slammed against the ship's side and sent it skidding several feet closer to the carriage until the slack of the mooring cables on the other side was taken up. The driver looked startled and whipped his wolves into a steep turn. They strained in their harness and loped across the ice with the carriage in tow.

Arflane smiled unpleasantly.

With a wind as erratic as this, few captains would allow their ships out of their moorings, but he intended to sail anyway. It might be dangerous, but it would seem worse to Ulsenn and his relatives.

Manfred Rorsefne and the Ulsenns had got out of the carriage and were standing uncertainly, looking up at the ship, searching for Arflane.

Arflane turned away from them and went back to the bridge.

Fydur, the ship's bosun, saluted him as he began to climb the companionway. "Shall I send out a party to take the passengers aboard, sir?"

Arflane shook his head. "Let them make their own way on board," he told the bosun. "You can lower a gangplank if you like."

A little later he watched Janek Ulsenn being helped up the gangplank and along the deck. He saw Ulrica, completely swathed in her furs, moving beside her husband. Once she looked up at the bridge and he caught a glimpse of her eyes — the only part of her face not hidden by her hood. Manfred strolled along after them, waving cheerfully up at Arflane, but he was forced to clutch a line as the ship moved again in her moorings.

Within a quarter of an hour he had joined Arflane on the bridge.

"I've seen my cousin and her husband into their respective cabins, captain," he said. "I'm settled in myself. At last we're ready, eh?"

Arflane grunted and moved down the rail to starboard, plainly trying to avoid the young man. Manfred seemed unaware of this; he followed, slapping his gloved hands together and looking about him. "You certainly know your ships, captain. I thought the *Spirit* was as neat as she could be until you took over. We should have little trouble on the voyage, I'm sure."

Arflane looked around at Rorsefne.

"We should have no trouble at all," he said grimly. "I hope you'll remind your relatives that I'm in sole command of this ship from the moment she sails. I'm empowered to take any measure I think fit to ensure the smooth running of the vessel…"

"All this is unnecessary, captain." Rorsefne smiled. "We accept that, of course. That is the law of the ice. No need for details; you are the skipper, we do as you tell us to do."

Arflane grunted. "Are you certain Janek Ulsenn understands that?"

"I'm sure he does. He'll do nothing to offend you — save perhaps scowl at you a little. Besides, his legs are still bothering him. He's not entirely fit; I doubt if he'll be seen above deck for a while." Manfred paused and then stepped much closer to Arflane. "Captain — you haven't seemed yourself since you took this command. Is something wrong? Are you disturbed by the idea of the voyage? It occurred to me that you might think there was — um — sacrilege involved."

Arflane shook his head, looking full into Manfred Rorsefne's face. "You know I don't think that."

Rorsefne appeared to be disconcerted for a moment. He pursed his lips. "It's no wish of mine to intrude on your personal…"

"Thank you."

"It would seem to me that the safety of the ship depends almost wholly upon yourself. If you are in poor spirits, captain, perhaps it would be better to delay the voyage longer?"

The wind was whining through the top trees. Automatically, Arflane looked up to make sure that the yards were firm. "I'm not in poor spirits," he said distantly.

"I think I could help…"

Arflane raised the megaphone to his lips and bawled at Hinsen as he crossed the quarter deck.

"Mr Hinsen! Get some men into the mizzen to'g'l'nt yards and secure that flapping canvas!"

Manfred Rorsefne said nothing more. He left the bridge.

Arflane folded his arms across his chest, his features set in a scowl.

CHAPTER ELEVEN

UNDER SAIL

At dawn the next morning a blizzard blew in a great white sheet across the city and the forest of ships, heaping snow on the decks of the *Ice Spirit* till the schooner strained at her anchor lines. Sky and land were indistinguishable and only occasionally were the masts of the other vessels to be seen, outlined in black against the sweeping wall of snow. The temperature had fallen below zero. Ice had formed on the rigging and in the folds of the sails. Particles of ice, whipped by the wind, flew in the air like bullets; it was almost impossible to move against the blustering pressure of the storm. Loose canvas flapped like the broken flippers of seals; the wind shrilled and moaned through the tall masts and boats swung and creaked in their davits.

As a muffled tolling proclaimed two bells in the morning watch, Konrad Arflane, wearing a bandage over his mouth and nose and a snow visor over his eyes, stepped from his cabin below the bridge. Through a mist of driving snow he made his way forward to the bow and peered ahead; it was impossible to see anything in the swirling wall of whiteness. He returned to his cabin, passing Petchnyoff, the officer of the watch, without a word.

Petchnyoff stared after his skipper as the door of the cabin closed. There was a strange, resentful look in the first officer's eyes.

By six-thirty in the morning, as the bell rang five, the driving snow
had eased and weak sunshine was filtering through the clouds. Hinsen
stood beside Arflane on the bridge, a megaphone in his hand. The crew
were climbing into the shrouds, their thickly clad bodies moving slowly
up the ratlines. On the deck by the mainmast stood Urquart, his head
covered by a tall hood, in charge of the men in the yards. The anchor
men stood by their mooring lines, watching the bridge and ready to let
go.

Arflane glanced at Hinsen. "All prepared, Mr Hinsen?"

Hinsen nodded.

Aware that Rorsefne and the Ulsenns were still sleeping below,
Arflane said, "Let go the anchor lines."

"Let go the anchor lines!" Hinsen's voice boomed over the ship
and the men sprang to release the cables. The taut lines whipped away
and the schooner lurched forward.

"Set upper and lower fore to'g'l'nts."

The order was repeated and obeyed.

"Set stays'ls."

The staysails blossomed out.

"Set upper and lower main to'g'l'nts and upper tops'l."

The sails billowed and swelled as they caught the wind, curving
like the wings of monstrous birds, pulling the ship gradually away. Snow
sprayed as the runners sliced through the surface and the schooner
began to move from the port, passing the still-anchored ships near her,
dipping her bowsprit as she descended a slight incline in the ice, surging
as she felt the rise on the other side. Kites squawked, swooping and
circling excitedly around the top trees where the grandiose standard
of the Rorsefne stood straight in the breeze. In her wake the ship left
deep twin scars in the churned snow and ice. A huge, graceful creature,
making her stately way out of port in the early morning under only a
fraction of her sail, the ice in the rigging melting and falling off like a
shower of diamonds, the *Ice Spirit* left Friesgalt behind and moved north
beneath the lowering sky.

"All plain sail, Mr Hinsen."

Sheet by sheet the sails were set until the ship sped over the ice under full canvas. Hinsen glanced at Arflane questioningly; it was unusual to set so much canvas while leaving port. But then he noticed Arflane's face as the ship began to gain speed. The captain was relaxing visibly. His expression was softening, there seemed to be a trace of a smile on his lips and his eyes were beginning to brighten.

Arflane breathed heavily and pushed back his visor, exhilarated by the wind on his face, the rolling of the deck beneath his feet. For the first time since Ulrica Ulsenn had rejected him he felt a lifting of the weight that had descended on him. He half smiled at Hinsen. "She's a real ship, Mr Hinsen."

Old Kristoff, overjoyed at the change in his master, grinned broadly, more in relief than in agreement. "Aye, sir. She can move."

Arflane stretched his body as the ship lunged forward over the seemingly endless plateau of ice, piercing the thinning curtain of snow. Below him on the decks, and above in the rigging, sailors moved like dark ghosts through the drifting whiteness, working under the calm, fixed eye of Long Lance Urquart as he strode up and down the deck, his harpoon resting in its usual place in the crook of his arm. Sometimes Urquart would jump up into the lower shrouds to help a man in difficulties with a piece of tackle. The cold and the snow, combined with the need to wear particularly thick gloves, made it difficult for even the whale men to work, though they were better used to the conditions than were the merchant sailors.

Arflane had hardly spoken to Urquart since the man had come aboard to sign on. Arflane had been happy to accept the harpooner, offering him the berth of third officer. It had vaguely occurred to him to wonder why Urquart should want to sail with him, since the tall harpooner could have no idea of where the ship was bound; but his own obsessions had driven the question out of his head. Now, as he relaxed, he glanced curiously at Urquart. The man caught his eye as he turned from giving instructions to a sailor. He nodded gravely to Arflane.

Arflane had instinctively trusted Urquart's ability to command, knowing that the harpooner had great prestige among the whalers; he had no doubts about his decision, but now he wondered again why Urquart had joined the ship. He had come, uninvited, on the whale hunt. That was understandable maybe; but there was no logical reason why a professional harpooner should wish to sail on a mysterious voyage of exploration. Perhaps Urquart felt protective towards his dead father's daughter and nephew, had decided to come with them to be sure of their safety on the trip; the image of the Long Lance at old Rorsefne's graveside suddenly came back to Arflane. Perhaps, though, Urquart felt friendship towards him personally. After all, only Urquart had seemed instinctively to respect Arflane's troubled state of mind over the past weeks and to understand his need for solitude. Of all the ship's complement, Arflane felt comradeship only toward Urquart, who was still a stranger to him. Hinsen he liked and admired, but since their original disagreement on the *Ice Spirit* over two months earlier, he had not been able to feel quite the same warmth towards him as he might have done.

Arflane leaned on the rail, watching the men at work. The ship was in no real danger until she had to descend the plateau, and they would not reach the edge for several days sailing at full speed; he gave himself the pleasure of forgetting everything but the motion of the ship beneath him, the sight of the snow spray spurting from the runners, the long streamers of clouds above him breaking up now and letting through the early morning sunlight and glimpses of a pale red and yellow sky reflected by the ice.

There was an old saying among sailors that a ship beneath a man was as good as a woman, and Arflane began to feel that he could agree. Once the schooner had gotten under way, his mood had lifted. He was still concerned about Ulrica; but he did not feel the same despair, the same hatred for all humanity that had possessed him while the ship was being readied for the voyage. He began to feel guilty, now he thought back, that he had been so ill-mannered towards his officers and so irrational in his dealings with the crew. Manfred Rorsefne had been concerned that his mood would continue. Arflane had rejected the idea that he was in any kind of abnormal mood, but now he realized the truth of Rorsefne's statement of the night before; he would have been in no state to command the ship if his temper had not changed. It puzzled him that mere physical sensation, like the ship's passage over the ice, could so alter a man's mental attitudes within the space of an hour. Admittedly in the past he had always been restless and ill-tempered when not on board ship, but he had never gone so far as to behave unfairly towards the men serving under him. His self-possession was his pride. He had lost it; now he had found it again.

Perhaps he did not realize at that point that it would take only a glimpse or two of Ulrica Ulsenn to make him once more lose that self-possession in a different way. Even when he looked around to see Janek Ulsenn being helped up to the bridge by Petchnyoff, his spirits were unimpaired; he smiled at Ulsenn in sardonic good humour.

"Well, we're under way, Lord Ulsenn. Hope we didn't wake you."

Petchnyoff looked surprised. He had become so used to the skipper's surly manner that any sign of joviality was bound to set him back.

"You did wake us," Ulsenn began, but Arflane interrupted him to address Petchnyoff.

"You took the middle watch and half the morning watch, I believe, Mr Petchnyoff."

Petchnyoff nodded. "Yes, sir."

"I would have thought it would have suited you to be in your bunk by now," Arflane said as pleasantly as he could. He did not want an officer who was going to be half asleep when his watch came round again.

Petchnyoff shrugged. "I'd planned to get some rest in, sir, after I'd eaten. Then I met Lord Ulsenn coming out of his cabin…"

Arflane gestured with his hand. "I see. You'd better go to your bunk now, Mr Petchnyoff."

"Aye, aye, sir."

Petchnyoff backed down the companionway and disappeared. Ulsenn was left alone. Arflane had deliberately ignored him and Ulsenn was aware of it; he stared balefully at Arflane.

"You may have complete command of this ship, captain, but it would seem to me that you could show courtesy both to your officers and your passengers. Petchnyoff has told me how you have behaved since you took charge. Your boorishness is a watchword in all Friesgalt. Because you have been given a responsibility that elevates you above your fellows, it is no excuse for taking the opportunity to…"

Arflane sighed. "I have made sure that the ship is in the best possible order, if that's what Petchnyoff means," he commented reasonably. He was surprised that Petchnyoff should show such disloyalty; but perhaps the man's ties were, after all, closer to the ruling class of Friesgalt than to a foreign skipper. His own surliness over the past weeks must in any case have helped turn Petchnyoff against him. He shrugged. If the first officer was offended then he could remain so, as long as he performed his duties efficiently.

Ulsenn had seen the slight shrug and misinterpreted it. "You are not aware of what your men are saying about you, captain?"

Arflane leaned casually with his back against the rail, pretending an interest with the racing ice to starboard. "The men always grumble about the skipper. It's the extent of their grumbling and how it affects their work that's the thing to worry about. I've hired whaling men for this voyage, Lord Ulsenn — wild whaling men. I'd expect them to complain."

"They're saying that you carry a curse," Ulsenn murmured, looking cunningly at Arflane.

Arflane laughed. "They're a superstitious lot. It gives them satisfaction to believe in curses. They wouldn't follow a skipper unless they could colour his character in some way. It appeals to their sense of drama. Calm down, Lord Ulsenn. Go back to your cabin and rest your legs."

Ulsenn's lean face twitched in anger. "You are an impertinent boor, captain!"

"I am also adamant, Lord Ulsenn. I'm in full command of this expedition and any attempt to oust my authority will be dealt with in the normal manner." Arflane relished the opportunity to threaten the man. "Have the goodness to leave the bridge!"

"What if the officers and crew aren't satisfied with your command? What if they feel you are mishandling the ship?" Ulsenn leaned forward, his voice high-pitched.

Having so recently regained his own self-control, Arflane felt a somewhat ignoble enjoyment in witnessing Ulsenn losing his. He smiled again. "Calm yourself, my lord. There is an accepted procedure they may take if they are dissatisfied with my command. They could mutiny, which would be unwise; or they could vote for a temporary command and appeal to me to relinquish my post. In which case they must abandon the expedition, return immediately to a friendly city and make a formal report." Arflane gestured impatiently. "Really, sir, you must accept my command once and for all. Our journey will be a long one and conflicts of this kind are best avoided."

"You have produced the conflict, captain."

Arflane shrugged in contempt and did not bother to reply.

"I reserve the right to countermand your orders if I feel they are not in keeping with the best interests of this expedition," Ulsenn continued.

"And I reserve the right, sir, to hang you if you try. I'll have to warn the crew that they're to accept only my orders. That would embarrass you, I think."

Ulsenn snorted. "You're aware, surely, that most of your crew, including your officers, are Friesgaltians? *I* am the man they will listen to before they take such orders from — a foreign —"

"Possibly," Arflane said equably. "In which case, my rights as commander of this ship entitle me, as I believe I've pointed out, to punish any attempt to usurp my authority, whether in word or deed."

"You know your rights, captain," Ulsenn retaliated with attempted sarcasm, "but they are artificial. Mine are the rights of blood — to command the men of Friesgalt."

Beside Arflane, Hinsen chuckled. The sound was totally unexpected; both men turned to stare. Hinsen looked away, covering his mouth a trifle ostentatiously with one gloved hand.

The interruption had, however, produced its effect. Ulsenn was completely deflated. Arflane moved forward and took his arm, helping him towards the companionway.

"Possibly all our rights are artificial, Lord Ulsenn, but mine are designed to keep discipline on a ship and make sure that it is run as smoothly as possible."

Ulsenn began to clamber down the companionway. Arflane motioned Hinsen forward to help him; but when the older man attempted to take his arm, Ulsenn shook him off and made something of a show of controlling his pain as he limped unaided across the deck.

Hinsen grinned at Arflane. The captain pursed his lips in disapproval. The sky was lightening now, turning to a bright, pale blue that was reflected in the flat ice to either side, as the last shreds of clouds disappeared.

The ship moved smoothly, sharply outlined against a mirror amalgam of sky and ice. Looking forward, Arflane saw the men relaxing, gathering in knots and groups on the deck. Through them, moving purposefully, Urquart was shouldering his way towards the bridge.

CHAPTER TWELVE

OVER THE EDGE

Vaguely surprised, Arflane watched the harpooner climb to the poop. Perhaps Urquart sensed that his mood had changed now and that he would be ready to see him. The harpooner nodded curtly to Hinsen and presented himself before Arflane, stamping the butt of his great weapon down on the deck and leaning on it broodingly. He pushed back the hood of his coat, revealing his heap of matted black hair. The clear blue eyes regarded Arflane steadily; the gaunt, red face was as immobile as ever. From him came a faint stink of whale blood and blubber.

"Well, sir." His voice was harsh but low. "We are under way." There was a note of expectancy in his tone.

"You want to know where we're bound, Mr Urquart?" Arflane said on impulse. "We're bound for New York."

Hinsen, standing behind Urquart, raised his eyebrows in surprise. "New York!"

"This is confidential," Arflane warned him. "I don't propose to tell the men just yet. Only the officers."

Over Urquart's grim features there spread a slow smile. When he spun his lance and drove it point first into the deck it seemed to be a gesture of approval. The smile quickly disappeared, but the blue eyes were brighter. "So we sail to the Ice Mother, captain." He did not question the existence of the mythical city; quite plainly he believed firmly in its reality. But Hinsen's old, rugged face bore a look of heavy skepticism.

"Why do we sail to New York, sir? Or is the voyage simply to discover if such a place does exist?"

Arflane, more absorbed in studying Urquart's reaction, answered abstractedly. "The Lord Pyotr Rorsefne discovered the city, but was forced to turn back before he could explore it. We have charts. I think the city exists."

"And the Ice Mother's in residence?" Hinsen could not avoid the hint of irony in his question.

"We'll know that when we get there, Mr Hinsen." For a moment Arflane turned his full attention to his second officer.

"She'll be there," Urquart said with conviction.

Arflane looked curiously at the tall harpooner, then addressed Kristoff Hinsen again. "Remember, Mr Hinsen, I've told you this in confidence."

"Aye, sir." Hinsen paused. Then he said tactfully, "I'll take a tour about the ship, sir, if Mr Urquart wants a word with you. Better have someone keeping an eye on the men."

"Quite right, Mr Hinsen. Thank you."

When Hinsen had left the bridge, the two men stood there in silence for a while, neither feeling the need to speak. Urquart wrested his harpoon from the deck and walked towards the rail. Arflane joined him.

"Happy with the voyage, Mr Urquart?" he asked at length.

"Yes, sir."

"You really think we'll find the Ice Mother?"

"Don't you, captain?"

Arflane gestured uncertainly. "Three months ago, Mr Urquart — three months ago I would have said yes, there would be evidence in New York to support the doctrine. Now…" He paused helplessly. "They say that the scientists have disproved the doctrine. The Ice Mother is dying."

Urquart shifted his weight. "Then She'll need our help, sir. Maybe that's why we're sailing. Maybe it's fate. Maybe She's calling for us."

"Maybe." Arflane sounded doubtful.

"I think so, captain. Pyotr Rorsefne was Her messenger, you see. He was sent to you — that's why you found him on the ice — and when he had delivered his message to us, he died. Don't you see, sir?"

"It could be true," Arflane agreed.

Urquart's mysticism was disconcerting, even to Arflane. He looked directly at the harpooner and saw the fanaticism in the face, the utter conviction in his eyes. Not so long ago he had had a similar conviction. He shook his head sadly.

"I am not the man I was, Mr Urquart."

"No, sir." Urquart seemed to share Arflane's sadness. "But you'll find yourself on this voyage. You'll recover your faith, sir."

Offended for the moment by the intimacy of Urquart's remark, Arflane drew back. "Perhaps I don't need that faith any more, Mr Urquart."

"Perhaps you need it most of all now, captain."

Arflane's anger passed. "I wonder what has happened to me," he said thoughtfully. "Three months ago…"

"Three months ago you had not met the Rorsefne family, captain." Urquart spoke grimly, but with a certain sympathy. "You've become infected with their weakness."

"I understood you to feel a certain loyalty — a certain protective responsibility to the family," Arflane said in surprise. He realized that this understanding had been conjecture on his part, but he had been convinced that he was right.

"I want them kept alive, if that's what you mean," Urquart said noncommittally.

"I'm not sure I understand you…" Arflane began, but was cut short by Urquart turning away from him and looking distantly towards the horizon.

The silence became uncomfortable and Arflane felt disturbed by the loss of Urquart's confidence. The half-savage harpooner did not elaborate on his remark, but eventually turned back to look at Arflane, his expression softening by a degree.

"It's the Ice Mother's will," he said. "You needed to use the family so that you could get the ship. Avoid our passengers all you can from now on, captain. They are weak. Even the old man was too indulgent, and he was better than any that still live…"

"You say it was the Ice Mother," Arflane replied gloomily. "I think it was a different kind of force, just as mysterious, that involved me with the family."

"Think what you like," Urquart said impatiently, "but I know what is true. I know your destiny. Avoid the Rorsefne family."

"What of Lord Ulsenn?"

"Ulsenn is nothing." Urquart sneered.

Impressed by Urquart's warning, Arflane was careful to say nothing more of the Rorsefne family. He had already noted how much involved with the three people he had become. Yet surely, he thought, there were certain strengths in all of them. They were not as soft as Urquart thought. Even Ulsenn, though a physical coward, had his own kind of integrity, if it was only a belief in his absolute right to rule. It was true that his association with the family had caused him to forsake many of his old convictions, yet surely that was his weakness, not theirs? Urquart doubtless blamed their influence. Perhaps he was right.

He sighed and dusted at the rail with his gloved hand. "I hope we find the Ice Mother," he said eventually. "I need to be reassured, Mr Urquart."

"She'll be there, captain. Soon you'll know it, too." Urquart reached out and gripped Arflane's shoulder. Arflane was startled, but he did not resent the gesture. The harpooner peered into his face. The blue eyes were alight with the certainty of his own ideas. He shook his harpoon. "This is true," he said passionately. He pointed out to the ice. "That is true." He dropped his arm. "Find your strength again, captain. You'll need it on this voyage."

The harpooner clambered down from the bridge and disappeared, leaving Arflane feeling at the same time uneasy and more optimistic than he had felt for many months.

From that time on, Urquart would frequently appear on the bridge. He would say little; would simply stand by the rail or lean against the wheelhouse, as if by his presence he sought to transmit his own strength of will to Arflane. He was at once both silent mentor and support to the captain as the ship moved rapidly towards the edge of the plateau.

A few days later Manfred Rorsefne and Arflane stood in Arflane's cabin, consulting the charts spread on the table before them.

"We'll reach the edge tomorrow," Rorsefne indicated the chart of the plateau (the only detailed map they had). "The descent should be difficult, eh, captain?"

Arflane shook his head. "Not necessarily. By the look of it, there's a clear run down at this point." He put a finger on the chart. "If we steer a course north-east by north by three-quarters north we should reach this spot where the incline is fairly smooth and gradual and no hills in our way. The ice only gets rough at the bottom, and we should have lost enough momentum by then to be able to cross without much difficulty. I can take her down, I think."

Rorsefne smiled. "You seem to have recovered your old self-confidence, captain."

Arflane resented the suggestion. "We'd best set the course," he said coldly.

As they left his cabin and came out on deck they almost bumped into Janek and Ulrica Ulsenn. She was helping him towards the entrance to the gangway that led to their quarters. Rorsefne bowed and grinned at them, but Arflane scowled. It was the first time since the voyage began that he had come so close to the woman. She avoided his glance, murmuring a greeting as she passed. Ulsenn, however, directed a poisonous glare at Arflane.

His legs very slightly weak, Arflane clambered up the companionway to the bridge. Urquart was standing there, nursing his harpoon and looking to starboard. He nodded to Arflane as the two men entered the wheelhouse.

The helmsman saluted Arflane as they came in. The heavy wheel moved very slightly and the man corrected it.

Arflane went over to the big, crude compass. The chronometer next to it was centuries old and failing, but the equipment was still sufficient to steer a fairly accurate course. Arflane unrolled the chart and spread it on the table next to the compass, making a few calculations, then he nodded to himself, satisfied that he had been right.

"We'd better have an extra man on that wheel," he decided. He put his head around the door of the wheelhouse and spoke to Urquart. "Mr Urquart — we need another hand on the wheel. Will you get a man up here?"

Urquart moved towards the companionway.

"And put a couple more hands aloft, Mr Urquart," Arflane called. "We need plenty of lookouts. The edge's coming up."

Arflane went back to the wheel and took it over from the helmsman. He gripped the spokes in both hands, letting the wheel turn a little of its own accord as its chains felt the great pull of the runners. Then, his eye on the compass, he turned the *Ice Spirit* several points to starboard.

When he was satisfied that they were established on their new course, he handed the wheel back to the helmsman as the second man came in.

"You've got an easy berth for a while, sailor," Arflane told the new man. "I want you to stand by to help with the wheel if it becomes necessary."

Rorsefne followed Arflane out onto the bridge again. He looked towards the quarter deck and saw Urquart speaking to a small group of hands. He pointed towards the harpooner. "Urquart seems to have attached himself to you, too, captain. He must regard you as one of the family." There was no sarcasm in his voice, but Arflane glanced at him suspiciously.

"I'm not sure of that."

The young man laughed. "Janek certainly isn't, that's certain. Did you see how he glared at you as we went by? I don't know why he came on this trip at all. He hates sailing. He has responsibilities in Friesgalt. Maybe it was to protect Ulrica from the attentions of a lot of hairy sailors!"

Again Arflane felt uncomfortable, not sure how to interpret Rorsefne's words. "She's safe enough on this ship," he growled.

"I'm sure she is," Manfred agreed. "But Janek doesn't know that. He treats her jealously. She might be a whole storehouse full of canvas, the value he puts on her!"

Arflane shrugged.

Manfred lounged against the rail, staring vacantly up into the shrouds where one of the lookouts appointed by Urquart was already climbing towards the crow's nest in the mainmast royals.

"I suppose this will be our last day on safe ice," he said. "It's been too uneventful for me so far, this voyage. I'm looking forward to some excitement when we reach the edge."

Arflane smiled. "I doubt if you'll be disappointed."

The sky was still clear, blue and cloudless. The ice scintillated with the mirrored glare of the sun and the white, straining sails of the ship seemed to shimmer, reflecting in turn the brilliance of the ice. The runners could be heard faintly, bumping over the slightly uneven terrain, and sometimes a yard creaked above them. The mainmast lookout had reached his post and was settling himself into the crow's nest.

Rorsefne grinned. "I hope I won't be. And neither will you, I suspect. I thought you enjoyed a little adventure yourself. This kind of voyage can't be much pleasure for you, either."

The next day, the edge came into sight. It seemed that the horizon had drawn nearer, or had been cut off short, and Arflane, who had only passed close to the edge once in his life, felt himself shiver as he looked ahead.

The slope was actually fairly gradual, but from where he was positioned it looked as if the ground ended and the ship would plunge to destruction. It was as if he had come to the end of the world. In a sense he had; the world beyond the edge was completely unknown to him. Now he felt a peculiar kind of fear as the prow dipped and the ship began her descent.

On the bridge, Arflane put a megaphone to his lips.

"Get some grappling lines over the side, Mr Petchnyoff!" He shouted to his first officer on the quarter deck: "Jump to it!"

Petchnyoff hurried towards the lower deck to get a party together. Arflane watched as they began to throw out the grappling lines. The barbed prongs would slow their progress since all but the minimum sail had been taken in.

The grapples bit into the ice with a harsh shrieking and the ship began to lose speed. Then she began to wobble dangerously.

Hinsen was shouting from the wheelhouse. "Sir!"

Arflane strode into the wheelhouse. "What is it, Mr Hinsen?"

The two hands at the wheel were sweating, clinging to the wheel as they desperately tried to keep the *Ice Spirit* on course.

"The runners keep turning, sir," Hinsen said in alarm. "Just a little this way and that, but we're having difficulty holding them. We could go over at this rate. They're catching in the channels in the ice, sir."

Arflane positioned himself between the two hands and took hold of the wheel. He realized at once what Hinsen meant. The runners were moving along shallow, iron-hard grooves in the ice caused by the gradual descent of ice flows over the centuries. There was a real danger of the ship's turning side-on, toppling over on the slope.

"We'll need two more hands on this," Arflane said. "Find two of the best helmsmen we've got, Mr Hinsen — and make sure they've got muscles!"

Kristoff Hinsen hurried from the wheelhouse while Arflane and the hands hung on to the wheel, steering as best they could. The ship had begun to bump noticeably now and her whole deck was vibrating.

Hinsen brought the two sailors back with him and they took over. Even with the extra hands the ship continued to bump and veer dangerously on the slope, threatening to go completely out of control. Arflane looked to the bow. The bottom of the incline was out of sight. The slope seemed to go on forever.

"Stay in charge here, Mr Hinsen," Arflane said. "I'll go forward and see if I can make out what kind of ice is lying ahead of us."

Arflane left the bridge and made his way along the shivering deck until he reached the forecastle. The ice ahead seemed the same as the kind they were on at the moment. The ship bumped, veered and then swung back on course again. The angle of the incline seemed to have increased and the deck sloped forward noticeably. As he turned back, Arflane saw Ulrica Ulsenn standing quite close to him. Janek Ulsenn was a little further behind her, clinging to the port rail, his eyes wide with alarm.

"Nothing to worry about, ma'am," Arflane said as he approached her. "We'll get her out of this."

Janek Ulsenn had looked up and was calling his wife to him. With a hint of misery in her eyes, she turned back to her husband, gathered up her skirts and moved away from Arflane across the swaying deck.

It was the first time he had seen any emotion at all in her face since they had parted. He felt a certain amount of surprise. His concern for the safety of the ship had made him forget his feelings for her and he had spoken to her as he might have spoken to reassure any passenger.

He was tempted to follow her then, but the ship lurched suddenly off course again and seemed in danger of sliding sideways.

Arflane ran rapidly back towards the bridge, clambered up and dashed into the wheelhouse. Hinsen and the four sailors were wrestling with the wheel, their faces streaming with sweat and their muscles straining. Arflane grabbed a spoke and joined them as they tried to get the ship back on course.

"We're traveling too damned slowly," he grunted. "If we could make better speed there might be a chance of bouncing over the channels or even slicing through them."

The ship lurched again and they grappled with the wheel. Arflane gritted his teeth as they forced the wheel to turn.

"Drop the bolts, sir!" Hinsen begged him. "Drop the heavy anchors!"

Arflane scowled at him. A captain never dropped the heavy anchors unless the situation was insoluble.

"What's the point of slowing down, Mr Hinsen?" he said acidly. "It's extra speed we need — not less."

"Stop the ship altogether, sir — knock out the emergency bolt as well. It's our only chance."

Arflane spat on the deck. "Heavy anchors — emergency bolts — we're as likely to be wrecked using them as not! No, Mr Hinsen — we'll go down under full canvas!"

Hinsen almost lost control of the wheel again in his astonishment. He stared unbelievingly at his skipper.

"Full canvas, sir?"

The wheel jumped again and the ship's runners squealed jarringly as she began to lurch sideways. For several moments they strained at the wheel in silence until they had turned her back onto course.

"Two or three more like that, we'll lose her," the hand nearest Arflane said with conviction.

"Aye," Arflane grunted, glaring at Hinsen. "Set all sail, Mr Hinsen."

When Hinsen hesitated once more, Arflane impatiently left the wheel, grabbed a megaphone from the wall and went out onto the bridge.

He saw Petchnyoff on the quarter deck. The man looked frightened. There was an atmosphere of silent panic on the ship.

"Mr Petchnyoff!" Arflane bellowed through the megaphone. "Get the men into the yards! Full canvas!"

The shocked faces of the crew stared back at him. Petchnyoff's face was incredulous. "What was that, sir?"

"Set all sails, Mr Petchnyoff. We need some speed so we can steer this craft!"

The ship shuddered violently and began to turn again.

"All hands into the shrouds!" Arflane yelled, dropped the megaphone and ran back into the wheelhouse to join the men on the wheel. Hinsen avoided his eye, evidently convinced that the captain was insane.

Through the wheelhouse port, Arflane saw the men scrambling aloft. Once again they barely succeeded in turning the ship back on her course. Everywhere the sails began to crack down and billow out as they caught the wind. The ship began to move even faster down the steepening slope.

Arflane felt a strong sense of satisfaction as the wheel became less hard to handle. It still needed plenty of control, but they were having no great difficulty in holding their course. Now the danger was that they would find an obstruction on the slope and crash into it at full speed.

"Get onto the deck, Mr Hinsen," he ordered the frightened second officer. "Tell Mr Urquart to go aloft with a megaphone and keep an eye out ahead!"

The ice on both sides of the ship was now a blur as the ship gathered speed. Arflane glanced through the port and saw Urquart climbing into the lower yards of the foremast.

The huge ship leaped from the surface and came down again hard with her runners creaking, but she had become increasingly easier to handle and there were no immediate obstacles in sight.

Urquart's face was calm as he glanced back at the wheelhouse, but the crew looked very frightened still. Arflane enjoyed their discomfort.

He grinned broadly, his exhilaration tinged with some of their panic as he guided the ship down.

For an hour the schooner continued her rapid descent; it seemed that she sped down a slope that had no top and no bottom, for both were completely out of sight. The ship was handling easily, the runners hardly seeming to touch the ice. Arflane decided he could give the wheel to Hinsen. The second officer did not seem to relish the responsibility.

Going forward, Arflane climbed into the rigging to hang in the ratlines beside Urquart.

The harpooner smiled slightly. "You're in a wild mood, skipper," he said approvingly.

Arflane grinned back at him.

Before them, the ice sloped sharply, seeming to stretch on forever. On both sides it raced past, the spray of ice from the runners falling on deck. Once a chip of ice caught Arflane on the mouth, drawing blood, but he hardly felt it.

Soon the slope began to level out and the ice became rougher, but the ship's speed hardly slowed at all. Instead the great craft bounced over the ice, rising and falling as if carried on a series of huge waves.

The sensation added to Arflane's good spirits. He began to relax. The danger was as good as past. Swinging in the ratlines, he hummed a tune, sensing the tension decrease throughout the ship.

Some time later Urquart's voice said quietly: "Captain." Arflane glanced at the man and saw that his eyes had widened. He was pointing ahead.

Arflane peered beyond the low ridges of ice and saw what looked like a greenish-black streak cutting across their path in the distance. He could not believe what it was. Urquart spoke the word.

"Crevasse, captain. Looks like a wide one, too. We'll never cross it."

Since the last chart had been made, a crack must have appeared in the surface of the ice at the bottom of the slope. Arflane cursed himself for not having anticipated something like it, for new crevasses were common enough, particularly in terrain like this.

"And we'll never stop in time at this speed." Arflane began to climb down the ratlines to the deck, trying to appear calm, hoping that the men would not see the crevasse. "Even the heavy anchors couldn't stop us — we'd just flip right over and tumble into it wrong side up."

Arflane reached the deck, trying to force himself to take some action when he was full of a deeply apathetic knowledge that there was no action to be taken.

Now the men saw the crevasse as the ship sped closer. A great shout of horror went up from them as they, too, realized that there was no chance of stopping.

As Arflane reached the companionway leading to the bridge, Manfred Rorsefne and the Ulsenns hurried onto the deck. Manfred shouted to Arflane as he began to climb the ladder.

"What's happening, captain?"

Arflane laughed bitterly. "Take a look ahead!"

He reached the bridge and ran across to the wheelhouse, taking over the wheel from the ashen-faced Hinsen.

"Can you turn her, sir?"

Arflane shook his head.

The ship was almost on the crevasse now. Arflane made no attempt to alter course.

Hinsen was almost weeping with fear. "Please, sir — try to turn her!"

The huge, yawning abyss rushed closer, the deep green ice of its sides flashing in the sunlight.

Arflane felt the wheel swing loose in his grasp; the front runners left firm ground and reached out over the crevasse as the ship hurtled into it.

Arflane sensed a peculiar feeling, almost of relief, as he anticipated the plunge downward. Then, suddenly, he began to smile. The schooner was traveling at such speed that she might just reach the other side. The far edge of the crevasse was still on the incline, lower than the opposite edge.

Then the schooner had leaped through the air and smashed down on the other side. She rolled, threatening to capsize. Arflane staggered, but managed to cling to the wheel and swing her hard over. She began to slow under her impact, the runners scraping and bumping.

"We're all right, sir!" Hinsen was grinning broadly. "You got us across, sir!"

"Something did, Mr Hinsen. Here — take the wheel again."

When Hinsen had taken over, Arflane went slowly out onto the bridge.

Men were picking themselves up from where they had fallen. One man lay still on the deck. Arflane left the bridge and made his way to where the hand was sprawled. He bent down beside him, turning him over. Half the bones in the body were broken. Blood crawled from the mouth. The man opened his eyes and smiled faintly at Arflane.

"I thought I'd had it that time, sir," he said. The eyes closed and the smile faded. The man was dead.

Arflane got up with a sigh, rubbing his forehead. His whole body was aching from handling the wheel. There was a scuffle of movement as the hands moved to the rails to look back at the crevasse, but not one of them spoke.

From the foremast, where he still clung, Urquart was roaring with laughter. The harsh sound echoed through the ship and broke the silence. Some of the men began to cheer and shout, turning away from the rails and waving at Arflane. Stern-faced, the skipper made his way to the bridge and stood there for a moment while his men continued to cheer. Then he picked up his megaphone from where he had dropped it earlier and put it to his lips.

"All hands back aloft! Take in all sail! Jump to it!"

In spite of their excitement, the crew leaped readily to obey him and the yards were soon alive with scurrying men reefing the sails.

Petchnyoff appeared on the quarter deck. He looked up at his skipper and gave him a strange, dark look. He wiped his sleeve across his forehead and moved down towards the lower deck.

"Better get those grapples in, Mr Petchnyoff," Arflane shouted at him. "We're out of danger now."

He looked aft at the disappearing crevasse, congratulating himself on his good fortune. If he had not decided to go down at full speed they would have reached the crevasse and been swallowed by it. The ship had leaped forty feet.

He went back to the wheel to test and judge if the runners were in good order. They seemed to be working well, so far as their responses were concerned, but he wanted to satisfy himself that they had sustained no damage of any kind.

As the ship bumped to a gradual halt, all her sail furled, Arflane prepared to go over the side. He climbed down a rope ladder to the ice. The big runners were scratched and indented in places but were otherwise undamaged. He looked up admiringly at the ship, running his hand along one of her struts. He was convinced that no other vessel could have taken the impact after leaping the crevasse.

Clambering back to the deck, he encountered Janek Ulsenn. The man's lugubrious features were dark with anger. Ulrica stood just behind him, her own face flushed. Beside her, Manfred Rorsefne looked as amusedly insouciant as ever. "Congratulations, captain," he murmured. "Great foresight."

Ulsenn began to bluster. "You are a reckless fool, Arflane! We were almost destroyed, every one of us! The men may think you anticipated that crevasse — but I know you did not. You have lost all their confidence!"

The statement was patently false. Arflane laughed and glanced about the ship.

"The men seem in good spirits to me."

"Mere reaction, now that the danger's past. Wait until they start to think what you nearly did to them!"

"I'm inclined to think, cousin," Manfred said, "that this incident will simply restore their faith in their captain's good luck. The hands place great store on a skipper's luck, you know."

Arflane was looking at Ulrica Ulsenn. She tried to glance away, but then she returned his look and Arflane thought that her expression might be one of admiration; then her eyes became cold and he shivered.

Manfred Rorsefne took Ulrica's arm and helped her back towards the gangway to her cabin, but Ulsenn continued to confront Arflane.

"You will kill us all, Brershillian!" He was apparently unaware that Arflane was paying little attention to him. His fear had caused him to forget his humiliation of a few days before. Arflane looked at him calmly.

"I will certainly kill somebody one day." He smiled, and strode towards the foredeck under the admiring eyes of his crew and the enraged glare of Lord Janek Ulsenn.

With the plateau left behind, the ice became rough but easier to negotiate as long as the ship maintained a fair speed. The outline of the plateau was visible behind them for several days, a vast wall of ice rising into the clouds. The air was warmer now and there was less snow. Arflane felt uncomfortable as the heat increased and the air wavered, sometimes seeming to form odd shapes out of nothing. There were glaciers to be seen to all points ahead and, in the heat, Arflane became afraid that they would hit an ice break. Ice breaks occurred where the crust of the ice became thin over an underground river. A ship floundering in an ice break, since it had not been built for any kind of water, often had little chance of getting out and could easily sink.

As the ship moved on, traveling north-west by north, and nearing the equator, the crew and officers settled into a more orderly routine. Arflane's previous moods were forgotten; his luck was highly respected, and he had become very popular with the men.

Only Petchnyoff surprised Arflane in his refusal to forgive him for his earlier attitude. He spent most of his spare time with Janek Ulsenn; the two men could often be seen walking along the deck together. Their friendliness irritated Arflane to some extent. He felt that in a sense Petchnyoff was betraying him, but it was no business of his what company the young first officer chose, and he performed his duties well enough. Arflane even began to feel a slight sympathy for Ulsenn; he felt he should allow the man one friend on the voyage.

Urquart still had the habit of standing near him on the bridge and the gaunt harpooner had become a comfort to Arflane. They rarely talked, but the sense of comradeship between them had become very strong.

It was even possible for Arflane to see Ulrica Ulsenn without attempting to force some reaction from her, and he had come to tolerate Manfred Rorsefne's sardonic, bantering manner.

It was only the heat that bothered him now. The temperature had risen to several degrees above zero and the crew were working stripped to the waist. Arflane, against his will, had been forced to remove his heavy fur jacket. Urquart, however, had refused to take off any of his clothing and stoically bore his discomfort.

Arflane kept two lookouts permanently on watch for signs of thin ice. At night, he took in all sail and threw out grappling hooks so that the ship drifted very slowly.

The wind was poor and progress was slow enough during the day. From time to time mirages were observed, usually in the form of inverted glaciers, and Arflane had a great deal of difficulty explaining them to the men, who superstitiously regarded them as omens that had to be interpreted.

Until one day the wind dropped altogether, and they were becalmed.

CHAPTER THIRTEEN

THE HARPOON

They were becalmed for a week in the heat. The sky and ice glared shimmering copper under the sun. Men sat around in bunches, disconsolately playing simple games, or talking in low, miserable voices. Though stripped of most of their clothes, they still wore their snow visors. From a distance they looked like so many ungainly birds clustered on the deck. The officers kept them as busy as they could, but there was little to do. When Arflane gave a command the men obeyed less readily than before; morale was becoming bad.

Arflane was frustrated and his own temper was starting to fray again. His movements became nervous and his tone brusque.

Walking along the lower deck, he was approached by Fydur, the ship's bosun, a hairy individual with great dark beetling eyebrows.

"Excuse me, sir, sorry to bother you, but any idea how long we'll…"

"Ask the Ice Mother, not me." Arflane pushed Fydur to one side, leaving the man sour-faced and angry.

There were no clouds to be seen; there was no sign of the weather changing. Arflane, brooding again on Ulrica Ulsenn, stalked about the ship with his face set in a scowl.

On the bridge one day he looked down and saw Janek Ulsenn and Petchnyoff talking with some animation to Fydur and a group of the hands. By the way in which some of them glanced at the bridge, Arflane could guess the import of the conversation. He glanced questioningly at Urquart, who was leaning against the wheelhouse; the harpooner shrugged.

"We've got to give them something to do," Arflane muttered. "Or tell them something to improve their spirits. There's the beginnings of a mutiny in that little party, Mr Urquart."

"Aye, sir." Urquart sounded almost smug.

Arflane frowned, then made up his mind. He called to the second officer, at his post on the quarter deck.

"Get the men together, Mr Hinsen. I want to talk to them."

"All hands in line!" Hinsen shouted through his megaphone. "All hands before the bridge. Captain talking."

Sullenly the hands began to assemble, many of them scowling openly at Arflane. The little group with Ulsenn and Petchnyoff straggled up and stood behind the main press of men.

"Mr Petchnyoff. Will you come up here!" Arflane looked sharply at his first officer. "You too, please, Mr Hinsen. Bosun — to your post."

Slowly Petchnyoff obeyed the command and Fydur, with equally poor grace, took up his position facing the men.

When all the officers were behind him on the bridge, Arflane cleared his throat and gripped the rail, leaning forward to look down at the crew.

"You're in a bad mood, lads, I can see. The sun's too hot and the wind's too absent. There isn't a damned thing I can do about getting rid of the first or finding the second. We're becalmed and that's all there is to it. I've seen you through one or two bad scrapes already — so maybe you'll help me sweat this one out. Sooner or later the wind will come."

"But *when*, sir?" A hand spoke up; one of those who had been conversing with Ulsenn.

Arflane glanced grimly at Fydur. The bosun pointed a finger at the hand. "Hold your tongue."

Arflane was in no mood to answer the remark directly. He paused, then continued.

"Perhaps we'll get a bit of wind when discipline aboard this ship tightens up. But I can't predict the weather. If some of you are so damned eager to be on the move, then I suggest you get out onto the ice and pull this tub to her destination!"

Another man muttered something. Fydur silenced him.

Arflane leaned down. "What was that, bosun?"

"Wanted to know just what our destination was, sir," Fydur replied. "I think a lot of us…"

"That's why I called you together," Arflane went on. "We're bound for New York."

Some of the men laughed. To go to New York was a metaphor meaning to die — to join the Ice Mother.

"New York," Arflane repeated, glaring at them. "We've charts that show the city's position. We're going north to New York. Questions?"

"Aye, sir — they say New York doesn't exist on this world, sir. They say it's in the sky — or — somewhere…" The tall sailor who spoke had a poor grasp of metaphysics.

"New York's as solid as you and on firm ice," Arflane assured him. "The Lord Pyotr Rorsefne saw it. That was where he came from when I found him. It was in his will that we should go there. You remember the will? It was read out soon after the lord died."

The men nodded, murmuring to one another.

"Does that mean we'll see the Ice Mother's court?" another sailor asked.

"Possibly," Arflane said gravely.

The babble that broke out among the men rose higher and higher. Arflane let them talk for a while. Most of them had received the news dubiously at first, but now some of them were beginning to grin with excitement, their imagination captured.

After a while Arflane told the bosun to quiet them down. As the babble died, and before Arflane could speak, the clear, haughty tones of Janek Ulsenn came over the heads of the sailors. He was leaning against the mizzen mast, toying with a piece of rope. "Perhaps that is why we are becalmed, captain?"

Arflane frowned. "What do you mean by that, Lord Ulsenn?"

"It occurred to me to wonder that the reason we are getting no wind is because the Ice Mother isn't sending us any. She does not want us to visit Her in New York!" Ulsenn was deliberately playing on the superstition of the hands. This new idea set them babbling again.

This time Arflane roared to them to stop talking. He glowered at Ulsenn, unable to think of a reply that would satisfy his men.

Urquart stepped forward then and leaned his harpoon against the rail. Still dressed in all his matted furs, his blue eyes cold and steady, he seemed, himself, to be some demigod of the ice. The men fell silent.

"What do we suffer from?" he called harshly. "From cold impossible to bear? No! We suffer from *heat*! Is that the Ice Mother's weapon? Would She use Her enemy to stop us? No! You're fools if you think She's against us. When has the Ice Mother decreed that men should not sail to Her in New York? Never! I *know* the doctrine better than any man aboard. I am the Ice Mother's pledged servant; my faith in Her is stronger than anything you could feel. I know what the Ice Mother wishes; She wishes us to sail to New York. She wishes us to pay Her court so that when we return to the Eight Cities we may silence all who doubt Her! Through Captain Arflane She fulfills Her will; that's why I sail with him. That's why we all sail with him. It's our destiny."

The harsh, impassioned tones of Urquart brought complete silence to the crew, but they had no apparent effect on Ulsenn.

"You're listening to a madman talk," he called. "And another madman's in command. If we follow these two our only destiny is a lonely death on the ice."

There was a blur of movement, a thud; Urquart's great harpoon flew across the deck over the heads of the sailors to bury itself in the mast, an inch from Ulsenn's head. The man's face went white and he staggered back, eyes wide. He began to sputter something, but Urquart vaulted over the bridge rail to the deck and pushed his way through the crowd to confront the aristocrat.

"You speak glibly of death, Lord Ulsenn," Urquart said savagely. "But you had best speak quietly or perhaps the Ice Mother may see fit to take you to Her bosom sooner than you might wish." He began to tug the harpoon from the mast. "It is for the sake of your kind that we sail. Best let a little of your blood tonight, my tame little lord, to console the Ice Mother — lest all your blood be let before this voyage ends."

With tears of rage in his eyes, Ulsenn hurled himself at the massive harpooner. Urquart smiled quietly and picked the man up to throw him, almost gently, to the deck. Ulsenn landed on his face and rolled over, his nose bleeding. He crawled back, away from the smiling giant.

The men were laughing now, almost in relief.

Arflane's lips quirked in a half smile, too; then all his humour vanished as Ulrica Ulsenn ran over the deck to her injured husband, knelt beside him and wiped the blood from his face.

Manfred Rorsefne joined them on the bridge.

"Shouldn't you have a little better control over your officers, captain?" he suggested blandly.

Arflane wheeled to face him. "Urquart knows my will," he said.

Hinsen was pointing to the south. "Captain — big clouds coming up aft!"

Within an hour the sails were filled with a wind that also brought chilling sleet, forcing them to huddle back into their furs.

They were soon under way through the grey morning. The crew were Arflane's men again. Ulsenn and his wife had disappeared below and Manfred Rorsefne had joined them; but, for the moment, Arflane insisted that all his officers stay with him on the bridge while he ordered full canvas set and sent the lookouts aloft.

Hinsen and Petchnyoff waited expectantly until he turned his attention back to them. He looked at Petchnyoff sombrely for a time; tension grew between them before he turned away, shrugging. "All right, you're dismissed."

With Urquart a silent companion beside him, Arflane laughed quietly as the ship gathered speed.

Two nights later Arflane lay in his bunk unable to sleep. He listened to the slight bumping of the runners over the uneven surface of the ice, to the sleet-laden wind in the rigging and the creak of the yards. All the sounds were normal; yet some sixth sense insisted that something was wrong. Eventually he swung from his bunk, climbed into his clothes, buckled his flenching cutlass around his waist, and went on deck. He had been ready for trouble of some kind ever since he had watched Petchnyoff, Ulsenn and Fydur talking together. Urquart's oratory would have had little effect on them, he was certain. Fydur might be loyal again, but Ulsenn certainly wasn't; on the few occasions when he had showed himself above decks it had been invariably with Petchnyoff.

Arflane looked up at the sky. It was still overcast and there were few stars visible. The only light came from the moon and the lights that burned dimly in the wheelhouse. He could just make out the silhouettes of the lookouts in the crosstrees, high above, the bulky forms of the lookouts forward and aft. He looked back at the wheelhouse. Petchnyoff should be on watch; he could see no-one but the helmsman on the bridge.

He climbed up and strode into the wheelhouse. The helmsman gave him a short nod of recognition. "Sir."

"Where's the officer of the watch, helmsman?"

"He went forward, sir, I believe."

Arflane pursed his lips. He had seen no-one forward but the man on watch. Idly he walked over to the compass, comparing it with a chart.

They were a full three degrees off course. Arflane looked up sharply at the helmsman. "Three degrees off course, man! Have you been sleeping?"

"No, sir!" The helmsman looked aggrieved. "Mr Petchnyoff said our course was true, sir."

"Did he?" Arflane's face clouded. "Alter your course, helmsman. Three degrees starboard."

He left the bridge and began to search the ship for Petchnyoff. The man could not be found. Arflane went below to the lower deck where the hands lay in their hammocks. He slapped the shoulder of the nearest man. The sailor grunted and cursed.

"What's up?"

"Captain here. Get on deck with the helmsman. Know any navigation?"

"A bit, sir," the man mumbled as he swung out of his hammock, scratching his head.

"Then get above to the bridge. Helmsman'll tell you what to do."

Arflane stamped back through the dark gangways until he reached the passengers' quarters. Janek Ulsenn's cabin faced his wife's. Arflane hesitated and then knocked heavily on Ulsenn's door. There was no reply. He turned the handle. The door was not locked. He went in.

The cabin was empty. Arflane had expected to find Petchnyoff there. The pair must be somewhere on the ship. No lights shone in any of the other cabins.

His rage increasing with every pace, Arflane returned to the quarter deck, listening carefully for any murmur of conversation which would tell him where the two men were.

A voice from the bridge called to him.

"Any trouble, sir?"

It was Petchnyoff.

"Why did you desert your watch, Mr Petchnyoff?" Arflane shouted. "Come down here!"

Petchnyoff joined him in a few moments. "Sorry, sir, I —"

"How long were you gone from your post?"

"A little while, sir. I had to relieve myself."

"Come with me to the bridge, Mr Petchnyoff." Arflane clambered up the companionway and pushed on into the wheelhouse. He stood by the compass as Petchnyoff entered. The two men by the wheel looked curiously at the first officer.

"Why did you tell this man that we were on course when we were three degrees off?" Arflane thundered.

"Three degrees, sir?" Petchnyoff sounded offended. "We weren't off course, sir."

"Weren't we, Mr Petchnyoff? Would you like to consult the charts?"

Petchnyoff went to the chart table and unrolled one of the maps. His voice sounded triumphant as he said, "What's wrong, sir? This is the course we're following."

Arflane frowned and came over to look at the chart. Peering at it closely, he could see where a line had been erased and another one drawn in. He looked at the chart he had consulted earlier. That showed the original course. Why should someone tamper with the charts? And if they did, why make such a small alteration that was bound to be discovered? It could be Ulsenn making mischief, Arflane supposed. Or even Petchnyoff trying to cause trouble.

"Can you suggest how this chart came to be changed, Mr Petchnyoff?"

"No, sir. I didn't know it had been. Who could have…?"

"Has anyone been here tonight — a passenger, perhaps? Any member of the crew who had no business here?"

"Only Manfred Rorsefne earlier, sir. No-one else."

"Were you here the whole time?"

"No, sir. I went to inspect the watch."

Petchnyoff could easily be lying. He was in the best position to alter the chart. There again, the helmsman could have been bribed by Manfred Rorsefne to let him look at the charts. There was no way of knowing who might be to blame.

Arflane tapped his gloved fingers on the chart table.

"We'll look into this in the morning, Mr Petchnyoff."

"Aye, aye, sir."

As he left the wheelhouse, Arflane heard the lookout shouting. The man's voice was thin against the sounds of the wind-blown sleet. The words, however, were quite clear.

"Ice break! Ice break!"

Arflane ran to the rail, trying to peer ahead. An ice break at night was even worse than an ice break in the day. The ship was moving slowly; there might be time to throw out grapples. He shouted up to the bridge. "All hands on deck. All hands on deck, Mr Petchnyoff!"

Petchnyoff's voice began to bellow through a megaphone, repeating Arflane's orders.

In the darkness, men began to surge about in confusion. Then the whole ship lurched to one side and Arflane was thrown off his feet. He slid forward, grabbing the rail and hauling himself up, struggling for a footing on the sloping deck as men yelled in panic.

Over the sound of their voices, Arflane heard the creaking and cracking as more ice gave way under the weight of the ship. The vessel dipped further to port.

Arflane swore violently as he staggered back towards the wheelhouse. It was too late to drop the heavy anchors; now they might easily help push the ship through the ice.

Around him in the night, pieces of ice were tossed high into the air to smash down on the deck. There was a hissing and gurgling of disturbed water, a further creaking as new ice gave way.

Arflane rushed into the wheelhouse, grabbed a megaphone from the wall and ran back to the bridge.

"All hands to the lines! All hands over the starboard side! Ice break! Ice break!"

Elsewhere Petchnyoff shouted specific orders to hands as they grabbed mooring cables and ran to the side. They knew their drill. They had to get over the rail with the cables and try to drag the ship back off the thin ice by hand. It was the only chance of saving her.

Again the ice creaked and collapsed. Spray gushed; slabs of ice began to groan upward and press against the vessel's sides. Water began to creep along the deck.

Arflane swung his leg over the bridge rail and leaped down to the deck. The starboard runners were now lifting into the air; the *Ice Spirit* was in imminent danger of capsizing.

Hinsen, half dressed, appeared beside Arflane. "This is a bad one, sir — we're too deep in by the looks of it. If the ice directly beneath us goes, we don't stand a chance..."

Arflane nodded curtly. "Get over the side and help them haul. Is someone looking after the passengers?"

"I think so, sir."

"I'll check. Do your best, Mr Hinsen."

Arflane slid down towards the door below the bridge, pushing it open and stumbling down the gangway towards the passengers' cabins.

He passed both Manfred Rorsefne's cabin and Ulsenn's. When he reached Ulrica Ulsenn's cabin he kicked the door open and rushed in.

There was no-one there.

Arflane wondered grimly whether his passengers had somehow left the ship before the ice break had come.

CHAPTER FOURTEEN

THE ICE BREAK

The monstrous ship lurched heavily again, swinging Arflane backwards into the doorframe of Ulrica Ulsenn's cabin.

Manfred Rorsefne's door opened. The young man was disheveled and gasping; blood from a head wound ran down his face. He tried to grin at Arflane, staggered into the gangway and fell against the far wall.

"Where are the others?" Arflane yelled above the sound of creaking and shattering ice. Rorsefne shook his head.

Arflane stumbled along the gangway until he could grab the handle of the door to Janek Ulsenn's cabin. The ship listed, this time to port, as he opened the door and saw Ulsenn and his wife lying against the far bulkhead. Ulsenn was whimpering and Ulrica was trying to get him to his feet. "I can't make him move," she said. "What has happened?"

"Ice break," Arflane replied tersely. "The ship's half in the water already. You've all got to get overboard at once. Tell him that." Then he grunted impatiently and grabbed Ulsenn by the front of his jacket, hauling the terrified man over his shoulder. He gestured towards the gangway. "Can you help your cousin, Ulrica — he's hurt."

She nodded and pulled herself to her feet, following him out of the cabin.

Manfred managed to smile at them as they came out, but his face was grey and he was hardly able to stand. Ulrica took his arm.

As they fought their way out to the swaying deck, Urquart joined them; the harpooner shouldered his lance and helped Ulrica with Manfred, who seemed close to fainting.

Around them in the black night, slabs of ice still rose and fell, crashing onto the deck, but the ship slipped no further into the break.

Arflane led them to the rail, grasped a dangling line and swung himself and his burden down the side, jumping the last few feet to the firm ice. Dimly seen figures milled around; over his head, the mooring lines running from the rail strummed in the darkness. Urquart and Ulrica Ulsenn were somehow managing between them to lower Rorsefne down. Arflane waited until they were all together and then jerked the trembling form of Janek Ulsenn from his shoulder and let the man fall to the ice. "Get up," he said curtly. "If you want to live you'll help the men with the lines. Once the ship goes, we're as good as dead."

Janek Ulsenn climbed to his feet; he scowled at Arflane and looked around him angrily until he saw Ulrica and Manfred standing with Urquart. "This man," he said, pointing at Arflane, "this man has once again put our lives in jeopardy by his senseless —"

"Do as he says, Janek," Ulrica said impatiently. "Come. We'll both help with the lines."

She walked off into the darkness. Ulsenn scowled back at Arflane for a second and then followed her. Manfred swayed, looking faintly apologetic. "I'm sorry, captain, I seem…"

"Stay out of the way until we've done what we can," Arflane instructed him. "Urquart — let's get on with it."

With the harpooner beside him he pushed through the lines of men heaving on the ropes until he found Hinsen in the process of hammering home a mooring spike.

"What are our chances?" Arflane asked.

"We've stopped the slide, sir. There's firm ice here and we've got a few pegs in. We might do it." The bearded second officer straightened up. He pointed to the next gang who were struggling to keep their purchase on their line. "Excuse me, sir. I must attend to that."

Arflane strode along, inspecting the gangs of sailors as they slipped and slithered on the ice, sometimes dragged forward by the weight of the ship; but now her angle of list was less than forty-five degrees and Arflane saw that there was a reasonable chance of saving the *Ice Spirit*. He stopped to help haul on a line and Urquart moved up to the next team to do the same.

Slowly the ship wallowed upright. The men cheered; then the sound died as the *Ice Spirit*, drawn by the mooring lines, continued to slide towards them under the momentum. The ship began to loom down.

"Get back!" Arflane cried. "Run for it!"

The crew panicked, skidding and sliding on the ice as they ran. Arflane heard a scream as a man slipped and fell beneath the side-turned runners. Others died in the same way before the ship slowed and bumped to a stop.

Arflane began to walk forward, calling back over his shoulder. "Mr Urquart, will you attend to the burial of those men?"

"Aye, aye, sir," Urquart replied from the darkness.

Arflane moved around to the port side of the great ship, inspecting the damage. It did not seem to be very bad. One runner was slightly askew, but that could be rectified by a little routine repair work. The ship could easily continue her journey.

"All right," he shouted. "Everybody except the burial gang on board. There's a runner out of kilter and we'll need a working party on it right away. Mr Hinsen, will you do what's necessary?"

Arflane clambered up a loose mooring line and returned to the poop deck. He took a megaphone from its place in the wheelhouse and shouted through it: "Mr Petchnyoff. Come up to the bridge, please."

Petchnyoff joined him within a few minutes. He looked enquiringly at Arflane. His deceptively foolish expression had increased and, seeing him through the darkness, Arflane thought he had the face of an imbecile. He wondered vaguely if, in fact, Petchnyoff were unstable. If that were the case, then it was just possible that the first officer had himself altered the course and for no reason but petty spite and a wish to create trouble for a captain he disliked.

"See that the ship's firmly moored while the men make the repairs, Mr Petchnyoff."

"Aye, aye, sir." Petchnyoff turned away to obey the order.

SAILING TO UTOPIA

"And when that's done, Mr Petchnyoff, I want all officers and passengers to assemble in my cabin."

Petchnyoff glanced back at him questioningly.

"See to it, please," Arflane said.

"Aye, aye, sir." Petchnyoff left the bridge.

Shortly before dawn the three officers, Petchnyoff, Hinsen, and Urquart, together with the Ulsenns and Manfred Rorsefne, stood in Arflane's cabin while the captain sat at his table and studied the charts he had brought with him from the wheelhouse.

Manfred Rorsefne's injury had not been as bad as it had looked; his head was now bandaged and his colour had returned. Ulrica Ulsenn stood apart from her husband who leaned against the bulkhead beside Petchnyoff. Urquart and Hinsen stood together, their arms folded across their chests, waiting patiently for their captain to speak.

At length Arflane, who had remained deliberately silent for longer than he needed to, looked up, his expression bleak. "You know why I have these charts here, Mr Petchnyoff," he said. "We've already discussed the matter. But most of you others won't understand." He drew a long breath. "One of the charts was tampered with in the night. The helmsman was misled by it and altered course by a full three points. As a result we landed in the ice break and we were almost killed. I don't believe anyone could have known we were heading for the break, so it's plain that the impulse to spoil the chart came from some irresponsible desire to irritate and inconvenience me — or maybe to delay us for some reason I can't guess. Manfred Rorsefne was seen in the wheelhouse and..."

"Really, captain!" Manfred's voice was mockingly offended. "I was in the wheelhouse, but I hardly know one point of the compass from another. I certainly could not have been the one."

Arflane nodded. "I didn't say I suspected you, but there's no doubt in my mind that one of you must have made the alteration. No-one else has access to the wheelhouse. For that reason, I've asked you all here so that the one who did change the chart can tell me. I'll take no disciplinary action in this case. I'm asking this so I can punish the helmsman on duty if he was bribed or threatened into letting the chart be changed. In the interests of all our safety it is up to me to find out who it was."

There was a pause. Then one of them spoke. "It was I. And I did not bribe the helmsman. I altered the chart days ago while it was still in your cabin."

"It was a foolish thing to do," Arflane said wearily. "But I thought it would have been you. Presumably this was when you were trying to get us to turn back."

"I still think we should turn back," Ulsenn said. "Just as I altered the chart, I'll use any means in my power to convince either you or the men of the folly of this venture."

Arflane stood up, his expression suddenly murderous. Then he controlled himself and leaned forward over the table, resting his weight on his palms. "If there's any more trouble aboard of that kind, Lord Ulsenn," he said icily, "I will not hold an inquiry. Neither will I ignore it. I will make no attempt to be just. I will simply put you in irons for the rest of the voyage."

Ulsenn shrugged and scratched ostentatiously at the side of his face.

"Very well," Arflane told them. "You may all leave. I expect the officers to pay attention to any suspicious action Lord Janek Ulsenn might make in future, and I want it reported. I'd also appreciate the co-operation of the other passengers. In future I will treat Ulsenn as an irresponsible fool — but he can remain free so long as he doesn't endanger us again."

Angered by the slight, Ulsenn stamped from the cabin and slammed the door in the faces of his wife and Manfred Rorsefne as they attempted to follow him.

Hinsen was smiling as he left, but the faces of Petchnyoff and Urquart were expressionless, doubtless for very different reasons.

CHAPTER FIFTEEN

URQUART'S FEAR

The ship sailed on, with the crew convinced of their skipper's outstanding luck. The weather was good, the wind strong and steady, and they made excellent speed. The ice was clear of glaciers or other obstructions as long as they followed old Rorsefne's chart closely and thus they were able to sail both day and night.

One day, as Arflane stood with Urquart on the bridge, they saw a glow on the horizon that resembled the first signs of dawn. Arflane checked the big old chronometer in the wheelhouse. The time was a few minutes before six bells in the middle watch — three in the morning.

Arflane rejoined Urquart on the bridge. The harpooner's face was troubled. He sniffed the air, turning his head this way and that, his flat bone earrings swinging. Arflane could smell nothing.

"Do you know what it means?" he asked Urquart.

Urquart grunted and rubbed at his chin. As the ship sped closer to the source of the reddish light Arflane himself began to notice a slight difference in the smell of the air, but he could not define it.

Without a word Urquart left the bridge and began to walk forward, hefting his harpoon up and down in his right hand. He seemed unusually nervous.

Within an hour the glow on the horizon filled half the sky and illuminated the ice with blood-red light. It was a bizarre sight; the smell on the breeze had become much stronger, an acrid, musty odour that was entirely unfamiliar to Arflane. He, too, began to feel troubled. The air seemed to be warmer, the whole deck awash with the strange light. Ivory beams, belaying pins, hatch-covers and the whale skulls in the prow all reflected it; the face of the helmsman in the wheelhouse was stained red, as were the features of the men on watch who looked questioningly up at him. Night was virtually turned to day, though overhead the sky was pitch black — blacker than it normally seemed now that it contrasted with the lurid glare ahead.

Hinsen came out onto deck and climbed the companionway to stand beside Arflane. "What is it, sir?" He shuddered violently and moistened his lips.

Arflane ignored him, re-entered the wheelhouse and consulted Rorsefne's map. He had not been using the old man's original, but a clearer copy. Now he unrolled the original and peered at it in the red, shifting light from the horizon. Hinsen joined him, staring over his shoulder at the chart.

"Damn," Arflane murmured. "It's here and we ignored it. The writing's so hard to read. Can you see what it says, Mr Hinsen?"

Hinsen's lips moved as he tried to make out the tiny printed words that Rorsefne had inscribed in his failing hand before he died. He shook his head and gave a weak smile of apology. "Sorry, sir."

Arflane tapped two fingers on the chart. "We need a scholar for this."

"Manfred Rorsefne, sir? I think he might be something of a scholar."

"Fetch him, please, Mr Hinsen."

Hinsen nodded and left the wheelhouse. The air bore an unmistakable stink now. Arflane found it hard to breath, for it carried dust that clogged his mouth and throat.

The light, now tinged with yellow, was unstable. It flickered over the ice and the swiftly traveling ship. Sometimes part of the schooner was in shadow, sometimes it was illuminated completely. Arflane was reminded of something that had frightened him long ago. He was beginning to guess the meaning of old Rorsefne's script well before Manfred Rorsefne, rubbing at his eyes with one finger, appeared in the wheelhouse.

"It's like a great fire," he said, and glanced down at the chart Arflane was trying to show him. Arflane pointed to the word.

"Can you make that out? Can you read your uncle's writing better than us?"

Manfred frowned for a moment and then his face cleared. "Fire mountains," he said. He looked at Arflane with some anxiety, his air of insouciance gone completely.

"Fire..." Arflane, too, made no attempt to disguise the horror he felt. Fire, in the mythology of the ice, was the arch-enemy of the Ice Mother. Fire was evil. Fire destroyed. It melted the ice. It warmed things that should naturally be cold.

"We'd better throw out the grapples, captain," Hinsen said thickly.

But Arflane was consulting the chart. He shook his head. "We'll be all right, Mr Hinsen, I hope. This course takes us through the fire mountains, as far as I can tell. We don't get close to them at all — not enough to endanger ourselves at any rate. Rorsefne's chart's been good up to now. We'll hold our course."

Hinsen looked at him nervously but said nothing.

Manfred Rorsefne's initial anxiety seemed over. He was looking at the horizon with a certain curiosity. "Flaming mountains," he exclaimed. "What wonders we're finding, captain!"

"I'll be happier when this particular wonder's past," Arflane said with an attempt at humour. He cleared his throat twice, slapped his hand against his leg and paced about the wheelhouse. The helmsman's face caught his attention; it was a parody of fear. Arflane forgot his own nervousness in his laughter at the sight. He slapped the helmsman on the shoulder. "Cheer up, man. We'll sail miles to starboard of the nearest if that chart's accurate!" Rorsefne joined in his laughter and even Hinsen began to smile.

"I'll take the wheel, sir, if you like," Hinsen said. Arflane nodded and tapped the helmsman's arm.

"All right, lad," Arflane told him as Hinsen took over. "You get below. You don't want to be blinded."

He went out onto the bridge, his face tense as he looked towards the horizon.

Soon they could see the individual mountains silhouetted in the distance. Red and yellow flames and rolling black smoke spouted from their craters and luminous crimson lava streamed down their sides; the heat was appalling and the poisoned air stung and clogged their lungs. From time to time a cloud of smoke would drift across the ship, making strange patterns of light and shadow on the decks and sails. The earth shook slightly and across the ice came the distant rumble of the volcanoes.

The scene was so unfamiliar to them that they could hardly believe in its reality; it was like a nightmare landscape. Though the night was turned almost as bright as day and they could see for miles in all directions, the light was lurid and shifted constantly, and when not obscured by the smoke they could make out the dark sky with the stars and the moon clearly visible.

Arflane noticed that the others were sweating as much as he. He looked for Urquart and saw the outline of the harpooner forward, unmistakable with his barbed lance held close to his body. He left the bridge and moved through the weird light toward Urquart, his shadow huge and distorted.

Before he reached the harpooner, he saw him fall to both knees on the deck near the prow. The harpoon was allowed to fall in front of him. Arflane hurried forward and saw, even in that light, that Urquart's face was as pale as the ice. The man was muttering to himself and his body was racked by violent shuddering; his eyes were firmly shut. Perhaps it was the nature of the light, but on his knees Urquart looked impossibly small, as if the fire had melted him. Arflane touched his shoulder, astounded by this change in a man whom he regarded as the soul of courage and self-control.

"Urquart? Are you ill?"

The lids opened, revealing prominent whites and rolling orbs. The savage features, scarred by wind, snow and frostbite, twitched.

To Arflane the display was almost a betrayal; he had looked to Urquart as his model. He reached out and grasped the man's broad shoulders, shaking him ferociously. "Urquart! Come on, man! Pull yourself out of this!"

The eyes fell shut and the strange muttering continued; Arflane furiously smacked the harpooner across the face with the back of his hand. "Urquart!"

Urquart flinched at the blow but did nothing; then he flung himself face forward on the deck, spreadeagled as if in cringing obeisance to the fire. Arflane turned, wondering why so many emotions in him should be disturbed. He strode rapidly back to the bridge, saying nothing to Manfred Rorsefne as he rejoined him. Men were coming out on deck now; they looked both frightened and fascinated as they recognized the source of the light and the stink.

Arflane raised the megaphone to his lips.

"Back to your berths, lads. We're sailing well away from the mountains and we'll be through them by dawn. Back below. I want you fresh for your duties in the morning."

Reluctantly, muttering among themselves, the sailors began to drift back below decks. As the last little knot of men climbed the companionway to their quarters, Janek Ulsenn emerged from below the bridge. He glanced quickly at Arflane and then moved along the deck to stand by the mizzen mast. Petchnyoff came out a few seconds later and also began to make his way toward the mizzen. Arflane bawled at him through the megaphone.

"To your berth, Mr Petchnyoff! It's not your turn on watch. The passengers can do what they want — but you've your duty to remember."

Petchnyoff paused, then glared at Arflane defiantly. Arflane motioned with the megaphone. "We don't need your help, thanks. Get back to your cabin."

Petchnyoff now turned towards Ulsenn, as if expecting orders. Ulsenn signed with his hand and in poor grace Petchnyoff went back below. Shortly afterwards Ulsenn followed him. Arflane reflected that they were probably nursing their imagined wrongs together, but as long as there were no more incidents to affect the voyage he did not care what the two men said to each other.

A little while later he ordered the watch changed and gave orders to the new lookouts to keep a special eye open for any sign of an ice break or the steam that would indicate one of the small warm lakes fed by underground geysers that would doubtless occur in this region. That done, he decided to get some sleep himself. Hinsen had been roused well before his turn on watch was due to begin, so Manfred Rorsefne agreed to share the morning watch with him.

Before he opened the door of his cabin, Arflane glanced back along the deck. The red, shadowy light played over Urquart's still prone figure as if in a victory dance. Arflane rubbed at his beard, hesitated, then went into his cabin and closed the door firmly behind him. He stripped off his coat and laid it on the lid of his chest, then went to the water barrel in one corner and poured water into a bowl, washing himself clean of the sweat and dust that covered him. The image of Urquart preyed on his mind; he could not understand why the man should be so affected by the fire mountains. Naturally, since fire was their ancient enemy, they were all disturbed by it, but Urquart's fear was hysterical.

Arflane drew off his boots and leggings and washed the rest of his body. Then he lay down on the wide bunk, finding it difficult to sleep. Finally he fell into a fitful doze, rising as soon as the cook knocked on the door with his breakfast. He ate little, washed again and dressed, then went out on deck, noticing at once that Urquart was no longer there.

The morning was overcast and in the distance the fire mountains could still be seen; in the daylight they did not look so alarming. He saw that the sails had been blackened by the smoke and that the whole deck was smothered in a light, clinging grey ash.

The ship was moving slowly, the runners hampered by the ash that also covered the ice for miles around, but the fire mountains were well behind them. Arflane dragged his body up to the bridge, feeling tired and ill. The men on deck and in the yards were also moving with apparent lethargy. Doubtless they were all suffering from the effects of the fumes they had inhaled the night before.

Petchnyoff met him on the bridge. The first officer was taking his turn on watch and made no attempt to greet him; Arflane ignored him, went into the wheelhouse and took a megaphone from the wall. He returned to the bridge and called to the bosun who was on duty on the middle deck. "Lets get this craft shipshape, bosun. I want this filth cleaned off every surface and every inch of sail as soon as you like."

Fydur acknowledged Arflane's order with a movement of his hand. "Aye, aye, sir."

"You'd better get the grappling anchors over the side," Arflane continued. "We'll rest in our lines for today while she's cleaned. There must be warm ponds somewhere. We'll send out a party to find them and bring us back some seal meat."

Fydur brightened up at the prospect of fresh meat. "Aye, aye, sir," he said emphatically.

Since they had been becalmed Fydur seemed to have avoided the company of Ulsenn and Petchnyoff, and Arflane was sure the bosun was no longer in league with them.

At Fydur's instructions the sails were taken in and the grappling anchors heaved over the side so that their sharp barbs dug into the ice, gradually slowing the ship to a stop. Then a party of mooring hands was sent over to drive in the pegs and secure the *Ice Spirit* until she was ready to sail.

As soon as the men were working on cleaning the schooner and volunteers had been called to form an expedition to look for the warm ponds and the seals that would inevitably be there, Arflane went below and knocked on the door of Urquart's small cabin. There was a stirring sound and a heavy thump from within, but no reply.

"Urquart," Arflane said hesitantly. "May I enter? It's Arflane."

Another noise from the cabin and the door was flung open, revealing Urquart standing, glaring. The harpooner was stripped to the waist. His long, sinewy arms were covered in tiny tattoos and his muscled torso seemed to be a mass of white scars. But it was the fresh wound across his upper arm that Arflane noticed. He frowned and pointed to it.

"How did this happen?"

Urquart grunted and stepped backwards into the crowded cabin that was little bigger than a cupboard. His chest of belongings filled one bulkhead and the other was occupied by the bunk. Furs were scattered over the bunk and on the floor. Urquart's harpoon stood against the opposite bulkhead, dominating the tiny cabin. A knife lay on top of the chest and beside it was a bowl of blood.

Then Arflane realized the truth, that Urquart had been letting his blood for the Ice Mother. It was a custom that had almost died out in recent generations. When a man had blasphemed or otherwise offended the Ice Mother, he let his blood and poured it into the ice, giving the deity some of his warmth and life. Arflane wondered what particular blasphemy Urquart felt he had committed; though doubtless it was something to do with his hysteria of the previous night.

Arflane nodded enquiringly at the bowl. Urquart shrugged. He seemed to have regained his composure.

THE ICE SCHOONER

Arflane leaned against the bunk. "What happened last night?" he asked as casually as he could. "Did you offend against the Mother?"

Urquart turned his back and began to pull on his matted furs. "I was weak," he grunted. "I lay down in fear of the enemy."

"It offered us no harm," Arflane told him.

"I know the harm it offered," Urquart said. "I have done what I think I should do. I hope it is enough." He tied the thongs of his coat and went to the porthole, opening it; then he picked up the bowl and flung the blood through the opening to the ice beyond.

Closing the porthole, he threw the bowl back on top of the chest, crossed to grasp his harpoon and then paused, his face as rigid as ever, waiting for Arflane to let him pass.

Arflane remained where he was.

"I ask only in a spirit of comradeship, Urquart," he said. "If you could tell me about last night…"

"You should *know*," Urquart growled. "You are Her chosen one, not I." The harpooner was referring to the Ice Mother, but Arflane was still puzzled. However, it was evident that Urquart did not intend to say anything more. Arflane turned and walked into the gangway. Urquart followed him, stooping a little to avoid striking his head on the beams. They went out on deck. Urquart strode forward without a word and began to climb the rigging of the foremast. Arflane watched him until he reached the upper yards, his harpoon still cradled in his arm, to hang in the rigging and stare back at the fire mountains that were now so far away.

Arflane gestured impatiently, feeling offended at the other's surliness, and went back to the bridge.

By evening the ship had been cleaned of every sign of the ash that had fouled her, but the hunting party had not returned. Arflane wished that he had given them more explicit instructions and told them to return before dusk, but he had not expected any difficulty locating a pond. They had taken a small sailboat and should have made good speed; now the Ice Spirit would have to wait until they returned and it was unlikely that they would travel at night, which meant that the next morning would doubtless be wasted as well. Arflane was to take the middle watch again and would need to be on duty at midnight. He decided, as the watch rang the four bells terminating the first dogwatch, that he would try to sleep to catch up on the rest he had been unable to get the previous night.

The evening was quiet as he took one quick tour around the deck before going to his cabin. There were a few muffled sounds of men working, a little subdued conversation, but nothing to disturb the air of peace about the ship.

Arflane glanced up as he reached the foredeck. Urquart was still there, hanging as if frozen in the rigging. It was more difficult to understand the strange harpooner than Arflane had thought. Now he was too tired to bother. He walked back towards the bridge and entered his cabin. He was soon asleep.

CHAPTER SIXTEEN

THE ATTACK

Automatically, Arflane awoke as seven bells were struck above, giving him half an hour before his spell on watch. He washed and dressed and prepared to leave his cabin by the outer door; then a knock came on the door that opened on the gangway between decks.

"Enter," he said brusquely.

The handle turned and Ulrica Ulsenn stood facing him. Her face was slightly flushed but she looked at him squarely. He began to smile, opening his arms to take her, but she shook her head as she closed the door behind her.

"My husband is planning — with Petchnyoff — to — murder you, Konrad." She pressed her hand against her forehead. "I overheard him talking with Petchnyoff in his cabin. Their idea is to kill you and bury your body in the ice tonight." She looked at him steadily. "I came to tell you," she said, almost defiantly.

Arflane folded his arms across his chest and smiled. "Thanks. Petchnyoff knows it's my turn on watch soon. They'll doubtless try to do it when I'm taking my tour around the deck. I wondered if they had that in mind. Well…" He went over to his chest, took out the belt that held his scabbarded flenching cutlass and buckled it on. "Perhaps this will end it, at last."

"You'll kill him?" she asked quietly.

"There'll be two of them. It's fair."

He stepped towards her and she drew away. He put out a hand and gripped the back of her neck, drawing her to him. She came reluctantly, then slid her arms around his waist as he stroked her hair. He heard her give a deep, racking sigh.

"I really didn't expect him to go this far," Arflane said after a moment. "I thought he had some sense of honour."

She looked up at him, tears in her eyes. "You've taken it all away from him," she said. "You have humiliated him too much…"

"From no malice," he said. "Self-protection."

"So you say, Konrad."

He shrugged. "Maybe. But if he'd challenged me openly I would have refused. I can easily kill him. I would have refused the chance. But now…"

She moaned and flung herself away from him onto the bunk, covering her face. "Either way it would be murder, Konrad. You've driven him to this!"

"He's driven himself to it. Stay here."

He left the cabin and stepped lightly on deck; his manner was apparently casual as he glanced around him. He turned and ascended the companionway to the bridge. Manfred Rorsefne was there. He nodded agreeably to Arflane. "I sent Hinsen below an hour ago. He seemed tired."

"It was good of you," Arflane said. "Do you know if the hunting party's returned yet?"

"They're not back."

Arflane muttered abstractedly, looking up into the rigging.

"I'll get to my own bunk now, I think," Rorsefne said. "Good night, captain."

"Good night." Arflane watched Rorsefne descend to the middle deck and disappear below.

The night was very still. The wind was light and made little sound. Arflane heard the man on the upper foredeck stamp his feet to get the stiffness from them.

It would be an hour before he took his second tour. He guessed that it would be then that Ulsenn and Petchnyoff would attempt to stage their attack. He went into the wheelhouse. As they were at anchor, there was no helmsman on duty; doubtless this was why the two men had chosen this night to try to kill him; there would be no witness.

Arflane climbed down to the middle deck, looking aft at the distant but still visible glow from the fire mountains. It reminded him of Urquart; he looked up to see the harpooner still hanging high above in the rigging of the foremast. He could expect no help from Urquart that night.

There was a commotion in the distance; he ran to the rail to peer into the night, seeing a few figures running desperately towards the ship. As they came closer he recognized some of the men from the hunting party. They were shouting incoherently. He dashed to the nearest tackle locker and wrenched it open, pulling out a rope ladder. He rushed back to the rail and lowered the ladder down the side; he cupped his hands and yelled over the ice.

"This way aboard!"

The first of the sailors ran up and grabbed the ladder, beginning to climb. Arflane heard him panting heavily. He reached down and helped the man aboard; he was exhausted, his furs torn and his right hand bleeding from a deep cut.

"What happened?" Arflane asked urgently.

"Barbarians, sir. I've never seen anything like them. They're not like true men at all. They've got a camp near the warm ponds. They saw us before we saw them... They use — *fire*, sir."

Arflane tightened his lips and slapped the man on the back. "Get below and alert all hands."

As he spoke, a streak of flame flew out of the night and took the man on lower-foredeck watch in the throat. Arflane saw it was a burning arrow. The man shrieked and beat at the flames with his gloved hands, then toppled backwards and fell dead on the deck.

All at once the night was alive with blazing arrows. The sailors on deck flung themselves flat in sheer terror, reacting with a fear born of centuries of conditioning. The arrows landing on the deck burned out harmlessly, but some struck the canvas and here and there a furled sail was beginning to flare. Sailors screamed as arrows struck them and their furs caught light. A man went thrashing past Arflane, his whole body a mass of flame. There were small fires all over the ship.

Arflane rushed for the bridge and began to ring the alarm bell furiously, yelling through the megaphone: "All hands on deck! Break out the weapons! Stand by to defend ship!"

From the bridge he could see the leading barbarians. In shape they were human, but were completely covered in silvery white hair; otherwise they seemed to be naked. Some carried flaming brands; all had quivers of arrows slung over their shoulders and powerful-looking bone bows in their hands.

As armed sailors began to hurry on deck, holding bows of their own and harpoons and cutlasses, Arflane called to the archers to aim for the barbarians with the brands. Further down the deck, Petchnyoff commanded a gang forming a bucket chain to douse the burning sails.

Arflane leaned over the bridge rail, shouting to Fydur as he ran past with an armful of bows and half a dozen quivers of arrows. "Let's have one of those up here, bosun!"

The bosun paused to select a weapon and a quiver and throw it up to Arflane, who caught it deftly, slung the quiver over his shoulder, nocked an arrow to the string and drew it back. He let fly at one of the brand-holding barbarians and saw the man fall to the ice with the arrow protruding from his mouth.

A fire arrow flashed towards him. He felt a slight shock as the thing buried itself in his left shoulder, but if there was pain he did not notice it in his panic. The flames unnerved him. With a shaking hand he dragged out the shaft and flung it from him, slapping at his blazing coat until the flames were gone. Then he was forced to grip the rail with his right hand and steady himself; he felt sick.

After a moment he picked up the bow and fitted another arrow to the string. There were only two or three brands to be seen on the ice now and the barbarians seemed to be backing off. Arflane took aim at one of the brands and missed, but another arrow from somewhere killed the man. Arrows were still coming out of the night; most of them were not on fire. The silvery coats of the barbarians made them excellent targets and they were beginning to fall in great numbers before the retaliating shafts of Arflane's archers.

The attack had come on the port side; now some premonition made Arflane turn and look to starboard.

Unnoticed, nearly a dozen white-furred barbarians had managed to climb to the deck. They rushed across the deck, their red eyes blazing and their mouths snarling. Arflane shot one and stooped to grasp the megaphone to bellow a warning. He dropped the bow, drew his cutlass and vaulted over the bridge rail to the deck.

One of the barbarians shot at him and missed. Arflane slammed the hilt of his sword into the man's face and swung at another, feeling the sharp blade bite into his neck. Other sailors had joined him and were attacking the barbarians, whose bows were useless at such close quarters. Arflane saw Manfred Rorsefne beside him; the man grinned at him.

"This is more like it, eh, captain?"

Arflane threw himself at the barbarians, stabbing one clumsily in the chest and hacking him down. Elsewhere the sailors were butchering the remaining barbarians who were hopelessly outnumbered.

The noise of the battle died away and there were no more barbarians to kill. On Arflane's right a man was screaming.

It was Petchnyoff. There were two fire arrows in him, one in his groin and the other near his heart. A few little flames burned on his clothes and his face was blackened by fire. By the time Arflane reached him, he was dead.

Arflane went back to the bridge. "Set all sail! Let's move away from here."

Men began to scramble eagerly up the masts to let out the sails that were undamaged. Others let go the anchor lines and the ship began to move. A few last arrows rattled on the deck. They glimpsed the white forms of the barbarians disappearing behind them as the huge ship gathered speed.

Arflane looked back, breathing heavily and clutching his wounded shoulder. Still there was little pain. Nonetheless it would be reasonable to attend to it. Hinsen came along the deck. "Take charge, Mr Hinsen," he said. "I'm going below."

At his cabin door Arflane hesitated, then changed his mind and moved along to pass through the main door into the gangway where the passengers had their cabins. The gangway joined the one which led to his cabin, but he did not want to see Ulrica for the moment. He walked along the dark passage until he reached Ulsenn's door.

He tried the handle. It was locked. He leaned back and smashed his foot into it; the exertion made his wounded shoulder begin to throb painfully. He realized that the wound was worse than he had thought.

Ulsenn wheeled as Arflane entered. The man had been standing looking out of the port.

"What do you mean by...?"

"I'm arresting you," Arflane said, his voice slurred by the pain.

"For what?" Ulsenn drew himself up. "I..."

"For plotting to murder me."

"You're lying."

Arflane had no intention of mentioning Ulrica's name. Instead he said: "Petchnyoff told me."

"Petchnyoff is dead."

"He told me as he died."

Ulsenn tried to shrug but the gesture was pathetic. "Then Petchnyoff was lying. You've no evidence."

"I need none. I'm captain."

Ulsenn's face crumpled as if he were about to weep. He looked utterly defeated. This time his shrug was one of despair. "What more do you want from me, Arflane?" he said wearily.

For a moment Arflane regarded Ulsenn and pitied him, the pity tinged with his own guilt. The man looked up at him almost pleadingly. "Where's my wife?" he said.

"She's safe."

"I want to see her."

"No."

Ulsenn sat down on the edge of his bunk and put his face in his hands.

Arflane left the cabin and closed the door. He went to the door that led out to the deck and called two sailors over. "Lord Ulsenn's cabin is the third on the right. He's under arrest. I want you to put a bar across the door and guard it until you're relieved. I'll wait while you get the materials you need."

When Arflane had supervised the work and the bar was in place with the door chained to it to his satisfaction, he walked down the gangway to his own cabin.

THE ICE SCHOONER

Ulrica had fallen asleep in his bunk. He left her where she lay and went to her cabin, packing her things into her chest and dragging it up the gangway under the curious eyes of the sailors on guard outside Ulsenn's door. He got the chest into his cabin and heaved it into place beside his; then he took off his clothes and inspected the shoulder. It had bled quite badly but had now stopped. It would be all right until morning.

He lay down beside Ulrica.

CHAPTER SEVENTEEN

THE PAIN

In the morning the pain in his shoulder had increased; he winced and opened his eyes.

Ulrica was already up, turning the spigot of the big water barrel, soaking a piece of cloth. She came back to the bunk, face pale and set, and began to bathe the inflamed shoulder. It only seemed to make the pain worse.

"You'd better find Hinsen," he told her. "He'll know how to treat the wound."

She nodded silently and began to rise. He grasped her arm with his right hand.

"Ulrica. Do you know what happened last night?"

"A barbarian raid, wasn't it?" she said tonelessly. "I saw fire."

"I meant your husband — what I did."

"You killed him." Again the statement was flat.

"No. He didn't attack me as he'd planned. The raid came too soon. He's in his cabin — confined there until the voyage is over."

She smiled a little ironically then. "You're merciful," she said finally, then turned and left the cabin.

A little while later she came back with Hinsen and the second officer did what was necessary. She helped him bind Arflane's shoulder. Infection was rare on the iceplains, but the wound would take some time to heal.

"Thirty men died last night, sir," Hinsen told him, "and we've six wounded. The going will be harder with us so undermanned."

Arflane grunted agreement. "I'll talk to you later, Mr Hinsen. We'll need Fydur's advice."

"He's one of the dead, sir, along with Mr Petchnyoff."

"I see. Then you're now first officer and Urquart second. You'd better find a good man to promote to bosun."

"I've got one in mind, sir — Rorchenof. He was bosun on the *Ildiko Ulsenn*."

"Fine. Where's Mr Urquart?"

"In the fore rigging, sir. He was there during the fight and he's been there ever since. He wouldn't answer when I called to him, sir. If I hadn't noticed his breathing I'd have thought he was frozen."

"See if you can get him down. If not, I'll attend to it later."

"Aye, aye, sir." Hinsen went out.

Ulrica was standing near her trunk, looking down at it thoughtfully.

"Why are you so depressed?" he said, turning his head on the pillow and looking directly at her.

She shrugged, sighed and sat down on the trunk, folding her arms under her breasts. "I wonder how much of this we have engineered between us," she said.

"What do you mean?"

"Janek — the way he has behaved. Couldn't we have forced him to do what he did, so that we could then feel we'd acted righteously? Couldn't this whole situation have been brought about by us?"

"I didn't want him aboard in the first place. You know that."

"But he had no choice. He was forced to join us by the manner of *our* actions."

"I didn't ask him to plan to kill me."

"Possibly you forced him to that point." She clasped her hands together tightly. "I don't know."

"What do you want me to do, Ulrica?"

"I expect you to do no more."

"We are together."

"Yes."

Arflane sat up in his bunk. "This is what has happened," he said, almost defensively. "How can we change it now?"

Outside, the wind howled and snow was flung against the porthole. The ship rocked slightly to the motion of the runners over the rough ice; Arflane's shoulder throbbed in pain. Later she came and lay beside him and together they listened as the storm grew worse outside.

Feeling the force of the driving snow against his face and body, Arflane felt better as he left the cabin in the late afternoon and, with some difficulty, climbed the slippery companionway to the bridge where Manfred Rorsefne stood.

"How are you, captain?" Rorsefne asked. His voice was at once distant and agreeable.

"I'm fine. Where are the officers?"

"Mr Hinsen's aloft and Mr Urquart went below. I'm keeping an eye on the bridge. I'm feeling quite professional."

"How's she handling?"

"Well, under the circumstances." Rorsefne pointed upwards, through the rigging, partially obscured by the wall of falling snow. Dark shapes, bundled in furs, moved among the crosstrees. Sails were being reefed. "You picked a good crew, Captain Arflane. How is my cousin?" The question was thrown in casually, but Arflane did not miss the implication.

The ship began to slow. Arflane cast a glance towards the wheelhouse before he answered Rorsefne. "She's all right. You know what's happened?"

"I anticipated it." Rorsefne smiled quietly and raised his head to stare directly aloft.

"You..." Arflane was unable to frame the question. "How...?"

"It's not my concern, captain," Rorsefne interrupted. "After all, you've full command over all who sail in this schooner." The irony was plain. Rorsefne nodded to Arflane and left the bridge, climbing carefully down the companionway.

Arflane shrugged, watching Rorsefne walk through the snow that was settling on the middle deck. The weather was getting worse and would not improve; winter was coming and they were heading north. With a third of their complement short they were going to be in serious trouble unless they could make the best possible speed to New York. He shrugged again; he felt mentally and physically exhausted and was past the point where he could feel even simple anxiety.

As the last light faded Urquart emerged from below the bridge and looked up at him. The harpooner seemed to have recovered himself; he hefted his lance in the crook of his arm and swung up the companionway to stand by the rail next to Arflane. He seemed to be taking an almost sensual pleasure in the bite of the wind and snow against his face and body. "You are with that woman now, captain?" he said remotely.

"Yes."

"She will destroy you." Urquart spat into the wind and turned away. "I will see to clearing the hatch-covers."

Watching Urquart as he supervised the work on the deck, Arflane wondered suddenly if the harpooner's warnings were inspired by simple jealousy of Arflane's relationship with the woman who was, after all, Urquart's half-sister. That would also explain the man's strong dislike of Ulsenn.

Arflane remained needlessly on deck for another hour before eventually going below.

CHAPTER EIGHTEEN

THE FOG

Autumn rapidly became winter as the ship moved northwards. The following weeks saw a worsening of the weather, the overworked crew of the ice schooner finding it harder and harder to manage the vessel efficiently. Only Urquart seemed grimly determined to ensure that she stayed on course and made the best speed she could. Because of the almost constant snowstorms, the ship traveled slowly; New York was still several hundred miles distant.

Most of the time it was impossible to see ahead; when the snow was not falling, fogs and mists would engulf the great ship, often so thick that visibility extended for less than two yards. In Arflane's cabin the lovers huddled together, united as much by their misery as their passion. Manfred Rorsefne had been the only one who bothered to visit Janek Ulsenn; he reported to Arflane that the man seemed to be bearing his imprisonment with fortitude if not with good humour. Arflane received the news without comment. His native taciturnity had increased to the point where on certain days he would not speak at all and would lie motionless in his bunk from morning to night. In such a mood he would not eat and Ulrica would lie with him, her head on his shoulder, listening to the slow bump of the runners on the ice and the creak of the yards, the sound of the snow falling on the deck above their heads. When these sounds were muffled by the fog it seemed that the cabin floated apart from the rest of the ship. In these moments Arflane and Ulrica would feel their passion return and would make violent love as if there were no time left to them. Afterwards Arflane would go out to the fog-shrouded bridge to stand there and learn from Hinsen, Urquart or Manfred Rorsefne the distance they had traveled. He had become a sinister figure to the men, and even the officers, with the exception of Urquart, seemed uneasy in his presence. They noticed how Arflane had appeared to age; his face was lined and his shoulders stooped. He rarely looked at them directly but stared abstractedly out into the falling snow or fog. Every so often, apparently without realizing it, Arflane would give a long sigh and he would make some nervous movement, brushing rime from his beard or tapping at the rail. While Hinsen and Rorsefne felt concerned for their skipper, Urquart appeared disdainful and tended to ignore him. For his part, Arflane did not care whether he saw Hinsen and Rorsefne or not, but made evident efforts to avoid Urquart whenever he could. On several occasions when he was standing on the bridge and saw Urquart advancing, he hastily descended the companionway before the second officer could reach him. Generally Urquart did not appear to notice this retreat, but once he was seen to smile a trifle grimly when the door of Arflane's cabin closed with a bang as the harpooner climbed to the bridge.

Hinsen and Rorsefne talked often. Rorsefne was the only man aboard in whom Hinsen could confide his own anxiety. The atmosphere among the men was not so much one of tension as of an apathy reflected in the sporadic progress of the ship.

"It often seems to me that we'll stop altogether," Hinsen said, "and live out the rest of our lives in a timeless shroud of fog. Everything's gotten so hazy..."

Rorsefne nodded sympathetically. The young man did not seem so much depressed as careless about their fate.

"Cheer up, Mr Hinsen. We'll be all right. Listen to Mr Urquart. It's our destiny to reach New York..."

"I wish the captain would tell the men that," Hinsen said gloomily. "I wish he'd tell them something — anything."

Rorsefne nodded, his face for once thoughtful.

CHAPTER NINETEEN

THE LIGHT

The morning after Hinsen's and Rorsefne's conversation Arflane was awakened by the sound of knocking on the outer door of his cabin. He rose slowly, pushing the furs back over Ulrica's sleeping body. He pulled on his coat and leggings and unbolted the door.

Manfred Rorsefne stood there; behind him the fog swirled, creeping into the cabin. The young man's arms were folded over his chest; his head was cocked superciliously to one side. "May I speak to you, captain?"

"Later," Arflane grunted, casting a glance at the bunk where Ulrica was stirring.

"It's important," Manfred said, advancing.

Arflane shrugged and stepped back to let Rorsefne enter as Ulrica opened her eyes and saw them both. She frowned. "Manfred…"

"Good morning, cousin," Rorsefne said. His voice had a touch of humour in it which neither Arflane nor Ulrica could understand. They looked at him warily.

"I spoke to Mr Hinsen this morning," Rorsefne said, walking over to where Arflane's chest stood next to Ulrica's. "He thinks the weather will be clearing soon." He sat down on the chest. "If he's right we'll be making better speed shortly."

"Why should he think that?" Arflane asked without real interest.

"The fog seems to be dispersing. There's been little snow for some days. The air is drier. I think Mr Hinsen's experienced enough to make the right judgment by these signs."

Arflane nodded, wondering what was Rorsefne's real reason for the visit. Ulrica had turned over, burying her face in the fur of the pillows and drawing the coverings over her neck.

"How's your shoulder?" Rorsefne asked casually.

"All right," Arflane grunted.

"You don't appear well, captain."

"There's nothing wrong with me," Arflane said defensively. He straightened his stooped back a little and walked slowly to the bowl by the water barrel. He turned the spigot and filled the bowl, beginning to wash his lined face.

"Morale is bad on board," Rorsefne continued.

"So it seems."

"Urquart is keeping the men moving, but they need someone with more experience to make them do their best," Rorsefne said meaningly.

"Urquart seems to be managing very well," Arflane said.

"So he is — but that's not my point."

Surprised by the directness of Rorsefne's implication, Arflane turned, drying his face on his sleeve. "It's not your business," he said.

"Indeed, you're right. It's the captain's business, surely, to deal with the problems of his own ship. My uncle gave you this command because he thought you were the only man who could be sure of getting the *Ice Spirit* to New York."

"That was long ago," said Arflane obliquely.

"I'm refreshing your memory, captain."

"Is that all your uncle wanted? It would seem to me that he envisaged very well what would happen on the voyage. He all but offered me his daughter, Rorsefne, just before he died." In the bunk Ulrica buried her head deeper in the pillows.

"I know. But I don't think he completely understood either your character or hers. He saw something as happening naturally. He didn't think Janek would come with us. I doubt if my uncle knew the meaning of conscience in the personal sense. He did not understand how guilt could lead to apathy and self-destruction."

Arflane's tone was defensive when he replied, "First you discuss the condition of morale on board, and now you tell me what Ulrica and myself feel. What did you come here for?"

"All these things are connected. You know that very well, captain." Rorsefne stood up. Although actually the smaller he seemed to dominate Arflane. "You're ill and your sickness is mental and emotional. The men understand this, even if they're too inarticulate to voice it. We're desperately short-handed. Where we need a man doing the work of two, we find he'll scarcely perform what were his normal duties before the attack. They respect Urquart, but they fear him too. He's alien. They need a man with whom they feel some kinship. You were that man. Now they begin to think you're as strange as Urquart."

Arflane rubbed his forehead. "What does it matter now? The ship can hardly move with the weather as it is. What do you expect me to do, go out there and fill them full of confidence so they can then sit around on deck singing songs instead of mumbling while they wait for the fog to lift? What good will it do? What action's *needed*? None."

"I told you that Hinsen feels the weather's clearing," Rorsefne said patiently. "Besides, you know yourself how important a skipper's manner is, whatever the situation. You should not reveal so much of yourself out there, captain."

Arflane began to tie the thongs of his coat, his fingers moving slowly. He shook his head and sighed again.

Rorsefne took a step closer. "Go around the ship, Captain Arflane. See if the sailor in you is happy with her condition. The sails are slackly furled, the decks are piled with dirty snow, hatch-covers left unfastened, rigging badly lashed. The ship's as sick as you yourself. She's about ready to rot!"

"Leave me," Arflane said, turning his back on Rorsefne. "I don't need moral advice from you. If you realized the problem…"

"I don't care. My concern's for the ship, those she carries, and her mission. My cousin loved you because you were a better man than Ulsenn. You had the strength she knew Ulsenn didn't possess. Now you're no better than Ulsenn. You've forfeited the right to her love. Don't you sense it?"

Rorsefne went to the cabin door, pulled it open and stalked out, slamming it behind him.

Ulrica sat in the bunk and looked up at Arflane, her expression questioning.

"You think what he thinks, eh?" Arflane said.

"I don't know. It's more complicated..."

"That's true," Arflane murmured bitterly. His anger was rising; it seemed to lend new vitality to his movements as he stalked about the cabin gathering his outer garments.

"He's right," she said reflectively, "to remind you of your duties as captain."

"He's a passenger — a useless piece of cargo — he has no right to tell me anything!"

"My cousin's an intelligent man. What's more he likes you, feels sympathetic towards you..."

"That's not apparent. He criticizes without understanding..."

"He does what he thinks he should — for your benefit. He does not care for himself. He's never cared. Life is a game for him that he feels he must play to the finish. The game must be endured, but he doesn't expect to enjoy it."

"I'm not interested in your cousin's character. I want him to lose interest in mine."

"He sees you destroying yourself — and me," she said with a certain force. "It is more than you see."

Arflane paused, disconcerted. "You think the same, then?"

"I do."

He sat down suddenly on the edge of the bunk. He looked at her; she stared back, her eyes full of tears. He put out a hand and stroked her face. She took his hand in both of hers and kissed it.

"Oh, Arflane, what has happened...?"

He said nothing, but leaned across her and kissed her on the lips, pulling her to him.

An hour later he got up again and stood by the bunk, looking thoughtfully at the floor.

"Why should your cousin be so concerned about me?" he said.

"I don't know. He's always liked you." She smiled. "Besides — he may be concerned for his own safety if he thinks you're not running the ship properly."

He nodded. "He was right to come here," he said finally. "I was wrong to be so angry. I've been weak. I don't know what to do, Ulrica. Should I have accepted this commission? Should I have let my feelings towards you rule me so much? Should I have imprisoned your husband?"

"These are personal questions," she said gently, "which do not involve the ship or anyone aboard save ourselves."

"Don't they?" He pursed his lips. "They seem to." He straightened his shoulders. "Nonetheless, Manfred was right. You're right. I should be ashamed…"

She pointed to the porthole. "Look," she said. "It's getting lighter. Let's go on deck."

There were only wisps of fog in the air now and thin sunlight was beginning to pierce the clouds above them. The ship was moving slowly under a third of her canvas.

Arflane and Ulrica walked hand in hand along the deck.

The browns and whites of the ship's masts and rigging, the yellow of her ivory, all were mellowed by the sunlight. There was an occasional thud as her runners crossed an irregularity in the ice, the distant voice of a man in the rigging calling to a mate, a warm smell on the air. Even the slovenliness of the decks seemed to give the ship a battered, rakish appearance and did not offend Arflane as much as he had expected. The sunlight began to break rapidly through the clouds, dispersing them, until the far horizon could be made out from the rail. They were crossing an expanse of ice bordered in the distance by unbroken ranges of glaciers of a kind Arflane had never seen before. They were tall and jagged and black. The ice in all directions was dappled with yellow light as the clouds broke up and pale blue sky could be seen above.

Ulrica gripped his arm and pointed to starboard. Sweeping down from the clearing sky, as if released by the breaking up of the clouds, came a flock of birds, their dark shapes wheeling and diving as they came closer.

"Look at their colour!" she exclaimed in surprise.

Arflane saw the light catch the shimmering plumage of the leading birds and he, too, was astonished. The predominant colour was gaudy green. He had seen nothing like it in his life; all the animals he knew had muted colours necessary for survival in the icelands. The colour of these birds disturbed him. The glinting flock soon passed, heading towards the dark glaciers on the horizon. Arflane stared after them, wondering why they affected him so much, wondering where they came from.

Behind him a voice sounded from the bridge. "Get those sails set. All hands aloft." It belonged to Urquart.

Arflane gently removed Ulrica's hand from his arm and walked briskly along the deck towards the bridge. He climbed the companionway and took the megaphone from the hands of the surprised harpooner. "All right, Mr Urquart. I'll take over." He spoke with some effort.

Urquart made a little grunting sound in his throat and picked up his harpoon from where he had rested it against the wheelhouse. He stumped down the companionway and took a position on the quarter deck, his back squarely to Arflane.

"Mr Hinsen!" Arflane tried to put strength and confidence into his voice as he called to the first officer, who was standing by one of the forward hatches. "Will you bring the bosun up?"

Hinsen acknowledged the order with a wave of his hand and shouted to a man who was in the upper shrouds of the mainmast. The man began to swing down to the deck; together he and Hinsen crossed to the bridge. The man was tall and heavily built, with a neatly trimmed beard as red as Arflane's.

"You're Rorchenof, bosun on the *Ildiko Ulsenn*, eh?" Arflane said as they presented themselves below him on the quarter deck.

"That's right, sir — before I went to the whaling." There was character in Rorchenof's voice and he spoke almost challengingly, with a trace of pride.

"Good. So when I say to set all sail you'll know what I mean. We've a chance to make up our speed. I want those yards crammed with every ounce of canvas you can get on them."

"Aye, aye, sir." Rorchenof nodded.

Hinsen clapped the man on the shoulder and the bosun moved to take up his position. Then the first officer glanced up at Arflane doubtfully, as if he did not place much faith in Arflane's new decisiveness.

"Stand by, Mr Hinsen." Arflane watched Rorchenof assemble the men and send them into the rigging. The ratlines were soon full of climbing sailors. When he could see that they were ready, Arflane raised the megaphone to his lips.

"Set all sail!" he called. "Top to bottom, stem to stern."

Soon the whole ship was dominated by a vast cloud of swelling canvas and the ship doubled, quadrupled her speed in a matter of minutes, leaping over the gleaming ice.

Hinsen plodded along the deck and began to retie a poorly spliced line. Now that the fog had cleared he could see that there were many bad splicings about the ship; they would have to be attended to before nightfall.

A little later, as he worked on a second knot, Urquart came and stood near him, watching.

"Well, Mr Urquart — skipper's himself again, eh?" Hinsen studied Urquart's reaction closely.

A slight smile crossed the gaunt harpooner's face. He glanced up at the purple and yellow sky. The huge sails interrupted his view; they stretched out, full and sleek as a gorged cow-whale's belly. The ship was racing as she had not raced since the descent of the plateau. Her ivory shone, as did her metal, and her sails reflected the light. But she was not the proud ship she was when she had first set sail. She carried too many piles of dirty snow for that, her hatches did not fit as snugly as they had, and her boats did not hang as straight and true in their davits.

Urquart reached up with one ungloved hand and his red, bony fingers caressed the barbs of his harpoon. The mysterious smile was still on his lips but he made no attempt to answer Hinsen. He jerked his head towards the bridge and Hinsen saw that Manfred Rorsefne stood beside the captain. Rorsefne had evidently only just arrived; they saw him slap Arflane's shoulder and lean casually on the rail, turning his head from left to right as he surveyed the ship.

Hinsen frowned, unable to guess what Urquart was trying to tell him. "What's Rorsefne to do with this?" he asked. "If you ask me, we've him to thank for the captain's revival of spirit."

Urquart spat at a melting pile of snow close by. "They're skippering this craft now, between them," he said. "He's like one of those toys they make for children out of seal cubs. You put a string through the muscles of the mouth and pull it and the creature smiles and frowns. Each of them has a line. One pulls his lips up, the other pulls them down. Sometimes they change lines."

"You mean Ulrica Ulsenn and Manfred Rorsefne?"

Urquart ran his hand thoughtfully down the heavy shaft of his harpoon. "With the Ice Mother's help he'll escape them yet," he said. "We've a duty to do what we can."

Hinsen scratched his head. "I wish I could follow you better, Mr Urquart. You mean you think the skipper will keep his good mood from now on?"

Urquart shrugged and walked away, his stride long and loping as ever.

CHAPTER TWENTY

THE GREEN BIRDS

In spite of the uneasy atmosphere aboard, the ship made excellent speed, sailing closer and closer to the glacier range. Beyond that range lay New York; they were now swinging onto a course east by north, and this meant the end of their journey was in sight. The good weather held, though Arflane felt it unreasonable to expect it to remain so fine all the way to New York.

Across the blue iceplains, beneath a calm, clear sky, the *Ice Spirit* sailed, safely skirting several ice breaks and sometimes sighting barbarians in the distance. The silver-furred nomads offered them no danger and were passed quickly.

Urquart began to take up his old position on the bridge beside the skipper, though the relationship between the two men was not what it had been; too much had happened to allow either to feel quite the same spirit of comradeship.

Leaving twin black scars in the snow and ice behind her, her sails bulging, her ivory-decorated hull newly polished and her battered decks tidied and cleaned of snow, the ice schooner made her way towards the distant glaciers.

It was Urquart who first sighted the herd. It was a long way off on their starboard bow, but there was no mistaking what it was. Urquart jabbed his lance in the direction of the whales and Arflane, by shielding his eyes, could just make them out, black shapes against the light blue of the ice.

"It's not a breed I know," Arflane said, and Urquart shook his head in agreement. "We could do with the meat," the captain added.

"Aye," grunted Urquart, fingering one of his bone earrings. "Shall I tell the helmsman to alter course, skipper?"

Arflane decided that, practical reasons aside, it would be worth stopping in order to provide a diversion for the men. He nodded to Urquart, who strode into the wheelhouse to take over the great wheel from the man on duty.

Ulrica came up on deck and glanced at Arflane. He smiled down at her and signed for her to join him. She sensed Urquart's antipathy and for that reason rarely went to the bridge; she came up a little reluctantly and hesitated when she saw that the harpooner was in the wheelhouse. She glanced aft and then approached Arflane. "It's Janek, Konrad," she said. "He seems to be ill. I spoke to the guards today. They said he wasn't eating."

Arflane laughed. "Probably starving himself out of spite," he said. Then he noticed her expression of concern. "All right. I'll see him when I get the chance."

The ship was turning now, closing with the land whale herd. They were of a much smaller variety than any Arflane knew, with shorter heads in relation to their bodies, and their colour was a yellow-brown. Many were leaping across the ice, propelling themselves by unusually large back flippers. They did not look dangerous, though; he could see that before long they would have fresh meat.

Urquart gave the wheel back to the helmsman and moved along the deck towards the prow, taking a coil of rope from a tackle locker and tying one end to the ring of his harpoon, winding the rest of the rope around his waist. Other sailors were gathering around him, and he pointed towards the herd. They disappeared below to get their own weapons.

Urquart crossed to the rail and carefully climbed over it, his feet gripping the tiny ridge on the outer hull below the rail. Once the ship lurched and he was almost flung off.

The strange-looking whales were beginning to scatter before the skull-decorated prow of the huge schooner as, with runners squealing, it pursued the main herd.

Urquart hung, grinning, on the outside rail, an arm wrapped around it, the other poising the harpoon. One slip, a sudden motion of the ship, and he could easily lose his grip and be plunged under the runners.

Now the ship was pacing a large bull-whale which leaped frantically along, veering off as its tiny eyes caught sight of the *Ice Spirit* close by. Urquart drew back his harpoon, flung the lance at an angle, caught the beast in the back of its neck. Then the ship was past the creature. The line attached to the harpoon whipped out; the beast reared, leaping on its hind flippers, rolling over and over with its mouth snapping. The whale's teeth were much larger than Arflane had suspected.

The rope was running out rapidly and threatened to yank Urquart from his precarious position as the ship began to turn.

Other whaling hands were now hanging by one arm from the rail, drawing back their own harpoons as the ship approached the herd again. The chase continued in silence save for the noises of the ship and the thump of flippers over the ice.

Just as Arflane was certain Urquart was about to be tugged from the rail by the rope, the harpooner removed the last of the line from his waist and lashed it to the nearest stanchion. Looking back, Arflane saw the dying whale dragged, struggling, behind the ship by Urquart's harpoon. The other harpooners were flinging their weapons out, though most lacked the uncanny accuracy of Urquart. A few whales were speared and soon there were more than a dozen being dragged along the ice in the wake of the ship, their bodies smashing and bleeding as they were bounced to death on the ice.

Now the ship turned again, slowing; hands came forward, ready to haul in the catches. Ice anchors were thrown out. The schooner lurched to a halt, the sailors descended to the ice with flenching cutlasses to slice up the catch.

Urquart went with them, borrowing a cutlass from one of the hands. Arflane and Ulrica stood by the rail, looking at the men hacking at the corpses, arms rising and falling as they butchered the catch, spilling their blood on the ice as the setting sun, red as the blood, sent long, leaping shadows of the men across the white expanse. The pungent smell of the blood drifted on the evening air, reminding them of the time when they had first embraced.

Manfred Rorsefne joined them, smiling at the working, fur-clad sailors as one might smile at children playing. There was not a man there who was not covered from hand to shoulder with the thick blood; many of them were drenched in the stuff, licking it from their mouths with relish.

Rorsefne pointed to the tall figure of Urquart as the man yanked the harpoon from his kill and made with his right hand some mysterious sign in the air.

"Your Urquart seems in his element, Captain Arflane," he said. "And the rest of them are elated, aren't they? We were lucky to sight the herd."

Arflane nodded, watching as Urquart set to work flenching his whale. There was something so primitive, so elemental, about the way the harpooner slashed at the dead creature that Arflane thought once again how much Urquart resembled a demigod of the ice, an old-time member of the Ice Mother's pantheon.

Rorsefne watched for a few minutes more before turning away with a murmured apology. Glancing at him, Arflane guessed that the young man was not enjoying the scene.

Before nightfall the meat had been sliced from the bones and the blubber and oil stored in barrels that were being swung aboard on the tips of the lower yards. Only the skeletons of the slaughtered whales remained on the stained ice, their shadows throwing strange patterns in the light from the setting sun.

As they prepared to go below, Arflane caught a movement from the corner of his eye. He stared up into the darkening scarlet sky to see a score of shapes flying towards them. They flew rapidly; they were the same green birds they had encountered several days earlier. They were like albatrosses in appearance, with large, curved beaks and long wings; they came circling in to land on the bones of the whales, their beady eyes searching the bloody ice before they hopped down to gobble the offal and scraps of meat and blubber left behind by the sailors.

Ulrica gripped Arflane's hand tightly, evidently as unsettled by the sight as he. One of the scavengers, a piece of gut hanging from its beak, turned its head and seemed to stare knowingly at them, then spread its wings and flapped across the ice.

The birds had come from the north this time. When Arflane had first seen them they were flying from south to north. He wondered where their nests were. Perhaps in the range of glaciers ahead of them; the range they would have to sail through before they could reach New York.

Thought of the mountains depressed him; it was not going to be easy to negotiate the narrow pass inscribed on Rorsefne's chart.

When the sun set, the green birds were still feeding, their silhouettes stalking among the bones of the whales like the figures of some conquering army inspecting the corpses of the vanquished.

Chapter Twenty-One

The Wreck

There was a collision at dawn. Konrad Arflane was leaving his cabin with the intention of seeing Janek Ulsenn and deciding if the man really was ill when a great shock ran through the length of the ship and he was thrown forward on his face.

He picked himself up, blood running from his nose, and hurried back to Ulrica in his cabin. She was sitting up in the bunk, her face alarmed.

"What is it, Konrad?"

"I'm going to see."

He ran out on deck. There were men sprawled everywhere. Some had fallen from the rigging and were obviously dead; the rest were simply dazed and already climbing to their feet.

In the pale sunlight he looked towards the prow, but could see no obstruction. He ran forward to peer over the skull-decorated bowsprit. He saw that the forward runners had been trapped in a shallow crevasse that could not be seen from above. It was no fault of the lookouts that the obstruction had not been sighted. It was perhaps ten feet wide and only a yard or so deep, but it had succeeded in nearly wrecking the ship. Arflane swung down a loose line to stand on the edge of the opening and inspect the runners.

They did not seem too badly damaged. The edge of one had been cracked and a small section had broken away and could be seen lying

Sailing to Utopia

at the bottom of the crevasse, but it was not sufficient to impair their function.

Arflane saw that the crevasse ended only a few yards to starboard. It was simply bad luck that they had crossed at this point. The ice schooner could be hauled back, the runners turned and she would be on her way again, hardly the worse for the collision.

Hinsen was peering over the forward rail. "What is it, sir?"

"Nothing to worry about, Mr Hinsen. The men will have some hard work to do this morning, though. We'll have to haul the ship out. Get the bosun to back the courses. That'll give them some help if we can catch enough wind."

"Aye, aye, sir." Hinsen's face disappeared.

As Arflane began to clamber hand over hand up the rope, Urquart came to the rail and helped him over it. The gaunt harpooner pointed silently to the north-west. Arflane looked and cursed.

There were some fifty barbarians riding rapidly towards them. They appeared to be mounted on animals very much like bears; they sat on the broad backs of the beasts with their legs stretched in front of them, holding the reins attached to the animals' heads. Their weapons were bone javelins and swords. They were clad in furs but otherwise seemed like ordinary men, not the creatures they had encountered earlier.

Arflane dashed to the bridge, bellowed through his megaphone for all hands to arm themselves and stand by to meet the attack.

The leading barbarians were almost upon the ship. One of them shouted in a strange accent, repeating the words over and over again. Arflane realized, eventually, what the man was shouting.

"You killed the last whales! You killed the last whales!"

The riders spread out as they neared the ship, evidently planning an approach from all sides. Arflane caught a glimpse of thin, aquiline faces under the hoods; then the javelins began to clatter onto the deck.

The first wave of spears hurt no-one. Arflane picked one of the finely carved javelins up in either hand and flung them back at the fast-riding barbarians. He in turn missed both his targets. The javelins were not designed for this kind of fighting and the barbarians were so far proving a nuisance more than a positive danger.

But soon they began to ride in closer and Arflane saw a sailor fall before he could shoot the arrow from the bow he carried.

Two more of the crew were killed by well-aimed javelins, but the more sophisticated retaliation from the decks of the ship was taking its toll of the attackers. More than half the barbarians fell from their mounts with arrow wounds before the remainder withdrew, massing for a renewed attack on the port side.

Arflane now had a bow and he, Hinsen and Manfred Rorsefne stood together, waiting for the next assault. A little further along the rail stood Urquart. He had half a dozen of the bone javelins ranged beside him on the rail and had temporarily abandoned his own harpoon, which was more than twice the size and weight of the barbarian weapons.

The powerful legs of the bearlike creatures began to move swiftly as, yelling wildly, the barbarians rushed at the ship. A cloud of javelins whistled upwards; a cloud of arrows rushed back. Two barbarians died from Urquart's well-aimed shafts and four more were badly wounded. Most of the others fell beneath the arrows. Arflane turned to grin at Hinsen but the man was dead, impaled by a carved bone javelin that had gone completely through his body. The first officer's eyes were open and glazed as the grip on the rail that had kept him upright gradually relaxed and he toppled to the deck.

Rorsefne murmured in Arflane's ear, "Urquart is hurt, it seems."

Arflane glanced along the rail, expecting to see Urquart prone, but instead the harpooner was tearing a javelin from his arm and leaping over the rail, followed by a group of yelling sailors.

The barbarians were regrouping again, but only five remained unwounded. A few more hung in their saddles, several of them with half a dozen arrows sticking in them.

Urquart led his band across the ice, screaming at the few survivors. His huge harpoon was held menacingly in his right hand while his left gripped a pair of javelins. The barbarians hesitated; one drew his sword. Then they turned their strange mounts and rushed away across the ice before the triumphant figure of Urquart shouting and gesticulating behind them.

The raid was over, with less than ten men wounded and only four, including Hinsen, dead. Arflane looked down at the older man's body and sighed. He felt no rancour towards the barbarians. If he had heard the man who had shouted correctly, their whale hunt had destroyed the barbarians' means of staying alive.

Arflane saw the new bosun Rorchenof coming along the deck and signed for him to approach. The bosun saw the corpse of Hinsen and shook his head grimly, staring at Arflane a little resentfully as if he blamed the captain for the barbarian attack. "He was a good sailor, sir."

"He was, bosun. I want you to take a party and bury the dead in the crevasse below. It should save time. Do it right away, will you?"

"Aye, aye, sir."

Arflane looked back and saw Urquart and his band hacking at the wounded barbarians with exactly the same gusto with which they had butchered the whales the evening before. He shrugged and returned to his cabin.

Ulrica was there. He told her what had happened. She looked relieved, then she said: "Did you speak to Janek? You were going to this morning."

"I'll do it now." He went out of the cabin and along the gangway. There was only one guard on duty; Arflane felt it unnecessary to have more. He signed for the man to undo the padlock chaining the door to the bar. The broken door swung inwards and Arflane saw Ulsenn leaning back in his bunk, pale but otherwise apparently fit.

"You're not eating much food they tell me," he said. He did not enter the cabin but leaned over the bar to address the man.

"I haven't much need for food in here," Ulsenn said coldly. He stared unfalteringly at Arflane. "How is my wife?"

"Well," said Arflane.

Ulsenn smiled bitterly. There was none of the weakness in his expression that Arflane had seen earlier. The man's confinement appeared to have improved his character.

"Is there anything you want?" Arflane asked.

"Indeed, captain; but I don't think you would be ready to let me have it."

Arflane understood the implication. He nodded curtly and drew the door closed again, fixing the padlock himself.

By the time the ice schooner had been set on course the men were exhausted. A particularly dreamlike atmosphere had settled over the ship and when dawn came Arflane ordered full sail set.

The ship began to move towards the glacier range that could now be made out in detail.

The curves and angles of the ice mountains shone in the sunlight, reflecting and transforming the colours of the sky, producing a subtle variety of shades from pale yellow and blue to rich marble greens, blacks and purples. The pass soon became visible, a narrow opening between gigantic cliffs. According to Rorsefne's chart, the place would take days to negotiate.

Arflane looked carefully at the sky, his expression concerned. There seemed to be bad weather on its way, though it would pass without touching them. He hesitated, wondering whether to enter the gorge or wait; then he shrugged. New York was almost in sight; he wanted to waste no more time. Once through the pass their journey would be as good as over; the city was less than a hundred miles from the glacier range.

As they moved between the lower hills guarding the approach, Arflane ordered most of the canvas taken in and appointed six men to stay on watch in the bow, relaying sightings of any obstruction back to the wheelhouse and the four helmsmen on duty.

The mood of dreamlike unreality seemed to increase as the *Ice Spirit* drifted closer and closer to the looming cliffs of ice. The shouts of the bow lookouts now began to echo through the range until it seemed the whole world was full of ghostly, mocking voices.

Konrad Arflane stood with his legs spread on the bridge, his gloved hands gripping the rail firmly. On his right stood Ulrica Ulsenn, her face calm and remote, dressed in her best furs; beside her was Manfred Rorsefne, the only one who seemed unaffected by the experience; on Arflane's left was Urquart, harpoon cradled in his arm, his sharp eyes eagerly searching the mountains.

The ship entered the wide gorge, sailing between towering cliffs that were less than a quarter of a mile away on either side. The floor of the gorge was smooth; the ship's speed increased as her runners touched the worn ice. Disturbed by the sounds, a piece of ice detached itself from the side of one of the cliffs to starboard. It bounced and tumbled down to crash at the bottom in a great cloud of disintegrating fragments.

Arflane leaned forward to address Rorchenof, who stood on the quarter deck looking on in some concern.

"Tell the lookouts to keep their voices down as best they can, bosun, or we might find ourselves buried before we know it."

Rorchenof nodded grimly and went forward to warn the men in the bow. He seemed disturbed.

Arflane himself would be glad when they reached the other side of the pass. He felt dwarfed by the mountains. He decided that the pass was wide enough to permit him to increase the ship's speed without too much danger.

"All plain sail, Mr Rorchenof!" he called suddenly.

Rorchenof accepted the order with some surprise, but did not query it.

Sails set, the *Ice Spirit* leaped forward between the twin walls of the canyon, passing strange ice formations carved by the wind. The formations shone with dark colours; everywhere the ice was like menacing black glass.

Towards evening, the ship was shaken by a series of jolts; her motions became erratic.

"It's the runners, sir!" Rorchenof called to Arflane. "They must have been damaged more than we thought."

"Nothing to worry about, bosun," Arflane said calmly, staring ahead. It was getting colder, and the wind was rising; the sooner they were through the pass the better.

"We could easily skid, sir, and crash into one of the cliffs. We could bring the whole thing down on top of us."

"I'll be the judge of our danger, bosun."

The trio beside him on the bridge looked at him curiously but said nothing.

Rorchenof scratched his head, spread his arms, and moved forward again.

The ship was wobbling badly as the sky darkened and the great cliffs seemed to close in on them, but still Arflane made no attempt to slow her and still she moved under full sail.

Just before nightfall Rorchenof came along the deck with a score of sailors at his back.

"Captain Arflane!"

Konrad Arflane looked down nearly serenely. The ship was shuddering constantly now in a series of short, rapid bumps, and the helmsmen were having difficulty in getting sufficiently fast response from the forward runners.

"What is it, bosun?"

"Can we throw out anchor lines, sir, and repair the runners? At this rate we'll all be killed."

"There's no fear of that, bosun."

"We feel there is, sir!" It was a new voice; one of the sailors speaking. From around him came a chorus of agreement.

"Return to your posts," Arflane said evenly. "You have still to understand the nature of this voyage."

"We understand when our lives are threatened, sir," cried another sailor.

"You'll be safe," Arflane assured him.

As the moon rose the wind howled louder, stretching the sails taut and pushing the ship to even greater speed. They jolted and shuddered along the smooth ice of the canyon floor, racing past white, gleaming cliffs whose peaks were lost from sight in the darkness.

Rorchenof looked about him wildly as a precipice loomed close and the ship veered away from it, runners thumping erratically. "This is insanity!" he shouted. "Give us the boats! You can take the ship where you like — we'll get off!"

Urquart brandished his harpoon. "I'll give this to you unless you return to your posts. The Ice Mother protects us — have faith!"

"Ice Mother!" Rorchenof spat. "All four of you are mad. We want to turn back!"

"We cannot turn back!" Urquart shouted, and he began to laugh wildly. "There's no room in this pass to turn, bosun!"

The red-headed bosun shook his fist at the harpooner. "Then drop the heavy anchors. Stop the ship and give us the boats and we'll make our own way home. You can go on."

"We need you to sail the craft," Arflane told him reasonably.

"You *have* gone mad — all of you!" Rorchenof shouted in increasing desperation. "What's happened to this ship?"

Manfred Rorsefne leaned forward on the rail. "Your nerve has cracked, bosun, that's all. We're not mad — you are merely hysterical."

"But the runners — they need attention."

"I say not," Arflane called, and grinned at Urquart, slipping his arm around Ulrica's shoulders, steadying her as the ship shook beneath them.

Now the wind was howling along the canyon, stretching the sails till it seemed they would rip from their moorings. The *Ice Spirit* careened from side to side of the gorge, narrowly missing the vast ragged walls of the cliffs.

Rorchenof turned silently, leading his men below.

Rorsefne frowned. "We haven't heard the last of them, Captain Arflane."

"Maybe." Arflane clung to the rail as the helmsmen barely managed to turn the ship away from the cliffs to port. He looked towards the wheelhouse and shouted encouragement to the struggling men at the wheel. They stared back at him in fear.

Moments later Rorchenof emerged on deck again. He and his men were brandishing cutlasses and harpoons.

"You fools," Arflane shouted at them. "This is no time for mutiny. The ship has to be sailed."

Rorchenof called up to the men in the shrouds: "Take in the sail, lads!"

Then he screamed and staggered back with Urquart's massive harpoon in his chest; he fell to the deck and for a moment the others paused, staring in horror at their dying leader.

"Enough of this," Arflane began. "Go back to your posts!"

The ship swerved again and a rattling sound came from below as the steering chains failed momentarily to grip the runner platform. The ice cliffs surged forward and retreated as the helmsmen forced the *Ice Spirit* away.

The sailors roared and rushed towards the bridge. Arflane grabbed Ulrica and hurried her into the wheelhouse, closed the door and turned to see that Urquart and Rorsefne had abandoned the bridge, vaulting the rail and running below.

Feeling betrayed, Arflane prepared to meet the mutineers. He was unarmed.

The ship seemed now completely at the mercy of the shrieking wind. Streamers of snow whipped through the rigging, and the schooner swayed on her faulty runners. Arflane stood alone on the bridge as the leading sailors began to climb cautiously towards him up the companionway. He waited until the first man was almost upon him then kicked him in the face, wrestling the cutlass from his grasp and smashing the hilt into his skull.

A sheet of snow sliced across the bridge, stinging the men's eyes. Arflane bellowed at them, hacking and thrusting. Then, as men fell back with bloody faces and mangled limbs, Urquart and Rorsefne re-emerged behind them.

Urquart had recovered his harpoon and Rorsefne was armed with a bow and cutlass. He began, coolly, to shoot arrows into the backs of the mutineers. They turned, confused.

The ship rocked. Rorsefne was flung sideways; Urquart barely managed to grasp at a ratline for support. Most of the sailors were flung in all directions and Arflane slipped down the companionway, clinging to the rail and dropping his cutlass.

Once again the ship was racked by a rapid series of jerks. Arflane struggled up, his jacket torn open by the wind, his beard streaming. With one hand he held the rail; with the other he gesticulated at the sailors.

"Rorchenof deceived you," he shouted. "Now you can see why we must get through this pass as fast as we can. If we don't, the ship's finished!"

A sailor's face craned forward, his eyes as wild as Arflane's own. "Why? Why, skipper?"

"The snow! Once caught in the main blizzard, we are blind and helpless! Loose ice will fall from the cliffs to block the pass. Snow will gather in drifts and make movement impossible. If we're not crushed we'll be snowbound and stranded!"

Above his head a sail broke loose from its eyebolts and began to flap thunderously against the mast. The howl of the wind increased; the ship was flung sideways towards the cliff, seemed to scrape the wall before it slid into the centre of the gorge again.

"But if we sail on we'll smash into a cliff and be killed!" another sailor cried. "What have we to gain?"

Arflane grinned and spread his arms, coat swirling out behind him, eyes gleaming. "A fast death instead of a slow one if our luck's really bad. If our luck holds — and you know me to be lucky — then we'll be through by dawn and New York only a few days' sail away!"

"You *were* lucky, skipper," the sailor called. "But they say you're not the Ice Mother's chosen any more — that you've gone against Her will. The woman…"

Arflane laughed harshly. "You'll have to trust my luck — it's all you have. Lower your weapons, lads."

"Let the wind carry us through. It's our only chance." The voice was Urquart's.

The men began to lower their cutlasses, still not entirely convinced.

"You'd be better employed if you got into the shrouds and looked to your sails." Manfred Rorsefne shouted above the moan of the wind.

"But the runners…" a sailor began.

"We'll concern ourselves with those," Arflane said. "Back to work, lads. There'll be no vengeance taken on you when we're through the pass, I promise. We must work together — or die together!"

The sailors began to disperse, their faces still full of fear and doubt.

Ulrica struggled through the wheelhouse door and made her way along the dangerously swaying deck to clutch Arflane's arm. The wind whipped her clothes and the snow stung her face. "Are you sure the men are wrong?" she asked. "Wouldn't it be best…?"

He grinned and shrugged. "It doesn't matter, Ulrica. Go below and rest if you can. I'll join you later." Again the ship listed and he slid along the deck, fighting his way back to her and helping her towards the bridge.

When she was safely below he began to make his way forward, leaning into the wind, the snow stinging his face and half blinding him. He reached the bow and tried to peer ahead, catching only glimpses of the cliffs on both sides as the ship rocked and swerved on its faulty runners. He got to the bowsprit and stretched his body along it, supporting himself by one hand curled in a staysail line; with the other he stroked the great skulls of the whales, pressing his fingers against the contours of cranium, eye sockets and grinning jaws as if they could somehow transmit to him the strength they had once possessed.

As the snow eased slightly ahead he saw the black outlines of the ice cliffs in front of him. They seemed to be closing in, as if shifting on their bases, crowding to trap the ship. It was merely a trick of the eyes, but it disturbed him.

Then he realized what was actually happening. The gorge really did narrow here. Perhaps the cliffs had shifted, for the opening between them was becoming little more than a crack.

The *Ice Spirit* would not be able to get through.

He swung himself desperately along the bowsprit, conscious only of the careening, speeding ship, gasped and staggered across the deck till he reached the great gland of the steering pin and seized the heavy mallet that was secured beside it, began swinging at the emergency bolt. Urquart swayed towards him; he turned his head, bellowing across the deck.

"Drop the anchors! For the Ice Mother's sake, man — drop the anchors!"

Urquart raced back along the deck, finding men and ordering them to the stanchions to knock out the pegs that kept the twin blades of the heavy anchors clear of the ice.

Arflane looked up, his heart sinking. They were nearly into the bottleneck; there was hardly a chance now of saving the ship.

The bolt was shifting. Driving his arms back and forth, he swung the mallet again and again.

Suddenly the thing flew free. There was a high-pitched squealing as the runners turned inwards, ploughshare fashion; the ship began to roll and shudder violently.

Arflane raced back along the deck. He had done all he could; now his concern was for Ulrica's safety.

He reached the cabin as the ship leaped as if in some monstrous orgasm. Ulrica was there, and her husband beside her.

"I released him," she said.

Arflane grunted. "Come — get on deck. There's little chance of any of us surviving this."

There was a final violent crash; the ship's shuddering movement subsided, dying away as the heavy anchors gripped the ice and brought her to a halt.

Clambering out on deck, Arflane saw in astonishment that they were barely ten yards from the point where the ship would have been dashed against the walls of the cliffs or crushed between them.

But the *Ice Spirit's* motion had not ceased.

Now the great schooner began to topple as her port runners gave out completely under the strain, snapping with sharp cracks. With a terrifying groan the vessel collapsed onto her side, turning as the wind caught the sails, flinging her crew in a heap against the port rail.

Arflane grabbed Ulrica and curled his hand around a trailing rope.

His one concern now was to abandon the ship and save them both. He slid down the line and leaped clear onto the hard ice, dragging the woman with him away from the ship and against the wind.

Through the blizzard he could see little of either the cliffs or the bulk of the schooner.

He heard her crash into the side of the gorge and then made out another sound from above as pieces of ice, shaken free, began to slide downwards.

Eventually he managed to find the comparative shelter of an overhang by the far wall of the gorge. He paused, panting and looking back at the broken ship. There was no way of telling if any of the others had managed to jump free; he saw an occasional figure framed near the rail as the curtain of snow parted and swirled back. Once he heard a voice above the wind. It sounded like Ulsenn's.

"He wanted this wreck! He wanted it!"

It was like the meaningless cry of a bird. Then the wind roared louder, drowning it, as a great avalanche of ice began to fall on the ship.

The two huddled together under the overhang, watching the *Ice Spirit* as she was crushed by the huge collapsing slabs, jerking like a dying creature, her hull breaking, her masts cracking and splintering, disintegrating faster than Arflane could ever have believed; breaking up in a cloud of ice splinters and swirling snow against the towering, jagged walls of the ice mountains.

Arflane wept as he watched; it was as if the destruction of the ship signified the end of all hope. He pulled Ulrica to him, wrapping his arms around her, more to comfort himself than for any thought for her.

CHAPTER TWENTY-TWO

THE   TREK

In the morning the snow had stopped falling but the skies were heavy and grey above the dark peaks of the glaciers. The storm had subsided almost as soon as the *Ice Spirit* had been smashed, as if destroying the ship had been its sole purpose.

Moving across the irregular masses of snow and ice towards the place where the gorge narrowed and where the main bulk of the wreck had come to rest, Arflane and Ulrica were joined by Rorsefne and Ulsenn. Neither man was badly hurt, but their furs were torn and they were exhausted. A few sailors stood by the pile of broken fibreglass and metal as if they hoped that the ship might magically restore itself. Urquart was actually in the wreck, moving about like a carrion bird.

It was a cold, bleak day; they shivered, their breath hanging white and heavy on the air. They looked about them and saw mangled bodies everywhere; most of the sailors had been killed and the seven who remained looked sourly at Arflane, blaming his recklessness for the disaster.

Ulsenn's attitude to Arflane and Ulrica was remote and neutral. He nodded to them as they walked together to the wreck. Rorsefne was smiling and humming a tune to himself as if enjoying a private joke.

Arflane turned to him, pointing at the narrow gap between the cliffs. "It was not on the chart, was it?" He spoke loudly, defensively, as much for the benefit of the listening sailors as anyone.

"There was no mention of it," Rorsefne agreed, smiling like an actor amused by his lines. "The cliffs must have moved closer together. I've heard of such things happening. What do we do now, captain? There isn't a boat left. How do we get home?"

Arflane glanced at him grimly. "Home?"

"You mean to carry on, then?" Ulsenn said tonelessly.

"That's the most sensible thing to do," Arflane told him. "We're only some fifty miles or so from New York and we're several thousand from home…"

Urquart held up some large slivers of ivory that had evidently come from broken hatch-covers. "Skis," he said. "We could reach New York in a week or less."

Rorsefne laughed. "Indefatigable! I'm with you, captain."

The others said nothing; there was nothing left to say.

Within two days the party had traversed the pass and begun to move across the wide iceplain beyond the glacier range. The weather was still poor, with snow falling sporadically, and the cold was in their bones. They had salvaged harpoons and slivers of ivory to act as poles and skis; on their backs they carried packs of provisions.

They were utterly weary and rarely spoke, even when they camped. They were following a course plotted from a small compass which Manfred Rorsefne had found among the things spilled from his shattered traveling chest.

To Arflane space had become nothing but an eternal white plain and time no longer seemed to exist at all. His face, hands and feet were frostbitten, his beard was encrusted with particles of ice, his eyes were red and pouched. Mechanically he drove himself on his skis, followed by the others who moved, as he did, like automata. Thought meant simply remembering to eat and protect oneself from the cold as best one could; speech was a matter of monosyllabic communications if one decided to stop or change direction.

From habit he and Ulrica stayed together, but neither any longer felt much emotion.

In this condition it would have been possible for the party to have moved on, never finding New York, until one by one they died; even death would have seemed merely a gradual change from one state to another, for the cold was so bitter that pain could not be felt. Two of the sailors did die; the rest of the party left them where they fell. The only one who did not seem affected by exhaustion was Urquart. When the sailors died he made the sign of the Ice Mother before passing on.

None of them realized that the compass was erratic and that they were moving across the great white plain in a wide curve away from the supposed location of New York.

The barbarians were similar in general appearance to the ones who had attacked them after the whale killing. They were dressed all in white fur and rode white, bearlike creatures. They held swords and javelins ready as they reined in to block the little party's progress.

Arflane only saw them then. He swayed on his skis, peering through red-rimmed eyes at the grinning, aquiline faces of the riders. Wearily he raised his harpoon in an attitude of defense; but the weight was almost too much for him.

It was Urquart who yelled suddenly and flung one harpoon then another, swinging his own weapon from his shoulder as two barbarians toppled from their saddles.

Their leader shouted, waving to his men; they rode swiftly down on the party, javelins raised. Arflane thrust out his own harpoon to defend Ulrica but was knocked backwards by a savage slash across the face, losing his footing in the snow. A blow on his head followed and he lost consciousness.

CHAPTER TWENTY-THREE

THE RITES OF THE ICE MOTHER

There was pain in Arflane's head and his face throbbed from the blow he had received. His wrists were tied behind him and he lay uncomfortably on the ice. He opened his eyes and saw the barbarian camp.

Hide tents were stretched on rigid bone frames; the riding bears were corralled to one side of the camp and a few women moved about among the tents. The place was evidently not their permanent home; Arflane knew that most barbarians were nomads. The men stood in a large group around their leader, the personage Arflane had seen earlier. He was talking with them and glancing at the prisoners who had been bound together at the wrists and lay sprawled on the ice. Arflane turned his head and saw with relief that Ulrica was safe; she smiled at him weakly. Manfred Rorsefne was there and Janek Ulsenn, his eyes tightly closed. There were three sailors, their expressions wretched as they stared at the barbarians.

There was no sign of Urquart; Arflane wondered vaguely if they had killed him. Some moments later he saw him emerge from a tent with a small, obese man, striding towards the main gathering. It seemed then that Urquart had somehow gained their confidence. Arflane was relieved; with luck the harpooner might find a way to release them.

The leader, a handsome, brown-skinned young man with a beak of a nose and bright, haughty eyes, gesticulated towards Urquart as he and the short man pushed through the throng. Urquart began to speak. Arflane gathered that the harpooner was pleading for his friends' lives and wondered how the man had managed to win favour with the nomads. Certainly Urquart was considerably taller than any of them and his own primitive appearance would probably impress them as it impressed all who encountered him. Also, of course, he had been the only one to attack the barbarians; perhaps they admired him for his courage. Whatever the reason, there was no doubt that they were listening gravely to the harpooner as he spoke, waving his massive lance in the direction of the captives.

Eventually the three of them — the leader, the fat man and Urquart — moved away from the other warriors and approached Arflane and the rest.

The young leader was dressed all in fine white fur, his hood framing his face; he was clean-shaven and walked lithely, his back held straight and his hand on the hilt of his bone sword. The fat man wore reddish furs that Arflane could not identify; he pulled at his long, greasy moustachios and scowled thoughtfully. Urquart was expressionless.

The leader paused before Arflane and put his hands on his hips. "Ha! You head north like us, eh? You are from back there!" He spoke in a strange, lilting accent, and jerked his thumb towards the south.

"Yes," Arflane agreed, finding it difficult to speak through his swollen lips. "We had a ship — it was wrecked." He eyed the youth warily, wondering what Urquart had told him.

"The big sleigh with the skins on poles. We saw it — many days back. Yes." The youth smiled and gave Arflane a quick, intelligent look. "There are more — on top of a great hill — months back, eh?"

"You know the plateau of Eight Cities?" Arflane was surprised. He glanced at Urquart, but the harpooner's expression was frozen. He stood leaning on his harpoon, staring into the middle distance.

"We are from much further south than you, my friend," grinned the barbarian leader. "The country is getting too soft back there. The ice is vanishing and there is something yielding and unnatural beneath it. We came north, where things are still normal. I'm Donal of Kamfor and this is my tribe."

"Arflane of Brershill," he replied formally, still confused and wondering what Urquart had said at the barbarian conference.

"The ice is really melting further south?" Manfred Rorsefne spoke for the first time. "It's vanishing altogether?"

"That's so," Donal of Kamfor nodded. "No-one can live there." He gestured with his hand. "Things — push up — from this soft stuff. Bad." He shook his head and screwed up his face.

Arflane felt ill at the idea. Donal laughed and pointed at him. "Ha! You hate it too! Where were you going?"

Arflane again tried to get some sign from Urquart, but the man refused even to meet his eye. There was nothing to gain by being secretive about their destination and it might capture the barbarian's imagination. "We were going to New York," he said.

Donal looked astonished. "You seek the Ice Mother's court? Surely no-one is allowed there…"

Urquart gestured at Arflane. "He is the one. He is the Mother's chosen. I told you that one of us is fated to meet Her and plead our case. She is helping him to reach Her. When he does, the melting will stop."

Now Arflane guessed how Urquart had convinced the barbarians. They were evidently even more superstitious than the whaling men of the Eight Cities. However, Donal was plainly not a man to be duped. He nudged the fat man's shoulder with his elbow.

"We do what this Urquart says to test the truth, eh?" he said.

The fat man chewed at his lower lip, looking bleakly at Arflane. "I am the priest," he murmured to Donal. "I decide this thing."

Donal shrugged and took a step back.

The priest turned his attentions from Arflane to Ulrica and then to Manfred Rorsefne. He glanced briefly at the sailors and Janek Ulsenn, and began to tug at his moustache. He moved closer to Urquart and laid a finger on his arm. "Those are the two, then?" he said, pointing to Ulrica and Rorsefne.

Urquart nodded.

"Good stock," said the priest. "You were right."

"The line of the highest chiefs in the Eight Cities," Urquart said. "No better blood — and they are my kind." He spoke almost proudly.

"It will please the Ice Mother and bring us all luck. Arflane will lead us to New York and we shall be welcome."

"What are you saying, Urquart?" Arflane asked uneasily. "What sort of bargain have you struck for us?"

Urquart began to smile. "One that will solve all our problems. Now my ambition can be fulfilled, the Ice Mother mollified, your burden can be removed, we win the help and friendship of these people. At last it is possible to do what I have planned all these years." His savage eyes burned with a disturbing brilliance. "I have been faithful to the Mother. I have served Her and I have prayed to Her. She sent you — and you helped me. Now She gives me my right. And I, in turn, give Her Hers."

Arflane shivered. The voice was cold, soft, terrifying.

"What do you mean?" he asked. "How have I helped you?"

"You saved the lives of all the Rorsefne clan — my father, his daughter and his nephew."

"That was why you befriended me, I thought..."

"I saw your destiny, then. I realized that you were the servant of the Ice Mother, though at first you did not know it yourself." Urquart pushed back his hood, revealing his bizarre hair and his dangling bone earrings. "You saved their lives, Konrad Arflane, so that I might take them in my own way at my leisure. The time has come for vengeance on my father's brood. I only regret that he cannot be here, also."

Arflane remembered the funeral outside Friesgalt and Urquart's strange behaviour when he had flung the ice block down so savagely into old Pyotr Rorsefne's grave.

"Why do you hate him?" he asked.

"He tried to kill me." Urquart's tone was distant; he looked away from Arflane. "My mother was the wife of an inn-keeper. Rorsefne's mistress. When she brought me to him, asking him to protect me as is the custom, he had his servants carry me onto the ice to expose me. I heard the story years later from her own lips. I was found by a whaling brig and became their mascot. The tale was told in the top-deck taverns and my mother realized what had happened. She sought me out and found me eventually when I was sixteen years old. From then on I planned my revenge on the whole Rorsefne brood. That was more than a score of years ago. I am a child of the ice — favourite of the Ice

Mother. The fact that I live today is proof of that." Urquart's eyes burned brighter.

"That's what you told these people to make them listen to you!" Arflane whispered. He tested the thongs holding his wrists together, but they were tied tightly.

Urquart moved forward, ignoring Arflane. He drew his long knife from his sheath and stooped to cut the lines tying Ulrica and Manfred to the rest. Ulrica lay there, her face pale, her eyes incredulous and terrified. Even Manfred Rorsefne's face had become grim. Neither made a move to rise.

Urquart reached out and pulled the trembling woman to her feet, sheathed his knife and grabbed Rorsefne by the front of his tattered coat. Manfred stood upright with some dignity. There was a movement behind Arflane. He turned his head and saw that Ulsenn's hands had come free. In cutting the thongs, Urquart had accidentally released the man. Donal pointed silently at Ulsenn, but Urquart shrugged disdainfully. "He'll do nothing."

Arflane stared up unbelievingly at the gaunt harpooner. "Urquart, you've lost your reason. You can't kill them!"

"I can," Urquart said quietly.

"He must," the fat priest added. "It is the bargain he made with us. We have had bad luck with the hunting and need a sacrifice for the Ice Mother. The sacrifice must be the best blood." He smiled a trifle sardonically and jerked his thumb at Donal. "We need this one — he is all we have. If Urquart performs the ritual then the rest of you go free; or we come with you, whichever we decide."

"He's insane!" Arflane tried desperately to struggle to his feet. "His hatred's turned his brain."

"I do not see that," the priest said calmly. "And even if it were true it would not matter to us. These two will die and you will not. You should be grateful."

Arflane struggled helplessly on the ice, half rising and then falling back.

Donal turned with a shrug and the priest followed him, pushing Ulrica and Manfred Rorsefne forward. Urquart came last. Ulrica glanced back at Arflane. The terror had left her eyes and was replaced with a look of helpless fatalism.

"Ulrica!" Arflane shouted.

Urquart called without looking at Arflane. "I am about to cut your chains. I am paying the debt I owe you — I am freeing you!"

Arflane watched dumbly as the barbarians prepared for the ritual, erecting bone frames and tying the captives to them so that they were spreadeagled with their feet just above the ice. Urquart stepped forward, cutting expertly at Manfred's clothing as he would skin a seal until the young man was naked. In a way this was a merciful action, since the cold would soon numb his body. Arflane shuddered as he saw Urquart step up to Ulrica and begin to cut the furs from her until she, too, was bare.

Arflane was exhausting himself in his struggles to get to his feet. Even if he could rise there was nothing he could do, for the thongs held his wrists. As a precaution there were now two guards standing nearby.

He watched in horror as Urquart poised the knife close to Manfred Rorsefne's genitals; he heard Rorsefne shriek in pain and thresh in his bonds as Urquart cut his manhood from him. Blood coursed down the young man's thighs and Rorsefne fell forward, head hanging limply. Urquart brandished his trophy, hands reddened with blood, before tossing it away. Arflane remembered the old savage customs of his own people; there had not been a ritual of this kind performed for centuries.

"Urquart! No!" Arflane screamed as the harpooner turned to Ulrica. "No!"

Urquart did not appear to hear him. All his attention was on Ulrica as, with her eyes mad with fear, she tried unsuccessfully to shrink from the knife that threatened her breasts.

Then Arflane saw a figure leap up beside him, grab a javelin from one of the guards, and impale the man. The figure moved swiftly, turning to slice at Arflane's bonds with the sharp tip of the javelin while the other guard turned bewilderedly. Arflane was up then, his fingers grasping the guard's throat and snapping his neck almost instantly.

Ulsenn stood panting beside Arflane, holding the bloody javelin uncertainly. Arflane picked up the other spear and dashed across the ice towards Urquart. As yet no-one had seen what had happened.

Then the priest shouted from where he sat and pointed at Arflane. Several barbarians leaped up, but Donal restrained them. Urquart turned, his eyes mildly surprised to see Arflane.

Arflane ran at him with the javelin, but Urquart leaped aside and Arflane only narrowly missed sticking the weapon into Ulrica's body. Urquart stood breathing heavily, the knife raised; then he moved his head slowly towards the spot where his own huge harpoon lay, ready to finish the pair after the ritual.

Arflane flung the javelin erratically. It took Urquart in the arm. Still Urquart did not move, but his lips seemed to frame a question.

Arflane ran to where the many-barbed harpoon lay and picked it up.

Urquart watched him, shaking his head bewilderedly. "Arflane…?"

Arflane took the lance in both hands and plunged it into the harpooner's broad chest. Urquart gasped and seized the shaft, trying to pull the weapon from his body. "Arflane," he gasped. "Arflane. You fool! You kill everything…" The gaunt man staggered back, his pain-filled eyes still staring unbelievingly; and it seemed to Arflane then that in killing Urquart he killed all he had ever held to be valuable.

The harpooner groaned, his great body swaying, his ivory ornaments clattering as he was racked by his agony. Then he fell sideways, attempted to rise, and collapsed in death.

Arflane turned to face the barbarians, but they did not move. The priest was frowning uncertainly.

Ulsenn ran forward. "Two!" he called. "Two of noble blood. Urquart was the man's cousin and the woman's brother!"

The barbarians murmured and looked questioningly at their priest and their chief. Donal stood up, rubbing his clean-shaven chin. "Aye," he said. "Two it is. It is fair. Besides, we had better sport this way." He laughed lightly. "Release the woman. Attend to the man if he still lives. Tomorrow we go to the Ice Mother's court!"

Ulrica wept like a child as they cut her down. Arflane took her gently in his arms, wrapping her in her ripped furs. He felt strangely calm as he passed the stiff corpse of Urquart and carried the woman towards the tent that the priest led him to. Ulsenn followed him, bearing the unconscious body of Manfred Rorsefne.

When Ulrica lay sleeping and Manfred Rorsefne's wound had been crudely dressed, Arflane and Janek Ulsenn sat together in the close confines of the tent. Night had fallen but they made no attempt to rest. Both were pondering the bond that had grown between them in the few hours that had passed; both knew in their hearts that it could not last.

CHAPTER TWENTY-FOUR

N E W   Y O R K

It took them two weeks to find New York and in that time Manfred Rorsefne, his nervous system unable to withstand the shock it had received, died peacefully and was buried in the ice. Konrad Arflane, Ulrica Ulsenn and Janek Ulsenn rode in a group, with Donal and his fat priest close by; they had learned to ride the huge bears without much difficulty. They moved slowly, for the barbarians had brought their tents and women with them. The weather had become surprisingly fine.

When they sighted the slender towers of New York they stopped in astonishment. Arflane felt that Pyotr Rorsefne had been peculiarly uneloquent in describing them. They were magnificent. They shone.

The party came to a straggling stop and the bears scratched nervously at the ice, perhaps sensing their riders' mixed feelings as they looked at the city of metal and glass and stone soaring into the clouds. The towers blazed; mile upon mile of shining ice reflected their shifting colours and Arflane remembered the story, wondering how tall they must be if they stretched as far below the ice as they did above it. Yet his instincts were alarmed and he did not know why. Perhaps, after all, he did not want to know the truth. Perhaps he did not want to meet the Ice Mother, for he had sinned against Her in many ways in the course of the voyage.

"Well," Donal said quickly. "Let's continue."

Slowly they rode towards the many-windowed city jutting from the ice of the plain. As they moved nearer Arflane realized what it was that so disturbed him. An unnatural warmth radiated from the place; a warmth that could have melted the ice. Surely this was no city of the Ice Mother? They all sensed it and looked at one another grimly. Again they came to a halt. Here was the city that symbolized all their dreams and hopes; and suddenly it had taken on a subtle menace.

"I like this not at all," Donal growled. "That heat — it is much worse than the heat that came to the south."

Arflane nodded. "But how can it be so hot? Why hasn't the ice melted?"

"Let us go back," said Ulsenn. "I knew it was foolish to come here."

Instinctively Arflane agreed with him; but he had set out to reach New York. He had told himself that he would accept whatever knowledge the city offered. He had to go on; he had killed men and destroyed a ship to get here and now that he was less than a mile away he could not possibly turn back. He shook his head and goaded his mount forward. From behind him came a muttering.

He raised his hand and pointed at the slender towers. "Come — let's go to greet the Ice Mother!"

The riding bear galloped forward; behind him the barbarians began to increase their speed until all were galloping in a wild, half-hysterical charge on the vast city, their ranks breaking and spreading out, their cries echoing among the towers as they sought to embolden themselves. Ulrica's hood was whipped back by the wind; her unbound hair streamed behind her as she clung to her saddle. Arflane grinned at her, his beard torn by the wind. Ulsenn's face was set and he leaned forward in the saddle as if going to his death.

The towers were grouped thickly, with barely enough space between the outer ones for them to enter the city. As they reached the great forest of metal and glass they realized that there was something more unnatural about the city than the warmth that came from it.

Arflane's mount's feet skidded on the surface and he called out in amazement. "This isn't ice!"

The stuff had been cunningly made to simulate ice in almost every detail; but now that they stood on it they could tell that it was not ice;

and it was possible to look down through it and make out the dim shapes of the towers going down and down into the darkness.

Donal cried: "You have misled us, Arflane!"

The sudden revelation had shocked Arflane as much as the others. Dumbly, he shook his head.

Ulsenn charged forward on his mount to shake his fist in Arflane's face. "You have led us into a trap! I knew it!"

"I followed Pyotr Rorsefne's chart, that was all!"

"This place is evil," the priest said firmly. "We can all sense that. It matters not how we were deceived — we should leave while we can."

Arflane shared the priest's feeling. He hated the atmosphere of the city. He had expected to find the Ice Mother and had found instead something that seemed to stand for everything the Ice Mother opposed.

"Very well," he said. "We turn back." But even as he spoke he realized that the ground beneath them was moving downwards; the whole great plain was sinking slowly below the level of the surrounding ice. Those closer to the edge managed to leap their clumsy animals upwards and escape but most of them were left in panic as the city dropped lower into what was apparently a huge shaft driven into the ice. The shadows of the shaft's enormous sides fell across the group as they milled about in fear.

Arflane saw how Donal and Ulsenn were staring at him and realized that he was to be their scapegoat.

"Ulrica," he called, turning his mount to plunge into the mass of towers with the woman close behind him. The light grew fainter as they galloped through the winding maze; behind they heard the barbarians, led by Ulsenn and Donal, searching for them. Arflane knew instinctively that in their panic they would butcher him and probably Ulrica too; they had to stay clear of them. He had two dangers to face now and both seemed insuperable. He could not hope to defeat the barbarians and he could not stop the city sinking.

There was an entrance in one of the towers; from it streamed a soft light. Desperately he rode his beast through it and Ulrica came with him.

He found himself in a gallery with ramps curving downwards from it towards the floor of the tower far below. He saw several figures lower on the ramps; figures dressed from head to foot in red, close-fitting garments, wearing masks that completely covered their faces. They looked up as they heard the sound of the bears' paws in the gallery, and one of them laughed and pointed.

Grimly Arflane sent the creature half sliding down one of the ramps. He glanced back and saw that Ulrica had hesitated but was following him. The speed of the descent was dangerous; twice the bear nearly slid off the edge of the ramp and three times he nearly lost his seat on the animal's back, but when he reached the floor of the tower the masked men were gone.

As Ulrica joined him, looking in awe at the strange devices that covered the walls, he realized that the city was no longer in motion. He stared at the things on the wall. They were instruments of some kind; a few resembled chronometers or compasses while others were alive with flickering letters that meant nothing at all to him. His main interest at that moment was in finding a door. There seemed to be none. Was this, after all, the court of the Ice Mother and the red-clad creatures ghosts? From somewhere came faint laughter again, then from above an echoing yell. He saw Ulsenn riding rapidly down the ramp towards him; he was waving a flenching cutlass while Arflane had only a javelin.

Arflane turned to look into Ulrica's face. She stared back at him, then dropped her eyes as if in consent.

Arflane rode his bear towards Ulsenn as the man lunged at him with the cutlass. He blocked the blow with the javelin but the blade sheered off the head of the spear, leaving him virtually defenseless. Ulsenn swung clumsily at his throat, missed and was taken off balance. Arflane plunged the jagged shaft into his throat.

Ulrica rode up, watching silently as Ulsenn clutched at the wound then fell slowly from the back of the bear.

"That is the end of it now," she said.

"He saved your life," Arflane said.

She nodded. "But now it is over." She began to cry. Arflane looked at her miserably, wondering why he had killed Ulsenn then and not earlier, before the man had had the chance to show that he could be courageous. Perhaps that was why; he had, towards the end, become a true rival.

"A fine piece of bloodshed, stranger. Welcome to New York."

They turned. A section of the wall had vanished; in its place stood a thin figure. Its overlong skull was encased in a red mask. Two eyes glittered humorously through slits in the fabric. Arflane jerked up his javelin in an instinctive movement. "This is not New York — this is some evil place."

The figure laughed softly. "This is New York, indeed, though not the original city of your legends. That was destroyed almost two thousand years ago. But this city stands close to the site of the original. In many respects it is far superior. You have witnessed one of its advantages."

Arflane realized he was sweating. He loosened the thongs of his coat. "Who are you?"

"If you are genuinely curious, then I will tell you," replied the masked man. "Follow me."

CHAPTER TWENTY-FIVE

THE TRUTH

Arflane had wanted the truth; it was why he had originally agreed to Rorsefne's scheme; but now, as he stared around the luminous chamber, Ulrica's arm on his, he began to feel that the truth was more than he could accept. The red-masked figure left the room. The walls gleamed blindingly bright and a seated man appeared at the far end of the chamber. He wore the same red garments as the other, but he was almost a dwarf and one shoulder was higher than the other.

"I am Peter Ballantine," he said pleasantly. His pronunciation was careful, as if he spoke the words of a language he had recently learned. "Please sit down."

Arflane and Ulrica seated themselves gingerly on the quilted benches and were startled as the man's chair slid forward until he sat only a foot or two away from them. "I will explain everything," he said. "I will be brief. Ask questions when I have finished."

The world had grown decadent and a malaise had settled on the West so that people lost the will and eventually the means of survival. A peculiar society of stoics had grown up in the polar bases of the South Antarctican International Zone where Russian, American, British Commonwealth, Scandinavian and other research teams lived; and

Camp Century, the city the Americans had established under the Greenland ice cap. Nature, unbalanced by a series of wars in Africa and Asia, had swiftly begun to draw a healing skin of ice over her ruined surface. What had precipitated the ice age was primarily the bombs and the sudden change in the various radiations in the atmosphere. The men of the two polar camps had communicated for a while by radio but the radiation was too great to risk personal contact. For one reason and another, forced by their separate circumstances, the groups of survivors had chosen different ways of adapting to the change. The men of the Antarctic learned to adapt to the ice, making use of all their resources to build ships that could travel the surface without need of fuel, dwellings where one could live without need of special heating plants. As the ice covered the planet, they moved away from the Antarctic, heading towards the equator until, at length, they reached the plateau of the Matto Grosso and decided that here was an ideal location for permanent camp. In adapting to the conditions they had neglected their learning and within a few hundred years the creed of the Ice Mother had replaced the logic of the second law of thermodynamics which had shown logically what the people now believed instinctively — that only ice eternal lay in the future. Perhaps the adaptation of the Antarcticans had been a healthier reaction to the situation than that of the Arcticans who had tended to bury themselves deeper and deeper into their under-ice caverns, searching for scientific means of survival that would preserve the way of life they knew.

Among the last messages to be sent by the Arcticans to the Antarcticans was the information that the northerners had reached the stage where they could transport their city complex further south and that they intended to site it in New York. They offered help to the Antarcticans, but they refused it, stripping their radios to make better use of them. They had grown to feel easy with their life.

So the Arcticans refined their science and their living conditions until the city of New York was the result. The rapid growth of the ice was now just as rapidly reversing.

"It will take at least another two hundred years before any great area of land is cleared," Peter Ballantine explained. "Wildlife is returning, though, from eastern and western areas that were never entirely icebound."

THE ICE SCHOONER

Arflane and Ulrica had received the information almost expressionlessly. Arflane felt that he was drowning; his body and mind were numb.

"We welcome visitors, particularly from the Eight Cities," Ballantine continued.

Arflane looked up at him then. "You are lying. The ice is not melting. You speak heresies…"

"We offer only knowledge. What is wrong with that?"

Arflane said slowly: "I believe in the ice eternal, the doctrine that all must grow cold, that the Ice Mother's mercy is all that allows us to live."

"But you can see how wrong that idea is," Ballantine said gently. "Your society created those ideas to enable them to live the way they did. They needed them, but they no longer need them now."

"I understand," Arflane said. The depression that filled him was hard to overcome; it seemed that his whole life since he had first saved Rorsefne had led to this point. Gradually he had forsaken his old principles, allowing himself soft emotions, taking Ulrica in adultery, involving himself with others; and it was as if by forgetting the dictates of the Ice Mother he had somehow created this New York. Logically, he knew the idea was absurd but he could not shake himself clear of it. If he had lived according to his code, the Ice Mother would be comforting him at this moment; if he had listened to Urquart, last of the Ice Mother's true followers, and gone with him, they would have found the New York they expected to find. But he had killed Urquart in saving Ulrica's life. "You kill everything," Urquart had said as he died. Now Arflane understood what the harpooner had meant. Urquart had tried to change his course for him, but the course had led inevitably to Peter Ballantine and his logic and his vision of an earth in which the Ice Mother was dying, or already dead. If he could find Her…

Ulrica Ulsenn touched his hand. "He is right," she said, "that is why the people of the Eight Cities are changing — because they sense what is happening to the world. They are adapting in the way that animals do, though most of the animals — the land whales and the like — will not adapt in time."

"The land whales' adaptation was artificially stimulated," Ballantine said with some pride. "It was an experiment that was incidentally beneficial to your people."

Arflane sighed again, feeling completely dejected. He rubbed his sweating forehead and tugged at his clothes, resenting the heat of the place. He turned and looked at Ulrica Ulsenn, shaking his head slowly, touching her hand gently. "You welcome this," he said. "You represent what they represent. You're the future, too."

She frowned. "I don't understand you, Konrad. You're being too mysterious."

"I'm sorry." He glanced away from her and looked at Ballantine as he sat in the moving chair, waiting patiently. "I am the past," he said to the man. "You can see that, I think."

"Yes," said Ballantine sympathetically. "I respect you, but…"

"But you must destroy me."

"Of course not."

"I have to see it so." Arflane sighed. "I am a simple man, you see. An old-fashioned man."

Ballantine told him: "We will find accommodation for you both while you rest." He chuckled. "Your barbarian friends are still chasing around on the surface of the city like frightened lice. We must see how we can help them. In their case our hypnomats will doubtless be of more use than conversation."

CHAPTER TWENTY-SIX

N O R T H

The next day Peter Ballantine walked in the artificial gardens of the city with Ulrica Ulsenn. Arflane had looked at the gardens and declined to enter. He sat now in a gallery staring at the machines Ballantine had told him were the life-giving heart of the city.

"Just as your ancestors adapted to the ice," Ballantine was saying to the woman, "so you must re-adapt to its disappearance. You came north instinctively because you identify the north with your homeland. All this is natural. But now you must go south again, for your own good and the good of your children. You must give your people the knowledge we have given you; though it will take time they will gradually come to accept it. If they do not change they will destroy themselves in a reversion to savagery."

Ulrica nodded. She looked with growing enjoyment at the multitude of brightly coloured flowers around her, sniffed their scents in wonder, her nostrils the keener for never having experienced such perfume before. It made her feel lightheaded. She smiled slowly at Ballantine, eyes shining.

"I realize Arflane is disturbed just now," Ballantine continued. "There is a lot of guilt in his attitude; but there is no need for him to feel this. There was a purpose to all those inhibitions, but now it does not exist. That is why you must go south again, to tell them what you have learned."

Ulrica spread her hands and indicated the flowers. "This is what will replace the ice?" she said.

"This and much more. Yours and Arflane's children could see it if they wished to journey even further south. They could live in a land where all these things grow naturally." He smiled, touched by her childlike enjoyment of his garden. "You must convince him."

"He will understand," she said confidently. "What of the barbarians? Donal and the rest?"

"We have had to use less subtle and possibly less lasting methods on them. But they will help spread the ideas."

"I wish Arflane had not refused to come here," Ulrica said. "I'm sure he would like it."

"Perhaps," said Ballantine. "Shall we return to him?"

When Arflane saw them come back he rose. "When you are ready," he said distantly, "I would like to be taken back to the surface."

"I have no intention of keeping you here against your will," Ballantine said. "I will leave you together now."

He left the gallery. Arflane began to walk back to the apartment that had been set aside for them. He moved slowly, Ulrica beside him.

"When we go back to Friesgalt, Konrad," Ulrica said, taking his arm, "we can marry. That will make you Chief Ship Lord. In that position you will be able to guide the people towards the future, as Ballantine wants us to. You will become a hero, Konrad, a legend."

"I do not trust legends," he said. Gently he took her hand from his arm.

"Konrad?"

He shook his head. "You go back to Friesgalt," he told her. "You go back."

"What will you do? You must come back with me."

"No."

He moved as if to kiss her, then he checked himself.

"Our love..." Her voice shook. "Oh, Konrad!"

"Our love was immoral. We paid our price. It is over. I —"

He frowned as if he heard his own voice for the first time. He continued, almost amused. "I give myself to the Ice Mother. She has all my loyalty now."

She kissed his shoulder. She turned back towards the garden.

E P I L O G U E

The city rose to ground level and they disembarked. A storm was beginning to rise over the iceplains. The wind whistled through the tall towers of the city. Peter Ballantine helped Ulrica into the cabin of the helicopter that would take her most of the way back to Friesgalt.

There was a general confused bustling as the barbarians mounted up and began to turn their steeds towards the south. With a wave Donal led his men away across the plain.

Arflane watched them as they rode. There were skis on his feet, two lances in his gloved hands, a visor pushed up from his face; on his back was a heavy pack.

Ulrica looked out from the cabin. "Konrad…"

He smiled at her. "Good-bye, Ulrica."

"Where are you going?" she asked.

He gestured into the distance. "North," he said. "To seek the Ice Mother."

As the rotors of the machine began to turn he pushed himself around on his skis and dug the lances into the ice, sending his body skimming forward. He leaned into the wind as he gathered momentum; it had begun to snow.

The helicopter bumped as it rose into the air and tilted towards the south. Ulrica stared through the glass and saw him moving swiftly northwards. His figure grew smaller and smaller. Sometimes it was obscured by drifting snow; sometimes she glimpsed him, the lances rising and falling as he gathered speed.

Soon, he was out of sight.

THE BLACK CORRIDOR

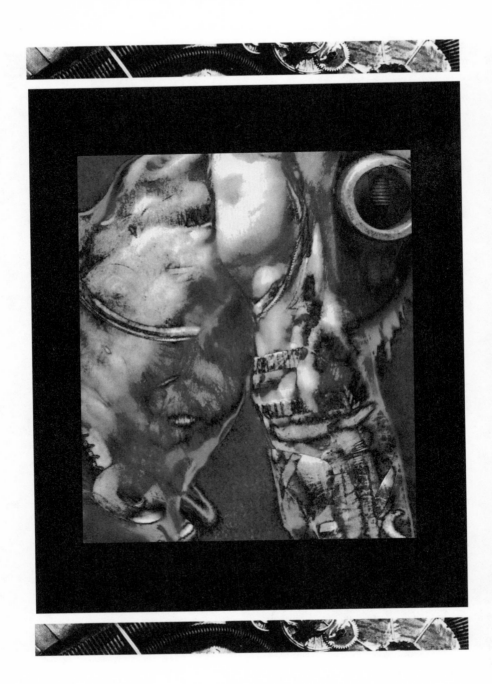

To the memory of Bob Calvert, a rare talent

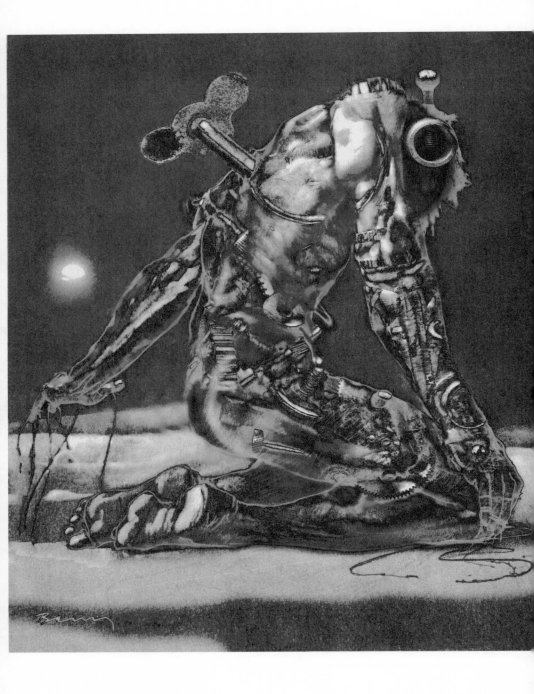

CHAPTER ONE

Space is infinite.
It is dark.

Space is neutral.

It is cold.

*

Stars occupy minute areas of space. They are clustered a few billion here. A few billion there. As if seeking consolation in numbers.

Space does not care.

*

Space does not threaten.

Space does not comfort.

It does not sleep; it does not wake; it does not dream; it does not hope; it does not fear; it does not love; it does not hate; it does not encourage any of these qualities.

Space cannot be measured. It cannot be angered. It cannot be placated. It cannot be summed up.

Space is there.

*

Space is not large and it is not small. It does not live and it does not die. It does not offer truth and neither does it lie.

Space is a remorseless, senseless, impersonal fact.

Space is the absence of time and of matter.

*

Through this silence moves a tiny pellet of metal. It moves so slowly as to seem not to move at all. It is a lonely little object. In its own terms it is a long way from its planet of origin.

In the solid blackness it gives off faint light. In that great life-denying void it contains life.

A few wisps of gas hang on it; a certain amount of its own waste matter surrounds it: cans and packages and bits of paper, globules of fluid, things rejected by its system as beyond reconstitution. They cling to its side for want of anything better to cling to.

And inside the spacecraft is Ryan.

Ryan is dressed neatly in regulation coveralls which are light grey in colour and tend to match the vast expanse of controls, predominantly grey and green, which surround him. Ryan himself is pale and his hair is mainly grey. He might have been designed to tone in with the ship.

Ryan is a tall man with heavy grey-black eyebrows that meet near the bridge of his nose. He has grey eyes and full, firm lips that at the moment are pressed tightly together. He seems physically very fit. Ryan knows that he has to keep himself in shape.

Ryan paces the spaceship. He paces down the central passageway to the main control cabin and there he checks the co-ordinates, the consumption indicators, the regeneration indicators and he checks all his figures, at length, with those of the ship's computer.

He is quietly satisfied.

Everything is perfectly in order; exactly as it should be.

Ryan goes to the desk near the ship's big central screen. Although activated, the screen shows no picture. It casts a greenish light onto the desk. Ryan sits down and reaches out towards the small console on the desk. He depresses a stud and, speaking in a clear, level voice, he makes his standard log entry.

"Day number one thousand, four hundred and sixty-three. Spaceship *Hope Dempsey* en route for Munich 15040. Speed holds steady at point nine of *c*. All systems functioning according to original expectations. No other variations. We are all comfortable.

"Signing off.

"Ryan, Acting Commander."

The entry will be filed in the ship's records and will also be automatically broadcast back to Earth.

Now Ryan slides open a drawer and takes from it a large red book. It is his personal logbook. He unclips a stylus from a pocket in his coveralls, scratches his head and writes, slowly and carefully. He puts down the date: December 24th, 2005 AD He takes another stylus from his pocket and underlines this date in red. He looks up at the blank screen and seems to make a decision.

He writes:

The silence of these infinite spaces frightens me.

He underlines the phrase in red.

He writes:

I am lonely. I am controlling a desperate longing. Yet I know that it is not my function to feel lonely. I almost wish for an emergency so that I could wake at least one of them up.

Mr Ryan pulls himself together. He takes a deep breath and begins a more formal entry, the third of his eight-hourly reports.

When he has finished, he gets up, puts the red logbook away, replaces his stylus neatly in his pocket, goes over to the main console and makes a few fine adjustments to the instruments.

He leaves the main control cabin, enters a short companionway, opens a door.

He is in his living quarters. It is a small compartment and very tidy. On one wall is a console with a screen that shows him the interior of the main control cabin. Set in the opposite wall is a double bunk.

He undresses, disposes of his coveralls, lies down and takes a sedative. He sleeps. His breathing is heavy and regular at first.

He goes into the ballroom. It is dusk. There are long windows looking out onto a darkening lawn. The floor gleams; the lights overhead are dim.

On the ballroom floor formally dressed couples slowly rotate in perfect time to the music. The music is low and rather sombre. All the couples wear round, very black spectacles. Their faces are pale, their features almost invisible in the dim light. The round black glasses give them a masklike appearance.

Around the floor other couples are sitting out. They stare forward through their dark glasses. As the couples move the music becomes quieter and quieter, slower and slower, and now the couples revolve more slowly too.

The music fades.

Now a low psalmlike moaning begins. It is in the room but it does not come from the dancers.

The mood in the room changes.

At last the dancers stand perfectly still, listening to the song. The seated men and women stand up. The chanting grows louder. The people in the room become angry. They are angry with a particular individual. Above the chanting, louder and faster, comes the beating of a rapid drum.

The dancers are angry, angry, angry...

Ryan awakes and remembers the past.

CHAPTER TWO

Ryan and Mrs Ryan shyly entered their new apartment and laid down the large, nearly brand-new suitcase. It came to rest on the floor of the lobby. They released the handle. The suitcase rocked and then was still.

Ryan's attention left the case and focused on the shining tub in which grew a diminutive orange tree.

"Mother's kept it well watered," murmured Mrs Ryan.

"Yes," said Ryan.

"She's very good about things like that."

"Yes."

Awkwardly Ryan took her in his arms. Mrs Ryan embraced him. There was a certain reserve in her movements as if she were frightened of him or of the consequences her action might provoke.

A feeling of tenderness overwhelmed Ryan. He smiled down at her upturned face, reached out his hand to stroke her jawline. She smiled uncertainly.

"Well," he said. "Let's inspect the family mansion."

Hand in hand they wandered through the apartment, over the pale gold carpets, past the simulated oak furniture of the living room to stare out through the long window at the apartment blocks opposite.

"Not too close," said Ryan with satisfaction. "Wouldn't it be terrible to live like the Benedicts — so near the next block that you can see right into their rooms. And they can see right into yours."

"Awful," agreed Mrs Ryan. "No privacy. No privacy at all."

They wandered past the wall-to-wall television into the kitchen. They opened cupboards and surveyed the contents. They pressed buttons to slide out the washing machine and the refrigerator. They turned on the infragrill, played with the telephone, touched the walls. They went into the two empty bedrooms, looking out of the windows, turning on the lights, their feet noisy on the tiles of the floors.

Last of all they went into the main bedroom, where the coloured lights of the walls shifted idly in the bright sunshine from the windows. They opened the wardrobes in which their clothes had been neatly laid out.

Mrs Ryan patted her hair in front of the huge convex mirror opposite the bed. Shyly they stood, looking out of the window.

Ryan pressed the button on the sill and the blinds slid down.

"Aren't the walls beautiful?" Mrs Ryan turned to look at the multicoloured lights playing over the flat surfaces.

"Not as beautiful as you."

She looked around at him. "Oh, you…"

Ryan reached out and touched her shoulder, touched her left breast, touched her waist.

Mrs Ryan glanced at the windows as if to reassure herself that the blinds were drawn and no-one could see in.

"Oh, I'm so happy," she whispered.

"So am I." Ryan moved closer, drew her to him, holding her buttocks cupped in his heavy hands. He kissed her lightly on the nose, then strongly on the mouth. His hand left her buttock and moved down her thigh, pushing up the skirt, feeling her flesh.

A flush came to Mrs Ryan's face as he eased her towards the new bed. She opened her lips and stroked the back of his neck. She sighed.

His thumb traced the line of her pelvis. She trembled and moved against him.

Then the Chinese jazz record started in the next apartment. The Ryans froze. Mrs Ryan was bent backwards with Mr Ryan's face buried in her neck. The clangour of the record, every note and every phrase, was as audible as if the music poured from their own glowing walls.

They broke apart. Mrs Ryan straightened her skirt.

"Damn them!" Mr Ryan raised his fists impotently. "Good God! Don't tell me that's the kind of neighbours we've got."

"Hadn't you better…?"

"What?"

"Couldn't you…?" She was confused.

"You mean…?"

"… go and speak to them?"

"Well, I…" He frowned. "Maybe this time I'll just hammer on the wall."

Slowly he took off his shoe. "I'll show them." He went to the wall and banged on it vigorously, stood back, shoe in hand, and waited.

The music stopped.

He grinned. "That did it."

Mrs Ryan took a deep breath and said, "I'd better unpack."

"I'll help you," said Ryan.

He left the bedroom and approached the suitcase. He took the handle in both hands and staggered back to where she was waiting.

Together they unpacked the residue of their honeymoon — the suntan lotions, the damp bathing suits, the tissue-wrapped gifts for their parents. They talked and they laughed as they took things out of the suitcase and put them away, but secretly they were sad as article after article came out. All the souvenirs of that sunny three weeks on an island where no-one else lived, where there was freedom from observation, the noise and demands of other people.

The suitcase was empty.

Mrs Ryan reached into the waterproof pouch at the back and produced the tapes they had processed when they reached the mainland heliport. He fetched the player from the dressing table and they went into the living room to play the tapes on the television.

In silence they looked at the pictures, drinking in the landscapes they showed. There were the mountains, there the great blue expanse of the sea, there the heaths.

There were almost no shots of Mr or Mrs Ryan. There were only the views of the silent crags, the sea and the moors of the island where they had been so happy.

A bird cried.

Somewhat shakily the picture swept upward towards the cloud-slashed sky. A kittyhawk dived into the distance. There was the sound of the breakers in the background.

Suddenly the picture cut out.

Mrs Ryan looked at Mr Ryan with tears in her eyes.

"We must go back there soon," she said.

"Very soon," he smiled.

And the Chinese jazz, as loud as ever, shrieked through the room.

The Ryans sat rigidly in front of the television screen.

Ryan clenched his teeth. "Jesus God, I'll —" He stood up. "I'll kill the bastards!" He gestured irresolutely. "There are laws. I'll call the police."

Mrs Ryan held his hand. "There's no need to speak to them, darling. Just put a note through their door. Warn them. They must have heard of the Noise Prevention Act. You could write to the caretaker as well."

Ryan rubbed his lips once.

"Tell them they could be heavily fined," said his wife. "If they're reasonable, they'll…"

"All right." Ryan pursed his lips. "This time that's what I'll do. Next time — and I mean it — I'll knock on the door and confront them."

He went into the living room to write the notes. Mrs Ryan made tea.

The Chinese jazz went on and on. Ryan wrote the notes with short, jerky movements of his pen.

… And I warn you that if this noise continues I will be forced to contact the police and inform them of your conduct. I have also told the caretaker of my intention. At very least you will be evicted — but you must also be aware of the heavy penalties you could receive under Section VII of the Noise Prevention Act of 1978.

He read back over the letter. It was a bit pompous. He hesitated. Perhaps if he…? No. It would do. He finished the letters, put them into envelopes and sealed them as Mrs Ryan directed the tea trolley into the living room. "That will do, thank you," she told it.

THE BLACK CORRIDOR

Suddenly the music stopped in mid-bar. Ryan looked at his wife and laughed. "Maybe that's the answer. Maybe it's robots making that row."

Mrs Ryan smiled. She picked up the teapot.

"Look, I'll do that," said Ryan, "if you'll just put these into the internal mail slot outside the front door."

"All right." Mrs Ryan replaced the pot. "But what shall I do if I meet them?" She nodded towards the neighbouring flat.

"Ignore them completely, of course. They surely won't try to involve you in conversation. You might as well ignore anybody else you meet outside. If we start making contact with all the people in this block we'll never have any bloody privacy."

"That's what mother said," said Mrs Ryan.

"Right."

She took the two letters and went out of the living room and into the lobby. Ryan heard the front door click open.

He straightened his head as he heard another voice. It was a woman's voice, high-pitched and cheerful. He heard Mrs Ryan mumble something, heard her footsteps as she entered hastily and shut the front door firmly.

"What on earth was that?" he asked as she returned to the living room. "It's like living in a zoo. Maybe it was a mistake…"

"It was the woman who lives on the other side of us. She was coming back with her shopping. She welcomed me to the block. I said thank you very much and slid back in here."

"Oh, Christ, I hope they're not going to pester us," said Ryan.

"I don't think so. She seemed quite embarrassed to be chatting with a stranger."

In cozy, uninterrupted silence the Ryans drank their tea and ate their sandwiches and cake.

When they had finished Mrs Ryan ordered the trolley back to the kitchen and she and Ryan sat together on the couch watching the tapes on the television. They were beginning to feel at ease in their little home.

Mrs Ryan smiled at the screen and pointed. There was a scene of cliffs, a cave. "Remember that old fisherman we found in there that day? I was never so startled in my life. You said —"

A steady knocking began.

Ryan swung around, seeking the source of the noise.

"Over here," said a voice.

Ryan got up. Outside the window was the head and torso of a man in overalls. His grinning red face was capped by a mop of clashing ginger hair. His teeth were ragged and yellow.

Mrs Ryan put her hand to her mouth as Ryan dashed to the window.

"What the bloody hell do you think you're doing, pushing your fucking face in our window without warning?" Ryan trembled with rage. "What's the matter with you? Haven't you ever heard of privacy? Can't we get a moment's peace and quiet? It's a bloody conspiracy?"

The man's grin faded as Ryan ranted on. His muffled voice came through the pane. "Look here," he said. "There's no need to be like that. I never knew you was back, did I? I was asked by the old lady to keep the windows clean while you was away. Which I have done without, if I may say so, any payment whatsoever. So before you complain about my bloody habits, I suggest you settle up."

"How much?" Ryan put his hand in his pocket. "Come on — how much?"

"Thirty pounds seven."

Ryan opened the window and put five-pound coins on the outside sill. "There you are. Keep the change. And while you're at it don't bother to come back. We don't need you. I'm going to clean the windows myself."

The man grinned cynically. "Oh, yeah?" He tucked the money into his overall pocket. "I hope you've got a head for heights, then. They're all telling me they're going to clean their own windows from now on. Have you seen them? Half of them don't do the outsides. They can't stand the height, see? You should see 'em. Filthy. You can hardly see out for the dirt. It must be like the black hole of Calcutta in most of them flats. Still, it's none of my business, I'm sure. If people want to live in the dark that's their affair, not mine."

"Too right," said Ryan. "You nosy bloody —"

The window cleaner's eyes hardened. "Look, mate —"

"Clear off," said Ryan fiercely. "Go on!"

The man shrugged, gave his yellow grin again and touched his

THE BLACK CORRIDOR

carroty hair sardonically in a salute. "Cheerio, then, smiler." He began to lower himself down the wall towards the distant ground.

Ryan turned to look at his wife. Mrs Ryan was not on the couch any more. He heard sobs and followed the sound.

Mrs Ryan was stretched across the bed, face down, weeping hysterically.

He touched her shoulder. "Cheer up, love. He's gone now."

She shrugged off his hand.

"Cheer up. I'll —"

"I've always been a *private* person," she cried. "It's all right for you — you weren't brought up like me. People in our neighbourhood never intruded. They didn't come poking their faces through windows. Why did you bring me here? *Why?*"

"Darling, I find it all just as distasteful as you do," Ryan told her. "Honestly. We'll just have to sort it out step by step. Show people that we like to keep to ourselves. Be calm."

Mrs Ryan continued to cry.

"Please don't cry, darling." Mr Ryan ran his hands through his hair. "I'll straighten things out. You won't see anyone you don't know."

She turned on the bed. "I'm sorry… One thing after another. My nerves…"

"I know."

He sat down on the edge of the bed and began to stroke her hair. "Come on. We'll watch a musical on TV. Then we'll…"

And as Mrs Ryan's sobs abated there came the familiar sound of the Chinese jazz. It was muted now, but it was still loud enough to lacerate the Ryans' sensitive ears.

Mrs Ryan moaned and covered her head as the tinkling, the jangling, the thudding of the music beat against her.

Ryan, helpless, stood and stared down at his weeping wife.

Then he turned and began to bang and bang and bang and bang on the wall until all the colours disappeared.

But the music kept on playing.

CHAPTER THREE

Mr Ryan has done his exercises, bathed, dressed and breakfasted.

He has left his cabin and has paced down the main passageway to the central control cabin. He has checked the co-ordinates, the consumption indicators, the regeneration indicators and run computations through the machine.

He seats himself at the tidy steel desk below the big screen that has no picture. Around him the dials and the indicators move unobtrusively.

Mr Ryan takes out the heavy red-covered logbook from its steel drawer. He unclips his pen.

Using the old-fashioned log appeals to his imagination, his sense of pioneerdom. It is the one touch of the historic, the link with the great captains and explorers of the past. The logbook is Ryan's poem.

He enters the date: December 25th, 2005 AD He underlines it. He begins to write the first of his eight-hourly reports:

Day number one thousand, four hundred and sixty-four. Spaceship Hope Dempsey *en route for Munich 15040. Speed steady at point nine of* c. *All systems functioning according to original expectations. No other variations. All occupants are comfortable and in good health.*

Under this statement Ryan signs his name and rules a neat line. He then stands up and reads the entry into the machine.

Ryan's report is on its way to Earth.

He likes to vary this routine. Therefore when he makes his next report he will do it orally first and write it second.

Ryan stands up, checks the controls, glances around and is satisfied that all is in order. Since embarkation on the *Hope Dempsey* three years ago he has lost weight and, in spite of his treatments under the lamps, colour. Ryan exercises and eats well and relatively speaking he is in the best possible condition for a man living at two-thirds Earth gravity. On Earth it would be doubtful if he could run a hundred yards, walk along the corridor of a train, move a table from one side of a room to another. His muscles are maintained, but they have forgotten much. And Ryan's mind, basically still the same, has also forgotten much in the narrow confines of the perfectly running ship.

But Ryan has his will. His will makes him keep to the perfect routine which will take the ship and its occupants to the star. That will has held Ryan, the ship and its instruments and passengers together for three years, and will hold them together, functioning correctly, for the next two.

Ryan trusts his will.

Thus, in the private and unofficial section of the red logbook, the section which is never read over to Earth, Ryan writes:

Today is Alex's ninth birthday — another birthday he will miss. This is very saddening. However it is the kind of sacrifice we must make for ourselves and for others in our attempt to make a better life. I find myself increasingly lonely for the company of my dear wife and children and my other old friends and good companions. Broadcasts from Earth no longer reach us and soon I shall be reduced, for stimulation, to those old shipmates of mine, my videotapes, my audiotapes and my books. But all this must be if we are to achieve our end — to gain anything worthwhile demands endurance and discipline. In three minutes it will be time to perform the duty I find most painful emotionally — and yet most essential. Every day I am seized by the same mixture of reluctance, because I know the distress it will cause me. And yet there is an eagerness to fulfill my task. I shall go now and do what I have to.

Ryan closes the red logbook and places it back in the steel drawer so that the near edges of the book rest evenly against the bottom of the drawer. He replaces his pen in his pocket and stands up. He glances once more at the controls and with a firm step leaves the room.

He walks up the metallic central corridor of the ship. At the end there is a door. The door is secured by heavy spin screws. Ryan presses a button at the side of the door and the screws automatically retract. The door swings open and Ryan stands for a moment on the threshold.

The room is a small one, instantly bright as the heavy door opens. There are no screens to act as portholes and the walls gleam with a platinum sheen.

The room is empty except for the thirteen long containers.

One of the containers is empty. Plastic sheets are drawn two-thirds of the way up over the twelve full containers. Through the semi-transparent material covering the remainder of the tops can be seen a thick, dark green fluid. Through the fluid can be seen the faces and shoulders of the passengers.

The passengers are in hibernation and will remain so until the ship lands (unless an emergency arises which will be important enough for Ryan to awaken them). In their gallons of green fluid they sleep.

At their heads is a panel revealing the active working of their bodies. On the plastic cover is a small identification panel, giving their names, their dates of birth and the date of their engulfment into suspended animation. On the indicator panel is a line marked DREAMS. On each panel the line is steady.

Ryan looks tenderly down into the faces of his family and friends.

JOSEPHINE RYAN. 9/9/1960. 7/3/2004. His wife. Blonde and plump-faced, her naked shoulders still pink and smooth.

RUPERT RYAN. 13/7/1990. 6/3/2004. The dark face of his son, so like his, the bony shoulders just beginning to broaden into manhood.

ALEXANDER RYAN. 25/12/1996. 6/3/2004. The fairer face of his younger son. Eyes, amazingly, still open. So blue. Thin shoulders of an active small boy.

THE BLACK CORRIDOR

Ryan, looking on the faces of his closest relatives, feels close to tears at their loss. But he controls himself and paces past the other containers.

SIDNEY RYAN. 2/2/1937. 25/12/2003. His uncle. An old man. False teeth, very white, revealed through open mouth. Eyes closed. Thin, wrinkled shoulders.

JOHN RYAN. 15/8/1963. 26/12/2003. Ryan's brother. Ryan thinks that now he is thinner, less muscular, he must look more like John than he has ever done, even when they were children. John has the same short face, thick brows. His exposed shoulders are narrow, knotted.

ISABEL RYAN. 22/6/1962. 13/2/2004. His brother John's first wife, her crowned teeth exposed in a snarl in her narrow jaw. Pale face, pale hair, pale, thin shoulders. Ryan feels a spasm of relief that Isabel is lying in her container instead of around him, erect and needlelike, talking to him in her high voice. Ryan does not notice the passing thought, does not need to correct himself.

JANET RYAN. 10/11/1982. 7/5/2004. So lovely. His brother John's second wife. Soft cheeks, soft shoulders, long wavy black hair suspended in the green fluid, a gentle smile through pink, generous lips, as if she were dreaming pleasant dreams.

FRED MASTERSON. 4/5/1950. 25/12/2003. Narrow face. Thin, narrow shoulders. Furrowed brow.

TRACY MASTERSON. 29/10/1973. 9/10/2003. Masterson's wife. A pretty woman, looking as stupid in her container as she did out of it.

JAMES HENRY. 4/3/1957. 29/10/2003. Shock of red hair floating, sea-green eyes open in the green fluid. Looking like some drowned merman.

Ryan moves past him and stops at the eleventh container.

IDA HENRY. 3/3/1980. 1/2/2004. Poor girl. Matted hair, pale brown. Sunken young cheeks, drooping mouth.

There are two arrested lives in that container, Ryan thinks. Ida, Henry's wife, and her coming child. What would be the result of that long gestation of mother and child, both in foetal fluid?

FELICITY HENRY. 3/3/1980. 1/2/2004. Henry's other wife and Ida's twin sister. Her hair is smoother and shinier, her cheeks less sunken than her sister's. Not pregnant.

Ryan reaches the last container and looks into it. The white bottom of the container shines up at him. Surrounded by his sleeping companions he has the urge to get into the container and try it out.

Suspecting his impulse, he squares his shoulders and walks firmly from the room. The door hisses shut behind him. He touches the stud that replaces the screws. He walks back down the silent corridor and re-enters the control cabin. He makes rapid notes on a small pad of paper he takes from his breast pocket. He moves to the computer and runs his calculations through.

If necessary the computer could be switched to fully automatic, but this is not considered good for the psychology of crew members.

Ryan nods with satisfaction when the replies come. He returns to the desk and puts the charts back in the drawer.

As he does this another spurt of paper comes from the computer. Ryan examines it.

It reads:

REPORT ON PERSONNEL IN CONTAINERS NOT SUPPLIED.

Ryan purses his lips and punches in the reports:

JOSEPHINE RYAN.   CONDITION STEADY.

RUPERT RYAN.   CONDITION STEADY.

ALEXANDER RYAN.   CONDITION STEADY.

SIDNEY RYAN.   CONDITION STEADY.

JOHN RYAN.   CONDITION STEADY.

ISABEL RYAN.   CONDITION STEADY.

THE BLACK CORRIDOR

JANET RYAN.   CONDITION STEADY.

FRED MASTERSON.   CONDITION STEADY.

TRACY MASTERSON.   CONDITION STEADY.

JAMES HENRY.   CONDITION STEADY.

IDA HENRY.   CONDITION STEADY.

FELICITY HENRY.   CONDITION STEADY.

****

*******YOUR OWN CONDITION****

suggests the computer.

Ryan pauses and then reports:

I AM LONELY.

The computer tells him instantly:

*******FILL YOUR TIME ACCORDING TO THE SUGGESTED PROGRAMME. IF THE CONDITION CONTINUES INJECT 1CC PRODITOL PER DIEM. DO NOT TAKE MORE. DISCONTINUE THE DOSAGE AS SOON AS POSSIBLE AND AT ALL COSTS AFTER 14 DAYS**

Ryan straightens his shoulders, signs off and walks away from the computer.

He walks down the corridor to his own accommodation. He inflates a red easy chair, sits down and presses a stud on the wall. The TV screen in front of him begins to roll off a list of its offerings. Films, plays, music, dancing and discussion and educational programmes. In his weakness Ryan does not choose the agricultural information he is committed to studying. He selects an old Polish film.

Soon the screen is full of people walking, talking, eating, getting on streetcars, watching scenery, kissing and arguing.

Ryan feels tears on his cheeks but he has an hour of relaxation due to him and he will take it, in whatever form it comes.

As Ryan watches, bearing his expected melancholy with stoicism, his mind wanders. He hears, echoing in his head, the report on his undead companions in their cavernous containers: *Josephine Ryan. Condition steady. Rupert Ryan. Condition steady. Alexander Ryan... Sidney Ryan... John Ryan... Isabel Ryan... Janet Ryan... Fred Masterson... Tracy Masterson... James Henry... Ida Henry... Felicity Henry...*

The parade of the faces he once knew passes in front of him. He imagines them as they were, before they were immersed in their half-life in the sea-green fluid.

CHAPTER FOUR

James Henry's pale hands, stubby and freckled, shook as he bent forward in his chair and stared into Fred Masterson's face.

"*Do* something, Fred, *do* something — that's what I'm saying."

Masterson gazed back, thin eyebrows raised cynically, long forehead creased by parallels of wrinkles. "Such as?" he asked after a pause.

Henry's hands clenched as he said: "Society is polluted physically and morally. Polluted by radioactivity we're continually told is within an acceptable level — though we see signs every day that this just isn't so. I cannot allow Ida or Felicity to bear children with the world as it is today. And worse, in a way, than the actual environment is the infinite corruption of man himself. Each day we grow more rotten, like sacks of pus, until the few of us who try to cling to the old standards, try to stay decent, are more and more threatened by the others. Threatened by their corruption, threatened by their violence. We're living in a mad world, Masterson, and you're advising patience..."

Beside him on the Ryans' couch were his two wives, tired, identically pale, identically thin, as if the split cell which produced them had only contained the materials for one healthy woman and had been forced to make two. As Henry spoke they both gazed at him from their pale blue eyes and followed every word as if he was speaking their thoughts.

Masterson did not reply to James Henry's tirade. He merely stared about him as if he were thoroughly tired of the discussion.

The furniture of the Ryans' living room had been pushed back against the walls to seat the group which met there every month.

The blinds were drawn and the lights were on.

Seated with his back to the window was Ryan's Uncle Sidney, a thin, obstinate old man with a tonsure of brown hair around his bald head. The rest of the group was seated around the other walls. The seat in front of the window, like the front row at public meetings, was always the last to be filled.

Fred Masterson and his wife, Tracy, who wore a well-cut black floor-length dress, the conservative fashion of the moment, and fully made-up black lips, sat opposite the Henry family on their sofa.

Next to Masterson sat John Ryan's first wife, Isabel. She was a dowdy, pinch-faced woman. On John's left sat his other wife, the beautiful Janet. Against the fourth wall were Ryan and his wife Josephine.

The women wore blacks and browns, the men were quietly dressed in dark-coloured tunics and trousers. The room, bare in the centre, entirely without ornament, had a dull look.

Ryan sat and worked out in his head some estimates for a new line of product. As a silence fell between James Henry and Fred Masterson, he turned his mind away from his business problems and said:

"This is, after all, only a discussion group. We haven't the power or the means to alter things."

Henry opened his green eyes wider and said urgently: "Can't you see, Ryan, that the days of discussion are practically over? We're living in chaos and all we're doing is talking about it. At the meeting next month —"

"We haven't agreed to a meeting next month yet," said Masterson.

"Well, if we don't we'll be fools." Henry crossed his legs in an agitated manner. "At the meeting next month we must urge that pressure —"

Tracy Masterson's face was taut with stress. "I've got to go home now, Fred."

Masterson looked at her helplessly. "Try to hang on…"

"No…" Tracy hunched her shoulders. "No. It's people all around me. I know they're all friends… I know they don't mean to…"

"A couple more minutes."

"No. It's like being shut up in a box."

She folded her hands in her lap and sat with her eyes downcast. She could say no more.

Josephine Ryan rose and took her by the arm. "I'll give you some pills and you can sleep in our bed. Come on, dear…" She drew the younger woman up by the arm and led her into the kitchen.

Henry looked at Masterson. "Well? You know why your wife is like this. It all dates from the time when she was caught up in that UFO demonstration in Powell Square. And that's an experience any one of us could have at any time — as things are now."

As he spoke there came the sound of chanting from nearby streets. A window broke in the distance and there were shouts. A noisy song began.

From the bedroom Tracy Masterson started to scream.

Fred Masterson got up, paused for a moment and then ran towards the sound.

The rest of the group sat frozen, listening as the hubbub came closer. In the bedroom Tracy Masterson screamed and shouted.

"NO.NO.NO.NO.NO.NO.NO.NO.NO."

Josephine Ryan came back, leaning against the doorway. "The pills will take effect soon. Don't worry about her. Who are the people in the street?"

No-one replied.

Tracy screamed again.

"Who are the people in the street?" Josephine moved further into the room. "Who?"

The noisy voices subsided, giving way to the same low chanting, in a minor key, which had begun the procession.

Now Ryan and his friends could hear some of the words.

"Shut up the land,
Shut up the sky.

THE BLACK CORRIDOR

We must be alone.
Strangers, strangers all must die.
We must be alone.
Alone, alone, alone.
Shut out the fearful, darkening skies.
Let us be alone.
No strangers coming through the skies.
We must be alone.
No threats, no fears,
No strangers here,
No thieves who come by night.
Alone, alone, alone."

"It's them, then. The Patriots." Mrs Ryan looked at the others. Again no-one replied.

The chanting was close under the windows now.

The lights went out. The room was left in complete darkness.

Tracy Masterson's screams had diminished to a whimper as the drug took hold.

"Bloody awful verses, whatever else..." Uncle Sidney cleared his throat.

The group sat surrounded by a chanting which seemed, in the utter darkness, to be coming from all over the room.

Suddenly it stopped.

There was the sound of running and sharp cries. Then a pitiful high screaming like the sound of an animal being killed.

Uncle Sidney stirred in his chair by the window and stood up. "Let's have a look out, then," he said calmly. His finger went to the button on the window sill.

As James Henry shouted "*No!*" Ryan was halfway across the room, arms stretched toward his uncle.

It was too late.

The blind shot up.

The window covering the whole of one wall was open to the night.

Ryan stood petrified in the middle of the floor as the flickering light cast by a thousand torches in the street played over him. Henry, half out of his seat, stood up and was completely still.

Josephine Ryan stood in the middle of the floor with the bottle of pills in her hand.

The dark-clad women sat in their seats without moving.

The cries and the terrible high scream went on.

Uncle Sidney looked down into the street. On the other side, in the high block opposite, all the windows were blinded.

"Oh, my God," said Uncle Sidney. "Oh, my God."

There was silence until Josephine Ryan said: "What is it?"

Uncle Sidney said nothing. He looked downward.

Mrs Ryan took a deep breath. She walked firmly over to the window. Ryan watched her.

She steeled herself, looked swiftly down into the street, stepped back. "It's too horrible. That really is too horrible."

Uncle Sidney's face was hard. He continued to watch.

The crowd had caught a young man of twenty, one of the people who lived in the block opposite. They had tied him to an old wooden door, propped the door against a great steel power supply post, drenched the door and the young man with petrol and set light to him.

The young man lay at an angle on the blazing door. He writhed and he screamed as the flames consumed him. The crowd pressed closely around, those in front being perpetually pushed too close to the flames by the people at the back who wanted to see. Their torches and the light cast over them by their human bonfire revealed chiefly men, most of them in their thirties and forties. The women among them were younger. All were dressed in dark, long clothing. In the front the people were crouched, tensely watching the young man burn.

A young woman with cropped blonde hair yelled: "Burn, stranger, burn." The men about her took up the cry. "Burn, burn, burn, burn!"

The young man writhed in the flames, gave a final, frantic twist of his body and was still.

When he had stopped screaming, the crowd became quiet. Apparently they were exhausted. They sat or stood about, breathing heavily, wiping their faces and hands and mouths.

*

Uncle Sidney pressed the blind button in silence. The blind slid down, blotting out the torches, the fire, the silent crowd below. He sat heavily in his chair.

The crackling of the fire could be heard in the Ryans' living room.

Mrs Ryan took her hand from her eyes, walked out to the kitchen and went to the sink. The men and women in the room heard her running water into a tumbler, heard her drink and put the tumbler into the dishwasher, heard the door of the washer close.

Uncle Sidney sat in his chair, looking at the floor.

"What did you want the blind open for?" James Henry demanded. "Eh?"

Uncle Sidney shrugged and continued to stare at the floor.

"Eh?"

"What difference does it make?" said Uncle Sidney. "What bloody difference…?"

"You had no right to expose us to that — particularly the women," said James Henry.

Uncle Sidney looked up and there were a few tears in his eyes. His voice was strained. "It happened, didn't it?"

"What's that got to do with it? We don't want to get involved. It's not even your home. It was Josephine's window which was uncovered when — this thing — took place. She'll be the one accused!"

Uncle Sidney didn't reply. "It happened, that's all I know. It happened — and it happened here."

"Very horrifying to see, no doubt," said Henry. "But that doesn't make any difference to the fact that the Patriots have got some of the right ideas, even if they do put them into practice in a very distasteful way." He sniffed. "Besides, some people enjoy watching that sort of thing. Revel in it. As bad as them."

Uncle Sidney's eyes expressed vague astonishment. "Do what?"

"What did you want to watch it for, then?"

"I didn't *want* to watch it."

"So you say…"

Masterson appeared in the doorway and said, "Tracy's gone to sleep at last. What's been happening? Patriots, was it?"

Ryan nodded. "They just burnt a man. Outside. In the street."

Masterson wrinkled his nose. "Bloody lunatics. If they really want to get rid of them there's plenty of legal machinery to help them."

"Quite," said Henry. "No need to take the law into their own hands. What bothers me is this odd anti-space notion of theirs."

"Quite," said Masterson. "They've been reassured time and time again that there are no alien bodies in the skies. They've been given a dozen different kinds of proof and yet they continue to believe in an alien attack."

"There could be some truth in it, couldn't there?" Janet said timidly. "No smoke without fire, eh?"

The three men looked at her.

"I suppose so," Masterson agreed. He made a dismissive gesture. "But it's extremely unlikely."

Mrs Ryan directed the trolley through the door. The group sat drinking coffee and eating cake.

"Drink up while it's hot." Mrs Ryan's voice had an edge to it.

Isabel Ryan flinched and said, "No thank you, Josephine. It doesn't agree with me."

Josephine's mouth turned down.

"Isabel hasn't been very well," her husband John said defensively.

Ryan tried to smooth things over. He smiled at Isabel.

"You're quite right to be careful," he said.

The whole group knew, from Isabel's demeanour, although no-one would have stated it, that Isabel was experiencing a phase where she supposed people were trying to poison her. She would eat and drink nothing she had not prepared herself.

Most of them knew what it was like. They had gone through the same thing at one time or another. It was best to ignore it.

Anyway, it wasn't unheard of for people who believed that sort of thing to be perfectly right. They all knew men and women who had imagined that they were being poisoned who later had died inexplicably.

"One of us ought to attend the next big meeting of the Patriots," said Ryan. "It would be interesting to know what they're up to."

"It's dangerous." John Ryan's face was stern.

"I'd like to know, though." Ryan shrugged. "It's best to investigate a thing, isn't it? We ought to find out what they're really saying."

"We'll go in a band, then," said James Henry. "Safety in numbers, eh?"

His wives looked at him fearfully.

"Right," said Masterson. "Time to tune into the report of the Nimmoite rally at Parliament. The government will fall tonight."

They watched the Nimmoite rally on the television. They watched it while more cries and shouts sounded from the street below. They watched as a group passed playing drums and pipes. They did not look around. They watched the Nimmoite rally until the President appeared in the House of Commons and offered his resignation.

CHAPTER FIVE

That night there were riots and fires all over the city.

The Ryans and their friends watched the riots and fires, sitting behind their closed blinds, staring at the large, bright wall which was their television.

The city was being ripped and battered and bloodied.

They drank their coffee and they ate their cake and they watched the men fall under the police clubs, watched the girls and boys savaged by the police dogs, heard the hooting and yelling of the looters, saw the fire service battling to control the fires.

The Ryans and their friends had seen a great many riots and fires in their lives, but never so many at a single time. They watched almost critically for a while.

But as the programmes wore on, Mrs Ryan became quieter and quieter, more mechanical in her presentation of coffee, of sugar, of things to eat.

It was when she saw her favourite department store go up in flames that she finally put her head in her arms and sobbed...

Mrs Ryan had been married for fourteen years.

For fourteen years she had carried the weight of her vigorous husband's moods and ambitions. She had reared children, battled with her fear of other people, of the outside, had made almost all family decisions.

She had done her best.

Now she wept.

Ryan was startled.

He went over and patted her, tried to comfort her, but she could not be stopped. She went on crying.

Ryan looked up from his wife and stared at Uncle Sidney. In front of them, unheeded, glass was smashing into the street, crowds were running and shouting, the top of the Monument, built to commemorate the Great Fire of 1666, was crowned with flames.

"Put her to bed," said Uncle Sidney. "You can't do or say anything effective. It's the situation that's getting her down. Put her to bed."

The group watched as sensible Josephine Ryan was supported out of the room by her husband. Josephine Ryan was about to be sedated and put to bed next to the unconscious Tracy Masterson.

Ida and Felicity Henry, seeing their senior woman carried off, became alarmed. Ida shuddered and Felicity said, "Where will it end?"

"You're becoming inhuman," said Uncle Sidney. "Switched off."

"In the grave unless we do something fast," James Henry said brutally. Apparently he hadn't heard Uncle Sidney.

"In the grave," he said again. "What are you two going to do, eh?" And he laughed nastily into the pale, identical faces of his two hapless wives.

Fred Masterson looked at Uncle Sidney and Uncle Sidney looked at Fred Masterson. They shrugged almost at the same time.

And there was Henry laughing as usual. As usual, leaning forward in his chair. As usual, springy, full of ideas, head crowned by that energetic mass of red hair which gave the impression of a man getting extra fuel from somewhere.

As James Henry pushed his features aggressively towards the faces of his tired twin girl brides it seemed impossible not to think that he was somehow plugged into their vital forces, in some manner draining off energy before it could reach the women to power their thin, narrow feet, their stooped backs, their limp hair, their lacklustre eyes.

Uncle Sidney, possessed by this thought, laughed heartily into the room.

"What the hell are you laughing at, Sidney?" demanded James Henry.

Uncle Sidney shook his head and stopped.

James Henry glared at him. "What was so funny, then?"

"Never mind," said Uncle Sidney. "It's enough to be able to laugh at all, the way things are."

"Then keep laughing, Sidney," said James Henry. "Keep at it, chum. You'll be fucking crying soon enough."

Sidney grinned. "So much for the good old values. Didn't you know there were ladies present?"

"What d'you mean?"

"Well, when I was a young man, we didn't use that sort of language in front of ladies."

"What sort of language, you old fool?"

"You said 'fucking', James," said Uncle Sidney, straight-faced.

"Of course I didn't. I don't believe in… A man has to have a very limited vocabulary if he needs to resort to swearing like that. What are you trying to prove, Sidney?"

Again the look of vague astonishment crept into Uncle Sidney's eyes. "Forget it," he said at length.

"Are you trying to start something?"

"I don't want to start anything more, no," said Uncle Sidney.

The television screen jumped from one scene to another. Fires and riots. Riots and fires.

James Henry turned to his wives. "Did I say anything objectionable?"

In unison they shook their heads.

He glared again at Uncle Sidney. "There you are!"

"Okay. All right." Uncle Sidney looked away.

"I proved I didn't say anything," said James Henry insistently.

"Fair enough."

"They're my witnesses!" He pointed back at his wives. "They told you."

"Sure."

"What do you mean, 'sure'?"

"I meant I believe you. I'm sorry. I must have misheard you."

James Henry relaxed and smiled. "You might apologize, then. To all of us, I should have thought."

"I apologize to all of you," Uncle Sidney said. "All of you."

Ryan watched from the doorway and he was frowning. He looked at Uncle Sidney. He looked at James Henry. He looked at Ida and Felicity. He looked at Fred Masterson. Then he looked at the television screen.

It was not so different. It was frightening. Nothing seemed real. Or perhaps it was that nothing seemed any more real than anything else.

He went towards the television with the intention of switching it off. Then he paused. He was overwhelmed with the feeling that if he turned the switch not just the television picture would fade, but also the scene in the room. He shuddered.

Mr Ryan shuddered, full of fear and hopelessness. Full of depression. Full of doubt.

It had been a bad day.

The day was really something of an historic day, he thought. Today marked a turning point in his country's history — perhaps the world's history.

Perhaps it was the beginning of a new Dark Age.

He came to a decision and reached forward to switch off...

CHAPTER SIX

Seated in his little cabin, the television flickering gently in front of him, the foreign voices speaking their lines, Ryan falls, against his will, into a doze.

Surely he knew, when he sat down, when he selected a film in an alien language, that this would be the result. Perhaps he did but would not acknowledge the thought.

Ryan, a man tormented by nightmares during his official hours of sleep, who rises every morning with the indefinable despair of a man who has dreamed of horrors he cannot even remember — Ryan is desperate for rest.

Through the caverns of his brain pound the sounds of heart and blood, the drums of life. He hears them dimly at first.

Ryan is standing in the ballroom.
The dance floor has a dull shine.
The lights in the candelabra are low.
They give off a bluish light.
Black streamers decorate the walls.
There are masks suspended at eye level on them.
The masks show human faces.

```
        K
          E
            E
              P
                      GOING
                  P
                E
              E
        K
```

The spaceship is on course for Munich.
Traveling at just below the speed of light.
The spaceship is on course for Munich.
I KNOW THAT I DES…
… DES SCIENCES — HISTOIRE DES SCIENCES — HISTOIRE
DES SCIENCES…

IT IS TRUE, HOWEVER
I AM WILLING TO TELL
WHOEVER WISHES TO KNOW
(*there is no need to tell — there is no-one to tell — it does not matter…*)

```
              K
            E
          E
        P
GOING
        P
          E
            E
              K
```

WHICH WAY?

In the ballroom the masks show human faces. Faces distorted by anger, lust and greed.

Suddenly one of the masks shows his wife Josephine, her face ferociously distorted. There is his youngest child, Alexander. His mouth is open, his eyes are blank. Alexander — a drooling idiot.

The couples are circling to the chanting music. It grows slower and slower and they revolve more and more slowly. They are dressed in dark clothes. They have the firm and well-defined faces of the practical, self-interested, well-fed middle classes. They are people of substance.

Their eyes are masked by the round sunglasses. The long closed windows at the end of the room look out into blackness. The music gets slower, the men and women revolve more slowly, so slowly they barely move at all.

The music almost stops.

There is the slow beating of a drum.

The music is heard more loudly. It is like a psalm sung by a chorus of monks. It is a funeral dirge, the song sung when a man is about to be buried.

The drums beat louder, the music quickens.

A high screaming note comes in and holds steady through the dirge.

The drum beats faster, the music quickens.

The high screams grow louder.

The dancers bunch in the middle of the room, staring towards the window through their round, black, covered eyes. They begin to talk quietly among themselves. They are discussing something and looking at the window.

ON THE NIGHT OF THE FAIR THERE WAS AN ACCIDENT.

Q: WHAT WAS THE EXACT NATURE OF THE CATASTROPHE?

ON THE NIGHT OF THE MARINOS AN ACCIDENT

Q: WHAT WAS THE EXACT NATURE OF THE CATASTROPHE?

ON A NIGHT IN MAY AN ACCIDENT

Q: WHAT WAS THE EXACT NATURE OF THE CATASTROPHE?

ON AND ON MAY ACCIDENT

    Q: WHAT WAS THE EXACT NATURE OF THECATASTROPHE?

ONE MAY ACCIDENT

    Q: WHAT WAS THE EXACT NATURE OF THE CATASTROPHE?

ONE MAY ACCEPT

    Q: WHAT WAS THE EXACT NATURE OF THE CATASTROPHE?

ONE MACE IT

    Q: WHAT WAS THE EXACT NATURE OF THE CATASTROPHE?

ONE ACED

    Q: WHAT WAS THE EXACT NATURE OF THE CATASTROPHE?

ONE A

    Q: WHAT WAS THE EXACT NATURE OF THE CATASTROPHE?

ONE

    Q: WHAT WAS THE EXACT NATURE OF THE CATASTROPHE?

WON

    Q: WHAT WAS THE EXACT NATURE OF THE CATASTROPHE?

WIN

    Q: WHAT WAS THE EXACT NATURE OF THE CATASTROPHE?

IN

    Q: WHAT WAS THE EXACT NATURE OF THE CATASTROPHE?

N

    Q: WHAT WAS THE EXACT NATURE OF THE CATASTROPHE?

NO ANSWER AVAILABLE

NO ANSWER AVAILABLE

NO ANSWER AVAILABLE

END OF SESSION. PLEASE CLEAR ALL PREVIOUS JUNK AND
RESET IF REQUIRED.

They are still looking at the window.

Ryan finds himself and his wife and their two children standing in front of the window. His arm is around Josephine on one side and his other arm spans the shoulders of the two boys on the other.

The crowd is talking about them. Ryan feels fear for his wife and children. The crowd talks more angrily, looks at Ryan and his family.

The scream behind the music is louder, the singing more urgent, the drum beats faster, faster, faster.

THE SPACESHIP IS ON COURSE FOR MUNICH. ON COURSE TRAVELING AT JUST BELOW THE SPEED OF LIGHT.

THE SPACESHIP IS ON COURSE FOR MUNICH.

CONDITION STEADY
CONDITION STEADY
CONDITION STEADY

The light flashes on and off as if trying to warn him of something rather than to reassure him. He frowns at the big sign. Is there something wrong with the hibernating personnel? Something he has not noticed? Something the instruments have not registered?

And Ryan awakes sweating in his red, inflatable chair and stares blindly at the minute, flat figures on the television screen.

His body is limp and his mouth is dry.

He licks his lips and sighs aloud.

Then he sets his mouth in a firm line, switches off the set and leaves the room.

His feet echo along the passageway. He reaches a cubicle containing a long white bed. He straps himself on and is massaged.

When he is finished his body aches and his mind is still not clear. It is now time for Ryan to eat. He returns to his room and gets food. He eats and he tastes nothing.

When he has finished he raises the cover over the porthole screen in his room and looks out through the simulated window into the vastness of space.

For a second he feels that he sees a dark figure out there in the void. He clears his vision rapidly and stares out at the stars.

He cannot see the planet that he and his companions are bound for. He has been in space for three years. He will be in space for another two years. And he cannot see his destination yet. He has only the word of the space physicists that it exists and that it can support the thirteen lives he carries with him.

A planet of Barnard's Star, Munich 15040.

He is alone in space, in charge of his ship and the lives of the other twelve. He is more than halfway to his destination.

The sudden remembrance of what he has done sweeps over him. Along with his fear, with the torment caused by the solitude, Ryan feels pride. He causes the cover to sweep down over the "porthole". He leaves his room and walks into the control room to continue his duties.

But he cannot get rid of the lingering feeling of depression, the sense of something not done.

This sense of a task unfulfilled makes him work with even greater intensity, even greater efficiency.

He frowns.

There is still something left undone.

He rechecks everything. He runs tests through the computer. He inspects every instrument and double-checks it to make sure it is reading accurately.

Everything is perfect.

He has forgotten nothing.

The feeling almost disappears.

CHAPTER SEVEN

When he has read his report into the machine Ryan goes to the desk beneath the screen and opens the drawer where his red logbook is lying ready for his remarks.

First he sits down at his desk and hums a song as he completes some calculations. He works quickly and mechanically to complete his task. He lays it aside, satisfied.

He has fifteen minutes free now. He produces the red logbook from the drawer again, rules a line under his formal report and writes:

Alone in the craft I experience the heights and depths of emotion untempered by the needs of less mechanical work than I do now, uninterrupted by the presence of others.

He reads this over, frowns, shrugs, continues:

This means deep pain and being a prey to my own feelings. It also means great joy. An hour ago I stared out of my porthole at the enormous vista and recollected what I — what we as a group — have done to save ourselves. My mind goes back to how we were, and forward to what we will be.

Ryan's stylus hovers over the page. He makes writing motions over the book, but he cannot phrase his thoughts.

At length he gives up, rules another line under his entry, shuts the book and replaces it in the drawer.

He changes his mind, gets the book out again and begins to write rapidly:

The world was sick and even our group was tinged with unhealthiness. We were not lilywhite. We sold out some of our ideals. But perhaps the difference was that we knew we were selling out. We admitted what we were doing and so remained rational when almost everyone else had gone insane.

It is true, too, that we became somewhat hardened to the horrors around us, shut them out — even condoned some of them — even fell in with the herd from time to time. But we had our objectives — our sense of purpose. It kept us going. However, I don't deny that we dirtied our hands sometimes. I don't deny that I got carried away sometimes and did things that I now am inclined to regret. But perhaps it was worth it. After all, we survived!

Perhaps that is all the justification needed.

We kept our heads and we are now on our way to colonize a new planet. Start a new society on cleaner, more decent, more rational lines.

Cynics might think that an impossible ideal. It will all get just as bad in time, they'd say. Well, maybe it won't. Maybe this time we really can build a sane society!

None of us is perfect. Especially this crew! We all have our rows and we all have qualities that the others find annoying. But the point is that we are a family. Being a family, we can have our arguments, our strong disagreements — even our hatreds, to a degree — and still survive.

That is our strength.

Ryan yawns and checks the time. He still has a few minutes of free time to spare. He looks at the paper and begins to write again:

When I look back to our days on Earth, particularly towards the end, I realize just how tense we were. The ship routine has relaxed me, allowed me to realize just what I had become. I don't like what I became. Perhaps one has to become a wolf, however, to fight wolves. It will never happen again. There were times, I cannot deny, when I lost hold of my ideals — even my senses. Some of the events are hazy — some are almost completely forgotten (though doubtless one of my relatives or friends will be able to remind me). I can hardly believe that it took such a short time for society to collapse.

That was what caused the trauma, of course — the suddenness of it all. Obviously, there were signs of the coming crises, and perhaps I should have taken more heed of those signs — but then all chaos suddenly broke loose throughout the world! What we tut-tutted at in the manner of older people slightly disconcerted by the changing times I now realize were much more serious indications of social unrest. Sudden increases in population, decreases in food production — they were the old problems that the Jeremiahs had been going on about for years — but they were suddenly with us. Perhaps we had been deliberately refusing to face the problem, just as people had refused to consider the possibility of war with Germany in the late thirties. We Homo sapiens have a great capacity for burying our heads in the sand while pretending to face out the issue.

Ryan smiles grimly. It's true, he thinks. People under stress usually start dealing with half a dozen surrogate issues, leaving the real issues completely untouched because they're too difficult to cope with. Like the man who lost the sixpence in the house but decided to look for it outside because the light was better and he would thus save his candles.

He adds in his log:

And there's always some bloody messiah to answer their needs — someone whom they will follow blindly because they are too fearful to rely on their own good sense. It's like Don Quixote leading the Gadarene Swine!

Ryan chuckles aloud.

Leaders, fuhrers, duces, prophets, visionaries, gurus... For a hundred years the world was ruled by bad poets. A good politician is only something of a visionary — essentially he must be a man who sees the needs of people in practical and immediate terms and tries to do something about them. Visionaries are fine for inspiring people — but they are the worst choice as leaders — they attempt to impose their rather simple visions on an extremely complicated world! Why have politics and art become so mixed up together in the last hundred years? Why have bad artists been given nations as canvases on which to paint their tatty, sketchy, rubbish? Perhaps because politics, like religion before it, was dead as an effective force and something new had to be found. And art stood in until whatever it was turned up. Will something turn up? It's hard to say. We'll probably never know on Munich 15040 if the world survives or not.

Thank God we had the initiative to get this ship on her way to the stars!

No more time for writing. Ryan puts the logbook away quickly and begins his regular check of the ship's nuclear drive, running a check on virtually every separate component.

He taught himself the procedure for running the ship. He was not trained as an astronaut. No-one planned that he should be the man standing in the control cabin at that particular moment.

THE BLACK CORRIDOR

Until comparatively recently Ryan was, in fact, a businessman. A pretty successful businessman.

As he does the routine checking, he thinks about himself before he even conceived the idea of traveling into space.

He sees himself, a strongly built man of forty, standing with his back to the vast plate glass window of his large, thickly carpeted office. His heavy, healthy face was pugnacious, his back was broad, his thick, stubby-fingered hands were clasped behind his back.

Where Ryan is now a monk — a man dedicated to his ship and his unconscious companions, a man charged, like a cleric in the Dark Ages, with preserving the knowledge and lives contained in this moving monastery — then he was a man almost perpetually in a state of combat.

Ten thousand years before he would have been a savage standing in front of his pack, hair bristling, teeth bared, bone club in hand.

Instead, Ryan had been a toymaker.

Not a kindly old peasant whittling puppets in a pretty little cottage. Ryan had owned a firm averaging a million pounds a year in profits, producing toy videophones, plastic hammers, miniature miracles of rocketry, talking lifesize dolls, knee-high cars with automatic gear changes, genuine all electric cooking machines, real baaing sheep, things which jumped, sped, made noises and broke when their calculated lifespan was over and were thrown secretly and with curses by parents into the rapid waste disposal units of cities all over the western world.

Ryan pressed the button which connected him with the office of his manager, Owen Powell.

Powell appeared on the screen. He was on his hands and knees on the office floor watching two dolls, three feet high, walk about the carpet. As he heard the buzz of the interoffice communicator he was saying to one of the dolls: "Hello, Gwendolen." As he said "Hello, Ryan," the doll replied, in a beautifully modulated voice, "Hello, Owen."

"That's the personalized doll you were talking about, is it?" Ryan said.

"That's it." Powell straightened up. "I knew they could do it if they tried. Lovely, isn't she? The child voice-prints her in the shop on its birthday, say. After that she can give any one of twenty-five responses to the child's questions — but only to the one child. Imagine that — a doll which can speak, apparently intelligently, *but only to you*. The kids go mad about it."

"If the price is right," Ryan said.

Powell was an enthusiast, a man who would really, if he had not had a twenty thousand pound a year job with Ryan, have been perfectly happy carving toys in an old peasant's hut. He looked disconcerted by Ryan's discouraging remark.

"Well, maybe we can get the price down to twenty pounds retail. What would you say to that?"

"Not bad." Ryan deliberately gave Powell no encouragement. Powell was a man who would work hard for a smile and stop working when you gave it, reasoned Ryan. Therefore it was better to smile seldom in his direction.

"Never mind all that now." Ryan rubbed his eyebrows. "There's plenty of time to get it right before Christmas when we'll try a few out, see how they go and produce a big line by spring for the following Christmas."

Powell nodded. "Agreed."

"Now," said Ryan, "I want you to do two things for me. One — get in touch with the factory and tell Ames to use the Mark IV pin on the Queen of Dolls. Two — ring Davies and tell him we're stopping all deliveries until he pays."

"He'll never keep going during August if we do that," objected Powell. "If we stop delivering, he'll have to close down, man. We'll only get a fraction of what he owes us!"

"I don't care." Ryan gestured dismissively. "I'm not letting Davies get away with another ten thousand pounds' worth of goods so that he'll pay us in the end, if we're lucky. I will not do business on that basis. That's final."

"All right." Powell shrugged. "That's reasonable enough."

"I think so." Ryan broke the connection.

He reached into his desk and took out a bottle of green pills. He poured water into a glass from an old-fashioned carafe on his immaculate desk. He swallowed the pills and put the glass down. Unconsciously he resumed his stance, head jutting slightly forward, hands behind back. He had a decision to make.

*

Powell was a good manager.

A bit sloppy sometimes. Forgetful. But on the whole efficient. He was not quarrelsome, like the ambitious Conroy, or withdrawn, like his last manager, Evers.

What he had mistaken at first for decent behaviour, respect for another man's privacy, had gone beyond reason in Evers.

When a manager refused to speak to the firm's managing director on the interoffice communicator — broke the connection consistently, in fact — business became impossible.

Ryan could certainly respect his feelings, sympathize with them as it happened — so would any other self-respecting person. But facts were facts. You could not run a business without talking to other people. Strangers they might be, uncongenial they might be, but if you couldn't stand a brief conversation on the communicator, then you were no use to a firm.

Ryan reflected that he himself was finding it increasingly distasteful to get in touch with many of his key workers but, since it was that or go under, he forced himself to do so.

Powell was certainly a good manager.

Inventive and clever, too.

On the other hand, Ryan thought, he had come to hate him.

He was childish. There was no other word for it. That open countenance, that smile, a smile which said that he would take to anybody who took to him. There was something doglike about it. Just pat him on the head and he would wag his tail to and fro, jump up and lick your face. Sickening, really, Ryan thought to himself. It made you feel sick to think about it. He had no reticences, no reserves. A man shouldn't be so friendly.

And, of course, Ryan thought, when you looked at the facts, it all came down to Powell's being Welsh. That was the Welshman for you — open-faced and friendly when they spoke to you and clannishly against you behind your back.

The Welsh gangs were some of the worst in the city. Ryan reflected that he had not bought his machine gun, and taught his wife and elder son how to use it, just for fun. That was the Welsh — all handshakes and smiles when you met them, and all the time their sons were stoning your relatives three streets away.

Ryan tapped his teeth together. Old Saunders of Happyvoice had shaken him a bit when he had got on the communicator just to warn him about Powell.

"It might help," he had said, "if that manager of yours, Powell, changed his name. You can't deny it sounds Welsh and there's been an awful lot of trouble with those Welsh Nationalists recently. Between ourselves, it only needs one word from a competitor of yours — say Moonbeam Toys — via their PRO, and you'll be branded in the Press as an employer of Welsh labour. And that's never likely to help sales — because people remember. Just at that critical moment when they're choosing between one of your products and one of another firm's — they remember. And then they don't buy a Ryan Toy. See what I mean? One word from you to old Powell and he'll change his name to Smith and you're in the clear."

Ryan had smiled and made bluff assurances. When he had cut off the communicator two thoughts came to him.

One, he knew Powell would be first confused and then obstinate about changing his name.

Two, and worse, Saunders did not think for one instant that Powell was a Welshman. He just thought he had an unfortunate name.

Ryan realized that he was right out on a limb. Where his competitors refused to take on employees with suspect names, however impeccable their backgrounds, Ryan had an actual living, breathing Welshman working for him. Someone who could quite easily be a Nationalist, working for the Welsh cause (a somewhat obscure cause as Ryan saw it). It was bloody ridiculous. How could he have got so out of touch? Why hadn't he thought of it?

Ryan frowned. No — it was stupid. Powell was too absorbed in his work to worry about politics. He was the last person to get involved in anything like that.

Still, a name was a name. The Nationalists had been causing quite a bit of trouble lately and things had really got bad with the assassination of the King. The Welsh Nationalists had claimed it was their work. But other groups of extremists had also made the same claim.

From a practical point of view, Ryan thought, Powell was an embarrassment. No question of it. Yet he couldn't fire a man on suspicion.

Ryan's face took on an over-rosy tinge and his thick hands gripped each other a little more firmly behind his back.

I'm in fucking trouble here, he thought.

He pinched his nose and then reached out to buzz for his personnel manager.

Frederick Masterson was sitting at his desk working on a graph. Masterson was, in physical terms, the exact complement to Ryan. Where Ryan was thickset and ruddy, Masterson was tall, thin and pale. As the communicator buzzed in his office he dropped the pencil from his long, thin hand and looked at the screen in alarm. Seeing Ryan, a thin smile came to his lips.

"Oh, it's you," he said.

"Fred. I want details of any staff we employ with foreign or strange-sounding names — or foreign backgrounds of any kind. Just to be on the safe side, you realize. I'm not planning a purge!" He laughed briefly.

"Just as well." Masterson grinned. "Your name's Irish, isn't it, begorrah!"

Ryan said, "Come off it, Fred. I'm no more Irish than you are. Not a single relative or ancestor for the past hundred years has even seen Ireland, let alone come from it."

"I know, I know," said Fred. "Call me Oirish agin and Oi'll knock ye over the hade wid me shillelagh."

"Skip the funny imitations, Fred," Ryan said shortly. "The firm's at stake. You know how bloody small-minded a lot of people are. Well, it seems to be getting worse. I just don't want to take any chances. I want you to probe. If necessary turn the whole department over to examining personnel records for the slightest hint of anything peculiar. Examine marriages, family background, schooling, previous places of employment. No action at this stage. I'm not planning to victimize anyone."

"Not at the moment," said Masterson, a funny note in his voice.

"Oh, come off it, Fred. I just want to be prepared. In case any competitors start going for us. Naturally I'll protect my employees to the hilt. This is one way of making sure I can protect them — against any scandal, for a start."

Masterson sighed. "What about those with Negro blood? I mean the West Indians got around a bit before they were all sent back."

"Okay. I don't think anyone's got anything against blacks at the moment, have they?"

"Not at the moment."

"Fine. But you never know…"

"No."

"I want to protect them, Fred."

"Of course."

Ryan cut the communicator and sighed.

An image flashed into his mind and with a start he remembered a dream he had had the previous night. It was funny, the way you suddenly remembered dreams long after you had dreamed them.

It had been to do with a cat. His old house where he had lived with his parents. It had had a big, overgrown back garden and they had kept several cats. The dream was to do with the air rifle he had had and a white and ginger cat — an interloper — that had entered the garden. Someone — not himself, as he remembered the dream — had shot the cat. He had not wanted to shoot the cat himself, but had gone along with this other person. They had shot the cat once and it had been patched up by neighbours. There had been a piece of sticking plaster on its left flank. The person had fired the gun and badly wounded the cat but the animal had not appeared to notice. It had still come confidently along the wall, tail up and purring, towards the French windows. It had had a big bloody wound in its side, but it hadn't seemed to be aware of it.

The cat had entered the house and come into the kitchen, still purring, and eaten from the bowl of one of the resident cats.

Ryan had not known whether to kill it to put it out of its misery or whether to let it be. It hadn't actually seemed to be in any misery, that was the strange thing.

Ryan shook his head. A disturbing dream. Why should he remember it now?

THE BLACK CORRIDOR

He had never, after all, owned a white and ginger cat.

Ryan shrugged. Good God, this was no time for worrying about silly dreams. He would have to do some hard thinking. Some realistic thinking. He prided himself that if he was nothing else he was a pragmatist. Not an ogre. He was well-known for his good qualities as an employer. He had the best staff in the toy industry. People were only too eager to come and work for Ryan Toys. The pay was better. The conditions were better. Ryan was much respected by his fellow employers and by the trades unions. There had never been any trouble at Ryan Toys.

But he had the business to consider. And, of course, ultimately the country, for Ryan's exports were high.

Or had been, thought Ryan, before the massive wave of nationalism had swept the world and all but frozen trade, save for the basic necessities.

Still, it would pass. A bit of a shake-up for everybody. It wasn't a bad thing. Made people keep their feet on the ground. One had to know how to ride these peculiar political crises that came and went. He wasn't particularly politically minded himself. A liberal with a small *l* was how he liked to describe himself. He had an excellent profit-sharing scheme in the factory, lots of fringe benefits, and an agreement with the unions that on his death the workers would take over control of the factory, paying a certain percentage of profits to his dependants. He was all for socialism so long as it was phased in painlessly. He steadfastly refused to have a private doctor and took his chances with the National Health Service along with everybody else. While he was not over-friendly with his workers, he was on good terms with them and they liked him. This silly racialistic stuff would come and go.

The odds were that it wouldn't affect the factory at all.

Ryan took a deep breath. He was getting over-anxious, that was his trouble. Probably that bloody Davies account preying on his mind. It was just as well to take a stiff line with Davies, even if it meant losing a few thousand. He would rather kiss the money good-bye if it meant kissing good-bye to the worries that went with it.

He buzzed through to Powell again.

Powell was once again on his knees, fiddling with a doll.

"Ah," said Powell, straightening up.

"Did you take care of those couple of items, Powell?"

"Yes. I spoke to Ames and I phoned Davies. He said he'd do his best."

"Good man," Ryan said and switched off hastily as a delighted grin spread over Powell's face.

CHAPTER EIGHT

Ryan is working on a small problem that has come up concerning the liquid regeneration unit in the forward part of the ship. It is malfunctioning slightly and the water has a slight taste of urine in it. A spare part is needed and he is instructing the little servorobot to replace the defunct element.

That was what had saved him, of course, he thinks. His pragmatism. He had kept his head while all around people were losing theirs, getting hysterical, making stupid decisions — or worse, making no decisions at all.

He smiles. He had always made quick decisions. Even when those decisions were unpalatable or possibly unfashionable in terms of the current thinking of the time. It was his basic hard-headedness that had kept him going longer than most of them, allowed him to hang on to a lot more, helped him to the point where he was now safely out of the mess that was the disrupted, insane society of Earth.

And that is how he intends to remain. He must keep cool, not let the depression, the aching loneliness, the weaker elements of his character, take him over.

"I'll make it," he murmurs confidently to himself. "I'll make it. Those people are going to get their chance to start all over again."

He yawns. The muscles at the back of his neck are aching. He wriggles his shoulders, hoping to limber the muscles up. But the ache remains. He'll have to do something about that. Must stay fit at all costs. Not just himself to think of.

He isn't proud of everything he did on Earth. Some of those decisions would not have been made under different circumstances.

But he didn't go mad.

Not the way so many of the others did.

He stayed sane. Just barely, sometimes, but he made it through to the other side. He kept his eyes clear and saw things as they really were while a lot of other people were chasing wild geese or phantom tigers. It was a struggle, naturally. And sometimes he had made mistakes. But his common sense hadn't let him down — not in the long run.

What had someone once said to him?

He nodded to himself. That was it. *You're a survivor, Ryan. A natural bloody survivor.*

It was truer now, of course, than ever before.

He was a survivor. *The* survivor. He and his friends and relatives.

He was making for the clean, fresh world untainted by mankind, leaving the rest of them to rot in the shit heap they had created.

Yet he mustn't feel proud. Pride goeth before a fall... Mustn't get egocentric. There had been a good deal of luck involved. It wasn't such a bad idea to test himself from time to time, run through that Old Time Religion stuff. The seven deadly sins.

Check his own psyche out the way he checked the ship.

CHECK FOR *Pride*.

CHECK FOR *Envy*.

CHECK FOR *Sloth*.

CHECK FOR *Gluttony*.

... and so forth. It didn't do any harm. It kept him sane. And he didn't reject the possibility that he *could* go insane. There was always a chance. He had to watch for the signs. Check them in time. A stitch in time saves nine.

That was how he had always operated.

And he hadn't done badly, after all.

REPAIR COMPLETED reports the computer. Ryan is satisfied.

"Congratulations," he says cheerfully. "Keep up the good work, chum."

The point was, he thinks, that he, unlike so many of the rest, had never been to a psychiatrist in his life. He'd been his own psychiatrist. *Gluttony*, for instance, could indicate some kind of disturbance that came out in obsessive eating. Therefore if he found himself overeating, he searched for a reason, hunted out the cause of the problem. It was the same with work. If it started to get on top of you, then stop — take a holiday. It meant you could work better when you got back and didn't spend all your time bawling out your staff for mistakes that were essentially your own creation.

He presses a faucet button and samples the water. He smacks his lips. It's fine.

He is relaxing. The disturbing dreams, the sense of depression, have been replaced by a feeling of well-being. He has compensated in time. Instead of looking back at the bad times, he is looking back at the good times. That is how it should be.

CHAPTER NINE

Masterson flashed Ryan about a week after he had begun his check-up.

Ryan had been feeling good for days. The Davies matter was settled. Davies had paid up two-thirds of the amount and they had called it quits. To show no hard feelings Ryan had even paid off the mortgage on Davies' apartment so that he would have somewhere secure to live after he had sold up his business.

"Morning, Fred. What's new?"

"I've been doing that work you asked for."

"Any results?"

"I think all the results are in. I've drawn up a graph of our findings on the subject."

"How does the graph look?"

"It'll come as a shock to you." Masterson pursed his lips. "I think I'd better come and talk to you personally. Show you the stuff I've got. Okay?"

"Well — of course — yes. Okay, Fred. When do you want to come here?"

"Right away?"

"Give me half an hour."

"Fine."

Ryan used the half hour to prepare himself for Masterson's visit, tidying his desk, putting everything away that could be put away, straightening the chairs.

When Masterson arrived he was sitting at his desk smiling.

Masterson spread out the graph.

"I see what you mean," said Ryan. "Good heavens! Just as well we decided to do this, eh?"

"It confirms what I already believed," said Masterson. "Ten percent of your employees, chiefly from the factories in the North, are actually of wholly foreign parentage — Australian and Irish in the main. Another ten percent had parents born outside England itself, i.e. in Scotland, Wales and the Republic of Ireland. Three percent of your staff, although born and educated in England, are Jewish. About half a percent have Negro or Asiatic blood. That's the general picture."

Ryan rubbed his nose. "Bloody difficult, eh, Masterson?"

Masterson shrugged. "It could be used against us. There are a number of ways. If the government offers tax relief to firms employing one hundred percent English labour, as they're talking of doing, then we aren't going to benefit from the tax relief. Then there are wholesalers' and retailers' embargos if our rivals release this information. Lastly there're the customers."

Ryan licked his lips thoughtfully. "It's a tricky one, Fred."

"Yes. Tricky."

"Oh, fuck, Fred." Ryan scratched his head. "There's only one solution, isn't there?"

"If you want to survive," said Fred, "yes."

"It means sacrificing a few in order to protect the many. We'll pay them generous severance pay, of course."

"It's something like twenty-five percent of your employees."

"We'll phase them out gradually, of course." Ryan sighed. "I'll have to have a talk with the unions. I don't think they'll give us any trouble. They'll see the sense of it. They always have."

"Make sure of it," said Masterson, "first."

"Naturally. What's up, Fred? You seem fed up about something."

"Well, you know as well as I do what this means. You'll have to get rid of Powell, too."

"He won't suffer from it. I'm not a bloody monster, Fred. You've got to adjust though. It's the only way to survive. We've got to be realistic. If I stood on some abstract ideal, the whole firm would collapse within six months. You know that. The one thing all political parties are agreed on is that many of our troubles stem from an over-indulgent attitude toward foreign labour. Whichever way the wind blows in the near future, there's no escaping that one. And the way our rivals are fighting these days, we can't afford to go around wearing kid gloves and sniffing bloody daffodils."

"I realize that," said Masterson. "Of course."

"Powell won't feel a thing. He'd rather be running a doll hospital or a toyshop anyway. I'll do that. I'll buy him a bloody toyshop. What do you say? That way everybody's happy."

"Okay," said Masterson. "Sounds like a good idea." He rolled up the charts. "I'll leave the breakdown with you to go over." He made for the door.

"Thanks a lot, Fred," Ryan said gratefully. "A lot of hard work. Very useful. Thanks."

"It's my job," said Masterson. "Cheerio. Keep smiling." He left the office.

Ryan was relieved that he had gone. He couldn't help the irrational feeling of invasion he had whenever anyone came into his office. He sat back, humming, and studied Masterson's figures.

You had to stay ahead of the game.

But Masterson had put his finger on the only real problem. He disliked the idea of firing Powell in spite of the man's unbearable friendliness, his nauseating candour, his stupid assumption that you only had to give one happy grin to open the great dam of smiles swirling about in everyone.

Ryan grinned in spite of himself. That summed up poor old Powell, all right.

As a manager, as a creative man, Powell was first class. Ryan could think of no-one in the business who could more than half fill his place.

He wasn't any trouble. He was content. A willing worker putting in much longer hours than were expected of him.

But was that just his good-heartedness? Ryan wondered. A light was dawning. Now he could see it. Powell was probably just grateful to have a job! He knew that no-one in any business would employ him.

Just like a bloody Welshman to hang on and on, not letting you know the facts, creeping about, getting good money out of you, not letting you know that his very presence was threatening to ruin your business. Trying to make himself indispensable in the hopes that you'd never find out about him and fire him. Pleasant and agreeable and co-operative. Maybe even a front for some sort of Welsh Nationalist sabotage. Then — the knife in the back, the bullet from the window, the enemy in the alley.

Stop it, Ryan told himself. Powell wasn't like that. He didn't need to build the man up into a villain to justify sacking him. There was only one reason for sacking him. He was an embarrassment. He could harm the firm.

Ryan relaxed.

He sat down at his desk, opened a drawer and took out his packed lunch. He opened the thermos flask and poured himself a cup of coffee. He placed his meal on the miniature heater in the lower compartment of the luncheon box.

Thank God, he thought, for the abolition of those communal lunches with other businessmen, or the firm's executives.

Thank God that communal eating had finally died the death. What could have been more disgusting than sitting munching and swallowing with a gang of total strangers, sitting there staring at their moving mouths, offering them items — wine, salt, pepper, water — to make their own consumption more palatable, talking to them face to face as they nourished themselves. The conversion of the canteens had provided much-needed office space as well.

Ryan took a fork and dug into the plate. The food was now thoroughly heated.

Once he had eaten he felt even more relaxed. He had thought it all out. He didn't waste time when it came to decisions. No point in moralizing.

He wiped his lips.

The problem had assumed its proper proportions. It would cost him a bit in golden and silver handshakes, but it was worth it. He could probably get cheaper staff anyway, considering the huge volume of unemployment, and recoup his losses by the end of the year.

This way everybody gains something. Nobody loses.

He picked up the sheets of names and figures and began to study them closely.

CHAPTER TEN

That's how it was, thinks Ryan. A cop-out, now he looked back, but a graceful cop-out. No-one got badly hurt. It could have been worse. It was the difference between a stupid approach and an intelligent approach to the same problem.

It had been the same when he had got the group out of that riot at the Patriot meeting. When had that been? January. Yes, January, 2000. The civilized world had been expecting the end. There had been all the usual sort of apocalyptic stuff, which Ryan had dismissed as a symptom of radical social change. He had not been able to believe then that things were going to get worse. There had been penitential marches through the streets. Even scourgings, public confessions.

And January had been the month of that oddball move to close the camps for foreigners. The camps had been decently maintained. The people lived as well as anyone outside the camps — perhaps better in certain circumstances. It had also been the month when the Patriots had tried to open the camps up to more people — to a more sinister, less identifiable group.

Ryan remembers the crowd in Trafalgar Square. A crowd of fifty thousand strong, covering the square, pushed up the steps of the National Gallery and St Martin's, pushed inside the gallery and the church, right up against the altar. The crowd had blocked the streets all around. It was horrifying. Disgusting. People like rats in a box.

Even now Ryan feels sick, remembering how he felt then.

He and the group had gone along, but they were now regretting it.

Whenever the crowd got too noisy or violent the troops fired over their heads.

It had been snowing. The searchlights played over the plinth where the leading Patriots stood and they flashed over the heads of the crowd, picked up large flakes of snow as they drifted down on the dense mass of people.

The Patriot leaders, collars of their dark coats turned up, stood in the snow looking over the crowd. And as they spoke their voices were enormously amplified. Deafeningly amplified; reaching all the way up the Mall to where Queen Anne sat in her lonely room, hearing the words on TV and from the meeting itself a quarter of a mile away; reaching all the way down Whitehall to Parliament itself.

Parliament. That discredited institution.

They are turning on each other now, thought Ryan, looking at the faces of the Patriots. There were signs of dissension there if he wasn't mistaken. There would be a split soon.

But meanwhile there were the usual speeches, coming distorted into the mind partly because of the amplification system, partly because of the wind, partly because of the usual ungraspable political clichés the speakers used.

The snow kept falling on the upturned faces of the crowd — an orderly crowd of responsible people. There were few interrupters. The presence of the troops and the paid Patriot Guards made sure of that.

Colin Beesley, Patriot leader and Member of Parliament, stood up to speak.

Beesley, a large, thickset man in a long black overcoat and a large hat, was an extremist. His political manner was of the old school — the Churchillian school which still touched many people who wanted their politicians to be "strong". His tone was ponderous. His words, spoken slowly and relatively clearly, were portentous.

Unlike the others, he did not speak generally about the Patriot cause, for he had come to make a fresh statement.

THE BLACK CORRIDOR

As he began to speak the wind dropped and his words came through with a sudden clarity — over the crowd in the square, the crowds in the streets, down as far as Westminster, along to Buckingham Palace, as far as Piccadilly Circus in the other direction.

"Aliens among us," he said, his head lowered and thrust towards the crowd. "There are aliens among us. We do not know where they come from. We do not know how they landed. We do not know how many there are. But we do know one thing, my friends, people of England — they are among us!"

Ryan, standing uncomfortably in the middle of the crowd in the square grimaced skeptically at his friend Masterson who stood beside him. Ryan couldn't believe in a group of aliens contriving to land on Earth without anyone's knowledge. Not when the skies were scanned for invaders from special observation posts built all over the country. But Masterson was listening seriously and intently to Beesley.

Ryan turned his attention back to the platform.

"We cannot tell who they are, yet they are among us." Beesley's voice droned on. "They look like us, sound like us — in every respect they are human — but they are not human. They are non-human — they are anti-human." He paused, lowered his voice. "How, you say, do we know about the aliens? How have we found out about the existence of this pollution, of these creatures who move about our society, like cancer cells in a healthy body? We know by the evidence of our own eyes. We know the aliens exist because of who they are, what happens when they are about.

"Otherwise how can we explain the existence of chaos, bloodlust, law-breaking, riot, revolution in our midst? How can we explain the little children battered to death by the fanatics of Yorkshire? The waves of rioting and looting all over the West Country? The satanic practises of religious maniacs in the Fens? How can we explain the hatred and the suspicion, the murder rate — now three times what it was five years ago, a full ten times what it was in 1990? How can we explain the fact that we have so few children when a few years ago the birth rate had doubled? Disaster is upon us! Who is stirring up and fomenting all this disorder, bloodshed and ruin? Who? Who?"

Ryan, glancing into the faces of the people about him, could almost believe they were listening seriously. Were they? Or was the presence of the troops and the Patriot Guards preventing them from cat-calling or just walking away from this nonsense?

He looked at the faces of the police around the platform. They were staring up at Beesley — brute-faced men listening to him with close attention. Ryan, scarcely able to believe it, realized that Beesley's story of the hidden invaders was being taken seriously by the majority of the vast crowd. As Beesley went on speaking, describing the hidden marauders, makers of chaos in their midst, the crowd began to murmur in agreement.

"Their bases are somewhere," Beesley went on. "We must find them, fellow patriots. We must eliminate them, like wasp nests…"

And there came from the crowd a great hissed susurrus "Yesssss."

"We must find the polluters and wipe them out forever. Whether they come from space or are the agents of another Power, we do not know as yet. We must discover where they originate!"

And the crowd, like a cold wind through the ruins, answered "Yessssss."

He's lost them, thought Ryan skeptically, *if he doesn't give them something a bit more concrete than that. He's got to tell them how to pick out these menacing figures they have to destroy.*

"Who are they? How do we find them?" asked Beesley. "How? How? How indeed?" His tone became divinely reasonable. "You all know, in your heart of hearts, who they are. They are the men — and women, too; make no mistake, they are women as well — who are different. You know them. You can tell them at a glance. They look different. Their eyes are different. They express doubt where you and I know certainty. They are the men who associate with strangers and people of doubtful character, the men and women who throw suspicion on what we are fighting for. They are the skeptics, the heretics, the mockers. When you meet them they make you doubt everything, even yourself. They laugh a lot, and smile too often. They attempt, by jesting, to throw a poor light on our ideals. They are the people who hang back when plans are suggested for purifying our land. They defend the objects of our patriotic anger. They hang back from duty. Many are drunkards, licentious scoffers. You know these people, friends. You know them — these men who have been sent here to undermine a righteous society. You have always known them. Now is the time to pluck them out and deal with them as they deserve."

And, before he had finished speaking, the crowd was in uproar. There were shouts and screams.

Ryan poked Masterson, who was staring incredulously at the platform, in the ribs. "Let's get out," he said. "There's going to be trouble."

"Only for the aliens," said James Henry at his other elbow. "Come on, Ryan. Let's sniff 'em out and snuff 'em out."

Ryan looked at Henry in astonishment. Henry's green eyes were ablaze. "For crying out loud, Henry..."

He turned to his brother John. John looked back vaguely and suddenly, under the gaze of his elder brother, seemed to pull himself together. "He's right," said John. "We'd better think of getting home. This is real mass hysteria. Jesus Christ."

Henry's mouth hardened. "I'm staying."

"Look —" Ryan was jolted by the crowd. Snow fell down his neck — "Henry. You can't possibly —"

"Do what you like, Ryan. We've heard the call to deal with these aliens — let's deal with them."

"They wouldn't be likely to come here tonight, would they?" Ryan shouted. Then he stopped, realizing that he was beginning to answer in Henry's terms. That was the first step towards being convinced. "Good God, Henry — this is too classic for words. We're rational men."

"Agreed. Which makes our duty even clearer."

The crowd was pushing the four men backwards and forwards. The men had to shout to be heard over the roar of the rabble.

"James — come home and talk it over. This isn't the place..." Ryan insisted, standing his ground with difficulty. From somewhere came the sound of gunfire. Then the gunfire stopped. Ryan found he was shouting into relative silence. "You won't take that 'aliens' nonsense seriously when you've got a drink inside you back at our flat!"

A man put his head over Henry's shoulder. His red face was flushed. "What was that, friend?" he said to Ryan.

"I wasn't talking to you."

"Oh, no? I heard what you said. That's of interest to *everyone* here. You're one of them, if you ask me."

"I didn't." Ryan looked contemptuously at the sweating face. "But we're all entitled to our own opinions. If you think it's true, I won't argue with you."

"Shut up," Masterson cried, tugging at Ryan's sleeve. "Shut up and come home."

"Bloody alien!" the red-faced man shouted. "A bloody nest of them!"

Instantly, it seemed to Ryan, the crowd was on them. He came rapidly to a decision, keeping his head even in this situation.

"Calm down all of you," he said in his most commanding voice. "My point is that we might make mistakes in this situation. The aliens have to be found. But we need to work systematically to find them. Use a scientific approach. Don't you see — the aliens themselves could be stirring things up for us — making us turn on each other."

The red-faced man frowned. "It's a point," he said grudgingly.

"Now I believe that if there are aliens here tonight they are not going to be in the middle of the crowd. They are going to be on the edges, trying to sneak away," Ryan continued.

"That seems reasonable," said James Henry. "Let's get after them."

Ryan led the way shouting with the rest.

"Aliens! Aliens! Stop the aliens! Get them now. Over there — in the streets!"

Pushing through the crowd was like trying to trudge through a quagmire. Every step, every breath Ryan took was painful.

Ryan led them, pace by pace, through the packed throng, up the steps into the National Gallery and, as the crowd thinned out in the galleries themselves, through a window at the back, through yards, over walls and car parks until they escaped the red-faced man and his friends and were finally in the moving mass of Oxford Street.

Only James Henry didn't seem aware of what Ryan had done. As they reached Hyde Park he pulled at Ryan's torn coat.

"Hey! What are we supposed to be doing? I thought we were going after the aliens."

"I know something about the aliens that wasn't mentioned tonight," Ryan said.

"What?"

"I'll tell you when we get back to my place."

When they finally reached Ryan's flat they were exhausted.

"What about the aliens, then?" James Henry asked as the door closed behind them.

"The worst aliens are the Patriots," said Ryan. "They are the most obvious of the anti-humans."

Henry was puzzled. "Surely not…"

Ryan took a deep breath and went to the drinks cabinet, began fixing drinks for them all as they sat panting in the chairs in the living room.

"The Patriots…" murmured Henry. "I suppose it's just possible…"

Ryan handed him his drink. "I thought," he said, "that the discoveries in space would give us all a better perspective. Instead it seems that the perspective has been even more narrowed and distorted. Once people only feared other races, other nations, other groups with opposed or different interests. Now they fear everything. It's gone too far, Henry."

"I'm still not with you," James Henry said.

"Simply — paranoia. What is paranoia, Henry?"

"Being afraid of things — suspecting plots — all that stuff."

"It can be defined more closely. It is an *irrational* fear, an *irrational* suspicion. Often it is in fact a refusal to face the *real* cause of one's anxiety, to invent causes because the true cause is either too disturbing, too frightening, too horrible to face or too difficult to cope with. That's what paranoia actually is, Henry."

"So?"

"So the Patriots have offered us a surrogate. They have offered us something to concentrate on that is nothing really to do with the true causes of the ills of society. It's common enough. Hitler supplied it to the Germans in the form of the Jews and the Bolsheviks. McCarthy supplied it to the Americans in the form of the Communist Conspiracy. Even our own Enoch Powell supplied it in the form of the West Indian immigrants in the sixties and seventies. There are plenty of examples."

James Henry frowned. "You say they were wrong, eh? Well, I'm not so sure. We were right to get rid of the West Indians when we did. We were right to restrict jobs to Englishmen when we did. You have to draw the line somewhere, Ryan."

270   SAILING TO UTOPIA

Ryan sighed. "And what about these 'aliens' from space, then? Where do they fit in. What are they doing to the economy? They are an invention — a crude invention, at that — of the Patriots to describe anyone who is opposed to their insane schemes. Where do you think the term 'witch-hunt' comes from, Henry?"

James Henry sipped his drink thoughtfully. "Perhaps I did get a bit over-excited…"

Ryan patted him on the shoulder. "We all are. It's the strain, the tension — and it is particularly the uncertainty. We don't know where we're going. We've no goals, because we can't rely on society any longer. The Patriots offer certainty. And that's what we've got to find for ourselves."

"You'd better explain," John Ryan said from his chair. "Have you got any suggestions?"

Ryan spread his hands. "That was my suggestion. That we find a goal — a rational goal. Find a way out of this mess…"

And Ryan, now sitting at his desk in the great ship, reflects that it was that evening which was the turning point, that decision which brought him to where he is now, aboard the spaceship *Hope Dempsey*, heading towards Munich 15040, Barnard's Star, at point nine of *c*…

CHAPTER ELEVEN

There is no sound here in space. No light. No life. Only the dim glow of distant stars as the tiny craft moves, so slowly, through the great neutral blackness.

And Ryan, as he goes methodically about his duties, thinks with a heavy heart of the familiarity and warmth of his early years — of the births of his children, of studying their first schoolbooks, talking to his friends in the evenings at their apartment, of his wife, now resting like some comfortable Sleeping Beauty, unaware of him in the fluids of her casket.

Just a pellet traveling through space, thinks Ryan. Nearly all the living tissue contained in the pellet is unconscious in the waters of the caskets. Once they had moved and acted. They had been happy, until the threats had become obvious, until life had become unbearable for them…

Ryan rubs his eyes and writes out his routine report. He underlines it in red, reads it into the machine, sits down again before the logbook.

He writes:

Another day has passed.

I am frightened, sometimes, that I am becoming too much of a vegetable. I am an active man by nature. I will need to be active when we land. I wonder if I have become too passive. Still, this is idle speculation…

His speculations were never idle, he reflects. The moment the problem was clearly seen, he began to think along positive lines. The problem was straightforward: society was breaking down and death and destruction were becoming increasingly widespread. He wished to survive and he wished for his friends and family to survive. There was nowhere in the world that could any longer be considered a safe refuge. Nuclear war was bound to arise soon. There had been only one answer: the stars. And there had been only one project for reaching the stars. Unmanned research craft had brought back evidence that there was a planetary system circling Barnard's Star and that two of those planets were in many respects similar to Earth.

The research project had been United Nations sponsored — the first important multilateral project between the Great Powers...

It had been a last attempt to draw the nations of the world together, to make them consider themselves one race.

Ryan shakes his head.

It had been too late, of course.

Ryan writes:

... I keep fit as best I can. An odd thought just popped into my head. It gives some idea of how closely one has to watch oneself. It occurred to me that a way of keeping fit would be to wake one of the other men so that we could have sparring matches, play football or something like that. I began to see the "sense" of this and began to rationalize it so that it seemed advantageous to all concerned to wake, say, my brother John. Or even one of the women... There are several ways of keeping fit and alert — getting exercise. Ridiculous, undisciplined ideas! It is just as well I keep the log. It helps me keep perspective.

He grins. A great way of cheating on old John. He'd never know...

He shudders.

Naturally, he couldn't...

There was Josephine, too. It would betray the whole idea of the mission if he betrayed them...

I think I'll go and take a cold shower! he writes jokingly. He signs the book, underlines his entry in red, closes the book, puts it neatly away, gets up, makes a last check of the instruments, asks the computer a couple of routine questions, is satisfied by the answers, leaves the control cabin.

THE BLACK CORRIDOR

*

True to his word, Mr Ryan has his cold shower. It does the trick. He feels much better. Humming to himself he enters his own cabin, selects the tape of Messiaen's *Turangalila Symphony* and sits down to listen to the strange and beautiful melodies of the Ondes Martenot.

By the Sixth Movement (*Jardin du sommeil d'amour*) he is asleep...

The gallery is vast and made of solid platinum.

He paces it.

It is the bridge of a massive ship. But the ship does not sail across the ocean. It sails through foliage. Dark, tangled foliage. Foliage that the Douanier himself might have painted. Menacing foliage.

Perhaps it is a jungle river. A river like the Amazon or one of those mysterious, unmapped rivers of New Guinea that, as a boy, he had wished to explore.

Ship... foliage... river...

He is alone on the ship, but for the sound of the engines, strangely melodic, and the cries of the unseen birds in the jungle.

He leans over the rail of the bridge, looking for the waters of the river. But there are no waters. Beneath the ship is only vegetation, crushed and bent by the passage of the great vessel.

The ships rolls.

He falls and from somewhere comes a sound that is oddly sympathetic. Something is pitying him.

He rejects the pity.

He falls to the ground and the ship passes on.

He is alone in the jungle and he hears the sounds of lumbering monsters in the murk. He searches with his eyes for the monsters, but he cannot see them, cannot trace the origin of their noise.

A woman appears. She is dark, lush, exotic. She parts her red lips and takes him by the hand into the shadowy darkness of the tropical foliage. Birds continue to cry and to squawk. He begins to kiss her wet, hot mouth. He feels her hand on his penis. He runs his hand into her crutch and her pants are wet with her juices. He tries to make love to her, but for some reason she is wary, expecting discovery. She will not remove her clothing. They make love as best they can. Then she gets up and leads him through the dark jungle corridors into a clearing.

They are in a bar. Girls — club hostesses or prostitutes, he cannot

274   SAILING TO UTOPIA

tell — fill the place. There are a few men. Probably ponces or gigolos. He feels at ease here. He relaxes. He puts his arm around the dark woman and puts his other arm around a young blonde with a lined, decaying face. Someone he knew.

All the faces, in fact, are familiar. He tries to remember them. He concentrates on remembering them. Dimly he begins to remember them...

AFTER THE FAIR THEY WERE ALL LEAD
    Q: PLEASE DEFINE SPECIFIC SITUATION
ARDOUR THE MORE THEY SANG AHEAD
    Q: PLEASE DEFINE SPECIFIC SITUATION
AH DO RE ME FA SO LA TI DI
    Q: PLEASE DEFINE SPECIFIC SITUATION
ARIA ARIADNE ANIARA LEONARA CARMEN
AMEN
    A: AMEN

AMEN
    AMEN. AMEN. AMEN.
AMEN.

        SUGGEST HOLD ON TIGHT
        SUGGEST HOLD ON TIGHT
        SUGGEST HOLD ON TIGHT

```
                              KEEP GOING
                              E          O
                              E          I
                              P          N
                                         G
                              G
                              O          K
                              I          E
                              N          E
                              GOING KEEP
```

THE SPACESHIP HOPE DEMPSEY IS EN ROUTE
   FOR MUNICH 15040

                  THE SPACESHIP

HOPE DEMPSEY IS EN ROUTE FOR MUNICH 15040
              IS GOING

EN ROUTE FOR MUNICH 15040 THE SPACESHIP
               NOWHERE

FOR MUNICH 15040 THE SPACESHIP
          MUST

HOPE DEMPSEY IS EN ROUTE
         BE SAFE

FOR MUNICH 15040
       MUST

THE SPACESHIP
      KEEP THEM

SPACESHIP
  SAFE

    SPACESHIP

SPACE   SAFE

SHIP   KEEP THEM

SAFE   SAFE

SHIP   THE SPACESHIP HOPE DEMPSEY IS EN ROUTE

SAFE   FOR MUNICH 15040 AND TRAVELING AT
             POINT

SHAPE   NINE OF C

SHIP   WE ARE ALL COMFORTABLE

SHAPE   WE ARE ALL

SPACE   SAFE

SHAPE   SPACESHIP SAFE

SHIP   SAFESHIPSAFE

SHAPE   SAFESHIPSHAPE

SAFE

SAFE

SAFE

SAFE

SAFE

SHIP

SHIP

SHIP

SHIP

SHAPE

SAFE

SHIP

SHIP

SAFE

SAFE

SHIP

SHIP

SAFE

SAFE

SHIP

SHIP

SAFE

SAFE

SHIP

SHIP

SAFE

SAFE

SHIP

SWEET
SAFE
SHIP
SPACE
SAIL
SPACE
SNAIL
PACE
SAFE
PACE
SNAIL
PACE
SPACE
SHIP
SAFE
PLACE
SPACE
SAFE
SMELL
TASTE
HASTE
RACE
WASTE
SPACE
SAVE
SPACE
SAFE
PLACE

SAFE	CASE	SPACE	PLACE
HATE	HEAT	SWEET	SAFE

SAILING TO UTOPIA

BRAIN
SHIP
TAME
WHIP
GOOD
TRIP
SPACE
SHIP
LET
RIP
SPACE
TRIP
HATE
TASTE
SPACE
FACE
HATE
HASTE
SPACE
RACE
HATE
FACE
SPACE
PLACE
HOT
DRIP
SPACE
SHIP
HATE

HEAT   SPACE   HEAT   SAFE   FEAT
SWEET   HATE   SAFE   HAZE

NOT TRUE * * * * * * * *
NOT TRUE * * * * * * * *
* * * * * * NOT TRUE *

NOT TRUE

"It's not fucking true!"

Ryan screams.

He wakes up.

The tape machine is humming rhythmically.

He shudders.

He has an erection.

His mouth is dry.

He has a pain above his left temple.

His legs are trembling.

His hands are gripping the plastic of his chair, pinching it in handfuls like a housewife inspecting a chicken.

The muscles at the back of his neck ache horribly.

He shakes his head.

What wasn't true?

The symphony has come to an end.

He gets up and switches off the machine, frowning and massaging his neck. He yawns.

Then he remembers the dream. The jungle. The women.

He grins with relief, recognizing the source of the exclamation — the denial with which he had woken himself up.

Just simple, old-fashioned guilt feelings, obviously.

He had considered waking Janet, cheating on his brother, had dreamed accordingly, had denied his feelings and had come awake with a start.

All that proved was that he had a conscience.

He stretches.

Scratching his head he leaves the cabin and goes to take another shower.

SAILING TO UTOPIA

As he washes, he smiles again. It's just as well to let those secret thoughts out into the open. No good burying them where they can fester into something much worse, catch him off his guard and possibly wreck the entire mission, maybe make him wake up the others. That would be fatal.

A wave of depression hits him. *It's bloody hard*, he thinks. *Bloody*.

He pulls himself together. His old reflexes are as good as ever. Keeping fit isn't just a matter of exercising the body. One has to exercise the brain, too. Make constant checks to be sure it's working smoothly.

He must be getting unduly sensitive, however, for his conscience was never that much of a burden to him!

He laughs. He knows what he must do.

It's the old trouble. The problem of leisure. It was unhealthy not to put your mind to something other than its own workings. He was developing the neuroses of the rich, the non-workers — or would start to, if he wasn't careful.

The dream is a warning.

Or rather his reaction to the dream is a warning. Tomorrow he will start studying the agricultural programmes, get interested in something other than himself.

Refreshed, his aches and pains vanishing, he returns to his cabin and sorts out the agricultural programmes ready for the next day.

Then he goes to bed.

CHAPTER TWELVE

Although he is alone on board, he faithfully follows all the rituals as if there were a full crew in attendance.

As a boy I used to swim through cold water in the streams that ran between the pines, he thinks.

At the time set for the daily conferences, he sits at the head of the table and reviews the few events and projected tasks with which he is involved.

He eats at the formal mealtimes, uses formal language in all his dealings with the ship, makes formal checks and radios formal log entries back to Earth. His only break with formal routine is the red logbook he keeps in the desk.

He makes the formal tours to the Hibernation Section (nicknamed "crew storage" by the personnel when they first came aboard).

As a young man I stood on hills in the wind and stared at moody skies, he thinks, *and I wrote awful, sentimental, self-pitying verse until the other lads found it and took the piss out of me so much I gave it up. I went into business instead. Just as well.*

He touches the button and the spin screws automatically retract.

I wonder what would have happened to me. Art thrives in chaos. What's good for art isn't good for business...

He pauses by the first container and looks into the patient face of his wife.

Mrs Ryan washed down the walls of her apartment. She was using the appropriate fluid. All the time she cleaned she kept her face averted from the long window forming the far wall of the apartment.

When she had finished cleaning she took the can of fluid back to the kitchen and put it on the right shelf.

Frowning uncertainly, she stood in the middle of the kitchen.

Then she drew a deep breath and she reached towards the shelf again, touching another can. The can was labeled PLANTFOOD.

She grasped the can.

She lifted it from the shelf.

She coughed and covered her mouth with her free hand.

She drew another breath.

She walked into the lobby and sprayed the orange tree that stood in its shining metallic tub. She went back into the living room, with its coloured walls, expensive, cushiony plastic chairs, the wall to wall TV.

She turned on the TV.

The wall opposite the window was instantly alive with whirling, dancing figures.

Watching them gyrate, Mrs Ryan relaxed a trifle. She looked at the can in her hand and put it down on the table. She watched the dancers. Her eyes were drawn back to the can, still lying on the table. She began to sit down. Then she stood up again.

Mrs Ryan's fresh forty-year-old's face crumpled slightly. Her lips moved. She had the expression of a resolute but frightened child, half-ready to cry if the expected accident occurred.

She picked up the can and walked to the wall-long window. With her eyes half-closed she located the button which controlled the raising and lowering of the blinds. With the room in darkness, she sprayed the plants on the windowsill.

She took the can back to the kitchen and placed it on the shelf.

THE BLACK CORRIDOR

She stood in the kitchen doorway for a while, staring into the darkness of the living room, lit only by the flicker of the TV. Then she crossed the room to the window and placed her hand on the button controlling the blind.

She turned her back to the window and found the button with her left hand.

There was a big production number on TV. She stared at it, unmoving.

Then she pressed the button and sprang away from the window as the blinds rushed up and the room was flooded with daylight again.

She hurried into the kitchen, turning off the TV as she went past. She made some coffee and sat down to drink it.

The room was silent.

The empty window looked out onto the apartment blocks opposite. Their empty windows stared back.

Few cars ran in the street between the blocks.

Inside the apartment, in the kitchen, Mrs Ryan sat with her coffee cup raised, like a puppet whose motor had cut out in mid-action.

The telephone buzzed.

Mrs Ryan sat still.

The telephone went on buzzing.

Mrs Ryan sighed and approached the instrument, set at head height on the kitchen wall. She ducked down against the wall and reached up to remove the mouthpiece.

"It's me. Uncle Sidney," said the voice from the screen above her head.

"Oh, it's you, Uncle Sidney," said Mrs Ryan. She backed away from the wall, still holding the mouthpiece, and sat down near the kitchen table.

"Don't come too close," said Uncle Sidney.

"Uncle Sidney," said Mrs Ryan pitifully. "I've asked you not to call during the day, when no-one's at home. After all, I don't know who you are. It might be anyone."

"I'm sorry, I'm sure. I just wanted to ask if you'd like to come over tonight."

"The car's being repaired," said Mrs Ryan. "He had to go by bus this morning. I told him not to, but he insisted. I don't know…"

Mrs Ryan broke off, a sadly bewildered look on her face.

There was silence.

Then she and Uncle Sidney spoke together:

"I've got to clean —" Mrs Ryan said.

"Can't you come —" said Uncle Sidney.

"Uncle Sidney. I've got to clean the front door today. And I know — I *know* that as soon as I open the door the woman from the next apartment will come out and pretend she's going to use the garbage disposal. Do you realize what it's like living next to a woman like that?"

Uncle Sidney's lined face dropped. "Well, if you won't visit your uncle you won't," he said. "Do you know how long it's been since I saw you and him and the kids? Three months."

"I'm sorry, Uncle Sidney." Mrs Ryan looked at the floor, noticing a smear on one of the tiles. "You wouldn't come to see us, I suppose…?"

"On my own?" Uncle Sidney said contemptuously.

He cut the connection. Mrs Ryan sat by the kitchen table holding the mouthpiece in her hand. She stood up slowly and replaced it.

It seemed to her that she could not get the cleaner and the spray from the cupboard. She could not cross the kitchen and go through the living room. She could not, alone, open the front door.

She could not open the front door.

She might…

Mrs Ryan's mind became dark, fearful, confused.

She was swept around the whirlpool of her brain, helpless and still, in spite of herself, struggling.

She could not open the door.

She could not.

Mrs Ryan uttered a low moan and went into the bedroom.

Even in daylight the walls shimmered with many colours. The bed was neatly covered with the white bedspread. The shining dressing table was clear. Mrs Ryan picked up the only sign of occupancy, a pair of Mr Ryan's outdoor shoes. She opened a concealed cupboard and threw them in violently. She ran to the window, pressed the button on the sill.

The blinds came down quickly.

The walls of the room glowed and flickered.

Mrs Ryan paced to and fro. Past the bed to the darkened window. Back from the window to the bed. Back and forth.

She stopped and turned on soft, soothing music.

She ran out of the room and locked the front door.

She came back into the bedroom, shut that door, lay down on the bed, listening to the music.

Even the music seemed slightly harsh today.

She closed her eyes and the faces came. She opened her eyes and reached towards the bedside cupboard, took out her sleeping pills, swallowed a pill and lay down again.

The music was almost raucous. She turned it off.

She lay in silence, waiting for sleep.

It was 11:23 AM.

CHAPTER THIRTEEN

Mrs Ryan began to dream.

She was walking across the field away from the house she had lived in when she was eight. If she turned around she could see her mother framed in the kitchen window, her head bent over the stove. Behind her she could hear the shouts of her brothers playing hide-and-seek.

Mrs Ryan trod over the springy turf, dreamily floated over the bright grass. She could hear birds singing in the trees at the edges of the field.

Mrs Ryan was floating, floating over the fields, far from the house. How sunny it was. How the birds sang. She was walking again. She turned to look for the house but she was too far away. She could not see it. The sky was darkening. She could only dimly see the trees on either side of the field. She seemed to hear a noise; a babble of talk. At once, ahead of her, she saw a dark crowd approaching, talking among themselves. As they came closer she could still not distinguish one person from another. She had the impression that there were men, women and children. But the mass was still a dark blur of heads, bodies, limbs, formless and faceless. The crowd advanced, the cackle of voices growing louder.

She stood transfixed in the field.

And the voices grew clearer.

"Look. There she is. She's there. She's really there."

She felt the mood of the crowd change.

She felt a terrible fear.

"She's there. That's her. That's her. She's there. She's there."

She stood rooted to the spot, her legs too heavy to carry her.

"She's there. She's there. That's her. That's her."

The dark crowd began to run towards her. It yelled and cried out.

She could hear high, vengeful screams from the women. The crowd was almost on her.

And Mrs Ryan awoke with a start in her bedroom in the light of the shimmering walls. She looked at the clock.

It was 11:31 AM.

Trembling, she lay there on the white bedspread, fighting her way out of the dream. She gazed blankly at the walls, blinking her eyes to rid herself of the image of the black, blank faces of that terrible crowd. She rose and walked heavily from the room.

She went into the kitchen and took a pill to clear her head. Sighing, she removed the can of cleaner from the shelf, walked through the living room, out into the lobby and up to the front door. She put her hand on the latch.

Mrs Ryan hesitated, stiffened her back and opened the front door. She crept outside, into the long corridor.

The corridor was bright and white. It stretched away from her on either side. Set in the walls were the doors, all painted in fresh, dark colours.

Slowly Mrs Ryan began to spray cleaner on the surface of the door. Once the door was covered with the white film she began to rub it off, faster and faster.

Nearly done, she thought to herself, *nearly done. Thank God, thank God. Soon finished. Thank God.*

Very slowly the blue door of the apartment opposite began to open. A woman looked through the crack of the door. She and Mrs Ryan stared at each other in shock. The woman's hand went to her mouth. Mrs Ryan recovered herself first.

Leaving the door half covered in white cleaning fluid she ran back inside her apartment and slammed the door. Almost at the same moment the other woman shut her own door.

Mrs Ryan stood in the middle of her kitchen, gasping for breath. "That bitch," she said aloud. "That bitch. What does she want to persecute me for? Why does she always do that to me? Spying on me all the time. Bitch, bitch, bitch."

She went to the shelf, took down a bottle of capsules and swallowed two. She went into the living room and fell down on the plastic couch. She switched on the TV.

There was a picture of a family eating a turkey dinner. The turkey and its trimmings were laid out brightly on a gay table. The family — parents and three teenage children — were joking. Mrs Ryan watched the programme with a faint smile curling around her mouth.

She was soon asleep.

It was 11:48 AM.

The boys woke her up.

She told them what had happened and they told Ryan.

Ryan was sympathetic.

"You need a holiday, old girl," he said. "We'll see what we can do."

"I'd rather not," she said. "I prefer to stay at home. It's just — the *interference* from the neighbours. I'm proud of my home."

"Of course you are. We'll see what we can do."

It was 7:46 PM.

"Time passes so slowly," she said.

"It depends how you look at it," he replied.

She suffered a lot, thinks Ryan. *Maybe I could have been more helpful.*

He shrugs the thought off. A pointless exercise. There was nothing to be gained from self-recrimination. If one didn't like what one had done, the best thing was to decide not to do it again and leave it at that. That was the pragmatic attitude. The scientific attitude.

He looks down at the sleeping face of his wife and he smiles tenderly, touching the top of the container.

Even her condition improved once they had decided on their goal. She was basically a sensible woman. Her condition was no different from that of millions of others in the cities all over the world.

If they had taken one of the abandoned houses in the country, perhaps she would have been happier. But probably not. The isolation of the places beyond the cities was pretty unbearable.

She had liked the country as a girl, of course. That was partly what the dream was about, he guessed. That dream of hers. It had recurred relatively frequently. Not unlike that recurring dream of his.

He starts to pace between the containers, checking them automatically.

What is time, after all? Do we meet in our dreams?

Pointless, mystical speculation.

Everything seems to be in order. The containers are functioning correctly. Ryan yawns and stretches, fighting off the sinking feeling in his stomach, ignoring the impulse to wake at least some of the occupants of the containers. They must not be awakened until the ship nears the planet that is its destination.

This is his penance, his test, his reward.

He has one last look at his sleeping boys, then he leaves the compartment and makes his way back to the main control cabin, sends his report back to Earth. All is well aboard the spaceship *Hope Dempsey*.

He writes a short entry in his red logbook:

On the other side of those thin walls is infinite space. There is no life for billions of miles. No man has ever been more alone.

In his cabin he takes three pills, disposes of his clothes, lies down.

As he begins to fall asleep a numb, desperate feeling tells him that tonight could be another of those nights of fitful, nightmare-ridden sleep. His routine demands that he sleep regularly. His health will break if he does not. Ryan lies on his narrow couch willing himself not to rise. The pills take effect and Ryan sleeps.

He dreams that he is in his office. It is dark. He has drawn the blinds to shut out the city noise and the view of the shining office towers opposite. He sits at his desk doing nothing. His hands are curled on the desk before him. The fingernails are torn. He is afraid.

He sees his wife in their apartment. She is sitting in the darkened living room doing nothing.

He sees the bedroom in which his two sons lie sleeping under heavy sedation. The youngest, five-year-old Alexander, groans in his sleep, thrusts an arm, thin as a Foreigner's, out of the covers. The arm dangles lifelessly down from his bed. He moans again. His brother Rupert, who is twelve, lies on his back, eyes half open in his coma, staring blindly at the ceiling.

Back in the living room Ryan sees the hunched figure of his wife. Again he sees himself sitting at his office desk staring into the half dark.

The family is waiting.

It is waiting in fear.

It does not know what to expect.

There is a scratching noise behind him. Ryan, half-paralyzed with terror, turns slowly around to see what it is. He faces the window now. The blind is shaking, as if it were being blown by the wind. There is something behind the blind, something from outside, trying to enter the office. Ryan breathes in, holds his breath hard in some animal instinct to make himself so immobile that he will not be noticed. The blind shakes and shakes. A bony hand comes through the fabric, leaving no gap or tear, merely sliding through as if the material were smoke, or air. Ryan gazes at the hand. It belongs to an old woman, thin fingered, with pronounced tendons. The nails are painted red. There are three large rings: two diamond ones on the middle finger, a large amethyst on the slender, slightly curved, little finger. The hand appears to part the blind and a face peers in.

It is the face of an old woman. The wrinkled eyelids are carefully painted blue. The mouth is blackened, the lined cheeks powdered. The old woman looks Ryan straight in the eyes and smiles, revealing yellow teeth, the edges slightly serrated with age. Ryan stares at the old woman. She continues to give him a confidential, intimate smile.

Her hand appears again, through another part of the blind.

It holds a pair of round, dark glasses.

The hand moves toward her face. It places the glasses over her eyes. Then the hand disappears through the blind again, leaving no gap or rent in it.

The old, blackened mouth continues to smile below the obliterated eyes.

Then the old woman's face, in the centre of the blind, begins to droop. The smile disappears, the lips begin to curve in a snarl.

Ryan is terrified.

He cannot scream.

He wants to say the following words:

I — DID — NOT

— but he cannot.

He cannot say the...

I —

He gets up from his bed. He is sweating. Naked, he leaves the cabin and walks down the bright corridor, enters the main control cabin and stares at the dancing, shifting indicators, at the ever busy computer.

He listens to the faint hum of the engine which is propelling the little pellet of steel through the void.

The computer has left him a message. He walks over to the machine and reads it.

It says:

***************THERE IS A LOSS OF COMMUNICATION**************
***************98765432100000000000""""""""""/***********
*****A LOSS**""""""""""""PLEASE ENSURE THAT IN FUTURE***INFORMATION
IS GIVEN IN THE CORRECT FORM""""""REPEAT THE**CORRECT FORM""""""""WHAT
IS THE EXACT NATURE OF THE******SITUATION REPEAT WHAT IS THE EXACT
NATURE OF THE******SITUATION REPEAT WHAT IS THE EXACT NATURE OF
THE*******SITUATION""""""""""""""""""""""""""""""""""""********

Uncomprehendingly Ryan stares at the message.

What has gone wrong?

He has carried out his duties impeccably.

His days have been dedicated to order, the routine of the ship.

What has he done wrong?

Or — worse — what mistake can be occurring inside the computer?

He rips off the printout and reads it, seeking a clue. It has all the fluency and random lack of sense of a message from a ouija board.

And as he reads the computer spills out more:

*********I CANNOT READ YOUR LAST MESSAGE UNLESS************
**********INFORMATION IS GIVEN IN THE CORRECT FORM""""""""I

CANNOT**ASSIST""""""""""PLEASE REPEAT YOUR LAST MESSAGE IN THE****CORRECT FORM***

Wearily Ryan organizes the machine to rerun his last message. It reads:

******TRIUMPHANT IN THE BLOODY SKY AND THE HUMAN FORM*IS NO MORE*

I must control this sort of thing, thinks Ryan.

He wanders to the desk and takes out his red logbook. He writes:

I must keep better control of things.

He struggles back to the computer and realizes he has left his red logbook on the desk. He weaves back to the desk and carefully, but with great difficulty, puts the book in its drawer. Slowly, he closes the door. He returns to the computer. He erases the messages as best he can by condemning them to the computer's deepest memory cells. He walks wearily from the control room.

I must control this sort of thing.

I must forget these nightmares.

I must maintain order.

It could wreck the computer and then I would be finished.

Everything depends on me.

Triumphant in the bloody sky and the human form...

Ryan weeps.

He paces the corridor, back to his prison, takes three more pills and sleeps.

He dreams of the factory. A huge hall, somewhat darker in Ryan's dream than it was in reality. It is filled with large silent machines. Only the throbbing of the tiled floor indicates the activity of the machines.

At the end of each machine is a large drum into which spill the parts used in the making of Ryan Toys.

There are the smooth heads, legs, arms and torsos of dolls; the woolly heads, legs and torsos of lambs, tigers and rabbits; the metal legs, heads and torsos of mechanical puppets. There are the tiny powerpacs for the bellies of Ryan Toys; there are the metal parts for Ryan Toys dredgers, oilpumps, spacecraft; there are the great, shining grinning heads of Rytoy Realboys and Rytoy Realgirls; the great proboscises of Rytoy Realphants.

The vast machines turn out their parts steadily and inexorably. As each drum fills it glides away and is replaced by another which is, in turn, steadily filled.

Ryan is a witness to this scene. He knows that he will be involved if they find out.

He sees a white-coated mechanic walk along the files of machines and disappear through a door at the end of the hall.

Did the mechanic notice him?

The drums roll away and are replaced by empty ones.

Suddenly Ryan sees the parts rise, as if in weightlessness. They join together, assembling in mid-air. As each toy is completed, or as completed as it can be with the parts available, it sinks to the floor of the hall and begins to operate.

A row of golden haired Realboys, lifesize but armless, revolve slowly, singing *Frère Jacques* in their high voices.

A cluster of woolly lambs gambol mechanically, raising and dipping their heads.

On the floor the large trunks of the Realphants plunge and rise.

The spacecraft hover a foot above the floor, emitting humming noises.

Ryrobots strut and clank about, running into the machines and toppling over. Two great heaps of musical building blocks chime out the letters printed on their sides —

I AM A

I AM M

I AM U

The piles fall and tumble as Ryan kicks them.

The Realgirls link hands and dance around him, tossing their blonde curls. The Ryan Battlewagons run about the floor, shooting their miniature missiles.

Ryan looks fondly at the action, music and chatter of his toys. The whole of the tiled floor is being gradually covered with toys in motion. All these things are Ryan's — made and sold by Ryan.

He looks at the building blocks and smiles. Some have fallen and spelled out: AMUSEMENT.

In the middle of this cheerful scene, Ryan ceases to dream and falls fast asleep.

In accordance with the regulations ensuring that no member of the government or the civil service could be identified save by his rank (thus ensuring the absence of blackmail, bribery, favour-seeking and/ or giving and so forth) the Man from the Ministry wore a black cloth over his face. It had neat holes for his eyes and his mouth.

Ryan, sitting behind his office desk, contemplated the Man from the Ministry somewhat nervously.

"Will you have a cup of tea?" he asked.

"I think not."

Ryan could almost see the expression of suspicious distaste on the man's face. He had made a tactical blunder.

"Ah..." said Ryan.

"Mr Ryan..." began the official.

"Yes," said Ryan, as if in confirmation. "Yes, indeed."

"Mr Ryan — you seem unaware that this country is in a state of war..."

"Ah. No."

"Since Birmingham launched its completely unprovoked attack on London, Mr Ryan, and bombed the reservoirs of Shepperton and Staines, the official government of South England has had to requisition a great deal of private industry if it has been discovered that it has not been contributing to our war effort as efficiently as it might..."

"That's a threat, is it?" Ryan said thickly.

"A friendly tip, Mr Ryan."

"We've turned over as fast as we can," Ryan explained. "We *were* a bloody toy factory, you know. Overnight we had to change to manufacturing weapons parts and communications equipment. Naturally we haven't had a completely smooth ride. On the other hand, we've done our best..."

"Your production is not up to scratch, Mr Ryan. I wonder if your heart is in the war effort? Some people do not seem to realize that the old society has been swept away, that the Patriots are bent on ordering an entirely new kind of nation now that the remnants of the alien groups have been pushed back beyond the Thames. Though attacked from all sides, though sustaining three hydrogen bomb drops from France, the Patriots have managed to hold this land of ours together. They can only do it with the full co-operation of people like yourself, Mr Ryan."

"We aren't getting the raw materials," Ryan said. "Half the things we need don't arrive. It's a bloody shambles!"

"That sounds like a criticism of the government, Mr Ryan."

"You know I'm a registered Patriot supporter."

"Not all registered supporters have remained loyal, Mr Ryan."

"Well, I *am* loyal!" Ryan half believed himself as he shouted at the Man from the Ministry. He and the group had decided early on that the Patriots would soon hold the power and had taken the precaution of joining the party. "It's just that we can't work more than ten bloody miracles a day!"

"You've got a week, I'm afraid, Mr Ryan." The official got up, closing his briefcase. "And then it will be a Temporary Requisition Order until our borders are secure again."

"You'll take over?"

"You will continue to manage the factory, if you prove efficient. You will enjoy the status of any other civil servant."

Ryan nodded. "What about compensation?"

"Mr Ryan," said the official grimly, wearily, "there is a discredited cabinet that fled to Birmingham to escape retribution. Among other things that was discovered about that particular cabinet was that it was corrupt. Industrialists were lining their pockets with the connivance of government officials. That sort of thing is all over now. All over. Naturally, you will receive a receipt guaranteeing the return of your business when the situation has been normalized. We hope, however, that it won't have to happen. Keep trying, Mr Ryan. Keep trying. Good luck to you."

Ryan watched the official leave. He would have to warn the group that things were moving a little faster than anticipated.

He wondered how things were in the rest of the world. Very few reports came through these days. The United States were now Disunited and at war. United Europe had fragmented into thousands of tiny principalities, rather as England had. As for Russia and the Far East the only information he had had for months was that a horde thousands of times greater than the Golden Horde was sweeping in all directions. Possibly none of the information was true. He hoped that the town of Surgut on the Siberian Plain was still untouched. Everything depended on that.

Ryan got up and left the office.

It was time to go home.

CHAPTER FOURTEEN

When he awakes he feels relieved, alert and refreshed. He eats his breakfast as soon as he has exercised and walks to the control room where he runs through all the routine checks and adjustments until lunch time.

After lunch he goes to the little gym behind the main control cabin and vaults and climbs and swings until it is time to inspect Hibernation.

He unlocks the door of Hibernation and makes a routine and unemotional check. A minor alteration is required in the rate of fluid flow on Number Seven container. He makes the alteration.

Again the routine checks, the reiteration during the normal conference period.

He then does two hours' study of the agricultural programmes. He learns a great deal. It is a much more interesting subject than he would have guessed.

Then it is time to report to the computer and read the log through to Earth, if anyone is left on Earth to hear it.

He makes the last of his reports for this period:

"Day number one thousand four hundred and sixty-six. Spaceship *Hope Dempsey* en route for Munich 15040. Speed steady at point nine of *c*. All systems functioning according to original expectations. No other variations. All occupants are comfortable and in good health."

Ryan goes to the desk and takes out his red logbook. He frowns. Scrawled across a page are the words:

I MUST KEEP BETTER CONTROL OF THINGS.

It hardly looks like his writing. Yet it must be.

And when did he write it? He has not had time to make any entries in the log until now. It could have been at any time today. Or last night. He frowns. When...?

He cannot remember.

He takes a deep breath and he rules two heavy red lines under the entry, writes the date below it and begins:

All continues well. I maintain my routine and am hopeful for the future. Today I feel less bedeviled by loneliness and have more confidence in my ability to carry out my mission. Our ship carries us steadily onwards. I am confident that all is well. I am confident

He stops writing and scratches his head, staring at the phrase, above the entry.

I MUST KEEP BETTER CONTROL OF THINGS.

I am confident that my period of nightmares and near-hysteria is over. I have regained control of myself and therefore

He considers tearing out this page and beginning it afresh. But that would not be in accord with the regulations he is following. He sucks his lower lip...

am doubtless much more cheerful. The above phrase is something of a puzzle to me, for at this point I cannot remember writing it. Perhaps I was under even greater stress than I imagined and wrote it last night after finishing the ordinary entry. Well, it was good advice — the advice of this stranger who could only have been myself!

It gives me a slightly eery feeling, however, I must admit. I expect I will remember when I wrote it. I hope so. In the meantime there is no point in my racking my brains. The information will come when my unconscious is ready to let me have it!

Otherwise — all O. K. The gloom and doom period is over — at least for the time being. I am in a thoroughly constructive and balanced state of mind.

He signs off with a flourish and, humming, puts the book in the desk, closes the drawer, gets up, takes a last look around the control room and goes out into the passage.

Before returning to his cabin, he goes to the library and gets a couple of educational tapes.

In his cabin, he studies the programmes for a while and then goes to sleep.

He is on the new planet. A pleasant landscape. A valley. He is working the soil with some sort of digging instrument. He is alone and at peace. There is no sign of the spaceship or of the other occupants. This does not worry him. He is alone and at peace.

Next morning he continues with his routine work. He eats, he makes his formal log entries, he manages to get an extra hour of study. He is beginning to understand the principles of agriculture.

He returns to the control room to make the last of his reports — the standard one — which, according to his routine, he first enters in his logbook and then reads out to the computer. He then sits down and picks up his stylus to begin his private entry. He enters the date.

Another pleasant and uneventful day spent largely in the pursuit of knowledge! I am beginning to feel like some old scholar. I can understand the attraction, suddenly, in the pursuit of information for its own sake. In a way, of course, it is an escape — I can see that even the most sophisticated sort of academic activity is at least in part a rejection of the realities of ordinary living. My studies, naturally, are perfectly practical, in that I will need a great deal of knowledge about every possible kind of agriculture when we

The computer is flashing a signal. It wants his attention.

Frowning, Ryan gets up and goes over to the main console.

He reads the computer's message.

*******CONDITION OF OCCUPANTS OF CONTAINERS NOT*****REPORTED**

Ryan gasps. It is true. For the first time he has not checked the hibernation compartment. He realizes now that he was so caught up in his studies he must have forgotten. He replies to the computer:

*****REPORT FOLLOWS SHORTLY********************************

SAILING TO UTOPIA

Reproving himself for this stupid lapse, relieved that the computer is programmed to check every function he performs and to remind him of any oversights, he marches along the corridor to the hibernation room.

He touches the stud to open the door.

But the door remains closed.

He presses the stud harder.

Still the door does not open.

Ryan feels a moment's panic. Could there be someone else aboard the ship? A stowaway of some kind who...?

He rejects the notion as stupid. And then he returns to the main control cabin and gives the computer a question.

******HIBERNATION COMPARTMENT DOOR WILL NOT OPEN*****PLEASE ADVISE***

There is a pause before the computer replies:

******EMERGENCY LOCK EFFECTIVE"""""""YOU MUST******************
********DEACTIVATE AT MAIN CONSOLE************************

Ryan licks his lips and goes to the main console. He scans the door plan and sees that the computer is correct. He touches a stud on the console and cuts off the emergency lock. Was the mistake his or the computer's? Perhaps the emergency lock was activated at the same time as he made the mysterious log entry.

He returns to the hibernation room and opens the door.

He enters the compartment.

CHAPTER FIFTEEN

The containers gleam a pure, soft white.

He walks to the first and inspects it. It contains his wife.

JOSEPHINE RYAN. 9/9/1960. 7/3/2004.

His blonde, pink-faced wife, blue eyes peacefully closed, lies in her green fluid. She looks so natural that Ryan half expects her to open her eyes and smile at him. Josephine, heart of the ship, so glad to be setting out on her great adventure, so glad to be free from the torture of living in the city with its unbearable atmosphere of hostility.

Ryan smiles as he remembers the eager step with which she came aboard on the day of the take-off, how she had lost, almost overnight, the sadness and the fear which had afflicted her — indeed, which had been afflicting them all. He sighs. How pleasant to be together again.

RUPERT RYAN. 13/7/1990. 6/3/2004.

ALEXANDER RYAN. 25/12/1996. 6/3/2004.

Ryan walks fairly quickly past the containers where his two sons' immature faces gaze in startlement at the bright ceiling.

SIDNEY RYAN. 2/2/1937. 25/12/2003.

Ryan stares for a while at the wrinkled old face, lips slightly drawn back over the false teeth, the thin musclely old shoulders showing above the plastic sheet drawn over the main length of the containers.

JOHN RYAN. 15/8/1963. 26/12/2003.

ISABEL RYAN. 22/6/1962. 13/2/2004.

Isabel. Still weary looking, even though at peace…

JANET RYAN. 10/11/1982. 7/5/2004.

Ah, Janet, thinks Ryan with a surge of affection.
    He loved Josephine. But, by God, he loved Janet passionately.
    He frowns. The problem had not been over when they went into hibernation. It would take a great deal of self-discipline on his part to make sure that it did not start all over again.

FRED MASTERSON. 4/5/1950. 25/12/2003.

TRACY MASTERSON. 29/10/1973. 9/10/2003.

JAMES HENRY. 4/3/1957. 29/10/2003.

IDA HENRY. 3/3/1980. 1/2/2004.

FELICITY HENRY. 3/3/1980. 1/2/2004.

Everything is as it should be. Everybody is sleeping peacefully. Only Ryan is awake.

He blinks.

Only Ryan is awake because it is better for one man to suffer acute loneliness and isolation than for several to live in tension.

One strong man.

Ryan raises his eyebrows.

And leaves Hibernation.

Ryan reports to the computer:

JOSESPHINE RYAN. CONDITION STEADY.

RUPERT RYAN. CONDITION STEADY.

ALEXANDER RYAN. CONDITION STEADY.

SIDNEY RYAN. CONDITION STEADY.

JOHN RYAN. CONDITION STEADY.

ISABEL RYAN. CONDITION STEADY.

JANET RYAN.

          CONDITION STEADY.

      FRED MASTERSON. CONDITION STEADY.

      TRACY MASTERSON. CONDITION

               STEADY.

   JAMES

               HENRY

   CONDITION STEADY.

   IDA HENRY. CONDITION STEADY

   FELICITY HENRY. CONDITION

            STEADY.

The computer says:

******EARLIER YOU REPORTED YOURSELF LONELY*****"""""""""DOES THIS CONDITION STILL/OBTAIN***************************************

Ryan replies:

******CONDITION EASIER SINCE THEN****************************

He moves to his desk and picks up his diary.

He writes:

land.

A short while ago the computer reported an oversight of mine. I'd forgotten to report on the condition of the personnel. The first time I've done anything like that! And the last, I hope. Then I discovered that the emergency locks in Hibernation had been sealed and I had to come back and unseal them. I must have done that, too, when I made the above entry. I feel relaxed and at ease now. The previous mistakes and, I suppose, mild blackouts must have been the result of the strain which I now seem to have overcome.

Ryan winds up the entry, closes the log, puts it away, leaves the control room.

He goes to his cabin and sets aside the educational tapes. *Too much concentration*, he thinks. *Mustn't overdo it. It's incredible how one has to watch the balance. A very delicate equilibrium involved here. Very delicate.*

He starts to watch an old Patriot propaganda play about the discovery of a cell of the Free Yorkshire underground and its eventual elimination.

He turns it off.

He hears something. He turns his head from the viewer.

It is a year since he heard a footstep not his own.

But now he can hear footsteps.

He sits there, feeling sweat prickle under his hair, listening to what seems to be the sound of echoing steps in the passage outside.

There is some stranger aboard!

He listens as the steps approach the door of the compartment. Then they pass.

He forces himself out of his chair and gets to the door. He touches the stud to open the door. It opens slowly.

Outside the passageway stretches on both sides, the length of the ship's crew quarters. The only sound is the faint hum of the ship's system.

Ryan gets a glass of water and drinks it.

He switches the viewer back on, half smiling. Typical auditory hallucination of a lonely man, he thinks. The programme ends.

Ryan decides to get some exercise.

He leaves his cabin and makes for the gym.

As he walks along the corridor he feels footsteps moving behind him. He ignores the feeling with a shrug.

Then comes a moment's panic. He gives way to the impulse to turn sharply.

There is, of course, no-one there.

Ryan reaches the gym. He has the impression that he is being watched as he runs through his exercises.

He lies down on a couch for fifteen minutes before beginning the second half of the exercise routine.

He remembers family holidays on the Isle of Skye. That was in the very early years, of course, before Skye was taken over as an experimental area for research into algae food substitutes. He remembers the pleasant evenings he and Josephine used to have with Tracy and Fred Masterson. He remembers the evening walks through the roof gardens with his wife. He remembers Christmases, he remembers sunsets. He remembers the smell of the rain on the fields of the place where he was born. He remembers the smell of his toy factories — the hot metal, the paint, the freshly cut timber. He remembers his mother. She had been one of the victims of the short-lived Hospitals Euthanasia Act. The act had been repealed by the Nimmoites during their short period of power. The only sensible thing they did, thinks Ryan.

He sleeps.

Once again he is on the planet, in the valley. But this time he is panic-stricken that the ship and the others have left him. He begins to run. He runs into the jungle. He sees a dark woman. He is in his own toy factory among the dancing toys.

He takes pleasure at the sight of these things he has made. They all function together so joyfully. He sees the musical building blocks. They still spell out a word.

AMU…

With dawning fear he hears, above the bangs and clangs of the mechanical toys, the drone of the dirgelike music which in other dreams accompanies the dancers in the darkened ballroom.

The music rises, almost drowning out the sounds made by the moving toys. Ryan feels himself standing rooted with fear in the middle of his gyrating models. The music grows louder. The toys spin to and fro, round and round. They begin to climb on top of each other, lamb on dredger, girl doll on piles of bricks, making a huge pyramid close to him. The pyramid grows and grows until it is at the level of his eyes.

The music grows louder and louder.

In his terror Ryan anticipates a point in the music when the pyramid of still-moving toys collapses on him.

He struggles to free himself from the toils of little mechanical bodies.

As he struggles he awakes. He lies there and hears himself groan:

"I thought they were over. I've got to do something about it."

He gets off the couch and abandons the idea of exercise.

He stares around at the exercising machines. "I can remain master of myself," Ryan says.

"I can."

He goes back to the control room, adjusts various dials, checks that his time devices are working accurately and makes the following statement to the computer:

*********I AM TROUBLED BY NIGHTMARES*************************

The computer replies:

******I KNOW THIS"""""""INJECT 1CC PRODITOL PER*****DIEM""""""""DO NOT TAKE MORE""""""""DISCONTINUE THE DOSE**AS SOON AS POSSIBLE AND AT ALL COSTS AFTER 14 DAYS****

Ryan rubs his lips.

Then he bites the nail of his right forefinger.

Ryan paces the ship.

Passageways, engine room, supplies room, exercise room, control room, own cabin, spare cabins, observation room, library...

He does not look at the door of the hibernation room. He does not walk along the passage towards the door.

He continues his angry prowling for half an hour or more, trying to collect his thoughts.

The footsteps follow him most of the time. Footsteps he knows do not exist.

Echoing up and down the passageways he begins to hear fragments of the voices of his companions, the men and women now suspended in green fluid in the containers that must remain sealed until planetfall.

"Daddy! Daddy!" cries his youngest child Alexander.

Ryan hears the thud of his feet in the passage. He overhears an argument between Ida and Felicity Henry: "Don't keep telling me how you feel. I don't want to know," Felicity snaps at her pregnant twin sister. "You don't realize what it's like," says the other on a familiar note of complaint. "No, no. I don't," he hears Felicity say hysterically. He hears the noise of a slap and Ida's weeping. A door bangs. "Let me see to it, Ryan," he hears James Henry say impatiently. The voice seems to echo all over the ship. He hears Fred and Tracy Masterson's feet coming rapidly along the passageway. His wife Josephine is behind them. "Daddy! Daddy!" The child's feet come scudding up to him. Ryan turns his head this way and that. Where are the sounds coming from?

Janet Ryan sings, far away.

"Homeward bound, where the fields are like honey…"

Ryan cannot hear the words properly. He cranes his neck to listen, but the words are still indistinct. Uncle Sidney is singing too. "There was a man who had a mouse, hi-diddle-um-tum-ti-do; he baked it in an apple pie; there was a man who had a mouse…"

Isabel Ryan's voice comes from somewhere around him. "I can't bear any more!"

Then the rumble of John Ryan, his brother, talking to her, saying something Ryan cannot catch.

Janet singing.

Both boys are running, running, running…

And Ryan, in the centre of all this noise, sinks to the floor of the passage, cocks his head, listening to the voices.

As he crouches there it seems to him that the voices must be coming from the room at the end of the passage. Automatically he gets to his feet and with a stiff gait starts to walk up the passageway towards the door.

The voices grow louder.

"I hate to see a man playing at being indispensable. It benefits neither him nor the people about him," says James Henry.

"The Lord thy God is a jealous God and thou shalt have no other God than Him," advises Uncle Sidney.

"Never mind, dear, never mind," Isabel Ryan is telling someone.

Alexander is crying muffled sobs into the pillow.

Janet Ryan is singing in her high, clear voice: "Homeward bound, we're homeward bound, where the singing birds welcome such lovers as we…"

Ida and Felicity Henry are still arguing: "Take it." "I don't want to take it." "You must take it. It's what you need." "I know what I need." "Be sensible. Drink it now."

As Ryan reaches the door, the voices rise. As he touches the stud, they are louder still.

Conversations, statements, songs, sobs, laughter, arguments, all coming towards him in an indistinguishable medley.

Then the door is open.

The noises cease abruptly and Ryan is left in the silence, staring at the thirteen containers, twelve full and labeled with the names and dates of the occupants.

The owners of the voices lie there quietly in their pale fluid. Ryan stands there in the doorway, suddenly realizing again that he is alone, that the noise has ceased, that he has opened the door at an unscheduled time…

His companions continue to sleep. Peaceful and unaware of the torment he is undergoing, they are all at CONDITION STEADY.

Which is more than I am, thinks Ryan. Tears come to his eyes.

From the door he cannot see the people in the containers.

He counts the containers. There are still thirteen. He looks at the thirteenth, his own. He draws in his breath. His lips curl back in a frightened, feral snarl. He steps out into the passageway and slams the heel of his hand against the door, shutting it.

He begins to run very slowly down the passage until he comes to the end.

Then he leans against a bulkhead, breathing heavily.

He gasps and gasps again. Then he straightens his back and sets off slowly for the control room.

I shall have to think about that injection. I might not be able to carry on without it. I'd hoped to hold out longer than this. Doesn't do to get too reliant on that sort of thing. It is supposed to be addictive, after all.

Maybe one dose will do the trick. One might be all I need.

At any rate, I daren't go on without it.

Ryan decides to have his first injection the next morning.

The Proditol is an enzyme-inhibiting substance that works directly on new cell matter entering the brain. It has the effect of preventing the release of harmful substances into the cells, substances causing lack of connection with the outside world and, thus, delusions. Ryan, partly for pride's sake, partly for reasons he does not fully understand, is very unwilling to take the drug.

But Ryan is dedicated to the ship, its occupants, its goal.

There is little he would not do in order to be able to continue with the steady schedule of the ship and fulfill his responsibility towards its occupants.

Ryan has made his decision.

Plenty of sleeping pills tonight and the Proditol tomorrow.

He goes to his sleeping compartment but then wanders back to the main control room.

He asks for details of the action of the drug.

*******1CC PRODITOL",",",1CC PRODITOL ALSO MA-19:::USSR*1CC PRODITOL IS A FAST ACTING DRUG OF THE ENZYME*****INHIBITOR VARIETY"""""""""IT BEGINS TO TAKE EFFECT*****WITHIN TEN MINUTES OF INJECTION""""""""""ITS FULL EFFECT*IS FELT WITHIN THE HOUR FOLLOWING""""""""AFTER THIS****THE MIND OF THE PATIENT SHOULD BE RELIEVED OF ALL****IMPRESSIONS OF A DELUSORY NATURE""""""""""IN THE*********SEVEREST CASES THE DRUG WILL CONTROL ADVERSE*********SYMPTOMS FOR 24 HOURS AFTER WHICH: IF DELUSIONS*******RETURN:A FURTHER INJECTION SHOULD BE ADMINISTERED*****IN MANY CASES THIS WILL NOT BE NECESSARY""""""""""IN NO**CIRCUMSTANCES: HOWEVER:SHOULD THE DRUG BE ADMINISTERED*DAILY FOR MORE THAN 14 DAYS**

Ryan acknowledges the message and walks to the control room's main "porthole". He activates the screen and looks out at space. The holographic illusion is complete.

Space and the distant suns, the tiny points of light so far away.

Ryan's brows contract.

He notices trails in the blackness. They appear to be wisps of vapour and yet they are plainly not escaping from the ship. It is something like smoke from an open fire, trailing in the dark.

He passes his hand across his eyes and peers forward again. The trails are still there.

He is alarmed. He casts his mind over the data he has accumulated, hoping to think of something that will account for the vapour.

Could it be left by the ships of another space-traveling race?

It must be a possibility.

Meanwhile the wisps continue to rise. There are more and more of them now. They swirl together, break apart and reform.

Ryan, to his horror, begins to hear a faint noise, a kind of buzzing and ringing in his ears. As the noise begins the gases begin to unite, to shape themselves. Once again Ryan passes a hand over his eyes.

The noises in his ears continue. As he looks out of the porthole once more a terrible suspicion comes over him.

And instantly, staring at him gravely, with a small, malicious smile on her lips, is the old woman. Her eyes are shielded by the round dark glasses. She is black-lipped, her old skin covered in powder. She puts the clawlike hand to the window and is gone.

Ryan gasps and is about to turn from the window in panic when he sees the shapes ahead of him. Out there in space are the whirling figures of his nightmare, the figures of the insane dancers in the darkened ballroom.

They are far away.

Ryan hears their music in his ears. As they dance, slowly and proudly, to the distant chant he watches, paralyzed, as they come closer to the ship.

He sees their stiff bodies, their plump, respectable faces, the expensive dark brocades of the women's dresses, the good dark suits of the men. He observes the well-nurtured upright bodies, the straight backs, the air of dignity and comportment with which they circle, so correctly, in time to the music.

The dark circles which are their eyes stare blindly at each other. Their faces are rigid below the dark glasses. They circle through the void towards Ryan and the music becomes louder, more solemn, more threatening.

"Daddy! Daddy!"

Alexander is crying.

Ryan is unable to move. Cold light falls on the dancers. They come closer to the ship, closer to Ryan, standing terrified at his window.

"Daddy!"

Ryan hears the insistent voice and frowns. Is Alex really up?

Ryan smiles. The boy was never one to stay in bed if he could help it.

But Alexander Ryan is not in bed. He is in hibernation.

The dancers dance on.

They are not real. Ryan realizes that he should give his attention to his son, not to the illusory dancers out there in space. They can't get in. They can't confront him. They can't take off, in one terrible gesture, the glasses which encircle their eyes, revealing...

"Get back to bed, Alex!"

They are very close now. The music slows. They are just a few paces from the ship. They turn to face Ryan with their blinded eyes. Slowly they take a step.

One step...

Two steps...

Three steps towards Ryan.

They are clustered, some thirty of them, a foot from Ryan, standing just outside the window. And then Ryan realizes with greater terror that it has been an illusion. The dancers are not outside. What he was seeing was a reflection in the window. The dancers are actually *behind* him. They have been in the ship all the time. He dares not turn. He stares instead into the mirror.

They stare back.

Then Ryan sees the others. Behind the crowd of dancers are his friends and relatives. All stare at him from blank eyes. All stare at him as if they do not know him. As if, indeed, he does not exist for them.

Josephine — her plump face expressionless, her blonde hair tumbling to her plump shoulders, cruel in her indifference.

His two sons, Alexander and Rupert, startled expressions in their round eyes. Uncle Sidney, his stringy arm gripping the two boys around their thin shoulders, his lips drawn back in a snarl, his eyes on an object somewhere above Ryan's head.

There are the Henry twins, one healthy, one tired by pregnancy, but hand in hand and staring through Ryan with identical hazel eyes. There is Tracy Masterson, looking vacuously past Ryan's left shoulder. There is Fred Masterson, Ryan's oldest friend, a sympathetic expression on his face. There is brother John, puzzled, tired, uncomprehending. There is Isabel, looking bitterly at John. There is James Henry, red hair gleaming in the mirror-light, glaring meaninglessly through Ryan.

And as he looks, Ryan sees the dancers in front take their last step towards him. He wheels to face them.

He stares into the cool, orderly control room. The screens, the dials, the indicators, the instruments, the computer console. Grey and green, muted colours, quiet...

He looks back at the porthole. There is only blackness.

In one way this seems worse to Ryan. He begins to beat at the porthole, howling and cursing.

"Where are you? Where are you? You shits, you cunts, you bastards, you bleeders, you fuckers, you horrors..."

They are there again. Not the dancers. Only his friends and relatives. But they still cannot see him.

He waves to them, mouths friendly words at them. They do not understand. They come a little closer.

And suddenly Ryan feels their malice, is shocked and horrified. He looks at them and his expression is puzzled. He tries to signal to them — that they know him, that he is their friend.

They crowd closer.

"*Let us in!*" they cry. "Let us in. Let us in. Let us in. Let us in. Let us in. Let us live. Let us in."

The clamour around the ship increases. Hands claw at the window. Hands tear their way through the fabric of the porthole.

"You fools! You'll destroy the ship. Be sensible. Wait!" Ryan begs them. "You'll bring the deaths of all of us! Don't — don't — don't!"

But they are ripping the whole of the wall away, exposing it to frigid space.

"You'll wreck the expedition! Stop it!"

They cannot hear him.

His throat is tight.

He faints.

THE BLACK CORRIDOR

CHAPTER SIXTEEN

Ryan is lying on the floor of the control room. His sleeve is rolled up and an ampoule of 1cc Proditol lies near him. The ampoule is empty.

He blinks. At some point he must have realized what he had to do to stop the hallucinations. He is impressed by his own strength of will.

"How are you now?"

He knows the voice. He feels fear, then relief. It is his brother John's voice. He looks up. His jacket has been folded under his head.

John, stalwart and stolid, looks down at him.

"You *were* in a bad way, old son!"

"John. How did you wake up?"

"Something to do with the computer, I think. There's probably an emergency waking system if anything happens to the man on duty."

"I'm glad of that. I was a real idiot to carry on on my own. I realized everything else about my condition except the extent of the strain. I was insisting to myself that I didn't need anyone else to help me."

"Well, you're okay now. I'll help you. You can go into hibernation if you like…"

"No, that won't be necessary," Ryan says hastily. "I'll be able to manage now I've got someone to share my troubles with." He laughs feebly. "It's just plain old-fashioned loneliness." He shudders. He still thinks he can see things in the corners of his eyes. "I hope."

"Of course," says John. He is convinced; he isn't just trying to humour Ryan. John was always a hard man to convince, therefore Ryan is satisfied.

"Thank God for the emergency system, eh?" says John a trifle awkwardly.

"Amen to that," says Ryan.

He wishes the emergency system had awakened that other member of John's family, his young wife Janet. If someone had to be awake... He dismisses the thought and gets up. Being with John is almost like being alone, he thinks, for John is not the most voluble of men. Still...

Ryan gets up. John is efficiently checking the instruments.

"You'd better get off to your bed, old chap," says John. "I'll look after things here."

Gratefully Ryan goes to his cabin.

He lies in the dark, grateful for the drug which has driven away his visions, slightly nervous of the fact that John has joined him.

John probably knows about the affair he had with Janet, John's younger wife. Perhaps he doesn't care.

Then again, perhaps he does. John isn't a particularly vengeful man, but it would be just as well to be on guard.

Ryan remembers the other affair he'd had. The affair with Sarah Carson — old Carson's daughter...

Carson's toy business had been Ryan's closest competitor. Carson was chairman of Moonbeam Toys and had known Ryan for years. They had both started off with Saunders Toys in the old days and had been running pretty much neck and neck ever since. Their rivalry had been a friendly one and they often met for lunch or dinner before the habit of communal eating became unfashionable. When that happened they would still converse over the video.

Carson became a fanatical Patriot one day and, as far as Ryan was concerned, no longer worth speaking to. But by this time it was evident that the Patriots were by far the most powerful political group in the country and Ryan decided it would do him no harm to be Carson's friend. He even attended some meetings with Carson and other Patriots, registering himself as a member.

It was at one of these meetings that he met Sarah, a tall, beautiful girl of twenty-two, who did not seem convinced by her father's views.

Josephine was going through a particularly bad time, as were the two boys. All three of them spent two-thirds of the day under sedation and Ryan himself, though he sympathized with their problems, needed some form of relaxation.

The form of relaxation he chose was Sarah Carson. Or, rather, she chose him. The moment she saw him, she made a heavy play for him.

They took to meeting at an all-but-finished hotel. For a few pounds they could hire a whole suite. The bottom had dropped out of the hotel business by that time. Very few people trusted hotels or liked to leave home.

Sarah pulled Ryan out of his depression and gave him something to look forward to at night. She was passionate and she had stamina. Ryan took to sleeping during the day.

Ryan used the Patriot meetings as an excuse and continued, with Sarah and her father, to turn up at several.

Then Carson had an argument with the rest of his group. Carson had lately formed the opinion that the Earth, far from being a planet circling through space, was in fact a hollowed-out "bubble" in an infinity of rock. Instead of walking about on the outside of a sphere, we were walking about on the inside of one.

Carson went off to form his own group and soon had a healthy following who shared the Hollow Earth belief with him. Sarah continued to go with her father to his meetings (she knew he had a weak heart and also acted, sometimes, as his chauffeur).

Then Carson formed the impression that Ryan was an enemy. Sarah told Ryan this.

"It's the old story — if you're not with me, you're against me. He's getting a bit funny lately," she said. "I'm worried about his heart." She stroked Ryan's chest as they lay together in the hotel bed. "He's told me to stop seeing you, darling."

"Are you going to?"

"I think so."

"Just to humour him? He's eligible for a nut-house now, you know. Even the bloody Patriot fanatics think he's barmy."

"He's my old dad," she said. "I love him."

"You're hung up on him, if you ask me."

"Darling, I wouldn't have gone for you if I didn't have a hefty father complex, would I?"

Ryan felt anger. Stupid old fool, Carson! And now his daughter trying to put him down.

"That was clever," he said bitterly. "I didn't know you had such sharp knives in your arsenal."

"Come off it, darling. You brought it up. Anyway, I was only joking. You're not at all bad for your age."

"Thanks."

He got up, scowling.

He put a glass under the tap in the washbasin and filled it with water. He sipped the water gingerly and then threw it down the sink. "Christ, I'm sure they're putting something in the water, these days."

"Haven't you heard?" She stretched out in the bed. Her body was near-perfect. She seemed to be taunting him with it. "There's everything in the water — LSD, cyanide, stuff to rot your brain — you name it!"

He grunted. "Sure. I think it's probably just dead rats..." He got his shirt and began to put it on. "It's time we were going. It's nine o'clock. The curfew starts at ten."

"You don't want one last fuck? For old time's sake?"

"You mean it, then? About not seeing each other again?"

"I mean it, darling. Make no mistake. The condition he's in, it would kill him..."

"He'd be better off dead."

"That's as may be." She swung her long legs off the bed and began to dress. "Will you give me a lift home?"

"For old time's sake..."

The mixture of rage and depression was getting on top of him. He tried to shrug it off, but it got worse. With all his business worries — production falling, custom declining, debts unpaid — he didn't need this. He knew there was no chance of her changing her mind. She was a direct girl. Her pass at him had been direct. Now the brush-off was direct. He hadn't realized how much she had been bolstering his ego. It was ridiculous to rely on something like that. But he had been. His feelings now told him so.

They left the hotel. The sun was red in the sky. His car was in the street outside. The curfew seemed pretty pointless, for there was hardly anyone in Oxford Street at all.

Ryan stood by the car looking at the ruins of the burnt-out department stores, the gutted office blocks, mementos of the Winter Riots.

Sarah Carson looked out of the window. "Admiring the view?" she said. "You're a bit of a romantic on the quiet, aren't you?"

"I suppose I am," he said as he climbed into the car and started the engine. "Though I've always considered myself a realist."

"Just a selfish romantic."

"You're making it harder than you need to," he said as he took the car down the street.

"Sorry. I'm not much of a sentimentalist. You can't afford to be, these days."

"You want me to take you all the way back to Croydon?"

"You don't expect me to *walk* through the Antifem zone, do you?"

"Zone? Have they got control of a whole area now?"

"All but. They're trying to set up their own little state in Balham — allowing no women in at all. Any woman they catch, they kill. Lovely."

Ryan sniffed. "They might have the right bloody attitude."

"Don't get morbid, sweetie. Can we go around Balham?"

"It's the quickest route since the Brighton Road got blown to bits in Brixton."

"Try going around the other side, then."

"I'll see."

They drove for a while in silence.

London was bleak, blackened and broken.

"Ever thought of getting out?" Sarah said as he drove down Vauxhall Bridge Road, trying to avoid the potholes. He had begun to feel slightly sick. Partly her, he thought, and partly the damned agoraphobia.

"Where is there to go?" he said. "The rest of the world seems to be worse off than England."

"Sure."

"And you need money to live abroad," he said. "Since nobody recognizes anyone else's currency any more, what would I live on?"

"You think people are going to buy a lot of toys this Christmas?" She was looking at the completely flattened houses on the right.

His depression and his anger grew. He shrugged. He knew she was right.

"You and my old dad are in the wrong business," she said cheerfully. "At least he had the sense to go into politics. That's a bit more secure — for a while, at any rate."

"Maybe." He drove over the bridge. It shook as he crossed.

"A strong wind'll finish that," she said.

"Shut up, Sarah." He gripped the wheel hard.

"Oh, God. Try to finish this thing off gracefully, darling. I thought you were such a good businessman. Such a cunning bastard. Such a cool bird, working out all the odds. That's what you told me."

"No need to throw it in my face. I've got plans, my love, that you haven't an inkling of."

"Not the spaceship idea!" She laughed.

"How —?"

"You didn't tell me, darling. I went through your briefcase a couple of weeks ago. Are you really serious? You're going to take thirteen people to Siberia and steal that U.N. spaceship that's been standing idle for the last year?"

"It's ready to go."

"They're still bickering over who owns what bit of it and whose nationals have got a right to go in it. It'll never take off."

Ryan smiled secretly.

"You're nuttier than my old man, sweetie!"

Ryan scowled.

"Wait till I tell my friends," she said. "I'll be dining out on it for weeks."

"You'd better not tell anyone, my love." He spoke through his teeth. "I mean it."

"Come *on*, darling. We all have our illusions, but this is ridiculous. How would you fly one of those things?"

"It's fully automatic," he said. "It's the most sophisticated piece of machinery ever invented."

"And you think they're going to let you pinch it?"

"We're already in touch with the people at the station," he said. "They seem to agree we can do it."

"How are you in touch with them?"

"It's not hard, Sarah. Old-fashioned radio. For some time a few scientifically minded pragmatists like myself have been working towards a way of getting out of this mess, since it seems impossible to save the human race from sinking back to the Dark Ages..."

"You could have saved it once," Sarah said, turning to look directly at him. "If you hadn't been so bloody careful. So bloody selfish!"

"It wasn't as simple as that."

"Your generation and the generation before that could have done something. The seeds of all this ridiculous paranoia and xenophobia were there then. God — such a waste! This century could have been a century of Utopia. You and your mothers and fathers turned it into Hell."

"It might look like that..."

"Darling, it *was* like that."

He shrugged.

"And now you're getting out," she said. "Leaving the mess behind. Your talk of 'pragmatism' is so much bloody balls! You're as much an escaper as my poor daft old dad! Maybe more of one — and less pleasant, for that — because you might fucking succeed!"

They were driving through Stockwell. The sun was setting but no street lighting came on.

"You feel guilty because you're letting me down, don't you?" he said. "That's what all this display is about, isn't it?"

"No. You're a good fuck. But I never cared much for your character, darling."

"You'll have to go a long way to find a better one in these dark days." He tried to say it as a joke, but it was evident he believed it.

"Selfish and opinionated," she said. "Pragmatism. Ugh!"

"I'll drop you off here then, shall I?"

He stopped the car. It sank on its cushion of air.

She peered out into the darkness. "Where's 'here'?"

"Balham," he said.

"Don't play games, darling. Let's get this over with. You were taking me all the way to Croydon, remember."

"I'm a bit tired of your small-talk — darling."

"All right." She leaned back. "I'll button my lip, I promise. I'll say nothing until we get to Croydon and then I'll give you a sweet thank you."

But he had made his decision. It wasn't malice. It was self-preservation. It was for Josephine and the boys, and for the group. He wasn't enjoying what he was doing.

"Get out of the car, Sarah."

"You take me bloody home the way you said you would!"

"Out."

She looked into his eyes. "My God, Ryan…"

"Go on." He pushed her shoulder, leaned over her and opened the door. "Go on."

"Jesus Christ. All right." She picked up her handbag from the seat and got out of the car. "It's something of a classic situation. But a bit too classic really. The sex war's hotted up in this part of the world."

"That's your problem," he said.

"I'm not likely to get out of this alive, Ryan."

"That's your problem."

She took a deep breath. "I won't tell anyone about your stupid spaceship idea, if that's what's worrying you. Who'd believe me, anyway?"

"I've got a family and friends to worry about, Sarah. They believe me."

"You dirty shit." She walked off into the darkness.

They must have been waiting for her all the time because she screamed — a high-pitched, ugly scream — she cried out for him to help her. Her second scream was cut short.

Ryan closed the door of the car and locked it. He started the engine and switched on the headlights.

THE BLACK CORRIDOR

He saw her face in the lights. It stuck out above the black mass of Antifems in their monklike robes.

It was only her face.

Her body lay on the ground, still clasping her handbag.

Her head was on the end of a pole.

CHAPTER SEVENTEEN

Ryan lies in his bunk with his logbook and his stylus. He has been there for two days now. John comes in occasionally, but doesn't bother him, realizing that he does not want to be disturbed. He lets Ryan get his own food when he wants to and looks after the running of the ship. To make sure that Ryan rests, he has even turned off the console in Ryan's cabin.

Ryan spends most of his time with the logbook. He removed it from the desk originally to make sure that John didn't come across it.

He reads over the first entry he made when he brought it back to the cabin.

What I did to Sarah can be justified, of course, in that she could have ruined this project. I had to be sure nothing wrecked it. The fact that we are all safe and aboard is evidence that I took the right precautions — trusting no-one outside the group — making sure that everything was done with the utmost secrecy. We kept contact only with the Russian group — about the last outpost of rational humanity that we knew about.

Would I have done it in that way if she had not turned me down in such an unpleasant manner? I don't know. Considering the state of things at the time, I behaved no worse, no less humanely, than anyone else. You had to fight fire with fire. And if it — and certain other things — is on my

*conscience, at least it isn't on anyone else's conscience. The boys are clean.
So is Josephine. So are most of the others...*

He sighs as he reads the entry over. He shifts his body in the bunk.

"All right, old chap?"

John has come, as silently as ever, into the cabin. He looks a trifle tired himself.

"I'm fine." Ryan closes the book quickly. "Fine. Are you all right?"

"I'm coping very well. I'll let you know if anything crops up."

"Thanks."

John leaves. Ryan returns his attention to the log, turning the pages until he comes to a fresh one.

He continues writing:

*There is no doubt about it. I have blood on my hands. That's probably
the reason I've been having bad dreams. Any normal, halfway decent man
would. I took it on myself to do it, at least. I didn't involve anyone else.*

*When we hijacked the Albion transport, I had hoped there would be no
trouble. Neither would there have been, I think, if the crew had been all
English. Incredible! I always knew the Irish were excitable, but that stupid
fellow who tried to get the gun from me in mid-air deserved all he got. He
must have been Irish. There's no other explanation. I was never a racist,
but one has to admit that there are certain virtues the English have which
other races don't share. I suppose that is racialism of a sort. But not the
unhealthy sort. I was horrified when I heard that the foreigners in the camps
were being starved to death. I would have done something about it if I could.
But by that time it had gone too far. Maybe Sarah was right. Maybe I could
have stopped it if I hadn't been so selfish. I always considered myself to be
an enlightened man — a liberal man. I was known for it.*

He stops again, staring at the wall.

*The rot had set in before my day. H-bombs, nuclear radiation, chemical
poisoning, insufficient birth control, mismanaged economics, misguided
political theories. And then — panic.*

*And no room for error. Throw a spanner in the works of a society as
sophisticated and highly tuned as ours was and — that's it. Chaos.*

*They tried to bring simple answers to complicated problems. They looked
for messiahs when they should have been looking at the problems. Humanity's
old trouble. But this time humanity did for itself. Absolutely.*

It is odd, he thinks, *that I will never know how it all turned out. Just as well, of course, from the point of view of our kids. We left just in time. They were bombing each other to smithereens...*

Another few days, he writes, *and we wouldn't have made it. I timed it pretty well, all things considered.*

Ryan had led the party out to London Airport, where the big Albion transport was preparing to take off on its bombing mission over Dublin. They were all in military kit for Ryan was posing as a general with his staff.

They had driven straight out onto the runway and were up the steps and into the plane before anyone knew what had happened.

At gunpoint Ryan had told the pilot to take off.

Within a quarter of an hour they were heading for Russia...

It had been over the landing strip on the bleak Siberian Plain that the Irishman — he must have been an Irishman — had panicked. How an Irishman had managed to remain under cover without revealing his evident racial characteristics, Ryan would never know.

For two hours Ryan had sat in the co-pilot's seat with his Purdy automatic trained on the pilot while Henry and Masterson looked after the rest of the crew and John Ryan and Uncle Sidney stayed with the families.

Ryan was tired. He felt drained of energy. His body ached and the butt of the gun was slippery with the sweat from his hands. He felt filthy and his flesh was cold. As the Albion came down through the clouds he saw the huge spaceship standing on the launching field. It was surrounded by webs of gantries, like a caged bird of prey, like Prometheus bound.

His attention was on the ship when the Irish pilot leaped from his seat.

"You damned traitor! You disgusting renegade —" The pilot lunged for the gun, screaming at the top of his voice, his face writhing with his hatred and his insanity.

Ryan fell back, pressing the trigger. The Purdy muttered and a stream of tiny explosive bullets hit the pilot all over his chest and face and his bloody body collapsed on top of Ryan.

Pilotless, the big transport began to shake.

Ryan pushed the body off him and reached up to throw the lever that would put the plane automatically on Emergency Landing

Procedure. The plane's rockets fired and the transport juddered as its trajectory was arrested. It began to go down vertically on its rockets.

Ryan wiped the sweat from his lips and then retched. He had smeared the pilot's blood all over his mouth. He cleaned his face with his sleeve, watching as the plane neared the ground, screaming towards the overgrown airstrip to the north of the launching field.

John Ryan put his head into the cabin. "My God! What happened?"

"The pilot just went mad," Ryan said hoarsely. "You'd better check everyone's got their safety belts on, John. We're going to make a heavy landing."

The Albion was close to the ground now, its rockets burning the concrete strip. Ryan buckled his own safety belt.

Five feet above the ground the rockets cut out and the plane bellyflopped onto the concrete.

Shaken, Ryan got out of his seat and stumbled into the crew section. Alexander was crying and Tracy Masterson was screaming and Ida Henry was moaning, but the rest were very quiet.

"John," Ryan said. "Get the doors open and get everybody out of the plane as soon as possible, will you?" He still held the Purdy.

John Ryan nodded and Ryan went aft to where Masterson and Henry were covering the rest of the crew.

"What was all that about?" James Henry said suspiciously. "You trying to kill us all, Ryan?"

"The pilot lost his head. We had to make an emergency rocket-powered landing — vertical." Ryan looked over the rest of the crew — four boys and a woman of about thirty. They all looked scared. "Did you know your captain was Irish?" Ryan asked them. "And you were going to bomb Dublin? You can bet your life he was going to try to make a landing."

The crew stared at him incredulously.

"Well, it was true," Ryan said. "But don't worry. I've dealt with him."

The woman said, "You murdered him. Is that what you did?"

"Self-defense," said Ryan. "Self-defense isn't murder. All right, Fred — Henry — you go and help everybody get off this bloody plane."

The woman said, "He was no more Irish than I am. Anyway, what does it matter?"

"No wonder your people are losing," Ryan answered contemptuously.

When everyone was off the ship Ryan shot the crew. It was the only safe thing to do. While they were alive there was a chance that they would seize control of the Albion and do something foolish.

Tishchenko was a harried-looking man of about fifty. He gravely shook hands with Ryan and then guided him by the elbow across the barren concrete towards the control buildings. The wind was cold and moaned. Beyond the launching site, the plain stretched in all directions, featureless and green-grey. Ryan's people trudged behind them.

Tishchenko was the man whom Ryan had contacted originally. The contact had been made through Allard, who had been one of the people vainly trying to keep the U.N. together in the last days. Allard, an old schoolfriend of Ryan's, had been sent to a Patriot camp not long after he had put Ryan in touch with Tishchenko.

"It is a great pleasure," said Tishchenko as they entered the building that had been converted to living quarters. It was cold and gloomy. "And something of an achievement that, in the midst of all this insane xenophobia, a little international group of sane men and women can work together on a project as important as this one." He smiled. "And it's good to be able to look at a woman again, I can tell you."

Ryan was tired. He nodded, rubbing his eyes. One of the reasons the Russian group had been so eager to deal with his group was because of the number of women he could bring with him.

"You are weary?" Tishchenko said. "Come."

He led them up two flights of stairs and showed them their accommodation. Camp beds had been lined around the walls of three rooms. "It is about the best we can provide," Tishchenko apologized. "Amenities are few. Everything had to go to the ship." He went to the window and drew back the blankets that covered it. "There she is."

They gathered around the window and looked at the spacecraft. She towered into the sky.

"She has been ready to fly for two years." Tishchenko shook his head. "It has taken two years to provision her. The civil war here, and then the Chinese invasion, is what protected us. We were all but forgotten about..."

THE BLACK CORRIDOR

327

"Who else is here now?" Ryan asked. "Just Russians?"

Tishchenko smiled. "Just two Russians — myself and Lipche. A couple of Americans, a Chinese, two Italians, three Germans, a Frenchman. That's it."

Ryan drew a deep breath. He felt odd. The shock of the killings, he supposed.

"I'll be back in a few minutes to take you down to dinner," Tishchenko told him.

Ryan looked up. "What?"

"Dinner. We all eat together on the floor below."

"Oh, I see..."

"I couldn't," said Josephine Ryan. "I really couldn't..."

"We're not used to it, you see," said James Henry. "Our customs — well..."

Tishchenko looked puzzled and very slightly perturbed. "Well, if you'd like to arrange to bring the food up here, I suppose we can do that... Then perhaps we can meet after meals. You have been in the thick of things, of course. We have been isolated. We haven't really experienced..."

"Yes," said Ryan, "it has been very nasty. I'm sorry. Some of our social sicknesses have rather rubbed off on us. Give us a day or two to settle. We'll be all right then, I'm sure."

"Good," said Tishchenko.

Ryan watched him leave. He sensed a certain antipathy in the Russian's manner. He hoped there would not be trouble with him. Russians could not always be trusted. For one moment he wondered if they had been led into a complicated trap. Could this team of scientists just be after the women? Would they dispense with the men now that they had served their purpose?

Ryan pulled himself together. An irrational idea. He would have to watch himself more carefully. He had had no sleep for two nights. *Get some rest now*, he told himself, *and you'll be your old self in the morning.*

The thirteen English people and the eleven scientists toured the ship.

"It is all completely automatic," said Schonberg, one of the

Germans. He smiled and patted Alexander on the head. "A child could run it."

The English party, rested and more relaxed, was in better spirits. Even James Henry, who had been the most suspicious of all, seemed better.

"And your probes proved conclusively that there are two planets in the system capable of supporting human life?" he said to Boulez, the Frenchman.

The French scientist smiled. "One of them could be Earth. About the same amount of land and sea, very similar ecology. There was bound to be a planet like it somewhere — we were just lucky to discover one this early."

Buccella, one of the Italians, was taking a strong interest in pointing out certain features of the ship to Janet Ryan.

Typical Italian, thought Ryan.

He glanced at his brother John, who was listening carefully as Shan, the Chinese, tried to explain about the regeneration units. Shan's English was not very good.

Back in their own quarters, Ryan asked his brother: "Did you notice that Italian, Buccella, and Janet together?"

"What do you mean, 'together'?" John said with a grin.

Ryan shrugged. "It's your problem."

The preparations continued swiftly. News came in of massive nuclear bombardments taking place all over the globe. They took to working night and day, resting when they could no longer keep their eyes open. And at length the ship was ready.

Buccella, Shan and Boulez were going on the ship with the others. The rest were staying behind. Their job was to get the ship off the ground. They were taking over the duties of some fifty technicians.

Lift-off day arrived.

THE BLACK CORRIDOR

CHAPTER EIGHTEEN

Ryan scratches his nose with the tip of his stylus. He writes:

One could not afford to be sentimental in those days. Perhaps when we land on the new planet we can relax and indulge all those pleasant human vices. It would be nice to feel at peace again, the way one did as a child.

He shifts in his bunk and looks up.

"Good God, Janet. You're up!"

Janet Ryan smiles down at him. "We're all up. John thought it wisest."

"I suppose he knows what he's doing. It's not part of the original plan."

"John wants to see how it works out. Can I get you anything?"

He grins. "No thanks, love. I've got my Proditol to keep me cool. It seems to be working fine. I've been doing some pretty sober thinking since I decided to stay in bed for a bit."

"John says you'd got pretty obsessive — following ship routine to the point of your own breakdown…"

"I can see I was half crazy now. I'm very well — very relaxed."

"You'll soon be in control of things again." She smiles.

"I certainly will!"

SAILING TO UTOPIA

Janet leaves the cabin.

Ryan writes:

Janet has just been in to see me. Apparently brother John feels it's best for everybody to be up and about. I expect Josephine and the boys will be along soon. Janet looks as beautiful as ever. You couldn't really blame that Italian chap for going overboard for her... A sick joke that, I suppose. When I caught him with her in John's own cabin, I felt sick. The man was a complete stinker, playing around like that. He had to be dealt with. His friends had their eyes on the girls, too, that was plain. They were only waiting for a chance to get their hands on them while our backs were turned. I was a fool to trust a pack of foreigners. I know that now. It became evident that his friends were in on the plot with him, the way they took his part. They threatened the security of the whole mission with their utterly irrational intentions on the girls — and the boys, too, I shouldn't wonder. I suppose it was that they hadn't seen any women for so long. It went to their heads. They couldn't control themselves. In a way one can sympathize, of course. It showed just what a threat to the safety of the ship they were when they tried to steal my gun. I had to shoot Buccella then and his friends, when they wouldn't stop coming at me. We pushed the corpses through the airlock. Everybody agreed I had done the right thing.

He sighs. It has been hard, keeping control of everything for so long. Making unpleasant decisions...

Strange that Josephine and the boys haven't come in, yet. John is probably staging the wake-up procedure.

He closes the log and puts it and the stylus under his pillow. He leans back, looking forward to seeing his wife and children.

He dozes.

He sleeps.

He dreams.

Q: WHO ARE YOU KIDDING?
A: HAD A NOISE TROUBLE

He stands in the control room. He is sure he has forgotten something, some crucial operation. He checks the computer, but it is babbling nonsense. Puns and facetious remarks flow from it. He casts around for the source of the trouble, looks for a way to switch off the computer.

But it will not switch off. The life of the ship depends on the computer. But it is the ship or Ryan, as Ryan sees it. He starts to batter at the computer with a chair.

******YOURE KILLING ME**********HAHAHAHAHAHA*************

says the computer.

Ryan turns. Through the porthole he sees the dancers again, their faces pressed against the glass.

"You're in league with them," he tells the computer. "You're on their side."

*******I AM ON EVERYONES SIDE*************I AM A*****SCIENTIFIC INSTRUMENT******I AM UTTERLY PRAGMATIC**

says the computer.

"You're laughing at me now," Ryan says almost pathetically. "You're taking the piss out of me, aren't you?"

*******MY DUTY IS TO LOOK AFTER YOU ALL AND KEEP YOU SAFE AND SOUND"""""""REPEAT SAFE AND SOUND**********

"You cynical bugger."

He sees a sweet old lady shaking her head, a wry smile on her face. "Language," she says. "Language."

It is his mother. Her maiden name was Hope Dempsey. He christened the ship after her.

"You tell the computer to stop getting at me, Ma!" he begs.

"Naughty thing," says his mother. "You leave my little boy alone."

But the computer continues to mock him.

"You were never a sweet old lady anyway," says Ryan. She turns into the hag who haunts him and he screams.

Josephine stands over him. She is holding an empty ampoule of Proditol. "You'll feel better in a moment, darling," she says. "How are you now?"

"Better already," he says, smiling in relief. "You don't know how pleased I am to see you, Jo. Where are the boys?"

"They're not quite awake yet. You know it takes a bit of time." She sits on the edge of his bunk. "They'll be here soon. You should have woken us up earlier, you know. It's too much of a strain for one man — even you."

"I realize that now," he says.

She gives the old slightly nervous, slightly tender smile. "Take it easy," she says. "Let the Proditol do its stuff."

She catches sight of the red logbook sticking from under his pillow. "What's that, darling?"

"My logbook," he says. "A sort of private diary, really."

"If it's private…"

"I'd rather keep it that way until I've had a look through it. When I feel better."

"Of course."

"It's the only thing that kept me halfway sane," he explains.

"Of course."

With one hand supporting his head, Ryan lies in his bunk and writes:

Alexander and Rupert both look fit and well and everybody seems singularly cheerful. It seems as if we have all benefited from rest and with breaking ties with Earth. We feel free again. I can hear them bustling about in the ship. Laughter. A general mood of easy co-operation. What a change from the early days on the ship, when even Uncle Sidney seemed jealous of my command! Even sullen, suspicious old James Henry has an almost saintly manner! My morbid thoughts melt like snow in springtime. My obsession for Janet has disappeared — part of the same morbid mood, I suppose. James Henry's new attitude surprises me most. If it wasn't for the fact that everybody is in better spirits I'd suspect that he was once again harbouring plans to get rid of me and run the ship himself. It is amazing what a change of environment can do! John was wise to awaken everybody. Plainly, I had become too worried that the tensions would start up again. We're going to make a fine colony on New Earth. And thank God for Proditol. Those scientists certainly covered every angle. I've decided to put all morbid thoughts of the past out of my mind. I was a different person — perhaps a sick person — when I did what I did. To indulge in self-recrimination now is stupid and benefits nobody.

THE BLACK CORRIDOR

My breakdown was caused by the chaos that crept over society. It reflected the breakdown of that society. I could almost date its beginning for me — when our own air force (or, at least, what had been our own air force) dropped napalm and fragmentation bombs on London. My psyche, I suppose, reflected the environment.

But enough of that! I've made up my mind. No more morbid self-examination. No need for it now, anyway.

The days will pass more quickly now that everybody is up and about and so cheerful. We'll be landing on that planet before we realize it!

He signs the page, closes the book and tucks it under his pillow. He feels a little weak. Doubtless the effects of the drug. He sleeps and dreams that the ship has landed on the Isle of Skye and everyone is swimming in the sea. He watches them all swim out. James Henry, Janet Ryan, Josephine Ryan, Rupert Ryan, Sidney Ryan, Fred Masterson, Alexander Ryan, Ida and Felicity Henry, Tracy Masterson, Isabel Ryan, John Ryan. They are laughing and shouting. They all swim out into the sea.

A week passes.

Ryan spends less time writing in his logbook and more time sleeping. He feels confident that John and the others are running the ship well.

One night he is awakened by pangs of hunger and he realizes that nobody has thought to bring him any food. He frowns. An image of the Foreigners comes into his mind. He saw a camp only once, but it was enough. They were not being gassed or burned or shot — they were being systematically starved to death. The cheapest way. His stomach rumbles.

He gets up and leaves his cabin. He enters the storeroom and takes a meal pack from a bin. Chewing at the pack, he pads back to his cabin.

He has a slight headache — probably the effects of the Proditol. They have given him a dose every day for the past ten days or so. It will be time to finish the doses soon.

He sleeps.

CHAPTER NINETEEN

Ryan makes an entry in his log.

I have now been resting for two weeks and the difference is amazing. I have lost weight — I was too heavy anyway — and my brain has cleared. I have had insights into my own behaviour (amazing what a clever rationalizer I am!) and my body is relaxed. I will soon be ready to resume control of the ship.

Josephine enters. She is holding an ampoule of Proditol in her hand.

"Time for your shot, dear," she smiles.

"Hey! What are you trying to do to me?" He grins at her. "Fourteen days is the maximum period for that stuff. I don't need it any more."

Her smile fades. "One more shot can't do you any harm, dear, can it?"

He swings himself out of the bunk. "What's up?" he jokes. "Is there something you don't want me to know about?"

"Of course not!"

Ryan unfolds a suit from the pack in the cupboard. He lays it on the bed. "I'm going to take a shower," he says. "Then I'll go into the control room and see how everyone's getting along without me."

"You're not well enough yet, dear," says Josephine, her pink face anxious. "Please stay in bed a bit longer, even if you won't let me give you the Proditol."

"I'm fine." Ryan frowns. He feels a return of his old feelings of suspicion. Maybe he should have something more to keep him calm — yet if he has any more Proditol, he exceeds the dose and risks his life. "I'd like to stay in my bunk all the time." He smiles. "Honest, I would. But the suggested dosage period is over, Jo. I've got to get up sometime."

He leaves the cabin and takes his shower. He comes back in. Josephine has gone. She has laid out a fresh disposable suit on the bed. He puts it on.

He walks along the passage toward the main control room and he remembers that he has left his diary under his pillow. There is a chance that someone will give in to the temptation to read it. It would be better if no-one saw his comments. After all, some of them were pretty insane. Some of it was a bit like a prisoner of the Inquisition, confessing to anything that is suggested to him!

He smiles and returns to his cabin. He picks up the logbook and puts it in his locker, sealing the locker.

He still feels weak. He sits on the edge of the bunk for a moment.

For some time now he has been aware of a sound. Now it impinges on his consciousness. A high-pitched whine. He recognizes the noise. An emergency in the control room.

He gets up and runs out of his cabin, down the passage, into the main control room.

The computer is flashing a sign:

URGENT ATTENTION REQUIRED

urgent attention required.

James Henry is at the controls. He turns as Ryan enters. "Hello, Ryan. How are you now?"

"I'm fine. What's the emergency?"

"Nothing much. I'm coping with it."

"What is it, though?"

"A new circuit needed in the heat control unit in the hydroponics section. Cut out the emergency signal, would you?"

Ryan automatically does as Henry asks him.

Henry makes a few adjustments to the controls then turns to Ryan with a smile. "Glad to see you're okay again. I've been managing pretty well in your absence."

"That's great..." Ryan feels a touch of anger at Henry's slightly patronizing tone.

Ryan looks around the control room. Everything else seems to be as he left it at the time of his breakdown. "Where's everybody else?" he asks.

"Studying — resting — checking out various functions — standard ship routine."

"You seem to be working together very well," Ryan says.

"Better than before. We've got something in common now, after all."

Ryan feels a touch of panic. He doesn't know why. Is there something in Henry's tone? A sort of triumph? "What do you mean?"

Henry shrugs. "Our great mission."

"Of course," says Ryan. He sucks his lower lip. "Of course."

But what did James Henry really mean? Is it that they have got rid of him? Do they believe that he was the cause of their tension? Is that what Henry is insinuating?

Ryan feels his throat go dry. He feels his anger rising.

He controls himself. He isn't thinking clearly. He still needs to rest. Josephine was right.

"Well, keep up the good work, James," he says, turning to leave. "If there's anything I can do..."

"You could check the hibernation room some time," Henry says.

"What?" Ryan frowns.

"I said you could check the hydration loom — in hydroponics."

"Sure. Now?"

"Any time you feel like it."

"Okay. I'm still a bit shaky. I'll get back to my bunk, I think."

"I think you'd better."

"I'm perfectly all right now."

"Sure. But you could still do with some rest."

Ryan again controls his temper. "Yes. Well — I'll see you later."

"I'm here whenever you need me, captain."

Again the feeling that James Henry is mocking him, just as he used to, before it became intolerable…

He feels faint. No. Henry is right. He's still not properly recovered. He staggers back to his cabin.

He falls into his bunk.

He sleeps and he dreams.

He is in the control room again. James Henry stands there. James Henry is trying to supersede him. James Henry has always wanted to take over command of the group and of the spaceship. But James Henry is not stable enough to command. If he takes over from Ryan the whole safety of the ship becomes at risk. Ryan knows that there is only one thing to do to stop Henry's plotting against him.

He raises the Purdy automatic — the same gun that he used on the aircraft. He levels it at James Henry. He takes a deep breath and begins to squeeze the trigger.

The computer flashes:

URGENT ATTENTION REQUIRED

urgent attention required.

Henry turns. Ryan hides the gun behind his back. Henry signals to him to have a look at the computer. Ryan approaches it suspiciously.

******YOU ARE IN NO CONDITION TO COMMAND THIS******CRAFT''''''''''REPEAT YOU ARE IN NO CONDITION TO*******COMMAND THIS CRAFT''''''''''REPEAT YOU ARE IN NO******CONDITION TO COMMAND THIS CRAFT''''''''''TAKE ONE DOSE*1CC PRODITOL INSTANTLY AND REPEAT DOSE DAILY FOR***FOURTEEN DAYS''''''''''YOU ARE IN NO CONDITION TO******COMMAND THIS CRAFT''''''''''YOU ARE ENDANGERING THE****ENTIRE EXPEDITION IF YOU DO NOT FOLLOW THESE******* INSTRUCTIONS AT ONCE''''''''''REPEAT AT ONCE**

Ryan looks contemptuously at Henry. "You'll use anything to try to discredit me, won't you?"

Henry says calmly: "You are a sick man, Ryan. The computer's right. Why don't you…?"

Ryan raises the Purdy automatic and fires one bullet into Henry's skull. The man's head jerks back. He opens his mouth to say something.

Ryan fires again. James Henry falls.

Ryan scowls at the computer. "The next one's for you if you go on playing games with me, chum."

He turns the cut-out switch.

*******YOU ARE IN NO CONDITION TO COMMAND THIS******

URGENT ATTENTION REQUIRED

URGENT AT

Tension, tension everywhere

Nor any time to think

CRAFT"""""""""REPEAT YOU ARE IN NO CONDITION TO******************

There is d...

Q: WHAT IS THE EXACT NATURE OF THE CATASTROPHE?

Ryan wakes up, sweating. His suit is torn. The bunk is in a mess. He climbs off the bunk and stands on the floor, shaking. The Proditol just hasn't been enough. But he can't risk taking any more. He strips the bunk and disposes of the covers. He takes off his clothes and disposes of them.

A feeling of desperation engulfs him. Is he really incurable? Will he never shake the nightmares? He was sure he was better. And yet...

Suppose they haven't been giving him Proditol. Suppose they are deliberately poisoning him. No. Not his friends. Not his family. They couldn't be so cruel.

And yet hasn't he been cruel? Hasn't he done as much for expediency's sake?

He sobs, drawing in huge breaths.

Ryan falls on his bunk and weeps.

He weeps for a long while before he hears his brother John's voice.

"What's the matter, old chap?"

He looks up. John's face is sympathetic. But can he trust him?

"I'm still getting the nightmares, John. They're just as bad. Worse, if anything."

John spreads his hands helplessly. "You must try to rest. Take some sleeping pills. Try to sleep, for God's sake. There's nothing to worry about. The responsibility was too much for you. No one man should

have to bear such a burden. You're afraid that you might weaken —
but it is right to weaken sometimes. You expect too much of yourself,
old son."

"Yes." Ryan rubs at his face. "I've done my best, John. For all of
you."

"Of course."

"What?"

"Of course you have."

"People are never grateful."

"We're grateful, old chap."

"I'm a murderer, John. I murdered for your sake."

"You took too much on. It was self-defense."

"That's what I think, but…"

"Try to rest."

More tears fell from Ryan's eyes.

"I'll try, John."

The music has started again. The drums are beating. Ryan watches the
dancers circle about the control room. They are smiling fixed, insincere
smiles. James Henry dances with one of them. He has two holes in his
forehead.

Ryan wakes up.

The dream is so vivid that Ryan can hardly believe he did not shoot
James Henry. Obviously he didn't. John would have mentioned it. He
gets out of his bunk and pulls on a new suit of coveralls. He leaves the
cabin and goes to the control room.

It is empty, silent save for the muted noises of the instruments.
There is no sign of any sort of struggle.

Ryan smiles at his own stupidity and leaves the control room.

Only when he is back in his bunk does he realize that there should
have been someone on watch.

He frowns.

Things are relaxed. But should they be lax?

He feels he should go and check, but he is sleepy…

He awakes to find the smiling face of his wife Josephine bending over him.

"How are you?"

"Still rough," he says. "You were right. I should have stayed in my bunk longer."

"You'll be fit and well soon."

He nods, but he is not confident. She seems to understand this.

"Don't worry," she says softly. "Don't worry."

"I suspect everyone, Jo — even you. That's not healthy, is it?"

"Don't worry."

She goes toward the door. "Fred Masterson's thinking of dropping in later. Do you want to see him?"

"Old Fred? Sure."

Fred Masterson sits on the edge of Ryan's bunk.

"You're still feeling a bit under the weather, I hear," Fred says. "Still got the old persecution stuff, eh?"

Ryan nods. "I once heard someone say that if you had persecution feelings it usually meant you were being persecuted," he says. "Though not always from the source you suspect."

"That's a bit complicated for me." Fred laughs. "You know old Fred — simple-minded."

Ryan smiles slowly. He is pleased to see Fred.

"I cracked up once," Fred continues. "Do you remember? That awful business with Tracy?"

Ryan shakes his head. "No…"

"Come on — you remember. When I thought Tracy was having it off with James Henry. You must remember. When we'd only been on the ship for a month."

Ryan frowns. "No. I can't remember. Did you mention it?"

"Mention it! I should think I did! You helped me out of that one. It was you who suggested that Tracy would be better off if she was in hibernation."

"Oh, yes. Yes, I do remember. She was overwrought…"

"We all were. We decided that in order to ease the tension she should enter her container a bit earlier than scheduled."

THE BLACK CORRIDOR

"That's right. Of course…"

"Off course," says Masterson.

Ryan looks at him. "You're not… you're not having a joke with me are you, Fred?"

"Why should I do that?"

"I'm still getting a touch of the trouble I had earlier. Auditory hallucinations. It's nasty."

"I bet it is."

Ryan turns in the bunk. "I'm a bit tired now, Fred."

"I'll be off, then. See you. Keep smiling."

"See you," says Ryan.

When Masterson has gone, he frowns. He really doesn't remember much about Tracy and Masterson's problems with her.

It begins to dawn on him that he might not be as disturbed as he thinks. If he is in a bad way, might not some of the others be in equally poor shape? Maybe Fred Masterson has a few delusions of his own to contend with?

It is a likely explanation. He had better be careful. And he had better humour Fred next time he sees him.

He begins to worry.

If they are all in bad shape, then that could threaten the smooth running of the ship. It is up to him to get well soon, keep a careful eye on the others.

People under stress do odd things, after all. They get peculiar paranoid notions. Like James Henry's…

Next time he sees John, he'll suggest, reasonably, that James Henry have another spell of hibernation. For his own sake and the sake of the rest of them. It could be suggested quite subtly to James.

CHAPTER TWENTY

Ryan's dreams continue.

Once again he is in the control room. Most of his dreams take place in the control room now. He stares through the porthole at the void, at the dancers with their round black glasses, at his friends and family who stand behind the dancers. Sometimes he sees the old woman.

When occasionally he wakes — and it is not very often now — he realizes that he must be under heavy sedation.

He hears the music — the high-pitched music — and it makes his flesh crawl. Dimly he wonders what is happening to him, what his one-time friends, his treacherous family are doing to him. There is now no question in his mind that he is the victim of some complicated deception, that he has been victim to this deception perhaps even before the spaceship took off, certainly after it left Earth.

He does not know why they should be working against him, however; particularly since he is the chief engineer of their salvation.

He is too weak, too drugged to do more than speculate about their plans.

Was that why they were all originally put into hibernation?

He seems to remember something about that now. Was that why

THE BLACK CORRIDOR

he was so insistent that they should not be wakened until the end of the journey? Could be.

But he had to crack up temporarily. The ship's emergency system awakened John, who awakened the others, and now they are in control, they have him in their power.

It is even possible that they are not his family and friends at all, but could have brainwashed him into thinking they are. He remembers that old Patriot rally.

"They look like us, sound like us — in every respect they are human — but they are not human…"

God! It couldn't be true!

But what other explanation is there for the strange behaviour of the rest of the personnel on board the *Hope Dempsey*?

Ryan moves restlessly on the bunk. He has cracked up — no doubt about that. And the reason, too, is obvious — strain, overwork, too much responsibility. But there is no such explanation, when he thinks about it, for the behaviour of the others.

The others are mad.

Or they are…

… not human.

"No," he murmurs. "Not Josephine and the boys. I'd realize it, surely. Not Janet, warm little Janet. Not Uncle Sidney and John and Fred Masterson and the women. And James Henry half believed the Patriots. He couldn't be one. Unless he was so cunning he…"

He rolls on the bunk.

"No," he groans. "No."

John comes into the cabin. "What's the matter, old son? What's bothering you now?"

Ryan looks up at him, wanting to trust his brother, wanting to confide in him, but he can't.

"Betray me…" he mutters. "You've betrayed me, John."

"Come off it." John tries to laugh. "What would I want to betray you for? How could I betray you? We're on your side. Remember the old days? Us against the world? The only ones who could see the terrible state the world was in. The only ones who had a plan to deal with it. Remember your apartment? The last bastion of rationalism in an insane world…"

But John's tone seems to be mocking. Ryan can't be sure. His brother was always straightforward. Not like him to take that tone — unless this man is not his brother John.

"We were an élite, remember?" John smiles. "Sane, scientific approaches to our problems…"

"All right!"

"What did I say?"

"Nothing."

"I was only trying to help."

"I bet you were. You're not my bloody brother. My brother wouldn't… couldn't…"

"Of course I'm your brother. East Heath Road. Remember East Heath Road where we were born? There was actually a heath there in those days. Hampstead Heath. There used to be a fair there on Bank Holidays. You must remember that…"

"But do you?" Ryan looks directly at the man. "Or are you just very good at learning that sort of information? Eh?"

"Come on, old son…"

"Leave me alone, you bastard. Leave me alone or I'll —"

"You'll what?"

"Get out."

"You'll what?"

"Get out."

AFTER THE FAIR WE KIDDED HER…

Q: PLEASE DEFINE SPECIFIC SITUATION

AFTER THE PAIR WE KIDS WERE…

Q: PLEASE DEFINE SPECIFIC SITUATION

AFTER A PEAR WE DID THE…

Q: PLEASE DEFINE SPECIFIC SITUATION

AFTER A LAIR WE RID THE…

Q: PLEASE DEFINE SPECIFIC SITUATION

AFTER THE AFFAIR WE KILLED HER.

*******THANK YOU***

"NO!"

NO   O   NO   NO   NO
NO   N   NO   NO   NO
NO   O   NO   NO   NO
NO   N   NO   NO   NO
NO   O   NO   NO   NO
NON   NO   NO   NO
NO   O   NO   NO   NO
NO   N   NO   NO   NO
NO   O   NO   NO   NO
NO   N   NO   NO   NO
NO   O   NO   NONONONO   NONONONO

"NO!"

Ryan rises from his bunk. He is weak, he is trembling. He vomits. He vomits over the floor of his cabin.

I need help.

He staggers from the cabin into the main control room.

It is empty.

No-one on watch.

The computer is flashing its signal:

URGENT ATTENTION REQUIRED

URGENT ATTENTION REQUIRED

URGENT ATTENTION REQUIRED.

He is suspicious of the computer.

Warily he approaches it.

The computer says:

*******CONDITION OF OCCUPANTS OF CONTAINERS NOT******REPORTED'''''''''''REPEAT CONDITION OF OCCUPANTS OF*******CONTAINERS NOT REPORTED'''''''''''REPORT YOUR OWN*********CONDITION'''''''''''REPEAT REPORT YOUR OWN CONDITION******LOG NOT FILED*SIXTEEN DAYS'''''''''''CONDITION OF OCCUPANTS OF**

Ryan is astonished.

It is plain to him that whoever else is running the ship, they are not running it as efficiently as he had been doing.

He replies to the computer:

*******OCCUPANTS NO LONGER IN CONTAINERS'''''''''''''''MY*****OWN CONDITION IS POOR''''''''''''I HAVE BEEN OUT OF********OPERATION FOR SIXTEEN DAYS''''''''''''WILL FILE REPORTS AS*SOON AS POSSIBLE''''''''''''PLEASE ACKNOWLEDGE**

He waits for a second. The computer replies.

*******THANK YOU''''''''''''LOOKING FORWARD TO HEARING*****YOUR LOG ENTRIES''''''''''''HOWEVER YOU ARE WRONG ABOUT****OCCUPANTS OF CONTAINERS''''''''''''THEY ARE STILL IN*******CONTAINERS''''''''''''SORRY TO HEAR YOUR OWN CONDITION*****POOR''''''''''''SUGGEST YOU SWITCH ME TO FULLY AUTOMATIC***UNTIL YOUR CONDITION IMPROVES''''''''''''DID YOU TAKE******RECOMMENDED DOSE PRODITOL''''''''''''REPEAT DID YOU TAKE***RECOMMENDED DOSE PRODITOL*****************************

Ryan is staring incredulously at the second part of the message. Automatically he replies:

*******YES I TOOK RECOMMENDED DOSE PRODITOL*****************

and before the computer replies he leaves the main control room and runs through the dark corridors of the ship until he comes to the hibernation room. He touches the stud and nothing happens. The emergency locks must again be operating. Someone has switched them on.

John?

Or someone pretending to be John?

He runs back to the main control room and switches off the emergency locks, runs back down the corridors to the hibernation room. He opens the door and dashes in.

There they are. As they were when he last saw them. Sleeping in the peace of the hibernation fluid.

Has he imagined…?

No. Someone locked the hibernation room before. Someone locked it again. There is at least one other person aboard. Probably the person posing as John.

He knew there was something odd about him.

An alien aboard.

It is the only explanation.

He realizes that he does not remember seeing any of the people together. Doubtless the creature can change shape.

He shudders.

He couldn't have imagined the creature because the Proditol cleared his delusions, at least for a while.

He stares around the hibernation room and he sees the Purdy pistol hanging on the wall. It is odd that it should be here. But providential. He goes to the wall and removes the pistol. It is low on ammunition, but there is some.

He leaves the hibernation room and returns to main control. Hastily he reports on the occupants of the containers.

Then he goes to look for the alien.

Just as he has on his routine inspections, he paces the ship, gun in hand. He checks every cabin, every cabinet, every room.

He finds no-one.

He sits down at the desk below the blank TV screen in the main control room and he frowns.

He realizes that he has no idea of the characteristics the alien may possess. He could live outside the ship in some ship of his own — attached like a barnacle, perhaps covering the airlock of the *Hope Dempsey*.

The big TV screen above his head is used for scanning the hull. Now he puts it into operation. It scans every inch of the hull. Nothing.

Ryan realizes he has eaten virtually nothing for two weeks. That explains his weakness. The creature, he remembers now, never brought him food. He only brought him drugs — and tried, in the shape of his wife Josephine, to administer more. Perhaps it was not Proditol at all...

Ryan clutches the back of his neck, massaging it. He holds the gun firmly in his other hand.

There is a polite cough from behind him.

He wheels.

Fred Masterson stands there — or a creature that has assumed the shape of Fred Masterson.

Ryan covers it with his gun, but he does not shoot at once.

"Ryan," says Fred Masterson. "You're the only one I can trust. It's Tracy."

Ryan hears himself saying, "What about Tracy?"

"I've killed her. I didn't mean to. We were having an argument and — I must have stabbed her. She's dead. She was having an affair with James Henry."

"What do you intend to do, Fred?"

"I've already done it. But I need your help as commander. I can't hide it from you. I put her in her container. You could say you suggested it. You could tell everybody she needed rest so you suggested she hibernate a little earlier than scheduled."

Ryan screams at him. "You're lying! You're lying! What do you know about that?"

"Please help me," says Masterson. "Please."

Ryan fires the pistol, careful not to waste ammunition.

'Masterson' falls.

Ryan smiles. His headache blinds him for a moment. He rubs his eyes.

He goes to see if 'Masterson' is dead.

'Masterson' has vanished. The alien cannot be killed.

Again Ryan feels sick. He feels defeated. He feels impotent.

His headache is worse.

He looks up.

The dancers are there. The group is there. The old woman is there.

Ryan screams and runs out of the control room, down the passage, into his cabin. He seals the cabin door.

He collapses on his bunk.

CHAPTER TWENTY-ONE

Sitting in the sealed cabin, Ryan tries to think things out.

There is no alien aboard. I am merely hallucinating. That is the most obvious explanation.

But it does not explain everything.

It does not explain why the door to the hibernation room was locked.

It does not explain why the Proditol did not work.

He blinks. *Of course. I had no Proditol. I merely deceived myself into believing I had had it. That was why I invented John's sudden awakening.*

And I suppose I could have switched on the emergency locks without realizing it.

The strain was too much for me. Some mechanism in my own brain tried to stop me working so hard. It invented the "help" so that I could relax for a couple of weeks, not worry about running the ship.

Ryan grins with relief. The explanation fits.

And thus I felt guilty about the personnel in the containers. Because I had "abandoned" them. My talk of their betrayal of me was really my belief that I had betrayed them...

Ryan looks down at the gun still clutched in his hand.

He shudders and throws it to the floor.

Uncle Sidney stands near the door.

"You're doing fine, aren't you?" he says.

"Go away, Uncle Sidney. You are an illusion. You are all illusions. Your place is in your container. I'll wake you up when we reach the new planet." Ryan leans back in his bunk. "Go on. Off you go."

"You're a fool," Uncle Sidney says. "You've been deceiving yourself all along. Well before you got into this predicament. You were as paranoid as anyone else on Earth. You were just better at rationalizing your paranoia, that's all. You don't deserve to have escaped. None of us deserves it. You're clever. But you're all alone now."

"It's better than having you lot around all the time." Ryan grins. "Go on. Get out."

"It's true," says Josephine Ryan. "Uncle Sidney's right. We were humouring you towards the end, you know. It didn't seem to make much difference to me and the boys whether we went up in an H-bomb attack or up in a spaceship. In a way I think I'd have preferred the H-bomb. I wouldn't have had to listen to your self-righteous pronouncements day in and day out until you…"

"Until I what?"

"Until…"

"Go on. Say it!" Ryan laughs in her face. "Go on, Jo — say it!"

"Until I went into hibernation."

"Bloody shrinking violet!" Ryan sneers at her. "If I'd had a stronger woman…"

"You needed one," she says. "I'll admit that."

"Shut up."

"You got rid of the strong one, didn't you?" says Fred Masterson. "Did her in, eh?"

"Shut up!"

"Just like you did James Henry in," says Janet Ryan, "after you helped Fred cover up Tracy's death. Shot him in the control room with that gun, didn't you?"

"Shut up!"

"You got worse and worse," says John Ryan. "We tried to help you. We put you under sedation. We humoured you. But you had to do it, didn't you?"

THE BLACK CORRIDOR

"Do what? Tell me?"

"Put me in hibernation," says John Ryan.

Ryan laughs. "You, too?"

Ida and Felicity Henry laugh harshly. Ida's hands are folded over her swollen abdomen. "You lost all your friends, didn't you, Ryan?" says Felicity. "You sold yourself the alien story, didn't you, in the end? After being so scornful about it, you swallowed it when you could least afford to."

"Shut up. You'll go, too."

"You've put us all in hibernation," says James Henry. "But we can still talk to you. We'll be able to talk to you again, when we wake up."

Ryan laughs.

"What are you laughing about, Dad?" says Alexander Ryan.

"Let us in on it, Dad. Go on!" says Rupert Ryan.

Ryan stops laughing. He clears his throat.

"Out you go, boys," he says. "You don't want to be involved in this."

"But we are involved," says Alex. "It's not our fault our dad's a silly old fart."

"She turned you against me," says Ryan.

"Anyone can see you're a silly old fart, Dad," Rupert says reasonably.

"I did my best for you," Ryan says. "I gave you everything."

"Everything?" says Josephine. She sniffs.

"Things will be different on the new planet. I'll have time for you and the boys." His tone is placatory. "I had so much work to do. So many plans to make. I had to be so careful."

"And you were." Isabel Ryan winks at him. "Weren't you?"

"You'd better shut up, Isabel. I warned you before to keep your mouth shut about that…"

He glances at Janet. Janet bursts out laughing. "I slept with you because I was shit scared of you," she says.

"Shut up!"

"I was afraid you'd do it to me, too."

"Do what?" He dares her. "What?"

She looks at the floor. "Put me in hibernation," she murmurs.

Ryan sneers at them all. "Not one with guts, is there? You all wanted to get rid of me. You all thought you could plan behind my back. But you forgot —" he taps his head — "I've got brains — I'm rational — I worked it out scientifically — pragmatically... I used a system, didn't I? And I beat you *all*!"

"You didn't get me," says Tracy Masterson.

Ryan screams.

Chapter Twenty-Two

Ryan is better now.

The hallucinations have passed. Some dreams still disturb him, but not seriously.

He paces the spaceship. He paces down the central passageway to the main control cabin and there he checks the co-ordinates, the consumption indicators, the regeneration indicators and he checks all his figures, at length, with those of the ship's computer.

Everything is perfectly in order; exactly as it should be.

Near the ship's big central screen is a desk. Although activated the screen shows no picture, but it casts a greenish light onto the desk. Ryan sits down and depresses a stud on the small console on his desk. In a clear, level voice he makes his standard log entry.

"Day number one thousand, four hundred and ninety. Spaceship *Hope Dempsey* en route for Munich 15040. Speed holds steady at point nine of *c*. All systems functioning according to original expectations. No other variations. We are all comfortable.

"Signing off.

"Ryan, Commander."

Ryan now slides open a drawer and takes from it a large red book.

It is a new book, with only one page filled in. He enters the date and underlines it in red.

He writes:

Another day without much to report. I am a little depressed, but I felt worse yesterday and I think my spirits are improving. I am rather lonely and sometimes wish I could wake someone else up so that we could talk a little together. But that would be unwise. I persevere. I keep myself mentally active and physically fit. It's my duty.

All the horror and humiliation and wretchedness of Earth is far behind us. We shall be starting a new race, soon. And the world we'll build will be a cleaner world. A sane world. A world built according to knowledge and sanity — not fear and guilt.

Ryan finishes his entry and neatly puts his book away.

The computer is flashing at him.

He goes over to it and reads.

REPORT ON PERSONNEL IN CONTAINERS NOT SUPPLIED.

A stupid oversight. Ryan punches in the reports:

JOSEPHINE RYAN.	CONDITION STEADY
RUPERT RYAN.	CONDITION STEADY
ALEXANDER RYAN.	CONDITION STEADY
SIDNEY RYAN.	CONDITION STEADY
JOHN RYAN.	CONDITION STEADY
ISABEL RYAN.	CONDITION STEADY
JANET RYAN.	CONDITION STEADY
FRED MASTERSON.	CONDITION STEADY

He hesitates for a moment, then he continues:

TRACY MASTERSON.	CONDITION STEADY.
JAMES HENRY.	CONDITION STEADY
IDA HENRY.	CONDITION STEADY
FELICITY HENRY.	CONDITION STEADY******

****

****YOUR OWN CONDITION

suggests the computer.

Ryan shrugs.

CONDITION STEADY

he reports.

Ryan sleeps.

He is in the ballroom. It is dusk and long windows look out onto a darkening lawn.

Formally dressed couples slowly rotate in perfect time to the music, which is low and sombre. All the couples have round, very black glasses hiding their eyes. Their pale faces are almost invisible in the dim light...

Ryan awakes. He smiles, wondering what the dream can mean.

He gets up and stretches. For some reason he remembers old Owen Powell, the man he had to dismiss, the man who killed himself. That gave him a bad turn at the time. Still...

He dismisses the thought. No point in dwelling on the past when the future's so much more important.

He switches on the agriculture programme. Might just as well do a bit of homework until he can get back to sleep.

He falls asleep in front of the screen.

The spacecraft moves through the silence of the cosmos. It moves so slowly as to seem not to move at all.

It is a lonely little object.

                Space is infinite.
                It is dark.

Space is neutral.

                It is cold.

THE DISTANT SUNS

To the memory of Arthur "Atom" Thompson
who helped illuminate our days

C H A P T E R   O N E

She was ready at last.

Colonel Jerry Cornelius of the United Nations Space Command stared at her with a mixture of love and trepidation. Today was the day when he would, once and for all, bind his fortune with hers. They were soon to become inseparable.

It was New Year's Day, 2021, and the sun was just beginning to rise over the vast expanse of silicon-concrete that was the Gandhi Space Launching Site a few miles north of Gandhinagar, India's capital city.

She was ready for blast-off.

The product of sixty years of intense technical and scientific development, the product of a concerted effort by all the nations of the Earth, she was beautiful. And she was inevitable.

Her birth, thought Jerry Cornelius, had been inevitable since that day in October 1957 when the first artificial satellite, Sputnik I, was put into orbit by the Soviet Union. It had been inevitable since 1969 when the booted feet of the American astronauts first sank into the ancient dust of the moon. It had been inevitable since 1980 and the first landing on Mars. It had been inevitable since 1985 and the first Russo-American mission to Venus.

She was a spaceship.

She was a gigantic spaceship, over a thousand feet long, larger than the largest ocean liner ever built, and her mission was the most breathtaking ever planned by the space scientists. Her mission was not to explore the Moon, not to visit Mars, not even to land on Pluto, farthermost of the planets that circled the sun. She had been designed to explore *beyond* the Solar System. She was ready to travel the vast depths of interstellar space — to journey billions of miles through the black, cold, silent vacuum until she reached *another* sun where she would explore the planets of the star men had named Alpha Centauri.

Alpha Centauri. Jerry turned his handsome head towards the sky but saw nothing save for the comfortingly familiar pink-tinged clouds of Earth. Alpha Centauri. A star so distant that it took a beam of light traveling at the rate of 186,000 miles per second over four *years* to reach Earth. And yet, perhaps even more astonishing, Alpha Centauri was a near neighbour to Earth, compared with stars such as Rigel, whose light now visible to the people of Earth had left the parent sun fifty years before Columbus discovered America.

Even Jerry, familiar since boyhood with the basic facts of astronomy and space science, could hardly conceive the magnitude of the project he was about to embark upon as he stared through the observation window of the Control Complex at the ship which was due, in a few hours' time, to bear him into the unknown.

She was a fine ship, designed to meet every possible eventuality during the course of her voyage, to withstand enormous heat and terrible cold, to operate effectively in the atmospheres of alien planets and at different gravities. She had been tested and re-tested. She had been tempered in the fires of Venus and the frozen methane of Neptune, hardened in the deepest oceans of Jupiter where gravity was twenty times greater than Earth's. And now she was being prepared for blast-off.

Helicopters buzzed around the cage of scaffolding containing the ship. Tiny figures moved up and down her hull. Huge fueling bowsers pumped in the nourishment for the nuclear reactor that was her engine.

Cornelius stood in a gallery overlooking the main Launch Control Centre and he watched the scores of men and women as they hurried back and forth across the floor, checking their instruments, making last minute adjustments to their consoles. Everything was calm on the surface, but there was a building atmosphere of tension as the moment of take-off came closer.

"All this, just to send three people on a journey." The voice was soft, amused, and Jerry recognized it. He turned, smiling.

"Hello, Cathy," he said to his wife. "Did the medic check you out all right?"

Cathy Cornelius spread her arms wide. "I'm as fit as a flea and ready to roll. No hitches so far."

"No." Jerry's voice dropped slightly and he frowned out at the spaceship that was to carry them to the stars. More than his own life was at stake — more than the life of his wife and the other member of the crew — perhaps the peace of the world was at stake. Not for nothing had the ship been christened *The Hope of Man*.

The world was on the brink of disaster.

Even though the United Nations had been working in accord for the past fifteen years; even though every nation on Earth was represented at the Council; even though war had been unknown since the late twentieth century — still a crisis loomed. Already China was threatening to leave the United Nations and America was muttering about using a "limited amount of force" to contain certain rebellious elements who were beginning to raise their voices throughout the world. The issues were clear enough. Essentially, there were two — Food and Living Space. There were too many people in the world. The planet was rapidly becoming overcrowded in spite of the efforts of the United Nations to implement birth-control, sea-farming, and all the other remedies conceived during the twentieth century to cope with the problem. It was now clear that these remedies had not been implemented quickly enough. It was impossible adequately to feed and house a large percentage of the world population. And the hungry masses were preparing to war on the more fortunate, threatening to destroy the stability that had been so hard-won, planning to get what they needed by means of violence. And if this violence did at last explode, it would spread so rapidly that the entire globe would be plunged into a destructive war that might even mean the end of humanity.

There was only one solution that the United Nations could see.

If the world was overcrowded, then new planets must be found — new planets in new solar systems — which could support human life.

This was the responsibility which weighed so heavily upon the shoulders of Colonel Jerry Cornelius. It was his job to find those planets and find them as quickly as possible so that even larger passenger ships could be built to take colonists to the stars where they could begin a new life with plenty of space and plenty of natural resources on fresh, new planets. And that was why the ship had been called *The Hope of Man*.

It was a desperate remedy. It was a remedy that should not have been necessary. If more people had listened to the voices of the prophets and visionaries in the twentieth century, then the situation might have been avoided. If people had learned to trust the new scientific instruments and methods that had been invented and discovered in the twentieth century, if the politicians had been convinced that their use was of absolute importance, if the people had overcome their superstitions concerning scientific farming methods, birth-control, computers, mechanized factories, if the educationists had concentrated on familiarizing people with the ideas of science, then perhaps the stability of the world would not now be threatened, and *The Hope of Man* would be about to embark on a simple exploration voyage, not on a critical journey to find a last-minute solution to the mess in which the world now found itself.

Jerry sighed. He resented the burden that had been placed on him by his immediate ancestors. They had spent so much time bickering amongst themselves that there was now no time to set things straight.

He put his arms around his wife and kissed her on the forehead. He smiled at her. "It's up to us, Cathy. I hope to God we succeed."

A deep, cynical chuckle broke from the throat of the short, thickset man who now approached them. "Let 'em rot in their own mire, Jerry. In a few hours, we'll be out of it — out there where it's clean and cold and beautiful. I hate the whole damned human race. I'd be glad to see 'em blow themselves up!"

Jerry smiled and shook hands with Professor Marek, the other member of the team. "Your bark's worse than your bite, you old rogue. You're really as soft as butter underneath all that hair."

Wryly, Frank Marek ran his hand through his mop of black hair and tried to smooth down his unruly black beard. "Well, you've got to admit, Jerry, it'll be a relief to get away from all this talk of war and rumours of war."

"In a way," Jerry agreed, "but one still feels — well — *involved* in it. It *is* almost like deserting the sinking ship in one way…"

"Deserting a ship in mid-ocean to go and look for land," Cathy reminded him. "It's not quite the same thing, is it, Jerry?"

"I suppose not." The chronometer on his wrist suddenly bleeped. "Oh, oh — that's the signal. We've got the worst ordeal of all to face now. It's time to meet the gentlemen of the Press!"

They entered the elevator that would take them down to ground level and the Press Room.

Behind them the sun suddenly touched the metal of the spaceship and turned it a blinding gold.

CHAPTER TWO

"Could you explain a little about the ship's 'brain', Professor Marek?" asked the representative of the Swedish *Aftonbladet*. "Is it true that the ship itself can actually think?"

"The ship is what we call a 'sentient vehicle', yes," Frank Marek said as he sat with his two companions in the deep comfort of the couch, completely surrounded by reporters, cameramen and photographers. "This means that it behaves in many ways like an animal — reacting to danger instinctively. Essentially its brain is a highly sophisticated computer. This is linked to what you might call a 'central nervous system' — the computer is aware of every function of the ship and at the first sign of anything — however tiny — going wrong, it will act to correct the fault. In some ways you could say that we will be traveling in the belly of an immense space-going whale — but a whale that possesses certain superhuman faculties!"

"And what about the atomic engines?" asked the *Pravda* correspondent. "Are they completely safe?"

"As safe as any reactor can be," replied the professor.

"And this new method of covering the distance in a matter of weeks." The interviewer for the BBC directed his tiny ring-mike at

Jerry Cornelius. "I thought Einstein had proved that it was impossible for a spaceship to exceed the speed of light, Colonel Cornelius."

"Einstein's reasoning is not, as far as we know, at fault," Jerry smiled. "The ship employs a device known as a 'space-warp', rather difficult to explain without recourse to some pretty complicated mathematical theorems. Essentially it has the effect of bending space — of folding space in on itself like a blanket, so that instead of traveling from one edge of the blanket to another in a linear way, we pass through the folded blanket to reach our objective." Jerry laughed at the puzzled expressions on the newsmen's features. "I told you it was hard to grasp, but the idea has existed for nearly a hundred years — only recently have scientists been able to come up with a means of making that idea reality. Therefore, though it would take us five or six years — perhaps much more — to reach Alpha Centauri by the *linear* method, we take advantage of the fact that space is *curved* — we make a short-cut, in fact — and should get to the new star system in five or six *weeks*."

"But this Space Warp device..." said the interviewer for TV Peking "... it has not been fully tested, I gather?"

"It's been as well tested as possible," Cathy said, "but obviously it hasn't been possible to test it under the conditions in which it will be used."

"So there is something of a risk?" said the *Times of India* correspondent.

"I suppose so," Cathy answered. She brushed a stray lock of auburn hair from her face.

"Would you say there was considerable danger?" asked the reporter from *The New York Herald Tribune*.

"We'll be able to tell you the answer to that one when we get back, gentlemen." Jerry smiled and got up. "Now, if you don't mind, I think we're due for our final briefing. See you again in six months' time, I hope."

The three astronauts made their way through the babble of last minute questions out of the Press Room and down the bare, white corridor to the Briefing Room.

"Phew!" Jerry mopped his forehead. "What an ordeal!"

"I thought you answered the questions pretty well considering how difficult it is to explain to the layman just how a ship like *The Hope of Man* works," Cathy said.

"They're right about the Warp, though," Marek added. "Those newsmen really sense where the hitch is, don't they? If the Warp goes wrong — we're in real trouble!"

"We could be finished," Jerry agreed. "But worse still — it might mean the finish of the world."

In sober silence they entered the Briefing Room. Field Marshal Hira was waiting for them. A tall, elegant man, his expression was grim. "Well," he said, "this is it. I hope you haven't decided to change your minds."

Jerry grinned. "It would be all the same if we had, wouldn't it?"

"Well, I don't need to tell you how desperate things are getting. The crisis is building virtually day by day. Even our most optimistic people at the U.N. think the balloon will go up within the year. Unless you can find at least one new planet that will support human life and return to tell us about it, I don't think there's much of a chance of averting disaster. One piece of good news from you, and it will give everybody something else to think about — will channel all that anger into something positive. There's nothing else to say — except good luck."

Hira shook them all by their hands, patted their backs and escorted them into the next room where their kit had been laid out.

As they were helped into their spacesuits, Jerry glanced at the chronometer on the wall. Just over an hour to go before blast-off. There was a tight feeling in the pit of his stomach.

Cathy smiled at him encouragingly, but even that could not change the mood of introspection into which he had fallen. He had volunteered for this mission three years before — volunteered in a spirit of idealism, because he had wanted to do something useful for humanity. But only now were the full implications dawning on him. Cathy had volunteered in the same spirit — that was how he had met her, fallen in love with her and married her in the space of a few months — and he knew that she, too, was suddenly feeling the weight of her responsibility.

Frank Marek on the other hand was whistling cheerfully as the assistants zipped him up in his bulky kit. Jerry wished he had the professor's healthy cynicism about the venture. But it was too important to him.

Trained as a biophysicist, Cornelius had spent his early years involved in research into nutrition, but the work had become steadily less satisfying and he had entered the United Nations Air Service and trained as a pilot flying planes of emergency rations to out-of-the-way parts of the globe. But still the itching sense of unfulfillment — still the sense that he was not making the best use of himself, either for his own benefit or for society's. At last the opportunity had arisen for him to join the Space Service. He had served on various missions to the nearer planets, doing valuable research and feeling fairly satisfied. But it was not until the Alpha Centauri mission had come up that he had realized that this was what he had been waiting for all his adult life. The training had been intense, grueling, sometimes heartbreaking, but it had been worth it. Cathy, trained as an ethnologist, had had a similar background, had studied ecology, also had experience of expeditions to Mars, Ganymede and Neptune. Marek, however, was something of an unknown quantity. A brilliant physicist, he had headed the team which had made the first descent into Jupiter's Red Spot and had also been the first to unravel the secret of the Rings of Saturn. He appeared to have no nerves at all and certainly understood a great deal more about the detailed workings of the ship than the others — yet he did not seem particularly interested in the mission. Perhaps that was just the front he presented to the world, Jerry decided.

At last they were completely clad in their spacesuits and, carrying their heavy helmets under their arms, they made for the door that led out to the space field itself.

The space field gleamed in the rays of the sun and the ship, still in its cage of steel girders, seemed a very long way away. The fuel bowsers had gone, the helicopters had vanished, the technicians had left. Everything seemed very quiet and still as they began the long walk across the silicon-concrete expanse, watched by a score of TV cameras, watched by the dozens of team members at work in the Control Complex — watched by the world.

The world watched. The world waited.

Upon the success or failure of this mission depended the fate of all mankind.

Jerry turned back once to look at the Complex, turned his head to stare up at the looming bulk of *The Hope of Man*, and he drew a deep breath, put his arm around Cathy's shoulders, winked bravely at Frank Marek and grinned.

"Here we go," he said, "All aboard, ladies and gentlemen — next stop — the stars!"

CHAPTER THREE

The three astronauts lay back in their acceleration couches waiting tensely for the final countdown that would launch them into the void of interstellar space.

Jerry Cornelius turned his helmeted head and looked at his wife, reached out a bulky, gloved hand to touch her once on the arm and smile.

Around them were the banks of screens, switches, indicator boards, knobs, dials, buttons, levers and all the rest of the electronic and nucleonic paraphernalia needed to run the most complex machine ever devised by man. As if operated by ghostly, invisible hands, buttons depressed themselves, switches clicked on or off, lights flashed, as the ship's delicate cybernetic system tested itself out. Only the set of controls to the left of the great semi-circular bank seemed dead. These were the controls for the mysterious Warp Drive that would take the ship into something the scientists vaguely called "hyperspace" where the journey would take weeks rather than years.

Nothing was known of hyperspace and the Warp was the one unknown factor that threatened danger for the expedition.

Frank Marek's harsh tones now issued from his helmet microphone. "We're all set to go, gentlemen."

He was speaking to Central Control whose job was to push the button that would send the ship into space.

"Get ready for the final countdown," came the voice over the intercom. "Thirty seconds to go."

Jerry suddenly felt relaxed. There was no turning back now. The decisions were out of his hands — at least until they reached Alpha Centauri. The tension went out of him and he studied the indicators almost absent-mindedly.

"Twenty seconds to go."

Cathy Cornelius shifted in her seat.

"Ten seconds to go. Prepare for ten second countdown."

Jerry thought of Earth. He thought of the overcrowding, the threat of starvation and war and the ultimate catastrophe. He thought of the friends he might never see again. And yet the strange sense of calm still filled him.

"TEN."

The volume increased as the final countdown started. It seemed to echo through his skull.

"NINE."

Automatically — operated by the ship's cybernetic system — relays clicked on the control board.

"EIGHT."

A television screen — one of thirty ranged above the control panel — flashed red — MAIN ROCKETS — MAIN ROCKETS — MAIN ROCKETS...

"SEVEN."

Jerry saw Professor Frank Marek's hands grip the sides of the acceleration couch.

"SIX."

A muted murmuring came from the bowels of the ship and Jerry sensed a faint tremor.

"FIVE."

Another screen began to flash green. ALL SYSTEMS AT GO — ALL SYSTEMS AT GO — ALL SYSTEMS AT GO...

"FOUR."

The murmuring grew slightly louder. A spasm went through the spacecraft.

THE DISTANT SUNS

"THREE."

Jerry drew a deep breath.

"TWO."

A high-pitched whispering sound came and went.

"ONE."

This was it.

"ZERO!"

The ship shuddered. Jerry felt his body pressed back against the acceleration couch, saw the screen flashing SHIP IN FLIGHT, heard a babble of sound over the intercom, felt a roaring in his ears. He took deep, long breaths as the pressure increased and all the sounds merged into one painful buzzing noise and his vision blurred so that it was impossible to make out details on the control panel in front of him. The ship was traveling so rapidly now that he had the equivalent of six times Earth's gravity pushing against him. But he was used to this — he had traveled through space before. A sensation of nausea filled him. His limbs felt like jelly and every bone and muscle in his body ached horribly. He knew that the others were suffering the same sensations.

And at last, mercifully, he blacked out.

When he came to, a feeling of well-being, equal to the feelings of discomfort he had experienced so recently, filled him. He knew that they had left Earth's atmosphere and were already in outer space. The TV screens were filled with faces — the faces of the technicians they had left behind at Ground Control. He loosened the straps around his space-suited body and they drifted in the weightlessness of space. He unclipped his space helmet and it began to drift away from his head as if through water. He reached out and caught it and the action caused his own body to begin to rise automatically from the couch.

"Order to Ship," he said calmly. "Switch to half gravity."

"Order implemented," came the reply, and Jerry drifted to the floor once again, though he still felt very light, since only the equivalent of half Earth's gravity had been switched on.

He crossed to Cathy's acceleration couch. She was just opening her eyes. She smiled when she saw him and he saw her lips move, heard a muffled sound from within her helmet. He shook his head to indicate that he couldn't understand her. She smiled again and unclipped her helmet, drew it over her head and shook out her auburn hair. "That wasn't too bad," she said. "I've known worse take-offs."

"This ship's got all the latest luxuries," Jerry grinned. He turned to see Frank Marek straightening himself on his couch and yanking off his helmet.

"I'm glad that's over," Marek said. "I hate these damned romper suits. They make me feel like a two-year-old baby."

Jerry turned his attention to the screens showing their rate of acceleration, position in space, rate of fuel consumption and so forth. "Everything looks as if it's going perfectly to plan. Let's see what Earth looks like." He raised his voice slightly. "Order to Ship — show view of Earth on Screen Eight."

Screen Eight came alive and there was Earth, all blue, white and green. They were still close enough to the mother planet to make out details of her continents, main cloud formations and so on, but they were moving away rapidly. Now they were passing through the Moon's orbit, with their speed steadily increasing, nearly a hundred million miles from the Sun. A tiny distance in terms of the enormous gulfs that lay between the stars.

The Hope of Man, traveling at a tremendous velocity, well over a thousand feet long, a great, gleaming thing of toughened titanium steel, that had looked too gigantic on Earth, was a mere speck in space — a mote of dust drifting rather slowly through the cosmic vacuum — apparently of no significance at all.

And space itself was not friendly. Space did not offer the comforts of Earth. Space was vast and cold and impersonal, uncompromising. Space could not be controlled, could not be tamed, could not be consoled or harnessed.

The Hope of Man was now traveling at a rate of 52,568 miles per second and had not yet reached its maximum speed which was 180,000 miles per second — just short of the speed of light. Only in the all-but frictionless vacuum of space could it reach these speeds, and only in space could its crew survive these speeds.

Soon they had passed the orbit of Mars and were traveling through the asteroid belt. This belt, made up of millions of pieces of rock, some more than fifty miles in diameter, ringed the sun. Earlier pioneer ships had been destroyed by the asteroids crashing into them, but *The Hope of Man* had been equipped to deal with them. At the first sign of any danger the whole ship radiated a screen of pure atomic energy which had the effect of vaporizing even the largest asteroid.

Jerry Cornelius sat in his control seat watching the television screens. Every so often there would come a blinding flash of colour as an asteroid came too close to the ship and the energy screen destroyed it. It was beautiful to watch and Jerry was fascinated.

Everything was going as smoothly as had been anticipated. The ship held its course steadily, still accelerating, still among the familiar planets of the Solar System.

As the ship left the asteroid belt behind, Jerry decided to get his first real look at space.

"Order to Ship — activate main observation port." He swiveled his chair at right angles to the control board and looked at the large circular Control Room. The wall of the ship seemed to flicker with a thousand points of colour and then gradually turned opaque and then transparent and Jerry stared suddenly at the blackness of space.

There it was. Infinity. And flung like a handful of diamonds on black velvet were the stars, bright and sharp and shining, their light undimmed by any atmosphere.

The stars. Offering what?

Peace?

Jerry pursed his lips.

The chance for the human race to expand — to colonize other worlds — to spread through the galaxy?

Statistically it was likely that there were other planets circling those distant suns — some of which could support human life, which were sufficiently Earthlike to be habitable.

But even if they were habitable, there was a question that few had bothered to answer.

What if they were already inhabited? What if creatures completely alien to Man already lived on those planets? Then there would be little chance of colonizing them peaceably.

Would the old pattern of colonialism begin all over again except on a larger scale? Would the people of Earth spread out in their spaceships to conquer and exploit whole planets?

Would they solve mankind's present problems only to begin the cycle on a larger scale?

Jerry sighed. He prayed that if they did find inhabitable planets they would not already be occupied, that they would not give rise to the old diseases that had plagued Man for centuries — the diseases of greed, of violence, of tyranny, of hate…

Catherine entered the Control Room and handed him a pressurized beaker containing vitamin concentrate. "You looked depressed, Jerry. What's up? You've seen the stars before."

He nodded. "I was just wondering what we'd find out there, Cathy. You never know. There could be people like us on the worlds we discover. Scientists say it's possible."

"In the universe everything's possible, darling," she smiled. "I don't think it's likely that we'll meet human beings out there, however."

Frank Marek entered the room. "I hope like Hell we don't! What a horrible suggestion. I've just got away from one lot. No, no — we'll be lucky if we find a planet that's even barely capable of supporting human life. We don't even know if Alpha Centauri has *any* planets yet!"

They were now passing through the orbit of Saturn and they could see the great planet clearly, as if below them — though essentially there was no such thing as "up" or "down" in space. The huge, purple-green sphere, surrounded by its rings of bright orange, yellow and blue, hung in the blackness, looking as much like a child's bauble as anything.

Frank Marek stared at the planet reminiscently as it disappeared behind them. "There's a funny world," he said. "I nearly died there." He shrugged. "I went on three expeditions to Saturn, you know."

Jerry and Cathy nodded. Marek had acted heroically on all three expeditions, according to those who had been with him. Thirty men had lost their lives attempting to explore Saturn, four spaceships had been lost for good.

Now Saturn was a diminishing dot in the left-hand corner of the observation porthole.

Jerry wondered how many would lose their lives in the exploration of the planets of Alpha Centauri. Of course the intention was not to land on the planets, but merely to check if any seemed capable of supporting human life, but there was still a possibility they might not

THE DISTANT SUNS

even reach the star that was their destination. Jerry glanced at the controls that lay to the right of the main control board, the controls that had not yet been activated. The controls to the Space Warp. The time was coming close when they would be activating them.

CHAPTER FOUR

Jerry joined Cathy in their cabin. It was Frank Marek's turn to take first watch and Jerry was grateful. He needed the sleep, he needed the comfort of Cathy beside him, he needed the sense of peace that he always experienced when Cathy was in his arms.

They were nine hours out from Earth and accelerating gradually all the time.

"Pleasant dreams," Jerry said to his wife. Her eyes were already beginning to droop. "Order to Ship — cabin light out please." The light dimmed. "When we wake up, Cathy, we'll have left the Solar System behind. An historic moment — the first people to go beyond the orbit of Pluto and we'll be sleeping through it!"

"Right now I'd rather sleep than witness *any* historic moment," Cathy murmured.

The bed modeled itself to their figures automatically and they were asleep at the same instant.

They were shocked awake by a bellow from the intercom. "Hey! Are you two lazy good for nothings still asleep? It's half-an-hour past my watch!"

Jerry grinned. At first, in his daze, he had thought the ship itself was talking to him.

THE DISTANT SUNS

But it was only Frank Marek.

"Okay, Frank, don't worry. We're on our way to relieve you."

Jerry sprang out of bed and went to the smooth wall of the cabin, passed his hand across a certain area and saw a shallow tray emerge from what had appeared to be a completely featureless expanse of metal. In the tray were a number of small dishes containing tablets of various colours. He took a magenta tablet and popped it into his mouth. He felt instantly more wakeful. The pill had contained his breakfast and his morning pick-me-up rolled into one. He moved along the wall and passed his hand over it again. This time a section of the wall moved downwards revealing a fully equipped shower. He stepped into the shower and washed quickly, stepping aside for Catherine to enter. Another motion of the hand and a tiny package dropped from the wall into his open palm. The package contained a fresh set of clothes, including the cobalt blue uniform of the United Nations Space Command.

"I'll see you in the Control Room," he told Catherine, waving to her. "Order to Ship — open cabin door, please." The door slid silently upwards and he passed through, walking down the long, steel corridor towards the nose of the ship where the main Control Room was situated.

He entered to find Frank Marek leaning on the globular star-chart that occupied the centre of the room. This chart was actually a completely accurate three-dimensional model of the region of space through which they would be passing in order to reach Alpha Centauri.

Marek nodded to Jerry wearily. "Sorry to shout like that, but I'm bushed, Jerry. Must get some sleep. Beginning to feel dizzy."

"Of course, Frank. Sorry I overslept. How are we doing?"

"We're on perfect course. Five hours out from Pluto. It's going to be your job to put her into Warp, Jerry. Think you can do it all right?"

"I've been trained for it, Frank." Jerry patted the older man's shoulder. "Don't worry. You'll wake up if anything goes wrong!"

"But I might be dead…" Frank tried to grin, but he was evidently worried about leaving the job of warping in Jerry's hands. "Maybe I should take a pill that will keep me awake…"

"It's better to sleep normally, Frank. You might be needed later — and it would be best if you're properly rested."

"You're right. See you, Jerry."

Frank Marek disappeared from the Control Room, half-staggering with tiredness. Jerry watched him go and then checked his chronometer against the chronometer above his head.

Another hour and he would have to activate the Space Warp.

Catherine joined him and they went through all the routines they had learned and re-learned on Earth. The ship was about to enter an area about which almost nothing was known — for "hyperspace" was merely a name to describe that limbo *between* Time and Space, that strange area that had no right to exist at all, that some called the Fifth Dimension.

The hour passed quickly. Too quickly for Jerry and his wife as they made preparations.

At last it was time to activate the Warp controls. Jerry switched on and watched the control board come alive with flashing lights, simulators and indicators. His instructions were to phase gradually into Warp Drive, but once the drive had been set at GO, there was no turning back. The ship's programming would do the rest, would see them into hyperspace and, with luck, out the other side, relatively close to Alpha Centauri.

But the Warp had never had a true test. They might disappear forever into that limbo. A new, horrifying death might await them. A death that their minds simply could not conceive — perhaps an eternity of different deaths in that timeless, spaceless place!

Jerry took a deep breath and glanced at Catherine as he began to punch the instructions out on the control panel.

He knew that this might be the last time he would ever look at his beautiful young wife again.

And he was suddenly filled with a sense of sheer terror.

They were about to leap blindly into the unknown — go where no living creature had been before.

Quelling the terror as best he could, Jerry pressed the final button. Now the programme was locked into the computer.

There was no turning back.

CHAPTER FIVE

There was no turning back.

Jerry poised himself over the Space Warp controls, his face bathed in the multicoloured lights that flickered from the console. Beside him, Catherine checked the normal operations of the ship, reading out co-ordinates in a rapid monotone.

They were in the gulf between the stars — in the empty, black, aching void of interstellar space, with the Solar System behind them and Alpha Centauri four light years ahead of them.

But it would not take them four years to reach the distant star, Sol's closest neighbour. It would take them perhaps four weeks — perhaps eternity.

Now the cybernetic ship itself began to speak. "Prepare for Warp Phase One."

Jerry's index finger rested on the appropriate button.

"Six seconds to go," sang the ship. "Five — four — three — two — one — zero."

Zero.

Jerry pressed the button and leaned back in his control couch, his eyes on the screens before him.

Nothing happened.

He glanced in puzzlement at Catherine.

Catherine had turned a deep, lustrous green; her eyes were mauve, staring in astonishment. The screens which had showed the blackness of space now swam with hazy colours. Strange shapes seemed to form and re-form on the screens. A high-pitched whine filled the ship.

Jerry felt nausea threatening to overwhelm him. The ship shuddered and groaned and Jerry's teeth ached horribly.

From somewhere a rasping voice said: "Prepare for Warp Phase Two. Five — four —"

It was the ship.

Desperately Jerry forced himself to concentrate on the control board before him. His finger found the second button.

"— three — two — one — zero."

He stabbed the button down.

His ears roared as if he was trapped in a gigantic waterfall. Bile rose in his throat and his eyes watered. A steady, rhythmic banging noise began to sound. At first he thought it was the ship's engines. Then he realized it was his own heart.

Catherine was shouting something. She was now bathed in a brilliant scarlet aura.

"*Jerry — Jerry* — look at the screens!"

He blinked and peered blearily at the screens. They were warping into the unknown regions of hyperspace. They were the first human beings to witness it. And it had a frightening beauty.

Space seemed to peel back on itself as great, blossoming splashes of colour poured through as if from the broken sides of a vat, merging with the darkness and making it iridescent so that sections shone like brass and others like silver, gold or rubies, the whole thing changing, changing constantly, erupting, flickering, vanishing, reappearing.

And the interior of the ship seemed to be subject to the same chaos that Jerry Cornelius witnessed outside it. The whole ship seemed filled with bright whiteness, the whole hull seemed to become transparent and against the darkness of the cosmos the spheres which began to roll by, flashing past like shoals of multicoloured billiard balls, were unrecognizable as any heavenly bodies Jerry had ever seen. Not asteroids by any means, not planets — they were too solid in colour and general appearance; they shone, but not with the glitter of reflected sunlight. And they passed swiftly by in hordes.

Moved by the beauty, astonished by the unexpected sight, Jerry couldn't voice the questions which flooded into his mind.

In the faint light that suddenly filled the ship, Catherine's silhouette could be seen in constant motion. The whining had ceased. The spheres now appeared on the screen and began to jump and progress more slowly. The picture jerked and one sphere, smoky blue in colour, began to grow until the whole screen itself glowed blue. Then it seemed to burst and the ship flashed towards the fragments, then through them, and saw —

"A star!" Jerry cried. "We'll burn up!"

The ship seemed to plunge into the very heart of the star, into the mass of waving flames. The flames — the word hardly described the curling, writhing wonder of those shooting sheets of fire. The control deck was not noticeably warmer, but Jerry felt his temperature rise just from the act of looking.

A roar of enigmatic laughter seemed to fill the ship, then fade, and then everything was deathly quiet. There was no sound at all.

Jerry turned his head again slowly, searching for Catherine.

She sat on an acceleration couch, her lips moving silently, her eyes staring, and it seemed to him then that she saw and heard something altogether different from the sensations that filled him.

Painfully he reached out to touch her arm. But she did not notice.

He spoke her name.

"C - a - t - h - e - r - i - n - e......."

The sound was a muffled echo, but she did not hear it.

"C - a - t - h - e - r - i - n - e......."

Again no reply.

Then everything went absolutely black and Jerry felt he was alone — alone in the blackness of space — completely and utterly alone — drifting, drifting, drifting…

Somehow he had become separated from the ship.

He was drifting in arbitrary configurations. He could not see. He could not hear. He could not speak. He could not feel. He could not smell. Even his sense of identity began to fade.

He made one last desperate effort to cry out. He uttered a soundless scream and emerald-green light blinded his eyes. He twisted convulsively and he was in the Control Room again.

Everything was normal save for the peculiar swirling colours on the screen. He glanced at the chronometer and then at Catherine, who was leaning against her acceleration couch panting heavily.

"How long...?" he began. It seemed to have lasted for eternity.

Yet the chronometer showed that barely three seconds had passed since he had thrown the Warp into Phase Two.

There was still a third phase — the final phase.

Cathy's eyes were wide with horror. "We can't make it Jerry. We can't."

He gritted his teeth. "There's no going back, Catherine. We've got to put her into Phase Three — and soon."

"But it's — it's — so terrifying!"

"We expected abnormal sensations. After all, we're entering a plane of existence that is completely alien to the universe we know."

"It will destroy us."

"We must take the risk, darling. We must."

He reached out and grasped her hand as the ship began to speak again.

"Prepare for Warp Phase Three," said the ship.

"No!" Cathy cried.

But Jerry detached his hand from hers and returned his attention to the control panel, every fibre of his being fighting the panic that threatened to overcome him, every element of his consciousness resisting the black madness that gnawed at the edges of his brain.

"Five — four — three — two — one — zero."

Jerry's shaking hand depressed the stud.

Something like an electric shock ran up his arm. The instruments danced crazily. The ship seemed to spin end over end. He felt as if he had left his body. A thousand fragmenting images of Catherine flickered before him.

A strange wailing sound filled his ears.

Around him the air was jeweled and faceted, glistening and alive with myriad colours, flashing, scintillating, swirling and beautiful.

THE DISTANT SUNS

And then a great sense of tranquility filled him — a feeling of peace as intense as the feeling of terror he had so recently experienced. He seemed to drift with the ship as if in a boat on a gentle stream in summer. He leaned back, his body relaxing.

He felt a cool hand on his forehead and looked up through sweet, golden light at Cathy. She was smiling down at him.

"Cathy…?"

"Jerry. Can you hear the music?"

He shook his head.

"It's wonderful — unearthly — are you sure you can't hear it."

He kissed her hand and smiled quietly. "No. I wish I could. Evidently, everybody experiences different sensations in the Warp…"

"It's a mental reaction, isn't it? Something happens to your mind?"

"That's my guess — the sensations are so alien to us that our senses attempt to translate them into ordinary experiences and fail completely. Even now, we are not undergoing any sort of normal experience. We…"

The ship screamed.

The golden light became shot through with veins of ghastly green. The ship began to bump as if it passed over a deeply rutted road. There was a sound like the deep-throated bellow of a great brass gong.

The Control Room seemed filled with terrifying beasts — like the beasts of Earth's ancient mythologies. They roared and croaked and cackled, beating their reptilian wings and baring their ferocious fangs. Jerry hugged Catherine close. She was shuddering in his arms, her face pressed against his chest.

"Oh, Jerry — when will it stop? When will it stop?"

The ship swayed and shook so that everything in it seemed to jangle and rattle. Waves of intense cold and blistering heat came and went.

And then it was over.

The Control Room looked slightly shaken about, but was otherwise normal. Catherine seemed a little disheveled, but none the worse for her ordeal. On the screens the colours had turned to soft, swirling pastel shades and the instruments showed that they were now passing through hyperspace at a subjective speed of 175,000 miles per second.

"My God!" Frank Marek came in. "I thought I was trapped in a nightmare. That was the Warp, was it? I don't want to do that too often."

He went to the main control panel and began checking the instruments.

"What's the matter, Frank?" Jerry noticed a frown on the older man's face.

"Sluggish responses in some places. You know how delicate the cybernetic system is — well, I'm worried. Just a minute. Order to Ship — please report any irregular functions in ship."

"Irregular function in engine section six. New cadmium rod req... req... req... requir... quired. Irregular function in cybersystem involving short-circuiting of synapse co-ordinates in — in — in..."

Frank looked significantly at the other two. "You know what that means, don't you? Something's gone wrong with the ship's brain. And we rely on that brain for all the main running of the ship. Jerry — Catherine — we're lost in hyperspace — lost in a crippled ship."

CHAPTER SIX

For a moment an expression of pure panic crossed Frank Marek's face and an hysterical note crept into his voice. "Without the ship's brain functioning properly, we could be marooned in space until we die!"

"Calm down, Frank," said Jerry Cornelius. "Every conceivable emergency is allowed for. You know that."

"But this is an *inconceivable* emergency, you fool!" Marek shouted. "The stresses of entering hyperspace have thrown the cybernetic system completely out. That's clear enough, isn't it?"

Jerry gripped the older man's shoulder. "The first thing we must do is to switch the ship to manual control. It's possible to navigate and land her without using the cybernetic system at all. We'll just have to work everything out on paper, that's all. It *can* be done, Frank."

"I know — it can be done in *normal* space. But this isn't normal space, Jerry." Catherine spoke quietly. "Frank might have a point, you know."

Hearing this, Marek seemed to calm down. "Can't you see, Jerry? We depend on the ship to tell us when to phase into hyperspace and when to phase out. How can we rely on its information even if it is capable of giving us the information in the first place?"

Jerry nodded. "Fair enough. But before we start to speculate, let's just make a few proper tests. It will take time. We'll have to get down to it right away. First we must cut out the main brain and control the ship ourselves. This means keeping a constant patrol. While one of us patrols the ship, checking for any signs of malfunctioning, the others must inspect the brain itself and see if we can put the damage right."

Marek rubbed his eyes with his stumpy hands. "I'm sorry, Jerry. You're quite right. That — that nightmare as we phased into hyperspace — it threw me into a panic. I acted like a fool."

Catherine put her arm around Marek's shoulders. "We were all badly shaken up by that. Come on — let's get busy."

"I'll make a tour of the ship," Jerry said. "You're more expert on cybernetics than me anyway, Frank."

He left them isolating the main brain of the ship and cutting out its power. He climbed into his spacesuit and began the slow journey down the length of the ship, down the metal corridors of the crew quarters until he reached the big steel hatch. It bore a red, stenciled sign:

HYDROPONICS SECTION. PLEASE PERFORM ALL DECONTAMINATION FUNCTIONS BEFORE AND AFTER LEAVING THIS AREA.

Jerry spun the manual controls of the hatch. At length it swung open and he entered the decontamination cubicle, closing the hatch behind him. He switched down the little lever that would start the decontamination process — cleaning his spacesuit of any organic material that was likely to upset the balance carefully preserved in the section he was about to enter.

The light in front of him blinked red and then changed to green, indicating that it was safe to proceed. He spun the controls of the second hatch and passed into the soft green light of the Hydroponics Section. This section was effectively a large greenhouse in which the ship's vegetable supplies were grown. But, in fact, the section did more than that. It actually replenished the oxygen supply of the ship by natural methods. Tall, fernlike plants, especially mutated for use on board spaceships, grew in special tanks of chemicals which supplied them with a carefully balanced diet of nutrients. It was like walking through some strange, artificial jungle — a jungle created by Science.

Jerry moved from tank to tank checking the instruments attached to the tanks, checking that everything was functioning as it should.

At last he reached the end of the Hydroponics Section and was satisfied that the journey into hyperspace had not adversely affected their food and oxygen supply. That was something!

At the next hatch he underwent the same decontamination procedures and passed through into another short corridor before he reached another hatch. This one was marked simply:

ENGINES

BEWARE OF HARMFUL RADIATION

ALL PERSONNEL MUST DON THE APPROPRIATE PROTECTIVE CLOTHING BEFORE ENTERING THIS SECTION. ALL OTHER NORMAL PRECAUTIONS MUST BE TAKEN.

There was a small locker near the door. Jerry opened it and drew a thin, membraneous covering over his spacesuit. This was a specially treated protective shield that would resist normal doses of nuclear radiation. Next Jerry checked the instruments set into the door. The radiation count was not high enough to be especially dangerous. He unlocked the door and swung it outwards, climbing clumsily through in his two layers of protective clothing, and closing it behind him.

The engines were all housed in grey, featureless boxes. According to the instruments, these, too, were functioning reasonably well, though not at the power Jerry might have expected.

Jerry passed through the dimly lit engine chambers until he came to the atomic pile itself. Although utilizing all modern miniaturization techniques, it was still a considerable size, towering over him, its top disappearing in the gloom of the ship's roof.

Jerry found trouble at last.

An emergency indicator was flashing wildly and now it became plain as to why the engines were not working at full power. The burnt-out cadmium rod, used to damp the reactor, had not been replaced. An emergency dampening procedure had taken place automatically and was attempting to hold the reaction down. Jerry had arrived just in time.

Swiftly, he switched over to manual control and began manipulating the handling tongs, removing the defective rod and replacing it with a new one. Normally the ship would have done this, but the damage to its cybernetic system had come just as it had been about to put things right. Jerry continued his tour of inspection through the various sections of the ship. Sometimes he paused to make a close check, but nothing else seemed seriously wrong. He could not speak for the internal workings of the ship, for only the instruments on the board in the Control Room could show what, if anything, was wrong. He turned and began to make his way back to the forward section of the ship.

CHAPTER SEVEN

The days passed swiftly on board *The Hope of Man* as the three people pored over their equations — equations that would have taken the ship itself only seconds to do. Meanwhile, Marek worked on the brain, testing all its functions over and over again until he was satisfied that it was working properly again and could begin the long series of tests, leading up to the moment when it could begin working at full capacity once more.

It was only when the cybernetic system was functioning properly that Marek relaxed. His face was set in lines of worry and concentration and there were deep rings under his eyes.

"I think she's okay," he said at last. "Two days to go before we're due to Warp into normal space. It was a close thing."

Jerry breathed a sigh of relief. "You've done an incredible job, Frank. You've almost certainly saved all our lives."

Marek frowned. "I suppose so. I wouldn't like to have to go through all that again. Now I suggest we get as much sleep as possible. We'll need all our energy for the ordeal of phasing back from hyperspace. It's a hell of a way to travel, isn't it…?"

Jerry laughed. "I wonder if we'll ever get used to it?"

With the ship working normally they were able to catch up with their sleep. Tension on board *The Hope of Man* began to increase, however, as the moment for phasing back came closer. Would they make it? And would they arrive in the area of space they had aimed at? Nobody knew.

The moment arrived.

This time Frank Marek sat at the Warp controls and Jerry and Catherine watched him from their couches. The ship began to speak its instructions. Frank Marek pressed the button.

The sensations began again. A thousand hallucinations came and went in a few seconds as the ship entered the first phase.

Jerry heard voices in his head during the second phase. They were the voices of all the people he had ever known. The voices of his dead grandparents, of his stern father, Bruno Cornelius, the chemist, of his mother, of his sister who had been killed in the Lunar Base disaster of 2018 and then, unable to bear the terrible agony, no longer needing to control himself in order to operate the Warp, he blacked out as the time came for the third and final phase.

He blacked out, not knowing if he would ever wake again.

"Look, Jerry! Look!" Catherine's voice.

Jerry opened his eyes and it seemed to him at first that he was back on Earth, lying on his back beneath the summer sun.

Then he realized that the main observation port was open and he was in normal space. But it was like no area of space he had ever seen.

For there before him, glowing a fiery orange, were *three* suns — suns very much like his own, but very close together, forming a sort of triangle in the sky.

"Then we made it," he said flatly, staring in wonder at the stars. "Three suns — the suns that make up Alpha Centauri. A triple star!"

"Yes, Jerry, we made it." Catherine said. "But not without cost."

"What do you mean?"

Catherine pointed to the far corner of the Control Room. Jerry peered into the shadows. Something was huddled there. A creature of some kind.

"What is it? How did that get aboard?"

"Look closer, Jerry," Catherine said grimly.

THE DISTANT SUNS

And then he recognized the huddled, shivering thing.

"My God! It's Marek — Frank Marek!"

From Marek's twisted lips there came a high-pitched giggling sound.

"We reached Alpha Centauri, Jerry. We reached it. I got us there, didn't I...?" The voice was Marek's, but it was also the voice of a small, demented child. "I got us here, Jerry..."

"The strain of the Warp jump proved too much for his brain," Catherine murmured. "I tried to get close to him. Tried to get him to take a sedative, but he won't let me touch him. We'll have to handle him together. If you can hold him, Jerry, I'll give him a shot from the hypogun."

Jerry got up and approached Frank cautiously.

"Don't touch me, Jerry, please," Frank whimpered. "Don't touch me. You know how much I hate human beings. You know I can't bear to be touched."

It was then that Jerry saw the gun in Frank's gloved hand — one of the weapons issued to them in case they should encounter danger on any of the planets they explored. It was a laser gun, capable of burning him to ashes in seconds.

Jerry paused, preparing to leap for the gun and get it away from the demented professor.

Had he come all the way to Alpha Centauri, risked the dangers of hyperspace, just to be killed by a madman with a pistol?

CHAPTER EIGHT

Marek giggled and motioned at Jerry with the laser gun.

"You're as bad as the rest. The human race is like a virus. It has infected one planet — now it seeks to infect the entire galaxy. I'll have no part of it. You are a cancer, Jerry — you and your like. And I have a cure for cancer — I'll burn it out with this."

The ship was hurtling towards the triple star that was Alpha Centauri. Light blazed and the Control Room was a mixture of intense brightness and deep shadow. Cathy stood tensely by the main control console while Jerry stood poised on the balls of his feet, staring warily at the space-maddened Marek.

"Marek — try to see sense. The hallucinations in hyperspace — they turned your brain. You're not rational. Please put the gun away, Marek."

"Shut up! You're my enemy. You — with your stupid ideals. Don't you realize the reason I came on this expedition? To be *alone!* To put four light years between myself and the rest of the human race! I no longer need either of you now!"

Suddenly Cathy shouted: "Our speed! We're traveling too fast!" She was pointing at the speed indicators.

Marek glared at her. "What does it matter if —?"

Jerry sprang.

He grasped the wrist of the hand holding the gun and forced it back, his face close against Marek's. The crazed eyes glared directly into his. The madman's finger squeezed the trigger and a beam of concentrated light left the gun and seared into the ceiling of the Control Room.

Desperately Jerry twisted the wrist. Marek's bearded face grimaced and his teeth clashed a few centimetres from Jerry's throat, his other hand clawing at Jerry's chest. Jerry's right hand grasped the barrel of the gun and wrenched it from Marek's grasp. He flung himself backwards, threw the gun to Cathy and then leapt forward to chop down at Marek's neck. The madman fell forward stunned, tried to get up and then collapsed face down on the deck.

The ship's siren was shrieking.

"Air escaping! Air escaping! Hull damaged in section fifteen."

Jerry tried to take in a deep breath of air, but there was no air left to breathe. He staggered towards the control console.

"Order to Ship," he gasped. "Order to Ship — instant emergency sealing procedure."

"Order received."

Cathy held the laser gun limply, leaning against the panel. The laser ray had burned a hole in the hull and that was why the air was escaping. Normally the ship would have acted automatically to reseal the hole, but evidently Marek's repairs to the cybernetic system had not been wholly successful.

Within seconds the siren had stopped and the ship's brain reported: "Air pressure returning to normal. Hull section temporarily repaired."

Between the two layers of titanium making up the ship's outer hull was a viscous pseudo-metallic substance that could be released to "plug" any small hole that might appear in the hull.

"Begin permanent repair operation," Jerry told the ship as he checked the instruments and gratefully breathed in the fresh supply of oxygen pumped into the cabin from the hydroponics section.

He switched to a view on the television screen of the outside of the hull at section fifteen. Within moments a small repair robot had left its special "kennel" in the outer hull and was crawling along towards the damaged area, its bright metal body glinting in the dazzling light of Alpha Centauri.

The little robot was soon busy "patching" the hull with a plate of titanium and Jerry returned his attention to Marek's prone body.

"We'd better restrain him in some way, I suppose," he said to Catherine.

She shrugged. "I suppose so. What shall we do — tie him up?"

They had not anticipated violence and thus were in no way prepared to deal with the problem that Marek now presented.

"Don't forget, Jerry," Catherine said in a low voice. "We're still heading towards Alpha Centauri at far too great a speed for safety."

Jerry had forgotten in the excitement. He knew it was too risky to decelerate suddenly, particularly with the hull weakened by the laser beam.

And yet — they *were* dangerously close to the nearest of the flaming orange spheres.

"We'll just have to slow down as rapidly as we dare," he said, "and slightly alter course at the same time."

He gave the necessary orders to the ship and then they picked up Marek and carried him back to the crew quarters. Catherine rolled up his sleeve and administered a strong sedative and then they lashed him to his bunk as best they could, returning speedily to the Control Room to check their speed and direction.

They were still traveling too fast. The huge, alien sun had grown to an enormous size in the main observation port. It blinded them.

Grimly Jerry closed the port. "It's the sun's gravity," he said. "It's pulling us towards it! Unless we think of something quickly, we're going to be drawn into the heart of the star and be vaporized in seconds!"

Catherine was checking the ship's co-ordinates.

"We'll just have to turn her completely round," she said. "Head back into deep space. Damn Marek. If he hadn't distracted us, we'd have anticipated all this. As it was, we emerged into ordinary space far closer to Alpha Centauri than we'd originally planned."

"It's a question of fuel, too," Jerry reminded her. "If we start moving away from the sun now, it will take an enormous amount of our fuel — and maybe leave us without enough to do what we came here to do."

"Perhaps even strand us here," Catherine agreed. She lifted her

THE DISTANT SUNS

head. "Order to Ship. Please scan all areas of space in the immediate vicinity. Use all screens."

"Order received."

Now they looked at areas of space away from the suns, desperately searching for signs of planets — planets where the ship might land and convert chemicals into fuel for the atomic pile that was the ship's source of power.

Suddenly Catherine pointed. "Look! Look at that, Jerry!"

A planet had appeared on one of the screens. It was a large planet — about the size of Jupiter. A planet of bright blue and white.

"Hold view on Screen Eight," Jerry commanded the ship. "Alter course for planetary body in view."

"Order received."

Now, as the ship obeyed the order, the blue planet grew larger on the screen. It was so much bigger than Earth that it was plain that the gravity must be considerably greater and that it would not be a habitable world for human beings, even if it was capable in other respects of supporting human life. But it *was* a planet and, if the worst came to the worst, they could always land the ship on it and send out robots to find the necessary chemicals to process for their fuel supply.

But now, as the ship approached the blue planet, they saw that it possessed several moons. And the moons themselves were larger than Earth!

Jerry pointed at a reddish coloured moon circling the planet. "That might be better to land on. The gravity would probably be about right. Order to Ship, close in on moon on Screen Five. Prepare to make preliminary survey."

"Order received."

Now the ship altered course slightly and headed for the red moon. Gradually they began to make out details. The redness seemed to come from a thick cloud layer. Soon the ship began to chant out the results of its preliminary checks.

"Gravity 1.7 Earth's. Atmosphere contains only minimum percentage oxygen — predominantly ammonia. Cannot support human life. Repeat, cannot support human life."

"I hadn't expected it to," grinned Jerry. The ship was principally programmed to discover Earth-type worlds. "Order to Ship — give me a complete breakdown of gases near the surface of the body, please."

The ship began to chant out the component gases of the moon's atmosphere.

Jerry frowned. "Doesn't sound too hopeful. It would take a long while to process that lot and I'm still worried about the weakened hull."

"Ship to commander — ship to commander. Reporting smaller body in view."

Now they could see it on the screen. A moon orbiting the red moon!

"Moons on moons!" Cathy smiled. "We're certainly getting a lot to choose from!"

The moon orbiting the red moon was about two-thirds the size of Earth and seemed to be rotating pretty rapidly on its own axis while it encircled its parent moon.

"Scientists predicted the possibility of moons being large enough to have moons encircling them," Jerry said in astonishment, "but I never expected to see something like it!"

"Gravity approximately .6 Earth's. Atmosphere primarily oxygen. Rotation approximately 18 hours. Orbit approximately 9 months. Can support human life. Repeat — *can support human life!*"

Jerry was unable to speak. He stared at Catherine and she stared back.

This is what they had come to Alpha Centauri to find. A world that could support human life. A new world — an unspoiled world. A world where people equipped with all the knowledge and science of the twenty-first century could begin afresh!

"Cathy!" Jerry murmured at last. "We've found it — we've found New Earth. And we found it almost by accident!"

He hugged his wife tightly and he was weeping with relief. All the strains of the voyage had been worthwhile.

"Ship to commander. Ship to commander. Fuel reserve dangerously low. Advise landing on Earth-type world. Advise landing on Earth-type world."

Jerry nodded. He put his arm around Cathy's shoulders. "Well, Cathy — this is it. Are you ready?"

She smiled her agreement.

"Order to Ship," said Jerry softly. "Prepare to make landing on Earth-type world."

"Order received."

They watched as the world came closer and closer.

The ship's instruments danced and clicked.

The world they approached was not the predominantly blue-green of Earth, but reflected the reddish light of the moon around which it circled. As they approached it they saw that there were clouds and below the clouds were what appeared to be large land areas and smaller areas of water. The land areas seemed chiefly coloured a kind of reddish-yellow.

Now they strapped themselves into their couches. The ship was ready to decelerate and circle the world on the fringes of its upper atmosphere in order for the crew to make preliminary surveys before landing.

As the ship slowed, Jerry felt the familiar sickening sensation. He grew dizzy, blacked out momentarily, and then it was over. The ship was circling the world, like some infinitely smaller moon.

Unstrapping himself from the couch, Jerry gave the ship orders to show the world's continents at close range.

Mountains and valleys appeared. Rivers and plains. Forests and lakes. All had a peculiarly *alien* quality, hard to define, though they were quite similar, at this range, to those on Earth.

They moved rapidly. Whole continents came and went. Jerry ordered the ship to decrease its speed even further. Now the planet below them passed less swiftly by. They were over an area that seemed to be a plateau similar to the Matto Grosso region on Earth, though covered with orange vegetation. It looked an ideal place for landing.

"I think we'll make planet-fall here," Jerry said to Catherine, turning his head to address his wife. "What do you think?"

"Seems fine," she agreed. "I'll — Good God! Jerry — look at that! Look at it Jerry, quickly, before we pass it!"

Jerry stared at the screen unable to believe his eyes.

He was looking at a city. A strange, ancient city that also looked somehow modern.

Then it was gone.

Jerry looked at his wife, unable to voice the thought that was in both their minds.

It seemed that New Earth was already inhabited. And it was too late to change their minds about landing. Already the ship was speaking.

"Preparing to land. Preparing to land."

Jerry let the ship continue with its landing procedures. There was nothing else to do. He could only hope that the inhabitants of this world were not hostile. His lips were dry as the ship began to descend towards the strange, orange plain.

CHAPTER NINE

The Hope of Man slid downwards through the thickening atmosphere of the strange satellite world — a world almost as large as Earth, yet dwarfed by the red planet about which it spun.

Flecks of orange cloud dappled the continents that sprawled beneath the spaceship and the sky turned rapidly from black to violet to blue.

A high, thin screaming filled the Control Room as the ship's listening devices transmitted the rush of heated gases across the outer hull.

Jerry Cornelius, staring at the massed banks of television screens above the instrument panels, licked his dry lips as he mentally pictured the slender tongue of fire that blazed from the rear propulsion tubes, the fire that supported thousands of tons of steel, plastics and titanium against the monstrous pull of the satellite's gravity.

He was helpless now. The brain of the ship was in full control of the landing procedure. He thought of Frank Marek's rage-distorted face and of the damage that the brain had suffered during their horrifying passage through hyperspace. Marek had repaired the brain, or so he claimed, and Cathy and Jerry had believed him.

But now Marek himself was unbalanced, a victim of the same forces that had overcome the ship. How long had he been affected before his attempt to kill his two companions?

"Jerry — is something wrong?"

He glanced up sharply and saw his wife's eyes gazing at him intently. Her pale face reflected some of his own tenseness. Jerry smiled, briefly.

"Sorry, darling. That business with Frank must have shaken me more than I realized. Blood and thunder isn't my line."

The voice of the ship broke in before she could reply. "*Stand by for landing! Three minutes to touchdown! Please secure your safety-webbing.*"

At the touch of a switch, the pilots' chairs lowered and extended themselves, becoming padded couches capable of cushioning their occupants against bumps or vibration, while a flexible web of rubbery strands closed about them like a folding flower.

Above Jerry's upturned face the landscape of the alien world expanded — flowing outwards to the borders of the television screens as the ship rushed stern-first towards the landing point. A storm of radiations and sonic pulses beat upon the earth below. They came from her complex instruments, probing, assessing the nature of the air, the soil and vegetation, the rock strata upon which the weight of the giant craft would rest.

Jerry's last, wry thought before ship and planet met was that it was fortunate they were not hoping to land unobserved; the people of the mysterious city glimpsed during their approach would scarcely be dull-witted enough to have missed their fiery, thunderous descent.

And then they were down.

The Hope of Man shuddered, settled a little, and was still.

Into the numbing silence that followed the shut-down of the engines crept a myriad lesser sounds. The groan and creak of cooling metal, the whirr of countless mechanical devices, and the faint crackling of burning vegetation borne to them through the sound pick-ups outside. Thick, purplish smoke drifted across the viewfield of the television scanners, shot through with rays of orange sunlight.

"Commander to Ship," said Jerry quietly. "Kill those fires. I want no smoke." He turned to Cathy. "If there are inhabitants in that city, I want to find them before they find us. They might be hostile. The ship's conspicuous enough without adding smoke-signals."

Cathy undid the web. "Please, Jerry — don't be such a pessimist."

She slid lithely from her couch. "Why should they want to harm us? What possible threat could we be to an entire world?"

Jerry rose, laughing. "That's my girl! Back on Earth they're ready to blow each other apart for the sake of a line on a map! Can you imagine how suspicious a lot of Earth people would be of an alien ship landing there? But you could be right. I hope so."

Cathy frowned slightly. "I'd better take a look at Frank. The sedative ought to be wearing off by now."

Jerry followed her along the narrow corridor to the living quarters. As the door slid aside and they stepped into the compact, cheerful room, he heard a voice muttering thickly. It was hardly recognizable as that of Frank Marek. Even though no words were distinguishable, the note of terror in the voice was clear.

Cathy hurried to the bunk where he lay, tied securely by Jerry, and quickly checked his pulse and temperature. He moved restlessly, straining against the tough cords, breathing harshly.

"How is he?"

Cathy spoke slowly. "Physically, he's fine. His pulse-rate's a little fast, but otherwise…" She paused. "Jerry, what can we do for him if his mind is still affected when he wakes?"

Jerry ran a hand over his thick blond hair. "The Lord only knows." He looked down at Marek's agitated face, bent over him, his mouth close to Marek's ear. "Frank. Frank, can you hear me?"

Marek stiffened. Then, very suddenly, his body relaxed, sagging in his bonds. He drew one great, gasping breath and then his eyelids fluttered open and he stared straight into Jerry's eyes. A smile curved on his broad mouth.

"Hello, Jerry. That third jump was a rough one, eh? I guess I must be getting old. How close are we to Centauri?"

Cathy, standing at the head of the bunk just out of range of Marek's vision, flashed a warning glance at Jerry and mouthed silently: "Amnesia."

"Pretty rough, Frank," said Jerry, with genuine relief. "You took a nasty tumble just as we went into hyperspace. Sorry we had to tie you down, but you were thrashing around quite a lot." He grinned. "I have bruises to prove it."

Marek became aware of the restraining cords for the first time. "Oh.

A hell of a situation for an old spaceman! I'll never live this down if the Astronauts' Club gets to hear of it." Abruptly his tone sharpened. "The engines have stopped. Are we in trouble?"

"No, Frank." Cathy came to his side as Jerry began to untie him. "Frank — we're down. We've landed upon an inhabitable world. Air and water and vegetation — and there may be other Earth-type worlds in this system!"

"Bullseye with the first shot, eh?" Marek grunted. He sat up, massaging his wrists, flexing his leg muscles. "Well, let's go and see what we've found. You haven't been outside yet, have you?"

"Not yet." Cathy sounded slightly piqued by his matter-of-fact reaction.

"We fired a few acres of grass, or whatever it is, when we touched down," explained Jerry. "I had the chemical-foam sprays turned on to smother the smoke and flames. Everything should be clear shortly."

"But there's more than that, Frank," Cathy declared. "*We saw a city!*"

"A city? You're certain?" Marek swung down from the bunk. He straightened and then swayed. Jerry caught his arm, steadying him. The older man shook his head irritably. "I'm all right. Just stiff, that's all. Lead on."

Blackened earth and rapidly drying patches of white foam surrounded the ship. At the limit of the scanner's range a faint orange haze blurred the horizon. Under a vivid blue sky the land lay empty and inviting. Jerry gave a last glance at the screens and said briskly, "According to the ship's analyses of soil and atmosphere everything out there looks good. So let's get started."

A short while later, clad now in the grey, silk-smooth coveralls designed for outdoor work, the trio stood in the airlock chamber, blinking in the glare of an alien sun. The air flooding into their lungs still carried the bitter smell of burnt vegetation, but a rich medley of scents underlay this. Already a feeling of exhilaration stirred the travelers, wiping out the memories of their recent troubles. Squatting far below them on the ashes was a sturdy six-wheeled vehicle, unloaded automatically from the ship's cargo compartment at Jerry's command. Light, powerful and capacious, it was the latest product of a long line of incredibly rugged carriers that had evolved during the wars of the twentieth century. Between the airlock and the carrier stretched a telescopic stairway of silvery metal. Marek gestured to it.

"Commander?"

"Without you, Frank, we'd probably still be wandering in hyperspace," Jerry smiled. "Yours should be the first foot to touch ground."

Marek grunted. "It strikes me," he said, "that we're both being unforgivably rude to a lady. After you, my dear."

Cathy did not hesitate. The two men followed her down the stairway.

Still thirty feet from the ground, Marek gasped. Jerry looked back as the older man faltered, then fell. Only Jerry's lightning-fast reflexes prevented him from being hurled headlong by the impact of the scientist's stocky body. With straining muscles he clung to the handrail. The dead weight of Marek dragging at his left arm, he gave an involuntary cry. Cathy turned. Now she sprang to his aid. Together they carried the inert body into the ship.

They did not leave *The Hope of Man* again that day.

Late in the evening Marek had recovered consciousness and seemed none the worse for his experience. But he agreed with Jerry when the latter suggested, on Cathy's advice, that he should remain with the ship while his younger companions carried out the preliminary survey of their new world. It had been a tiring day, but Jerry did not sleep well.

CHAPTER TEN

At a distance of three miles, the gleaming hull was still an impressive sight, towering up from a tangle of blue-green foliage. The carrier's sextuple wheels hissed along over dark, mossy growths still wet with the overnight rain and a cool breeze fluttered Cathy's auburn hair. With Jerry at the wheel they had made good time since leaving the ship, moving across a level plateau that invited speed.

Forests marched to right and left — strange bulbous "trees" that reminded them of the ancient pillars of Minoan palaces, crowned with fountainlike bursts of slender leaves, and a dense undergrowth of violet, blue and sepia stalks flowering about their roots.

The land that had seemed so empty on the television screens actually swarmed with life. Shining insectlike things as big as jack rabbits fled before their advance, leaping with dreamlike power on this low-gravity planet. Through the cloud-flecked sky moved creatures of breathtaking size, translucent and tenuous, trailing iridescent whiplike cilia. Cathy manipulated camera and sound recorder almost continuously, until Jerry accused her of being an interstellar tourist. She dug an elbow into his ribs in reply, and he fended her off with one hand, laughing.

In the middle of this mock struggle the carrier dipped into a shallow valley and executed a spectacular skid before Jerry regained full control of the wheel. They rocked to a halt and fell against each other in helpless mirth.

Thunder bellowed in the distance and was flung back from the far hills. It built up and up, a long crescendo of sound that could have only one source.

White-faced, Cathy stared at her husband. "My God, Jerry — *it's the ship!*"

Jerry had the carrier in motion already, the engine snarling as they raced up the slope. But even as they shot over the crest, a blinding pillar of fire leapt into the sky from the landing-site, higher and yet higher, becoming a bright point against the blue, an after-image on the eye and then — nothing.

Stunned, they sat there until the thunder died into silence.

"Could it have been an accident, Jerry?"

Jerry stirred, looked at her. "It could be. The ship's brain was never fully repaired... Damn it, Cathy, we both know that take-off wasn't an accident! Frank's up there now in full charge with his mind full of God knows what twisted ideas!"

"And now?"

He thumbed the engine into life, swung the carrier's blunt nose about to face the hazy horizon.

"The city, Cathy. Where else?"

Towards the close of the planet's short day, with their elongated shadow rippling over the plain before them they had their second view of the city.

The huge red primary of their satellite world had risen ponderously above the hills, fringing the plateau — a sullen, mottled ball suspended in the darkening sky, and beneath it the weird cluster of towers and domes crouched in the shadow.

Despite the warmth of her heated suit, Cathy shivered.

"It looks like a colossal cemetery. I'd almost prefer to spend the night in the carrier."

"Me, too," said Jerry. "If there were any lights over there they ought to be visible from here, but I can't see a glimmer."

The city seemed dead.

Then Jerry blinked, rubbing his eyes, craning his neck. He thought he had seen a flash of brightness — something...

He raised binoculars to his eyes. And then he saw it!

From out of the city walls came something great and glittering. A mechanism of metal and crystal that floated through the purple dusk. Dying sunlight caught facets of its complex surfaces as it turned, so that its shape fluctuated and never seemed the same from moment to moment.

"My God! An aircraft of some kind!"

Jerry reached for the curved stock of the laser rifle clipped to the carrier's side, placed the weapon in its swivel mounting at shoulder level.

The glittering machine came on.

A figure sat within it.

The glittering machine was even closer now, but Jerry couldn't get a strong impression of the figure occupying it. His hand gripped the stock of the laser rifle and he noted abstractedly that there was sweat on it.

Was the occupant of the flying machine human? Again this was difficult to judge.

Cathy put a hand on Jerry's shoulder. "Jerry — shouldn't we — shouldn't we make for cover or something?"

"Don't worry, Cathy — this laser rifle gives us plenty of protection should we need it. I'm counting on the fact that whoever it is in that aircraft is as curious about us as we are about them..."

The machine came to a halt about a hundred yards from their carrier and hovered in the twilight air, its crystal and metal body still catching some of the fading sunlight. Above it dark orange clouds crossed the sky. Somewhere a strange, unearthly cry sounded.

Now the machine began to descend to the reddish-yellow plain and landed.

Jerry and Cathy waited tensely.

Nothing happened for a moment.

Then there was a whine and part of the machine's canopy slid back. From the opening the figure emerged.

"It's a biped, at least," said Jerry.

The biped was tall and thin — about seven feet tall. It left the machine and with long, graceful movements came towards the carrier. It seemed clad in some sort of highly flexible metal cloth, with a mask covering its entire face.

Jerry's pulse-rate increased. He wiped the sweat from his left hand on his coveralls.

About five yards from them the figure stopped and raised one thin, metal-clad arm. A sonorous, echoing voice came from the helmet.

"*Yoasha, hana, canala…*"

Jerry shook his head, trying to indicate that he did not understand.

"*Yoasha, hana, canala…*" The voice seemed more insistent this time.

Again Jerry tried to show that he did not know what the creature was saying.

"*Yoasha, hana, canala — TEY!*"

The figure turned and pointed at his aircraft.

"He wants us to get in it," Cathy said. "Oh, Jerry — I wish…"

Jerry tightened his grip on the gun. "I'll compromise, I think." With gestures he tried to tell the creature that he would follow the aircraft back to the city in the carrier. You go — we follow.

The alien seemed to deliberate for a moment and then was apparently satisfied. He raised an arm.

"*Yoasha kompla.*"

He returned to his aircraft and it took off, flying only a few feet from the ground. Jerry started up the carrier and began to follow.

Now it was almost dark, but the outlines of the strange city could still be seen against the horizon. Jerry switched on the carrier's headlights.

"I hope they're friendly, Jerry," said Cathy with a little shudder.

"So do I. My God, they'd better be. Without the spaceship, we're stranded here forever."

"Why do you think Frank took off again?"

"Who's to say. His mind is unbalanced. He might even have forgotten we were down here. Maybe he plans to return…"

"The ship's already short of fuel. He never refueled. He hasn't a chance of getting back to Earth. No-one will ever know what became of us — or *The Hope of Man*."

"They'll send another ship out sooner or later," Jerry reassured her.

"But *will* they? You know how bad conditions were getting on Earth. It may be too late. War is bound to break out soon if we don't get back and tell them that there are planets out here that can be colonized."

Jerry could not reply to this. She was right. Unless a miracle happened, *The Hope of Man* was the last spaceship to leave Earth before the final cataclysm overwhelmed her.

CHAPTER ELEVEN

They were close to the city. And now it had taken on a menacing air. Its towers were huge, asymmetrical structures that seemed to have been built by madmen. There was something unnatural about every line of the architecture, every choice of colour or carving. And yet there was also a sense of great strength about it, of purpose and intelligence.

"Surely the people who built this are not human beings," Cathy murmured. "It really is — *alien*."

Jerry nodded. The crystal machine had reached the wall, a section of which was opening to admit it. He followed it through.

Strange smells, a peculiar mood.

They followed the machine through twisting, narrow streets, the towers rising high above them, threatening and gloomy.

Now at last the crystal machine stopped and the tall, thin alien got out, signaling for them to follow. Jerry took the laser rifle off its rest and handed another gun to Cathy. "Stay ready for trouble," he said.

The city was only illuminated by the light from the stars.

Jerry got out of the carrier and trod a surface very much like black marble, walking cautiously towards the alien, Cathy following immediately behind.

The alien entered a dark entrance of the nearest tower. Jerry took a deep breath and followed.

A faint luminescence filled the interior of the tower as they walked along a narrow passage and entered a hall with a surprisingly low ceiling — barely eight feet from the floor.

"Ugh!" Cathy sniffed. "The smell — it's horrid!"

"It is pretty strong," Jerry admitted. "Strange — all this sophisticated science and yet apparently no decent sanitation..."

Now the alien led them through a series of narrow corridors until it came to another chamber in which a thin light glowed, illuminating a series of barbaric murals which, though abstract, were subtly horrifying.

Cathy glanced away. "There's something very wrong about this place. It isn't just that it's an alien city — it somehow doesn't seem to be functioning in the way it was originally designed."

"I know what you mean." Jerry studied the murals. "Maybe..."

"*Yoasha chanda!*" The sonorous voice echoed and boomed. "*Yoasha chanda!*" The figure came to a dead stop and remained where it was without a muscle moving.

The air was full of tension as Jerry and Cathy waited for it to speak again or give them some signal. Minutes passed. Jerry checked his chronometer impatiently. The minutes became a quarter of an hour.

At length Jerry approached the figure. "What's happening? What are you playing at?"

There was no response.

He went around the alien and faced him. "What's going on, friend?"

Still no response.

The figure was completely immobile.

Jerry reached out to touch him. The alien made no effort to stop him. He touched dead, cold metal that sent a chill through his entire body. He pushed the alien against the chest. It rocked but otherwise made no movement.

"Is he — has he died, Jerry?" Cathy murmured.

Jerry frowned. "I'm not sure. Perhaps he isn't..." He reached up to touch the head. It was not a mask that the creature was wearing at all. The featureless helmet *was* its head. Jerry moved his hand down the alien's chest until his hand touched a small oval panel set in the metal.

With a fingernail he pulled at the panel. At last it swung out, revealing a set of controls of a bizarre design.

"A robot!" Cathy gasped. "It isn't a living creature at all! A metal man!"

Jerry nodded. "That means we have still to meet the true inhabitants of the city — presuming they exist."

"But why did the robot stop?"

"It's hard to say. Perhaps it was programmed to greet visitors and bring them to this part of the city. Perhaps its masters are away or dead or something, but it followed its original programme, bringing us here where, under normal circumstances, we would have been met by the people — or creatures — who live here. They are probably quite like us in appearance."

"How do you know that, Jerry?"

"Because the robot is fashioned in the form of a man. Why else would they design it in this way? Not the most practical design for a robot, you must admit!"

Cathy smiled. "I suppose you're right. What do we do now?"

"We explore. It's a good opportunity to take a look around while the inhabitants are away — if away they are."

"But why would they leave an entire city uninhabited?"

"Who's to explain the workings of an alien mind?"

"Perhaps something drove them from the city," Cathy suggested. "Something terrifying — that might still be here!"

"We'll have to risk that. We've no choice. We're here now, after all." Jerry gave her a reassuring smile. "Come on, Cathy."

They entered another tunnel and moved cautiously along it until, at length, they emerged into the air again. They were in an open courtyard formed by the inner walls of the tower. There were a number of entrances on every side of the courtyard. In the middle of the courtyard was a fountain. Jerry moved towards it and inspected it as best he could in the darkness.

"The water's dried up. It doesn't look as if it's been used for years. You're right, Cathy — the city does seem permanently deserted, and yet…" He frowned. "Don't you get the sense that it *is* inhabited? I do."

"I know what you mean," nodded his wife. "Ugh — this place gives me the shakes. Let's get back to our carrier, Jerry."

"Okay."

They made their way back through the corridors, past the immobile robot, along through the other passages until they came back to the entrance to the tower, the street and their carrier.

It was Cathy who noticed it first. "The aircraft, Jerry — it's gone."

It was true. The crystal flying machine was no longer there.

"Perhaps it returned automatically to wherever it came from," Jerry suggested.

Cathy shivered and climbed into the carrier. Then she shouted again.

"Jerry! Your binoculars. They've disappeared. Someone — or something — has taken them."

"Oh, they're probably just…" Jerry began to walk towards the carrier and then stopped.

From somewhere behind him had come a stealthy sound. A scuttling sound. A slithering sound. He wheeled round.

There was a giggle — high-pitched, insane. Jerry flicked the safety catch off the laser rifle.

"What's out there? Who are you?"

Again the giggle. Again the slithering sound. Jerry saw something moving in the shadows and he aimed his gun high, sending a beam of pure energy into the sky.

By its light he made out the shape.

If these were the inhabitants, then they had *not* made the robot in their own form.

Jerry gasped in horror!

Crouched in the seat of the carrier Cathy stared at the people of the city and panic swelled within her. She fought it down — forced her mind to accept what she saw.

They were human in shape — clearly, sickeningly human. Jerry, silhouetted against the blinding glare of the laser rifle, towered over a semi-circle of grotesque figures. Frozen in attitudes of shock by the sudden burst of light, the dark mass of their hunched bodies and their white, blank-eyed faces formed a nightmare tableau. In that first vivid glimpse Cathy could not distinguish between male and female, young and old. Their clothes were rags and tatters, smeared with a hundred hues in bizarre and gloomy patchwork. Around the necks of some, on cords, hung objects that quivered and glittered.

Without turning Jerry said quietly: "Put the spotlight on them, Cathy. But don't make any sudden movements."

The sound of his voice seemed to release her from a spell. Rising slowly she stepped into the rear section of the carrier. Unmasking the spotlight, she swung it smoothly about and clicked it into life. At the same moment, Jerry released the laser's trigger. Darkness rushed in around them. Across the spotlight's pale beam fell silver streaks of rain. The huddled group stirred suddenly, shuffling forward.

"Jerry — please get into the carrier!" Shadows danced across the tower walls as the spotlight responded to the tensing of Cathy's muscles.

"Steady, darling — relax." Jerry smiled grimly. "Remember I have the laser rifle and none of this bunch seems to be armed. I'm going to try to talk to them."

He drew a deep breath, swallowing hard as the acrid stench of the strangers filled his nostrils. Then, mimicking the tones of the robot guide as nearly as he could, he cried: "Yoasha chanda!"

The group halted.

A rapid gabbling broke out among them. Their heads bobbed, their hands moved in a disorganized way, rubbing and plucking at their garments. The rain increased, spattering on the black streets, rattling on the carrier's metal sides. Jerry waited in mingled wariness and despair. Who were these creatures? Had *they* built this massive and complex city, and if so, what had destroyed their humanity?

Cathy screamed.

He whirled, swinging the laser at hip level. A swarm of figures, like tattered apes, were pouring from the low doorway of a nearby tower. Two had already reached the carrier and were climbing aboard. The spotlight swiveled crazily as Cathy sprang aside from their clutching fingers. Jerry vaulted into the vehicle hearing a sudden wild uproar behind him.

"Start her up!" he yelled. "I'll hold them off!"

He plunged forward. Slavering and spitting, two creatures flung themselves in his path. Reluctant even now to use the laser beam upon them, he slammed the rifle-butt at the side of one man's head, dropped the other with a blow to the chest. A hand grabbed at his ankle. He fell, painfully, against the spotlight and rolled away from the swinging, flat-handed blows of his attackers. They were coming from both sides now, filling the night with an insane and toneless howling. Cathy felt an arm lock about her throat, dragging her head backwards. Gagging, she fought to start the engine, bracing her body against the pull. As the carrier jerked forward, she heard a thud and the choking pressure ceased. A body slithered from the carrier's side into the rain-slashed roadway. Jerry fell into the seat beside her, panting, shaking one raw-knuckled hand. They roared into a glassy wall of rain, wheels throwing up sheets of spray to either side. He jabbed a button and the windscreen extended itself to become a transparent canopy of tough plastic. The sound of shouting faded behind them, swallowed by the drumbeat of falling water. Cathy called above the din: "Are you hurt?"

"Scraped knuckles," he said. "Nothing more. Are you okay?"

A huge pillar loomed out of the rain, squarely in their path. Jerry made a futile, instinctive braking motion and then was thrown sideways as the carrier swerved. Cathy spun the wheel, feeling the vehicle swing wide under the weaker gravity. The headlights flared across twisting stairways, crazily angled walls, dark arches, an open gateway. They shot between jagged metallic columns into a dimly seen square. The carrier slowed, braked. Cathy fell back against the padded headrest, smiling wanly.

"I'm okay, thanks. But I can't take any more of this maniac's maze. Where are we going?"

Jerry laughed shortly. "I should know? Move over, darling — I'll take the wheel. What we need is to find an exit from this place without running into our little friends again. There must be more than one gateway in the city walls."

He eased the carrier forward and put the spotlight on remote control, sweeping the beam to and fro automatically. It seemed to penetrate the downpour only slightly more than did the headlamps.

"Try the detectors," Cathy suggested.

"Good idea — they may be of use now that we have space to maneuvre."

Jerry activated the twin telescopic antennae behind the canopy, and as an afterthought switched on the radio. On the carrier's console, a small screen began to glow, building up a ghostly image of their surroundings as the antennae pulsed signals into the night. Thunder banged somewhere overhead. The radio crackled. Cathy drew out a pocket mirror and grimaced at the disarray of her hair.

"Jerry, do you think we'll find anyone else in the city? Anyone — sane?"

He drove slowly, peering at the screen. "We certainly made a wonderful first contact back there, didn't we? A true meeting of minds…" His tone was light, but she sensed the worry behind his words. "No, Cathy, I can't see any hope of discovering intelligent life here. Did you recognize the objects those people were wearing around their necks?"

"No," she answered, faintly puzzled. "I didn't get a close look at them."

"I did! Those baubles were scientific instruments, Cathy — scientific instruments! Beautifully finished, too, so far as I could tell!"

A profound depression settled over her as the implications of his statement sank home.

"Then we're lost. Frank has marooned us on a world filled with — with — Morlocks!"

"Eh?" said Jerry, darting a glance at her. "Filled with *what*?"

"Morlocks," Cathy repeated. "They were characters in a nineteenth century novel. They looked like apes and operated vast machines in caves beneath the earth."

He grunted. "I doubt if our bunch were capable of running a clockwork train, let alone vast machines. Their clumsiness was the only thing that saved us."

She pointed at the screen. "Look!"

Shadowy green shapes filled the viewfield, a luminous barrier of spires, domes and arches, an architectural cliff. The distance indicator told Jerry that the reality lay slightly more than a mile ahead. He accelerated slightly: "Taking to the high ground is a good old military maxim when in doubt. That central archway looks as if it has an ascending ramp leading off from it. Maybe we can reach a level from which we can see a way to the walls."

On the screen, a rectangular blur detached itself from the background. It expanded as they watched. Abruptly it quivered, seemed momentarily to divide, and rippled into shapelessness. The radio

SAILING TO UTOPIA

emitted a deafening barrage of squeals and growls, mixed with a curious thudding like the beat of a giant heart.

"Whatever *that* was, it was big!" Jerry snapped. "And it was heading our way. I don't like the way it blanked out our detectors. Better get the laser rifle mounted, Cathy."

"The image split," she said. "There could be two of them."

"Then let's not hang around!" He sent the carrier surging forward, water cascading from its sleek sides. Cathy slid from the front seat into the retractable turret that served to hold telescope or gun. Deftly she fitted the laser into its mounting. The rain slammed against the plastic cupola in slanting white rods and the world was a glistening darkness. The rifle barrel jutting from the water-tight iris of the turret seemed a feeble threat to the forces raging in the night.

Blue-green lightning flamed through the lowering clouds, illuminating the square with theatrical vividness. Crests of towers and curves of domes gleamed ahead. Jerry caught his breath as a monstrous bulk moved into view to their left, parting the curtains of rain with a metallic prow. Thunder broke like an avalanche as the light blinked out. He gripped the wheel with aching hands and drove straight for the unseen distant doorway. The screen was useless now, a rectangle of flickering grey-green.

"Jerry! To your left!"

He jerked his head around as the laser blazed. Towering high above him rose a mass of metal, a whirling nightmare of blades and wheels from which waterfalls poured. Cursing, he spun the wheel, canting the carrier to the limits of its stability in a screeching turn. Something smashed into the stones of the square behind him and he felt the shock vibrate throughout the chassis.

Splinters clanged from the bodywork, rattled on the cupola. Cathy swung the bright flame of the laser, seeking a vital spot in the chaotic jumble of shape and shadow. A great arm, spiked with yard-long blades, swept across the canopy.

Jerry flinched. Glass shattered. Metal screeched.

And the spotlight went out.

The carrier bounced.

He was still fighting to control it when a pair of toothed jaws settled upon the canopy and bit into the steel-hard plastic.

THE DISTANT SUNS

The front wheels lost traction, spinning helplessly as the claw began to raise the vehicle clear of the ground.

"I can't stop it, Jerry! The laser doesn't do anything to it!" White faced, Cathy hung on to the rifle's butt, slashing with futile strokes of concentrated light at the armoured monster.

Cursing, Jerry reached for a red toggle-switch set into a recess in the console. "Get down!" he yelled. "I'm going to blow the canopy!"

She dropped into a crouch, arms wrapped about her head. He yanked the switch, and flung himself face-down upon the driving seat. A split-second later, the emergency release mechanism detonated the explosive bolts set around the cabin's perimeter. The canopy ruptured and bulged. The jaws of the grab clashed together as resistance vanished, and a violent thrust pushed the carrier earthwards. Dazed and deafened, Jerry groped for the controls.

Scarcely knowing what he was doing, he sent the vehicle rocketing forward. Before they had gone a hundred yards, the interior was awash, but they were not aware of the rain.

Somewhere ahead was refuge, and their minds had room for nothing else at that moment. The doorway was already visible in the headlamp beams.

Then, from the murk behind them, a titanic crash, like the meeting of worlds, shivered through the air. They looked at each other wide-eyed.

Cathy said:

"The second machine?"

Jerry's answering grin was close to a snarl. "It sounds as if it met the first one!"

Then they began to laugh, and the laughter became wild and hysterical till Cathy passed into tears. The carrier took the ramp easily, bearing them up into a vaulted interior where luminescent panels threw a cold, dim light at intervals along the way. Elaborate galleries and arcades wandered off into stygian gloom. Exterior noises faded, and the purr of the engine echoed back from unguessable depths and hollows of stone.

It was strangely soothing, and so they were lulled and unready when the final attack came.

"It's like an artificial mountain," whispered Cathy, now somewhat recovered. "Why would people want to shut themselves inside such a mass of stone?"

"Lord knows." Jerry's voice, too, was subdued. "Fear of the outer world, maybe?" He shook his head. "I'm no psychologist."

He was about to move off from the intersection of ramp and gallery, where they were parked, when a mass of dark figures erupted from a side tunnel only yards away. There was no time to escape, no space to use the gun. They went down under a squirming clawing tangle of bodies, choking on the sour stench of dirt and sweat. Jerry fought with scientific savagery and the superior strength of Earthly muscles, developed under a gravity-pull greater than anything known on this lighter world. He rose clear of the struggle for a moment, and had a strange, fleeting impression that the robot-guide they had encountered outside the city was standing some distance away, aloof and watching. It was his last clear thought for some time. Lights pierced the shadows, irregular, flickering lights of many colours that swiftly established a compelling rhythm. His opponents fell away from him, and lay huddled and inert. Thoughts leaped into his mind in wild disorder. A street in London he had known… years ago… pillared porticos… busy traffic. Then the scene darkened. There were craters, snow, a sea of mud. Cathy and Frank were there; he spoke to them and they answered and yet he knew somehow they were dead. And then it all faded, down, down into blackness and oblivion.

He woke. A girl in a short, silvery tunic leaned over him. She was small, pretty, hazel-eyed. Blonde hair framed her unsmiling face. As Jerry's eyes came fully open, her expression brightened. She said:

"My name is Lae-Pinu. Who are you?"

Jerry stared at her, speechless. She was speaking English — clear, fluent English! He tried to rise, but something held his head down. He reached up, and felt a cold metallic band clasping his temples. A wave of weakness overwhelmed him, and he fell back, down into the nightmare of death and ruin.

CHAPTER TWELVE

There was no hope. Man was lost. *The Hope of Man* was lost. There was no hope...

The phrases ran like a child's nursery rhyme through Jerry's mind as he came back to consciousness. When he awoke for the second time his brain was clear, but memories of the dream-images, the cratered streets of London and the dead-alive faces of Cathy and Frank, stayed with him. He raised a hand to his forehead. The metal circlet that had held his head down was gone. With an effort he put aside the thoughts of death and sat up slowly.

He was on a kind of dais against one wall of a large five-sided room. Directly opposite to this dais a tall, narrow doorway led off to unseen regions. Instruments lined the walls, huge dials marked in curving symbols that conveyed nothing to him. Above and between the dials luminescent panels glowed with a bluish light. In the centre of the floor, six people stood, regarding him intently. The foremost, a stocky, thick-necked man with long dark hair streaked with grey, pointed a peculiar translucent tube at Jerry.

"Stay there!" he ordered gruffly. "Tell us who you are and what you are doing here."

Jerry studied the group for a moment before replying. There were four men and two women, all clad in loose tunics and trousers of various colours. All six had light golden skin, and, save for one blonde woman, their hair was black. Altogether, despite their hostile expressions, they were a considerable improvement upon the other inhabitants of the city. His spirits rose.

"I am Colonel Jerry Cornelius, commander of the spaceship which landed on your world two days ago..."

The stocky man made a threatening gesture with the tube. "We do not understand you. Speak in Arvik!"

"Speak in *what?*" Jerry was at a loss.

"Arvik!" growled the spokesman. "The speech machine taught you while you slept. Speak in our tongue!"

And Jerry realized with a shock that the sounds the other's lips made were strange, but the words which formed in his own brain were clear and familiar. So *that* was the purpose of the metal circlet. A language-teaching device! Then the girl who had greeted him when he first awoke had spoken not in English but in Arvik! With the realization, knowledge of the alien language seemed to leap to his tongue. He repeated his opening words and continued:

"We came from the planet Earth, which circles a sun very close to your own solar system. We hoped to find a world similar to Earth. To meet a race so like ourselves is more than we had dreamed."

He paused. A young man in a yellow tunic turned to the blue-clad spokesman. They began a whispered conversation. Over their heads Jerry saw the girl Lae-Pinu standing in the doorway. She was barefoot and clad in the brief silvery garment he remembered. Her eyes were wide and troubled. As his glance met hers, she started and withdrew from sight. The whispering went on. Anxiety finally overrode Jerry's self-control. "Where is my wife?" he said sharply. "Where is Cathy? Is she safe?"

The stocky man looked at him coldly. "There was no woman. I know nothing of any woman. There was only you."

THE DISTANT SUNS

CHAPTER THIRTEEN

"Stranger!"

Jerry stirred, groaning. His head throbbed. A chill sickness assailed him. Gritting his teeth he braced one arm against the cell wall and rose, fighting down his nausea. Light filtered through the steel-barred window set in the locked door, casting faint shadows upon the stones. Beyond the bars a girl's blonde head was visible, her eyes only just above the level of the window's lower edge. He lurched toward the door.

"Lae-Pinu!" he croaked. "What's happening?"

"Please!" she whispered. "Do not make a noise!" She stepped back, glanced swiftly to left and right, came close to the bars again. "Quickly — take these."

Two rectangular objects wrapped in some kind of metal foil were thrust through the window. He took them, turned them over in his hands.

"What are they?"

"Food!" Lae-Pinu said. Again she surveyed the corridor. "They are coming for you soon — my father and the others. He does not believe your story. They will put you before the Judgment Wall to discover the truth."

"I told them the truth!" Jerry gripped the bars in frustration. "Tell me, has there been any news of my wife?"

"No. I heard my father say that there was no woman among the Sev-Alab — the creatures of the lower city — when we used the hypnosis machine upon them."

"But he couldn't be sure," said Jerry desperately. "With such a struggle going on and the hypnotic lights flickering, he could have overlooked her! The Sev-Alab may have carried her off when they recovered!"

Lae-Pinu looked to left and right again. "I do not know —"

He put one hand over hers where she held the grill.

"Lae-Pinu, please, you've got to help..."

She started back. "I must go! If my father finds me here he will punish me! Do not tell him of the food!"

Tears sprang into her dark eyes. Hurriedly, Jerry released her hand.

"I'm sorry," he said. "Of course I won't tell your father of this. I should be thanking you for what you've done already, instead of asking more."

Lae-Pinu looked at him wordlessly for a moment and then she was gone.

Jerry strained his ears for the sound of other footsteps, but heard nothing. He sat against the wall and began to peel off the metal foil. The mere knowledge that food was available filled him with a ravenous hunger. He could not remember how long it was since his last meal. It seemed incredible that only weeks ago he had walked across the Gandhi Space Launching Site in company with Cathy and Frank, full of dreams and hopes. The fate of Earth rested on their shoulders, or so the television commentators had declared. Jerry grinned without humour. And here he was, the world's saviour, locked in a cell on a nameless planet. He recalled the scene in the room of the language machine, how he had lost control and attempted to push his way through the group to begin his search for Cathy. The leader had pressed a stud on the translucent tube that he held and Jerry's nerves had burned with a fire so agonizing that he sweated at the memory. Then a numbness had enveloped his mind, and he had known no more until the sound of Lae-Pinu's voice awakened him.

The packages held two slabs of a dense, rough-surfaced substance that smelled faintly of coffee. Nibbling cautiously, he found the flavour quite palatable. The food might be drugged or poisoned, he realized — after all he knew nothing of this race's motives or customs — but he had to trust someone, and the girl seemed sincere. Why was she helping him? Again, without real knowledge of their alien ways, speculation was pointless. Maybe she saw him as an exotic novelty!

Voices echoed in the corridor. Hastily he crammed the last fragments of food into his mouth, crumpled the foil and wedged it into a crevice in the floor. With a last-minute inspiration, he lay down again, huddled in a corner. Sandaled feet slapped upon the stones outside. The lock whirred and a widening wedge of light fell across him. Through half-shut eyes he saw three men in the doorway. A voice said: "Does he sleep or did the neurogun kill him?"

"Stay back!" came the leader's familiar growl. "It could be a trick. A touch of the gun will tell us."

Before Jerry could move a white-hot pain flared in his chest. Mild as it was in comparison to the earlier dose, it still shattered his pretense of unconsciousness. Scrambling to his feet, he stood half-crouched, glaring at his captors. "What do you want now, you swine?" he shouted, hoarse with thirst and rage. Behind his anger, he coolly noted that the trio retreated a pace at the sight of him.

"Come out!" snapped the leader, flourishing the neurogun. "It is time for you to stand before the Judgment Wall. The truth of your story will be weighed there before the court of the Sev-Kalan, the people of the upper city. Come!"

Jerry came. They walked in triangular formation, Jerry in the centre, the blue-clad man at the apex behind him, gun in hand. Watery sunlight slanted across the long corridor at intervals, between squat stone pillars. Monstrous carvings covered the walls, leering through the shadows, with an occasional doorway or side-passage to relieve their oppressive weight.

Unconsciously Jerry straightened as they passed into a high open space where the corridor intersected a wide gallery. They climbed an endless flight of broad steps, came to a crossroads where massive metal doors blocked off all exits save one towering archway. Jerry's heart leaped. The carrier! It stood at the base of a great carved column, the jagged mounting of the broken spotlight glinting in the sunlight. A

SAILING TO UTOPIA

thrill of hope ran through him. If only he could reach the driving cab —

His footsteps must have faltered. Behind him a voice grated: "Keep moving!" He gritted his teeth and walked on. Through the archway, and into a room so vast that the several hundred people it held seemed lost and forlorn. Glowing panels lit the lower walls leaving the ceiling shrouded in darkness. As Jerry entered, his eyes were caught and held by an expanse of brass and crystal and rippling colour too great for the mind to grasp. It dominated one end of the cavernous hall, filling the space between with incomprehensible flashing signals. He did not need to be told that this was the Judgment Wall. It was also very obviously a gigantic computer.

A wide aisle led between rows of ornate benches to a tiered platform directly below the Wall. As Jerry strode along, he was acutely aware of hundreds of eyes fastened upon him, of a rising tide of muttering and whispered speculation. The audience was composed of men and women of all ages and he noticed a few children in the front rows. Tunics were the common dress for young and old. The ever-moving multihued beams gave an unreal quality to the scene, masking the contours of the room. He squinted into the rainbow haze, searching for stairways, avenues, exits.

Now the titanic complexity of the Wall was so near that Jerry could no longer discern the outer edges. A sentient mountain, veined with tubes of pulsing light, studded with a myriad trembling instruments cased in brass, it hung above him. For all his familiarity with the giant mechanisms of twenty-first century Earth, he could not repress an irrational fear that the Wall would topple, crushing him beneath its immeasurable weight.

On the highest tier of the platform stood two smooth, black, waist-high blocks. At a command from his gaoler, Jerry walked over to them and turned to face the crowd.

With the watching face of the computer Judge out of sight, he found himself oddly calm. He noticed that the tops of the blocks were worn into shallow depressions, as if by constant rubbing.

The stocky man, standing some distance away with the neurogun still trained upon Jerry, began to address the crowd.

"I speak in the name of the Great Judge. I, Lae-Varka, servant of

THE DISTANT SUNS

the Wall, bring the outlander prisoner before the all-seeing eye of the Great Judge, that the truth of his words may be weighed."

There was a cry of assent from the crowd below. Lae-Varka glanced at the desk console at the further side of the platform and frowned.

"Where is the Keeper of the Records?"

Slowly, reluctantly, Lae-Pinu emerged from the audience and climbed the steps. "I am here, my father." She wore now a dark red tunic. Her face was deathly pale, her lips compressed.

Lae-Varka turned to Jerry.

"Prisoner, you may tell your tale. The Keeper of the Records will translate your words into the sacred language of the Great Judge. When all is told, the Voice of the Wall will declare your fate. Stand now between the blocks and place your hands upon them."

Under the threat of the neurogun Jerry moved to obey. There was a sudden feminine cry.

"Do not touch them! The Wall sends death to those who touch the blocks!"

Heedless of the weapon, Jerry spun about. Lae-Pinu was standing by the console, her face contorted with terror. Her father swung the neurogun, yelling: "You have broken the Law of the Wall! You are not fit to live!"

He pointed the gun at Lae-Pinu's head.

CHAPTER FOURTEEN

On Earth, she would have died. Even as Jerry hurled himself at Lae-Varka, he saw the man's fingers tighten upon the butt of the weapon aimed at the girl's head. It was all very clear and very far away, out of reach. And then his flying body hit Lae-Varka and the smaller man went sprawling.

Gravity was the answer, Jerry thought, while he scrambled to retrieve the neurogun. Two-fifths of one gee, the difference between the pull of this world and Earth, the difference between life and death. A foot came swinging at his head. He dropped flat, caught the foot, twisted it and rolled. The owner crashed to the platform with a startled whoop. Two down and one to go. Lae-Varka, however, was not ready to be counted out. He came up, wild-eyed and breathing hard, as Jerry rose. The sight of the neurogun in the other's hand did not seem to register upon his mind. He rushed in, fingers hooked like claws. The Earthman took one pace forward, pivoted to the right. There was a meaty thud. Lae-Varka fell as if hit by a hammer. Jerry's left fist felt numb. He backed towards Lae-Pinu, bringing the gun to bear upon the audience.

"The next one to move will get this!"

The Sev-Kalan crowded to the base of the platform, surging to and fro as if checked by an invisible wall. He could almost feel their hatred beating up to him in waves. He looked sideways at the girl, at her taut, bloodless face, and realized with a sick horror that the hatred was directed as much at her as at himself. With deliberate curtness, he snapped: "You know this place — show me a way out! Hurry, girl!"

Lae-Pinu stared back at him. Her throat muscles worked convulsively but no sounds passed her lips. A small bright missile flashed out from the forest of waving arms below and rebounded from the console, missing her by inches. It was a thin-bladed knife. Jerry swallowed his pity, reached out and grabbed Lae-Pinu's tunic, shaking her small body like a doll.

"They're going to kill you! Run, girl! Run, damn you! I can't stop them!"

Colour flooded back into her face.

"To the left, " she said. "The stairway over there leads to an upper gallery —"

He was moving before she could finish the sentence. As they sprinted for the stairway, a roar of fury broke from the crowd. In a multicoloured wave the Sev-Kalan swept across the platform. Four men appeared at the foot of the steps as if from nowhere. Steel blades glinted. Coldly, Jerry squeezed the neurogun. The crowd, following after, parted and flowed around four stunned, twitching figures. Jerry pounded up the stairway, half-carrying the girl.

From that point onwards, Lae-Pinu took charge. A breathless succession of corridors, ramps and dusty rooms made Jerry's head reel. The howling of the crowd faded, muffled by the intervening stonework. Finally, in a room grimier than any they had previously crossed, Lae-Pinu halted.

"Up there," she panted, pointing. He looked up. Several feet above his head was a lightless opening roughly two yards high and a yard wide. It looked remarkably like an open grave. Jerry shrugged.

"Right," he said. "Up you go, then!"

She placed one foot in his linked hands. He heaved upwards, grunting. She soared with incredible ease, grasped the sill of the opening, and swung herself into it in a flurry of bare golden legs. Jerry backed off, took a short run, and leaped. A moment later, temporarily winded, he was lying beside her in thick, musty darkness. Presently, she tugged gently at his sleeve.

"We can go on, now."

Jerry sat up. "No, Lae-Pinu, wait. I must think. I must find my wife. God knows what may have happened to her. If your people haven't got her, then I must search the lower city."

Her voice sank to a whisper. "The Sev-Alab do not take people away. When they find someone alone, they kill him and leave the... the remains for us to discover. We have placed hypnosis machines and warning signals in all the ways leading from the lower levels, but each year they grow bolder.

He scrubbed the palms of his hands across his face, feeling the unfamiliar rasp of a thickening beard. He was suddenly weary and cold. Dully, he answered: "Then either your father was mistaken about Cathy not being with the hypnotized Sev-Alab, or someone else has —" He stopped. *Could* someone else have taken her? The words had stirred a dormant memory.

"Lae-Pinu," he said with a new urgency. "When Cathy and I were attacked, I thought I saw something just before the hypnotic lights dazzled me. A very tall, manlike figure, barely visible in the shadows. Just standing, like the robot that led us into the city when we first landed on your world. Would the robots hurt a human being, or carry him off?"

"Where... where did it go?" she asked, in a voice like that of a frightened child.

"I only saw it for a second or two." Jerry tried to speak casually, but her tone had filled him with foreboding. "It didn't move at all. Do you know anything about it?"

"Oh, Jeh-ree!" To his utter amazement and embarrassment, she threw herself against him, making sobbing, incoherent sounds of distress. He held her, letting the tears flow, waiting for her emotions to work themselves out. A small corner of his mind kept hoping that the noise she was making would not attract their pursuers. Presently she calmed and moved away, sniffling. Jerry took a handkerchief from an inside pocket, pressed it into her dimly seen hand.

"Use this."

Dabbing her face dry, she said quietly: "I'm sorry."

"For what?" he said. "After what you've gone through in the past hour, you needed to do that. I could shed a few tears myself!"

Crushing down his wild desire to learn the cause of her fear, he put a hand gently on her shoulder.

"Before you tell me what's wrong, lead us out of here. Things may look better in the daylight."

Lae-Pinu stood up. "You are not offended when I call you Jeh-ree?"

Jerry chuckled. "I've been called worse. You have a pretty good memory for names, young lady!"

"I am the Keeper of the Records," said Lae-Pinu with pride.

A few paces brought them to a metal grating which blocked the narrow tunnel. Despite corrosion, it swung back with little noise when the girl pushed it. Grey light filtered through the dimness from above as they emerged into a circular, vertical shaft that smelled faintly of dampness. High overhead, Jerry saw a pearly disc of sky. Lae-Pinu indicated a ladder of rusty rungs set in the stonework. "At the top of the shaft we will be in a part of the upper city that has been abandoned. I know it from ancient writings in the Records."

Jerry stuck the neurogun in his belt, ready to hand.

"Nevertheless, we'll play it safe," he told her. "Stay a few rungs below me and keep your head down until I give the all-clear."

The climb was accomplished without incident. Side by side, Jerry and Lae-Pinu stood upon a wide, windswept roof, drawing deep breaths of cool, moist air. Clouds raced low above the ragged towers that hemmed in their refuge. The suns, just past their zenith, gleamed intermittently through deep blue rifts. No living thing save themselves moved in all that bizarre landscape of stone, but Jerry did not linger. Only when they had found a turret room commanding a view of every possible line of approach did he relax. Lae-Pinu sat beside him in the baroque, crumbling interior, suddenly quiet. For a moment he studied her grave, dust-streaked face, and then he said: "All right, Lae-Pinu, go ahead. Tell me the worst."

The Hope of Man was falling. A sleek sentient cylinder of titanium-steel, she slid through the impalpable currents of interplanetary space, her nuclear engines silent. She was falling from apogee to perigee, from the outermost point of her elliptical orbit to the innermost, in a stupendous, suicidal swoop. Frank Marek savoured her fall. He was alive and well and alert. He was exalted and exultant. He was doomed.

Weightless, he floated in the disorder of the Control Room, staring through an unshielded vision port at the blue-white giant planet falling swiftly astern. He yelled into the dark cavern of the ship: "Who is your master? Who made you?"

And the ship answered in stunning, echoing amplification: "Marek! Marek! MAREK!"

Marek laughed. He laughed at Space, at the orange-tinted world he had left, at the wide, encircling Universe. Again he yelled to the ship that was now his creature: "What is the hope of Man?"

And the ship answered: "Death! Death is the hope of Man! Death, Death, DEATH!"

Marek was content.

"And so your older sister vanished just as mysteriously as did Cathy?"

Jerry spoke in a whisper. He lay in the narrow horizontal duct of a ventilator, Lae-Pinu at his side. Below them stood the carrier. They had left the turret several hours ago after deciding upon a plan of action, and found their way back to the intersection at the entrance to the Judgment Room. En route they had picked up supplies from the Sev-Kalan warehouses with little difficulty. Now they waited for nightfall, when the upper city would sleep.

"She disappeared four years ago," Lae-Pinu replied. "My father had no sons, and so he trained his eldest daughter in the lore of the Wall, for we are the traditional Keepers of the Records. Lae-Mura was his favourite. I had to take her place — it is the law — but he treated me as if Lae-Mura's loss was my fault. I hate him," she said with quiet intensity. "I hate the Wall and the whole cruel, stupid business. Sometimes I think that our people are as savage and mad as the beasts of the lower city. If it were not for fear of the Alanga, I would have fled outside the walls long ago."

Jerry watched a party of Sev-Kalan cross the space below. When they were out of sight, he said: "I know very little of this world of yours, but I cannot see why the presence of these beings, the Alanga, terrifies the Sev-Kalan. You tell me that they can enter and leave the city at will, and that no-one knows how they gain access. They take your people as offerings to some mysterious god called the All-Devourer, according to your records. Yet there is only the vaguest description of them there — tall, slender, moving without sound. Why has there never been an attempt to explore the hills where they are said to live?"

Lae-Pinu shrugged, helplessly. "We believe that the Alanga would wish us to do this. Then they would fall upon us in the wilderness and destroy us all. Sometimes I feel that would be better than our present existence."

He noted that her tone was now controlled and rational as she spoke of the beings, in contrast to the near-hysterical account she had given in the turret room when she had finally nerved herself to speak at all. Perhaps he was right, after all, in agreeing to her request to go with him when he made his bid to leave the city. Grimly, he said: "It's a chance I must take. If Cathy has been taken by the Alanga — and it seems almost certain that she has — I'll scour those hills from end to end, and God help whoever gets in my way!"

When complete silence reigned in the halls and passageways, Jerry uncoiled the rope they had brought, secured one end to a grating and cautiously lowered the other until it brushed the floor. Then, swiftly and stealthily, he descended, followed by the girl. They padded across the wide, cold expanse of paving to the carrier, climbed into the cab. Everything seemed to be in order. Jerry set the engine purring almost inaudibly. No trouble there. He was about to ease the carrier forward when a triumphant shout rang out from the great entrance of the Judgment Hall. With a thunderous, reverberating boom, massive metal doors dropped into place all around, sealing off every avenue.

Lae-Pinu shrieked: "Jeh-ree! My father has trapped us!"

Sev-Kalan poured from the Hall. At their head was Lae-Varka. In his right hand was the twin of Jerry's neurogun.

"Get down, Lae-Pinu!" Jerry yelled over the clamour of the oncoming mob. "This is going to be rough!"

As she dropped to the floor of the cab, he gunned the carrier forward, simultaneously triggering the distress siren to full voice. The effect at such close range was shattering. Lae-Varka made a wild, ludicrous attempt to aim the neurogun and cover his ears at the same time. Behind him the other men slowed, bewildered. Lae-Pinu, peering over the rim of the dashboard, cried: "Where can we go? They have closed all of the doors!"

"That's what your father thinks!" Jerry wrenched the carrier around in a tyre-twisting arc, aligned the nose on the long stairway directly opposite the Judgment Hall. "Hang on!"

And amid a bedlam of cursing and howling, he drove through the one exit the Sev-Kalan had never thought to close. Lae-Pinu cast one horrified look at the steep stone steps falling endlessly away beneath her, and buried her face in the cushioned seat. The carrier lurched over the brink. Never had Jerry been so acutely aware of sheer speed. The grey walls blurred, flowing by like an enclosing torrent. The six tyres, with their flexible, almost organic structure, absorbed the worst of the repeated shocks, but the jarring and the oscillation of the headlights were unpleasantly similar to the rhythms of the hypnotic machines. It was vertigo quite as much as logic that made him swing the vehicle from side to side of the slope to minimize the sickening pitching motion, converting their descent into a wide snaking series of S-bends. When they bounced off the final step and rolled to a halt in the high gallery he remembered, Jerry had some difficulty in uncurling his fingers from about the steering wheel. He grinned at the disheveled Lae-Pinu as she opened her eyes and sat up.

"I should have warned you that I used to be a street-car driver in San Francisco!"

"Sehan Francisco… what is that?" She was still slightly breathless.

Jerry began to cruise the carrier slowly along the gallery, searching for a continuation of the route down to ground level. "Sorry! San Francisco is the name of a town on my native planet. Parts of it are built on very steep hills. I went there once with my father when I was a kid."

"There is more than one town on your world? Why is that?" Lae-Pinu's curiosity overrode her fears. "Are they like Beya-Sev?"

He was silent for a moment, listening for sounds of pursuit. The engine purred softly and the wheels made a barely audible swish. Otherwise, silence. His mind examined the implications of her questions.

"There are many towns on my world. Surely there is more than one on yours? Doesn't Beya-Sev have any sort of contact with other communities?"

She looked at him blankly. "Why would there be other towns? Who would live in them?"

"Who would…?" Jerry did not complete the repetition of her query. He tried to quell an uneasy suspicion about the mental processes of the Sev-Kalan. An old saying ran through his mind: *Everybody's crazy except thee and me — and I have my doubts about thee!*

Aloud, he said: "On Earth — my world — there are several thousand million people. They live in communities of various sizes, from tiny villages with only a few dozen inhabitants up to great cities holding twenty or thirty millions. Very few cities have a sharply defined boundary like that of Beya-Sev. They sprawl over vast areas and are constantly growing."

Her eyes were huge with wonder. "But… but…" She seemed unable to formulate the question, whatever it was. Half to herself, she murmured: "All those faces!"

"I know," said Jerry. "I feel that way myself."

CHAPTER FIFTEEN

They were outside the city. It had been easy, after all, so easy that he could still scarcely believe it. The gallery had given them access to a descending ramp and a flat roof. Unwilling to face the dangers of the lower levels during darkness, he had driven across the roof in the hope of seeing some part of the city wall when daylight permitted. To his delight, the roof terminated at the inner surface of the wall, only a foot or so below the parapet. After that it had been a straightforward, if laborious, matter of unshipping the powered winch, anchoring it to a convenient drainage outlet, and allowing the carrier to roll, snail-like, down the slightly sloping outer face of the wall on the end of taut, tough cables. Lae-Pinu's part in the operation had chiefly consisted of standing watch, after a brief lecture on the use of the laser rifle, to see that no person or thing caught them unawares. Nothing did, but the night sounds and smells that rose from the hidden streets of Beya-Sev were not pleasant.

The dawn wind was cold. Jerry, shivering, turned up the heating of his suit. He rummaged in the lockers of the carrier for spare clothing for the girl. She was already hugging herself against the chill, and her legs, little protected by the short red tunic, were covered with gooseflesh. With strands of blonde hair trailing across her face, she had the pathetic look of a lost child. *Which is exactly what she is,* Jerry thought. He pushed the unwelcome thought away. Out here she was safe, at least, from her own people.

"Try this," he said, holding out Cathy's spare suit. Clumsily she struggled into the unfamiliar garments. Jerry heroically refrained from grinning at the result. Lae-Pinu looked with dismay at the flopping sleeves, the trouser-cuffs trailing over her toes. Tugging at the sagging blouse, she said: "Thank you. It is very warm." She carefully folded her tunic and tucked it into the locker. Climbing into the open cab as Jerry slid in behind the steering-wheel, she asked: "Is your wife very beautiful, Jeh-ree?"

"Very beautiful." He looked away from her, surveying the dark horizon. In a deliberately lighter tone, he added: "And very tall too!"

Lae-Pinu smiled faintly. Then, staring fixedly ahead at the mist-streaked land slowly emerging from night, she whispered: "I hope the Alanga have not harmed her."

God help them if they have, Jerry thought savagely. His fingers ran expertly over the control panel. The carrier moved off, drawing broad, glistening tracks across the wet, blue moss. An edge of sun lifted suddenly above the hills, laying orange light on the mist. The windscreen darkened, automatically reducing the glare to a tolerable level, and he flicked off the headlights. At an exclamation from the girl, he looked back. Beya-Sev shone. High overhead the strange, convoluted towers flung back the sun's rays, so blindingly bright that their outlines were already blurred by a shimmer of gold. He had an almost overwhelming impulse to turn back, to ransack the whole fantastic, evil structure for some sign of Cathy. He was deserting her, driving off on a wild hunt on the flimsiest of evidence...

"Tell me what you know about the Alanga's homeland," he said abruptly.

Lae-Pinu drew her gaze from the shining city with reluctance. "The towers are so beautiful," she breathed. "I have never seen them in this way before. If only my people could be here, outside the walls."

"They could be," Jerry told her. "It's my guess that they have shut themselves away in Beya-Sev for so long that they're as much afraid of open spaces as they are of the Alanga."

"You have not lived in Beya-Sev," Lae-Pinu answered with a note of reproof in her voice. "You have not had to lock doors and set guards every night upon the passageways. After my sister Lae-Mura was taken, my mother would not let me out of her sight for weeks."

"There are many cities like that upon Earth." He watched the colour of the hills deepen moment by moment, their slopes acquire solidity and perspective. "There'll be many more if the population keeps on increasing. Now, what can your records tell me about the Alanga?"

"They have secret ways into the city which no-one has ever discovered. My father searched tunnels and passages so old that even the Elders of our council could not recall them having been used, and I studied ancient maps, but we found nothing. There are parts of Beya-Sev which the maps do not show."

"How do you know that the Alanga live in those hills?" Jerry steered left, skirting a small lake where mist lingered. Something round and green skimmed across the water, sank again with a muffled "plop". Feathery black creatures rose from the further shore and flew into the orange haze with curious, barking calls. Lae-Pinu watched them go, and said:

"They have been seen from the upper city. We have a telescope with which our Elders study the lands around Beya-Sev. I remember when I was young seeing a party of Alanga crossing the valley below the hills. It was early in the morning, just like now."

"Where, exactly?" Jerry asked sharply.

She pointed to the right. "There — that hill higher than the rest, with streaks of red on its sides. I could not see very much of them, of course, because the telescope is old and doesn't work well."

Jerry stared at her. "You're sure they were Alanga? It couldn't perhaps have been a herd of animals, or shadows thrown by moving clouds?"

His voice must have had more of an edge than he had realized. Her face became sullen. She said, through barely opened lips: "Of course they were Alanga! I'm not a liar!" She moved to the other end of the seat and turned her back. Jerry choked down a strong urge to shake her. He contented himself, instead, with saying something brief, in English, to the passing scenery. They rolled on for ten miles more in funereal silence.

The signal came as the carrier was fording the broad, shallow stream that meandered around the stony feet of the hills. On the cab console a blue light began to blink in accompaniment to a series of high-pitched buzzes. Lae-Pinu was jolted from her moody pose as Jerry accelerated, sending the vehicle lunging up the bank, stones scattering from beneath the spinning wheels.

"What is it?" she exclaimed in alarm. "What has happened?"

"It's her!" Jerry cried. "It's Cathy! Oh, God, I hope she's all right!"

Lae-Pinu stood up, clutching at the windscreen, and was almost hurled overboard as the carrier swerved. "Where?" she asked eagerly. "Where is she?"

He gestured at the console. "That's her signal. She was carrying a miniature transmitter set to broadcast a distress signal. It can be operated by the wearer, or started automatically by being removed from the wearer's body — she wore it as a pendant. It must be very near — the signal is getting stronger."

Minutes later he leaped from the cab, ordering Lae-Pinu to remain in the parked carrier to watch the nearby slopes. His face was pale and set as he strode to the edge of the water. The soft mud there had been trampled and churned. Tiny pools had formed in the hollows. The marks were unlike any that he knew, but they were unmistakably those of animals. With cold fingers he groped in the mud and the clumped vegetation, hardly aware that the girl had joined him in his search. It did not take long to find it. Jerry straightened, holding the tiny, exquisitely constructed device and its attached necklace in the palm of his hand. There was mud on it, and something more. Lae-Pinu, coming close, touched the casing with a tentative finger. She looked up at Jerry's drawn, brooding features and said in a small, lost voice: "The mud... it has blood in it!"

CHAPTER   SIXTEEN

Marek whimpered. He floated through the curving spaces of *The Hope of Man*, weightless, in free fall. His body was curled in sleep, arms clasping knees, head tucked down upon his chest. A nimbus of dark hair waved about his face. Small things pursued him, borne on the eddying air-currents circulating through the ship. A flask trailed shining globes of liquor which collided constantly, breaking into ever-smaller droplets, creating a universe of mirrors. An endless succession of Mareks, tiny and distorted, revolved with their slow, spinning dance.

The ship murmured. Messages flashed along the intricate network of her electronic nerves. On the control console, screens glowed. Marek stirred, reaching out, groping at the air. His legs moved fitfully. He mumbled.

It was summer, and the broad avenues shimmered with sunlight. Dust eddied about the carefully spaced trees, rustled on the grey armour of the riot cars parked in their shadow. White-helmeted police slacked in the gun turrets, bored and sweating. Marek ran past them, shouting, his lips cracked and dry. They did not stir. His words died on the hot, still air. The avenue stretched before him interminably, a quivering mirage of glass and concrete, ponderous parallel rows of monuments to a dead political creed that he scarcely remembered. As the rocks swallow and compress green forests and transmute their substance into strange forms, so the pressures of the twenty-first century had seized and warped the social institutions of the twentieth, piling stress upon stress faster than their sagging structures could adjust. But it would all end soon. The world would be clean and clear. Why couldn't he make them hear? Why was his throat so constricted?

The ship was troubled. A programme had been fed into her circuits, locked into her immensely complex computer-brain. In a little while, the huge and beautiful automaton that was *The Hope of Man* would enter Phase One of the Warp, the first step into that strange sub-universe of hyperspace beyond the laws of orthodox cosmology. Of all the precautions taken by the gifted scientists who had designed her, working on the sketchiest of information about a region which could not be probed in advance, the most sternly enforced had been that regarding the proximity of matter. No-one really knew what might happen if the forces of the Warp were released within the area of distorted space surrounding a sun, but theoretical predictions were apocalyptic enough to deter the rashest of experimenters. Stripped of its esoteric mathematics, the warning had been impressed upon the mind of *The Hope of Man* — stellar mass and the Warp do not mix! And yet her master, Marek, had set her upon the path of destruction, initiating the sequence of spatial re-orientations that would culminate in the shift into hyperspace, while her present orbit led her with increasing speed towards the small planet that burned, remote and bright, in her vision screens. The ship was troubled, but meanwhile there were dangers that she could deal with. Her defenses went into action.

He had used his native tongue only rarely during the twenty years that had elapsed since he emigrated to the Californian Republic, and it was strange now to hear it all about him. The avenue was thronged with men, women and children, clad in the gay, casual clothes that were the universal form of summer dress. Flowers on a coffin lid, Marek thought, as he pushed his way through the crowd. He had come home, back to the continent of his youth, bearing a message. The message was liberation, liberation beyond the feeble dreams of the revolutionaries who roved Asia and the American States. The final liberation. The bombs were coming, the multiheaded missiles, the nuclear rain that would wash the Earth, sterilize it, cleanse it of the squirming, pullulating mass that was humanity. He came to a vast open square surrounding the pedestal of a statue built on a scale of paranoiac grandeur.

Standing amid the unheeding strollers, he cried his news, arms outflung to the sky. And it was true. The sky vanished, was wiped away by a fire intolerably bright that burned through his closed eyelids as the bombs exploded and exploded and exploded...

Marek awoke screaming. The screens above him flickered with brilliant, intermittent flashes as the atomic shield of the ship intercepted and vaporized fragments of rock and metal, the debris of the planet-forming processes, streaming eternally around the distant orange sun. There was nothing there to deflect him from his course. He shook his head as if to clear his vision, and looked across the Control Room at the chronometer. Phase One was near.

CHAPTER SEVENTEEN

"Jeh-ree?"

Jerry Cornelius looked away from the tiny transmitter resting in his palm. Lae-Pinu was watching him with an expression of concern. He realized that she had spoken to him more than once.

"I'm sorry," he said. "You were right, Lae-Pinu. The Alanga, whatever they are, do exist." He turned the device over, as if some fresh information might be gained by doing so. "We've got to assume that Cathy was wearing this up to the time it fell beside the stream. Let's examine the place for other signs."

They found the second group of prints almost immediately. Smaller, and sunk more deeply into the mud than were the others, they were plainly the tracks of a quadruped. At one point they had been obliterated by a broad furrow. Unskilled as he was in the art of reading signs, Jerry still felt fairly confident in assuming a solitary animal dragged down by a hunting pack. What sort of hunters, he wondered, and what was their prey? The unbidden thought came to him: had the object of the struggle been Cathy?

"There do not seem to be any marks made by people," Lae-Pinu said, hopefully. She moved her feet up and down as she spoke, apparently enjoying the feel of the mud between her toes.

"That's true," Jerry agreed, smiling. "Let's take that as an indication we're on the right trail." He felt illogically cheered by her words. "Hop back in the carrier, girl, and we'll take a look at the hill where you saw the Alanga. Wipe your feet first!"

She laughed, the first real expression of amusement that he had seen from her since first they met. She was, Jerry decided, a very pretty girl.

"It sucks, doesn't it?" she said, scrubbing at her feet with a handful of blue moss.

Jerry climbed into the driving seat. "The mud? Yes, I suppose it does. My paddling days are long gone! Is this the first time you've ever stood on natural ground?"

Lae-Pinu nodded. "There are a few small gardens in the upper city, but they are mostly dried up and withered. My mother told me that *her* mother had seen living flowers once in a garden, but that was long ago."

He backed the carrier away from the stream and turned it towards the hill with the red-streaked flanks that she had indicated. The slope was fairly gradual at first and they made good speed, climbing diagonally across the face of the range. It was close to high noon of this world's eighteen-hour day, but the air was cooled to a pleasant degree by a breeze off the hills. Vegetation thickened as they climbed, tough, slender trunks quite unlike the forests of the plateau, tangled and matted with wiry stems that bore black fruit. When he was forced to bulldoze his way through patches too extensive to make detouring practical, Jerry felt a quite unreasonable twinge of guilt as stems snapped and fell. Conditioned by his early training in the science of nutrition to regard plant life as something to be nurtured and protected, constantly outraged by the thoughtless burning and mutilation inflicted upon the Earth's oldest living things, the trees, he found it difficult to make a virtue of present necessity. To Lae-Pinu, on the other hand, the ride was clearly the greatest thing that had ever happened.

A thousand feet above the plain, they halted on an open, rocky ledge that commanded a view both upslope and down. Jerry swung out of the cab and stretched, breathing deeply. Walking to the edge of the rocks, he stared out across the flat immensity of the plateau to where the city lay like a discarded piece of jewelry, gleaming through the faint orange haze. The girl joined him, though she refrained from approaching the very brink of the drop. Jerry covertly studied her reaction to the panorama below.

"The city is so *small*," she said quietly.

"Like your world or mine, seen from space," Jerry answered. "But all the people, and their problems, remain as big as ever." Struck by a sudden thought, he said: "What is the name of your world? You never told me."

"Why, Beya, I think… I'm not really sure. Do all worlds have names?"

Once again, he was thrown mentally off-balance by her naïveté. He explained the origins of various planetary names to her, meanwhile speculating inwardly upon this new information. If Beya was a world, was Beya-Sev a "world-city"? And if so… He decided it was time to eat.

Lae-Pinu was fascinated by the many-coloured concentrates and liquids which had originally been carried in the deep-freeze compartments of *The Hope of Man*, and at first did not realize that they were edible. Jerry, picking up a chunk of the coffee-scented substance taken from the city storerooms, asked incredulously: "Is this the only form of food available in Beya-Sev?"

Licking a drop of pink ice-cream off her upper lip, she said: "The Great Judge has told us that it is all we need. It has always been there and always will be. Without it we would be like the Sev-Alab, the beasts of the lower city. By processes known only to the Great Judge, the elements of the food are drawn from water and air and rock."

My God, thought Jerry, it's like one of those old commercials from the days when some countries had so much food that people had to be seduced into eating it. He didn't ask what the diet of the Sev-Alab consisted of. He didn't really want to know. But he made a resolve to analyze the food as soon as circumstances permitted. After sampling it while a prisoner of the Sev-Kalan, he could vouch for its nutritional value. And the available food sources of Earth were all too few. Fine, said a small sardonic voice within him, all you have to do now is get it back there.

When evening came, the carrier was forging steadily upward on the steepening sides of the supposed Alanga hill. Spiny ridges, stained rust-red by minerals leached from upper slopes, jutted through the gnarled and gloomy thickets. Jerry had just begun to debate the wisdom of making camp for the night when a crackling rush of unseen bodies through the darkness ahead brought his heart into his mouth. He flicked on the headlights. Frozen almost in mid-stride, a group of weird beings looked blindly back at him with huge, dazzled yellow eyes. The tableau lasted no more than seconds. On legs — or were they legs and forearms? — that must in the larger specimens have been all of six feet long, they resumed their headlong flight into the scrub. Mournful, hooting cries drifted back to the two travelers. When Jerry's pulse had slowed to something like its normal rate, he said: "If those were your friends the Alanga, our chief difficulty will be catching them!"

"Oh no, they cannot be the Alanga. I have never heard of creatures like that before." Her voice was utterly serious.

With equal seriousness, he answered: "It's what may be chasing them that worries me. Be ready to use this."

He passed the neurogun to her. She was in the act of reaching for it when the deep blue arch of sky above seemed to burst apart. Light cascaded upon the hills, the plateau, the whole visible world. Colour vanished. The universe was molten silver and blackest ink. And silence. No thunder followed, no shock wave. Space, thought Jerry incoherently, even as he crouched numbly in the carrier's cab, explosion in space. Must have been outside the atmosphere or there would be blast. He heard Lae-Pinu shouting and saw, through watering eyes, some kind of struggle raging around the vehicle. His body responded to danger instinctively, but his mind had room for only one terrible, overwhelming realization — *The Hope of Man* was gone!

THE DISTANT SUNS

CHAPTER EIGHTEEN

The Hope of Man was gone! Jerry shook his head as if recovering from a blow. There was no time for despair. As the light of the great explosion faded from the sky, and his eyes began to function normally again, he saw a confusion of leaping, plunging bodies all around the carrier. Beasts and riders! The latter were undoubtedly human, their tall shapes wrapped in robes and leather. Several gripped short spears, while other weapons swung at their sides, slings, stone-tipped maces, bows. Their mounts were bizarre, high-backed and slim-legged with pendulous blue crests surmounting their narrow heads, a heavy fleece covering them almost to the feet. No rider had yet been unseated, but they were plainly having immense difficulty in controlling their fear-maddened beasts.

"The Alanga! The Alanga!" Lae-Pinu was clutching his arm, her mouth only inches away from his ear.

"You could be right!" Jerry shouted over the hubbub. He put the carrier into motion, heading uphill. "Whoever they are, I prefer to talk to them from a distance. Let's be off while they're busy."

For good measure, he sounded the distress siren and turned on every available light. As the carrier roared towards a gap in the scrub, the nearest mounts sheered away in panic. They had a brief glimpse of a rider's hawklike face as he swayed far out, clinging to his beast's thick wool and waving a spear. Jerry swung around him, expecting at any moment to feel a heavy point tearing into his flesh. Low branches raked across the windscreen. Wood splintered. The wheels rode up over tilted rocks, dropped jarringly to earth again. The tyres took a fresh grip, the superb engine responded, and within seconds they were clear of the disordered ambush. He did not stop until they had a large area of open space around them.

"Jeh-ree... Jeh-ree..." Lae-Pinu stopped, gulped for air. He could feel a fine trembling in her body as she rested against him. Two shocks so close together, he guessed, had produced an equally strong reaction. He put an arm about her shoulders, held her while the shaking subsided. Meanwhile, his eyes never left the broad stretch of hillside that lay below them, brilliantly lit by the headlamps. Voices and the snorting of animals drifted up the slope, but as yet no sign of pursuit. Despite the warm proximity of the girl, Jerry was suddenly acutely aware of loneliness. What was he doing on this alien hill, with a band of armed riders about to fall upon him? Where was Cathy? The destruction of *The Hope of Man*, being stranded upon this hostile world — all this could be borne if only she was safe, if only he could find her. He felt a fleeting pang of sorrow for Frank Marek. Something very terrible had happened to that courageous and brilliant scientist in the strange, distorted universe of hyperspace. Had that quality of misanthropy apparent in his nature, expressed chiefly in his ironic jokes about mankind's dreams of Utopia, been unchained, set free to dominate his reason? Might it be that Jerry and Cathy had suffered less grievously because of their rapport, the check-and-balance effect of contrasted but complementary personalities? He stared into the night, blinking away the weariness that weighted his eyelids. The fate of Earth was a far-away thing, abstract and unreal. Reality for the moment was Beya and Cathy and nothing else.

It was fortunate for Field Marshal Hira that the light which rushed outward from the Centaurian system at one hundred and eighty-six thousand miles per second would not reach his eyes for another four years, if at all. That brief, abnormal burst of energy, so different to the cold unchanging glitter of the distant suns, would have brought to his keen mind the same message that had appalled Colonel Jerry Cornelius.

THE DISTANT SUNS

449

He paced the upper promenade of the Control Centre Building, high above the silicon-concrete desert of the Gandhi Space Launching Site. White moonlight washed the artificial plain and the barren lands beyond. The burning heat of an Indian day had ebbed into the higher air, and a cool night breeze ruffled Hira's silvery hair. He walked with hands clasped behind his back, his brown eyes thoughtfully regarding the scarred beauty of the full moon. As on many other such nights, he fancied that he could discern, at the limit of vision, the cruciform pattern of Lunar One, the greatest concentration of research laboratories in the Solar System. From that point the eye of his imagination leaped, across meaningless millions of miles, to the triple fires of Centauri.

He realized, as never before, how difficult it was to *believe* in the stars. Traverse the planetary orbits, from the searing hell of sunward Mercury to the frozen solitude of Pluto, and the stars remained the same. Aloof, remote — and inaccessible? Not now, Hira told himself, not now. A few months more and the stars will be ours. If we can hold civilization together until then. Along the promenade a door slid open, sighed shut again. A tall, heavily built man emerged from the shadows, walking with precise, rapid strides. Hira paused.

The big man halted, saluted with a well-judged blend of formality and familiarity. "Perimeter report, sir."

"Yes, Major Armstrong?" Hira, sensing trouble, tried to read some meaning into the impassive Occidental face. As usual, he failed.

"Pressure building up on Sector Yellow North, sir. It could be nasty if it continues. Lieutenant Bruckner did a minicopter survey and says he spotted a Church of Relativity cell stirring things up. They're mostly States people in that sector, sir, with a few New Australasians. A bad mixture."

Field Marshal Hira nodded. "Any mixture that includes the Church of Relativity is a bad one. Einsteinian Fundamentalists are all we need to have a major action on our hands." He began to walk towards the nearest doorway. "You have the record with you? Good. Run it through in here."

In the softly lit, deserted room, Major Armstrong took a small plastic container from his pocket, clipped it into one of the visualizers which were standard fixtures throughout the Control Centre. At the touch of a switch, colour and movement flooded into the viewing prism. A Lilliputian three-dimensional version of the launching site flowed swiftly by as the remote-control camera in the tiny helicopter scanned the earth below. Yellow beacons gleamed ahead, spaced out along a tall metal-mesh fence that marked off the spacefield from the brown, dry plain. To right and left, diminished by distance, the lights of Sectors Red and Green glowed. Across the fence, all semblance of order was lost. Tents, inflatable plastic domes, motor-caravans, a hundred varieties of portable housing, darkened the plain for mile upon mile. Rivers of luminous colour ran through the huddled structures, winding along unplanned, crooked courses. Major Armstrong jabbed a thick forefinger at the prism.

"Watch them, sir, when I step up the magnification." He manipulated the visualizer controls, brought the scene rushing up towards them. Individual faces could be distinguished in the long processions that shuffled by. High above the heads of the crowd, illuminated signs bobbed on the ends of insulated poles. Hira read the gaudy inscriptions silently.

"THERE IS NO UNIVERSE BUT EINSTEIN'S"... "HYPERSPACE INVASION WILL DESTROY THE BALANCE OF CREATION"... "HOLES IN SPACE WILL SWALLOW OUR EARTH!"... "EINSTEIN EQUALS SANITY — HYPERSPACE IS HELL".

There were other, less coherent slogans, in a score of languages. A vast, formless chanting filled the loudspeaker, mingled with clashing strains from numberless musical instruments. Black, yellow, brown and white faces looked up to the hovering television eye. Anger deepened the wordless sounds that rose from the myriad throats, fists were raised, objects soared and fell back upon the surging mob. Flame stabbed suddenly, searingly bright. The eye swept about in a tight curve and headed back to the towering mass of Control Centre. The prism went dark.

"Those flashes," Hira said, "were laser pistols."

Armstrong straightened. "There were at least two rifles among them, too. For a movement that apparently didn't exist until a year ago, the Church of Relativity is remarkably well-equipped, sir."

Hira's brown eyes were hooded and introspective. He walked slowly to the door. Out on the promenade, he said: "How many people are around the field now?"

"At the last count, two million. The Einsteinians represent perhaps one-fiftieth of the total. Aerial reports estimate another million or so within a seventy-mile radius, converging upon the Site. Without the electrified fence there wouldn't be an unoccupied square yard of concrete by now."

"Two million…" Field Marshal Hira shook his head. In a voice that Armstrong had to strain to hear, he murmured: "What do they *want?* What do they think we can do? How do they propose to live out there?"

"They won't live, sir," Armstrong answered bluntly. "Some of the first arrivals, the ones who were here when *The Hope of Man* took off, before we had to erect the fence, are starving. They won't accept food or medical aid from anyone. They just wait." He wheeled, looked squarely at his commanding officer. "I'm not worried about them, not from a military point of view. It's the later arrivals, the crackpot organizations, the private armies, such as the Church of Relativity, that are the real threat. They've got the death-wish, or whatever the therapists call it nowadays, the will to destroy. God knows what satisfaction they get from it. But we'll stop them, sir, we'll stop them. Thank the Lord we have realists at the top of the United Nations in *this* century!"

Hira did not answer. From the distant perimeter came a rattle of gunfire. Lasers flashed. Three huge helicopters lifted from an unseen pad, rumbled away across the field. Flame blossomed somewhere beyond the fence and a pillar of oily smoke climbed between the watchers and the moon. The major swore. Hira snapped: "Major Armstrong, there is to be no firing back! Use sleep-gas if the fence is breached and have squads stand by to carry the rioters off the field before they recover. I'll court-martial any man, whatever his rank, who opens fire without a direct order from me!" He looked at the stars, those distant suns. Whatever *The Hope of Man* returns to, he thought, it won't be to a field reddened with the blood of frightened, deluded men, not so long as I retain command. I think you would call that a realistic attitude, Colonel Cornelius. We're the same kind of realist, you and I. But hurry — for the sake of humanity, hurry!

CHAPTER NINETEEN

"We can talk from here," Jerry said. He stood in the carrier's cab, one hand resting lightly on the laser rifle. At the edge of the scrub a rider sat his restless mount, his spear laid across the saddle. Between Earthman and Beyan ran a long, black, smoking furrow in the soil. Jerry pointed to it.

"You see what this weapon can do. I come in peace, seeking a lost companion. I have no wish to hurt anyone, but those who would bar my way must take the consequences."

He spoke in slow, carefully enunciated Arvik. Lae-Pinu had been astounded to discover that she shared a common language with the barbaric strangers, but to Jerry it meant the confirmation of certain theories he had formed about this world. As he waited for a reply, he kept a keen watch upon the riders bunched behind their spokesman, but they seemed content to wait on the outcome of the exchange.

"Beware, Jeh-ree!" the girl gasped suddenly. Jerry tensed at the same instant, as the Beyan began to raise the spear. Then, leaning forward over the animal's neck, he plunged the point into the ground. Straightening, he spread both arms wide, showing empty hands. In the glare of the headlamps, he was an imposing figure, taller and heavier than the Earthman, with flowing beard and shaven skull. Loose robes emphasized his bulk. Sonorously, his oddly accented words rolled across the intervening space.

"Man of a far land, we too are men of peace. I, Chailemm, speak for all when I say that we make you welcome. But know that there is no place for machines in our community, and the makers of machines. You must put aside these devices of evil, or perish, man and woman alike." He folded his arms and sat, a dark, monolithic figure of menace, in the saddle. "That is my word — I, Chailemm, Speaker for the Alanga!"

"Do not believe him, Jeh-ree!" Lae-Pinu said, imploringly. She looked from Jerry to the huge, motionless figure of the Alanga spokesman, her young face mirroring a struggle between trust and superstitious fear. "He is trying to trick you into surrendering your rifle! Then they will make prisoners of us for their evil god, the All-Devourer!"

Without glancing down, Jerry patted her shoulder. "Maybe he's lying, maybe not. Either way, Chailemm is a brave man, because he knows I could burn him down with this laser at any moment." His voice took on a grimmer note. "I'm inclined to believe him. But I'm not parting with the carrier or the rifle, not for any man or nation on Beya! *The Hope of Man* has gone, but Cathy still has to be found, and until that happens I go armed!"

"Stranger, what is your decision?" The deep tones were edged with impatience, though the man had not moved.

How much does he know, Jerry wondered, how deep is his ignorance of science? Can I bluff him into letting us go without bloodshed? Surely his people can have no conception of the cause of the explosion they've just seen? He spread his arms wide, empty palms showing plainly, in imitation of the Alanga's gesture.

"Speaker Chailemm, men of the Alanga, you have guessed correctly that I come from a far land. What you do not guess is that my land lies on another world, a world similar to your own, called Earth. My name is Jerry Cornelius, and I represent the people of Earth, who built the great ship in which myself and my companions voyaged through space. We come in peace, to warn you of a danger which threatens your people, and mine. You have just seen the first omen of that danger in the sky."

Now there was a stirring among the shadowy riders grouped beneath the branches. Several shot quick, seemingly apprehensive looks at the star-jeweled darkness overhead. Chailemm did not even turn his head.

"The girl has not come from this world you speak of, this Earth. She is of the Sev-Kalan, the people of the city. How does she come to be in your company, Jericornelius?"

There's nothing wrong with your eyesight, Chailemm, thought Jerry. Aloud, he said: "As our ship circled your world, we saw the city from above. We were seeking for signs of intelligent life, and so we came to Beya-Sev in the hope of finding beings with whom we could exchange information. However, the inhabitants were none too willing to help us. Catherine — my wife — vanished from the city, and if it had not been for the courage of Lae-Pinu, who has accompanied me, I would have been a prisoner there, or worse."

"So you think to find your wife in the hills, Jericornelius? Why should she be here?"

There was an undertone to the question, an extra shade of meaning that the Earthman sensed but could not pin down. Or was fatigue making his mind suspect subtleties where none existed? He sighed. Instead of exchanging fruitless cross-talk while Cathy faced God knew what dangers, how temptingly easy it would be to blast a way through these barbarians and pursue his own path into the night!

A split second later he regretted his indecision. With the faintest of hisses, a noosed rope flashed out of the darkness behind him like a striking snake. A violent tug pulled him off his feet and he thudded into the driving seat, half-winded. Lae-Pinu sprang across him, grabbing the butt of the laser rifle. He caught a glimpse of her pale face, her hazel eyes, wide and wild. The laser beam carved the upper air, scattering shadows across the slope. Animals squealed in terror, fighting away from the blinding ray, throwing their riders into confusion. Jerry fought frantically against the pull of the rope, his arms bound tightly against his sides, rage and despair goading his weary muscles. Lae-Pinu steadied the rifle, swept it down. A knotted cluster of branches exploded into flame above Chailemm's head as he struggled to control his mount. He leaped from the saddle, sending the beast galloping to safety with a powerful smack on the rump. At that instant, a second noose encircled the girl's shoulders and jerked her, threshing and sobbing, to join Jerry on the seat. The stealthy Alanga ropemen who had come upon them unseen, now sprang into the cab and began, very efficiently, to tie their

THE DISTANT SUNS

arms and wrists. Lae-Pinu fought with feet and teeth and voice until the men, not ungently, trussed her ankles, too.

"I'm sorry, Lae-Pinu," said Jerry, "I'm sorry." It sounded silly and useless even in his own ears, but she smiled while tears of anger still glistened on her cheeks.

"It is not your fault, Jeh-ree. Do not blame yourself."

Chailemm, mounted again, rode up alongside the carrier. He looked down at them from his great height, his bearded face enigmatic. Turning in the saddle, he shouted to the riders forming up once more on the hillside.

"Galdonn! Sechral! Come, take the man and the woman on your shambri. But beware — the beasts may not like the smell of the strangers!"

That detached, observing portion of Jerry's mind that continued to function even at the times of greatest stress, noted a new word. Shambri had not been part of the Sev-Kalan vocabulary implanted in his brain by the city's language-machine. Another indication that the Alanga and the city-dwellers had diverged from a common cultural beginning? Yet how, in the name of Creation, could a planetary culture consist of one mechanized community and a band of hill-dwelling hunters?

Snorting and stamping, two blue-crested shambri approached the carrier, their riders urging them forward with nudges and soothing words. The nearer Alanga was a smaller version of Chailemm, broad-shouldered and heavy, his youthful features half-hidden by a thick black beard. At his side rode a man several years his junior, slim and upright, his bright blue eyes unashamedly taking in every detail of the two prisoners and their vehicle. As the beasts, with skittish reluctance, came close to the cab, the younger man somehow contrived to place his mount between that of his companion and the carrier's side. It could have been accidental, but Jerry, noting the fleeting scowl that passed over the other's face, thought otherwise. The ropemen looked doubtfully from one man to the other, obviously wondering which of them to obey, but the interloper, grinning, said: "Leave the heavier burden to my brother Galdonn — his are the broader shoulders!"

Lae-Pinu had ceased to struggle and lay like a dead weight as the hunters lifted her. Sechral reached down and gathered her from their arms with an easy strength that belied his slightness. As her tight-lipped, tear-streaked face under its tousled mop of blonde hair came level with his own, he said lightly: "The Sev-Kalan are indeed crazy to allow their prettiest daughters to roam the hills at night! Or have they finally decided to quit that midden-heap on the plain and come out into the air?"

She spat at him. Laughing, he placed her, side-saddle, on the shambri's back, holding her with an arm about her waist. Turning away from the carrier, he called to Galdonn: "Take care, brother — do not tell yours that he has a pretty face! He may spit venom!"

Galdonn's reply was another, and even more interesting, example of cultural divergence. Then he dragged Jerry up like a sack and growled: "Hold to the fleece and do not try to dismount until I say so!"

Chailemm's deep tones rose above the noise of men and animals, and for a moment there was stillness.

"It is time that we were gone. Harn, the White One, will rise before morning and the Drigg will hunt by his light. It is not a propitious time to meet them, for their numbers will be many. Let us go!"

The shambri broke into long, smooth-swinging strides. Twisting his head about, Jerry had a final sight of the carrier, empty and silent, still blazing its headlamps into the tangled scrub. Presently, low-hanging branches intervened. The riders rounded a jagged wall of rock, and there was nothing more to be seen.

CHAPTER   TWENTY

"In the name of the Great Judge, woman, be silent!"

Lae-Varka thumped the table with the flat of his hand, making the dishes rattle. Particles of food sprayed from his lips. The small blonde woman seated at the far side of the room shook her head wearily, as if observing a familiar scene. Her reply, delivered in a low, monotonous whine, had the mechanical quality of a statement made many times before.

"Anger will not change the truth, husband. Our youngest daughter is gone, driven away by your cruelty. Now we have lost both of our children. Without someone to carry on the duties of the Varka, what will become of us? We are nothing... nothing!"

The stocky man wiped crumbs from his beard, violently.

"Do you think I do not know that — I, the Voice of the Great Judge, whose ancestors have served the Wall since Beya-Sev began? If you had given me sons instead of —"

He broke off at the sound of running feet in the corridor outside. A loud knocking followed. The woman rose and slid aside the bronze-paneled doors, admitting a slim man in yellow tunic and trousers. Agitatedly he bowed and then trotted to Lae-Varka's side.

SAILING TO UTOPIA

"Well, Lahl-Maghra, what is it, man? Speak, speak!"

"Speaker," Lahl-Maghra panted. "There is something wrong at the Wall! The Great Judge has given strange signals — we do not know what he requires of us!"

"Ha!" Lae-Varka barked. "The Elders may mumble and mutter that there is no place for a Speaker whose wife cannot give him heirs, but who do they run to when in doubt?" The woman began to speak. He waved a dismissing hand at her. "Be silent, wife! This is a man's business. Come, Lahl-Maghra!"

Once in the corridor, the acolyte's agitation became something closer to panic. At an angle of the passage, he paused and began to babble his story, but Lae-Varka pushed him ahead, saying brusquely: "Whatever it is, it can wait until we reach the Judgment Hall. I take it that the Elders still have tongues in their doddering heads!"

It required a massive effort of will to keep his façade of confidence intact when finally he strode through the towering doorway of the Judgment Hall and confronted the scene within. Seated on the dais below the vast face of the Great Judge, the six Elders of the Sev-Kalan were submerged in a sea of sombre yellow light, the colour of imminent peril in the code of the Wall. All other signals had disappeared. The few members of the community still awake at this hour were huddled in a small dark group in the front pews. Lae-Varka paced unhurriedly up the central aisle, ignoring their pallid, staring faces. Two women sobbed, somewhere in the gloom. He mounted the steps to the dais.

"What news have you?" He addressed the Elders without formality, noting, not for the first time, that the marks of senility were upon them, despite the fact that there was little difference in years between himself and the youngest of the six. Surely a man's life had been longer when Beya-Sev was newly built?

"You speak discourteously, but we forgive your error, for the occasion is one to disturb the reason of the strongest of men." The speaker was Borud-Brahn, oldest member of the upper city tribe. The careful phrasing of his rebuke could not disguise the quaver in his voice. Slumped in his chair, he regarded Lae-Varka with faded, watery eyes. "We can tell you little, other than what you see for yourself. Less than one quarter of an hour ago, the yellow signals began to cover the Wall. We await your interpretation of the words of the Great Judge."

Lae-Varka nodded. Seated at the desk console, he fell easily into a routine that he had not practised in several years, ever since his daughter had become Keeper of the Records. The information flowed from the vast storage banks of the Wall, becoming comprehensible as the console transformed the symbols into the language of men. Slowly, Lae-Varka's expression grew grim. Presently he rose and faced the silent assembly.

"What is the word of the Great Judge…" Borud-Brahn's query tailed off into inaudibility.

"The message," said Lae-Varka harshly, "is that within two nights and two days, Beya-Sev will be destroyed!"

CHAPTER TWENTY-ONE

The black beast paused upon the crest of the ridge, sniffing the air. Light from the huge pale planet on the horizon silvered the stiff ruff of hair that bristled upon its thick neck. As it swung its blunt, fanged snout from side to side, two red feral pin-points glowed under the heavy brows above the flaring nostrils. For a moment it stood, testing the rich odours that flooded from the tangled vegetation on the hillside. Then the muscular body stiffened. A low mewing issued from the barely open jaws. Where there had been only shadows, there was suddenly a pair, a quartet, a dozen black shapes. They coalesced, became a pack, flowed across the open ground towards the scrub.

"Slowly... slowly," Chailemm murmured, as he rode alongside the trail leader of the Alanga band. "If the Drigg are hunting tonight, this will be their hour. There is much fresh spoor to draw them."

The gaunt rider nodded. "Even so, Chailemm. The shambri are becoming uneasy." He patted the thick fleece on his mount's arching neck. "Trust these ears and long nose to give warning."

"When the Drigg hunt, I trust nothing." Chailemm turned his shambri about, rode back down the line of plodding animals. Reaching one that was doubly burdened, he said quietly: "How goes it, stranger?"

Jerry Cornelius glared at him. "It goes badly. What else do you expect with these on my wrists?" He flourished his bound hands before the Speaker's eyes, and was forced to make a hasty grab at the shambri's fleece to prevent himself from pitching out of the saddle.

Behind him the hunter, Galdonn, cursed. Craning his head around the Earthman's taller form, he growled: "How long must my beast suffer this fellow's weight? Cannot he be passed to someone else?"

"A reasonable request," said Chailemm. In a low but carrying voice, he called to a nearby rider. "Genli! Take the outlander upon your saddle to ease Galdonn's mount. Steady, now… take it slowly."

An amused chuckle sounded from the darkness close at hand. "Galdonn, my brother, you lack the quality of sympathy for this task. See how mine sleeps!"

And indeed Lae-Pinu did sleep, betrayed by her own weariness, her blonde head lolling on Sechral's shoulder. Galdonn's thick, black eyebrows drew together in a frown, but he said nothing, concentrating upon the awkward business of transferring Jerry from his own shambri to that of Genli. When the exchange was completed, he muttered: "Harn be thanked!" and promptly edged away. With Genli's hand to steady him, Jerry eased himself gingerly into the saddle. He had never cared for horseback riding, and the movement of the shambri was markedly more unsettling than that of any terrestrial animal he had ever sat upon. Scarcely had he gripped the neck-fleece when there came a sudden rustling in the bushes ahead. The shambri made a thin, bleating sound, and abruptly jerked its head up. Jerry slid sideways, fingers knotted in the shaggy pelt, muscles bulging with strain. Somewhere in the night, the trail leader blew two short, urgent notes on a carved horn.

"The Drigg hunt!" Genli's voice sounded, low-pitched and intense, in Jerry's ears. Without further signals, the Alanga drew together, forming a wedge. Spear-points bristled along its edges. Chailemm and the gaunt leader formed the apex, each with bows strung and arrows nocked. Unnoticed save by Sechral, Lae-Pinu awoke and gazed bewilderedly at the warlike scene. A clearing opened before the riders, and as they rode out into the white light of Harn, she seemed fully to recollect the situation. Sechral pressed her close as she instinctively attempted to draw away.

"Sit quietly, little one. There is danger all around us. Be still, and do not distract me from my duties." He spoke gently, almost casually, but his grip was unbreakable. She twisted her head about to look up at him. There was a half-smile on his dark, beardless face. His blue eyes flicked a brief glance at her, then returned to their scrutiny of the hillside. The bushes rustled again, and she felt a swift stab of fear.

With a crash, the tall stalks immediately before Chailemm collapsed. Giant figures shouldered through, trampling the foliage, brushing broken stems aside. The trail leader flung out his arms, crying: "Hold! Hold! Mahra! Mahra!"

"What is it?" Jerry asked, striving to see over the heads of the intervening riders. "What's happening?"

He had his answer almost before Genli could begin to reply. Into the clearing ran a band of familiar beings. Saucer-sized yellow eyes gleamed from simian faces, incredibly long forearms swung in unison with the shorter, sturdier hindlegs. The creatures loped across the open ground, uttering gabbling sounds of distress. Clinging to the long hair on the shoulders of several were their young, lightly furred and unsettlingly humanoid. Jerry knew them now. A band like this had crossed the path of the carrier only hours before. No-one tried to intercept them.

"They are the Mahra, outlander, the people of the forest," said Genli, no longer whispering. "Except at birthing time, they are harmless. But be ready, now, for tonight they are the quarry of the Drigg. Brace yourself!"

Something black came out of the forest. The horn brayed, high and hard. Polished stone spear-heads lifted, gleaming dully. The Drigg cast a look of crimson-eyed malevolence at the waiting beasts and men, and then ignored them. Lifting its head to the sky, it cried out, a high screaming that ended in a sound like the ripping of heavy cloth. Jerry's stomach contracted. Was this *thing* the source of the tracks where Cathy had crossed the stream? Sweat broke out upon his back and palms.

There was a sudden sound of indrawn breath, a collective movement of the shambri. The Drigg sprang. It seemed fantastically to multiply itself, becoming a twelve-headed fury. The Mahra scattered in panic, hopelessly. Jerry saw one female stumble. She recovered almost instantly, but the cub she carried had lost its grip upon her hair, and rolled over and over across the rocky ground. Under the very feet of

Sechral's mount a Drigg pounced, crunched the cub's skull with yellow fangs. Lae-Pinu shouted as the shambri reared, kicking and snorting. A foot caught the killer's blunt dark head. With blood-chilling speed the Drigg twisted aside and launched itself at Sechral and the girl. Bowstrings twanged. Sechral flung Lae-Pinu flat along the shambri's back, threw himself across her. She felt the shambri stagger under the impact of the Drigg's attack and bleat in agony. Then she was falling, with Sechral's arms still holding her fast.

"Cut me loose, damn you!" Jerry raged. "Cut me loose!" Helplessly he watched the pair roll clear of the mauled and dying shambri, saw the Drigg, studded with arrows, leap at them with bloodied jaws agape. On his knees, straddling the dazed girl, Sechral stabbed upward with his spear. A thick, claw-tipped foreleg smashed the weapon aside, ripping one leather sleeve to gory ribbons. The black beast rose above him, snarling hideously. There was a great shout, and a stone spear-point buried itself in the round, bristling head, transfixing the upper and lower jaws. Galdonn vaulted to earth, a long mace gripped in both broad hands. Evading the slashing claws, he swung the mace twice with ferocious skill. Bone snapped. The Drigg shuddered and fell.

"My thanks, brother." Sechral rose, swaying. Sweat shone on his bloodless face. Dark streams coursed down his torn arm, spattering the silvery grey of Lae-Pinu's coveralls. He stooped, reaching down a hand to her. Galdonn waited. Sechral staggered, recovered his balance, looked vaguely at his brother, and then his knees buckled. Galdonn, grinning wolfishly, caught him and raised him from the ground as if he were a child.

"I will take him." The voice was that of Chailemm. Galdonn stared straight into the eyes of the Alanga Speaker as he towered over the scene of death and pain.

As Chailemm began to dismount, Galdonn said: "No, my father. He rides with me."

"So be it. You have earned the right to decide." Chailemm took the limp form of his youngest son, held him while Galdonn remounted. Then he gave him over to the other's care. Turning to Lae-Pinu, who was sitting up and regarding the stiff and bloody corpse of the Drigg with horrified wonder, he said: "Now you, small one." Gently and without any apparent effort, he lifted her to the saddle of his shambri. For the first time since the action had begun, Jerry relaxed. He looked about him. What had become of the balance of the Drigg pack? Amazingly, they had not come to the assistance of their fellow. Shreds of flesh, some with clumps of hair attached, were strewn along one side of the clearing. Of the Mahra and their pursuers, there was no other sign. A pack of individualists, thought Jerry. God help the Alanga — and us — if the Drigg had acted differently. Twelve, working in unison, would have made mincemeat of our band, shambri included.

The riders formed up again, and they set off at an easy pace in deference to the wounded hunter. As Chailemm's mount passed him, Sechral gave Lae-Pinu the pale ghost of a smile. Jerry, riding at her other side, saw that she was weeping. He leaned over, perilously, and called: "Do not upset yourself too much, Lae-Pinu. These people are tough. He'll get over it!"

She looked back at him out of brimming hazel eyes. Between sniffs, she said huskily: "I was thinking of the little Mahra!"

They rode on under the white face of Harn.

CHAPTER TWENTY-TWO

"You lie! You lie!" Borud-Brahn was on his feet, his ponderous body shaking with the intensity of his anger. He pointed a gnarled hand at Lae-Varka. "It is a trick, a plot to usurp the authority of the Elders! Beya-Sev cannot be destroyed! The Great Judge protects us!"

Cries of approval sounded from the group of Sev-Kalan assembled in the Hall, cries that had a note of hysteria in them. Several people left their seats and threw themselves down at the foot of the platform, as if to be reassured by closer proximity to their fount of wisdom. Standing by the console, Lae-Varka spoke in controlled tones, but small muscles in his face and hands jerked and quivered.

"Old man, you are a fool. Your eyes show you plainly that disaster is upon us, but your brain is too withered to accept the truth. I am the servant of the Wall, and the Wall does not lie. Those who say otherwise reject the authority of the Great Judge. Do the Elders set themselves above the Guardian of Beya-Sev?"

"Does Lae-Varka set himself above the Council of the Elders?" snapped a small, sharp-faced man at the further end of the council table. "How do we know that he offers the correct interpretation of the Great Judge's words?"

Panting, Borud-Brahn demanded: "Tell us what is about to destroy Beya-Sev — if you can. What is the exact nature of the catastrophe?"

"Tell us!" cried a woman in the audience, and the crowd took up her words as if responding to a cue. "Tell us! Tell us, Voice of the Wall!"

Lae-Varka nodded, ignoring the agitated Elders. "You shall be told, if the Great Judge is willing." He sat down at the console desk again.

Time crawled by. The Sev-Kalan, audience and Elders alike, sat tensely in the yellow-lit cavern of the Judgment Hall, mutely waiting. Towering over all, the glittering instrumented precipice that was the controlling brain of the city shone a sombre and relentless light upon them. The console clicked. Lae-Varka pushed back his chair. For a moment he sat, head bowed. As a murmur began to rise in the Hall, he stood and once more faced the assembly. The harshness had gone from his voice, replaced by a curious note of resignation.

"Elders and citizens of Beya-Sev, the word of the Great Judge is this. An object of enormous mass approaches our world at a velocity beyond understanding. This object comes from the regions outside the atmosphere, where no life exists. When it enters the atmosphere, the Great Judge has calculated that it will create a disturbance sufficient to overthrow the walls of the city. That is our fate. There is nothing that can be done to prevent it."

The brief silence that followed shattered before a torrent of words. Men and women streamed from the Hall, carrying the dread news to the sleeping city. Borud-Brahn rounded upon Lae-Varka.

"The outlander who came to us with his fantastic tale of other worlds has done this! Did he not say that he and his people could move bodies through the airless spaces, against all reason? You, Lae-Varka, you were responsible for his keeping. Your carelessness allowed him to escape! And now we must suffer!"

The accused man made no reply. From the outer chambers and galleries came a sudden clangour. It grew rapidly in volume, a metallic thunder as of giant hammer-blows, battering upon the barriers that sealed off the upper city from the darkness below!

"What in blazes is going on down there?" The man from *The New York Herald Tribune* squinted into the glare of an Indian sun, as wind from the whirling rotors overhead whipped his words away. Below, the shadow of the big United Nations helicopter rippled over the myriad heads of the crowd, like a flat dark fish over pebbles. The scrape and shuffle of innumerable feet, the babble of a thousands of voices, blended in a featureless, ascending roar. From the starboard viewport, the red-bearded correspondent of the Swedish *Aftonbladet* said, wonderingly: "It looks like some kind of dance. But it's a pretty odd affair."

"An example of contagion by communication." The lanky *London Guardian-Times* representative spoke with his usual air of casual omniscience. Watching the slow, mindless whirlpool of human figures half-a-mile outside the Gandhi Space Launching Site's electrified fence, he continued: "The four AM satellite relay brought scenes of dancing mania in Southern China and Brazil. Our friends down there, lacking anything more constructive to do, no doubt were caught up by the craze and have imitated what they saw on their screens. That's our twenty-first century Earth — one big cozy electronic madhouse."

"Four AM?" said the technical expert from *Pravda*, brushing an ant off her white stretch-suit. "Don't you *ever* go to bed? And what is 'dancing mania', please?"

"We can go into question one later. As for question two, there are historical parallels for the spectacle we are witnessing. Europe in the Middle Ages, during the onset of the Black Death, is a good example. The Death — Bubonic plague — killed millions and shattered the structure of European society. Strange cults, irrational and perverted, arose in its wake. One notable symptom was a compulsion to dance which gripped crowds, without reason, so that they danced until they fell through sheer exhaustion."

"They are just going round and round and round," exclaimed *Aftonbladet*. "Thousands of them! Does anyone know the Skygrid count today?"

"Seven point four millions at 0800 hours," the *Herald Tribune* newsman informed him. "At that time, the robocopter had covered three-tenths of the perimeter. Then somebody blasted it down."

"Seven million people in less than a third of the total distance around the field! And still they are arriving!"

"I do not see the relevance of the effects of the Black Death, I am afraid." The tone of *Pravda's* remark was skeptical rather than apologetic.

"Me neither," grunted *Herald Tribune*.

"To answer our colleague's very pertinent question," said *Guardian-Times* reprovingly, "I would refer you to the excellent United Nations summary of fifty years' work upon the psychological effects of overcrowding. The Black Death has been eradicated, my friends, but Man has created a less tractable plague to replace it. Himself! The new scourge of humanity is — humanity."

"Hey, hey! Who is that?"

Conversation ceased at *Aftonbladet*'s cry. His eyes pressed to a binocular viewer, he was gesturing forward and down with one freckled, knuckly hand. Ahead, a colossal hemisphere swelled above the clustered tents and caravans, a dome as yellow as the Sun and only a little less bright. The Master Chapel of the Church of Relativity was an imposing sight, not least because of the military neatness of the lesser installations surrounding it and isolating it from the antlike, swarming disorder of the multitude. But to the reporters it was a familiar landmark in their daily survey of the fantastic scene at the Launching Site. Something else had drawn *Aftonbladet*'s attention. Peering through another viewer, *Herald Tribune* whistled. On the huge stage curving across the base of the dome stood a tall, regal, blonde-haired woman in her late fifties. A glittering cloth-of-gold kaftan draped her statuesque figure, a mass of necklaces and pendants hung with jeweled symbols encased her upper body. Men and women in plain yellow robes attended her, deferentially.

"That, kiddies," announced *Herald Tribune*, "is Sophie Gavin, the power behind the throne of Relativity, no less!"

"She is the wife of Minister Gavin, the leader of the Church?" asked *Pravda*.

"Indeed she is," said *Guardian-Times*, cutting in on *Herald Tribune*. "Her younger sister, Kate, married the designer of *The Hope of Man*, which must make for some interesting chat at family reunions. I don't like the look of this at all. There's entirely too much Relativity heavy artillery, both literal and figurative, concentrated here. I hope Marshal Hira has a good intelligence service."

"That's all for today, people." The bored voice of the pilot signaled the end of the daily flight. The helicopter swung in a wide arc, across the sprawling, motley multitude encamped on the sunbaked plain, over the gleaming strands of the fence, into the airspace above the shimmering, sterile vastness of the silicon-concrete launching field. Behind them, the tall, glittering figure on the curved stage stared enigmatically at the glass towers of the Control Centre. The dance went on.

CHAPTER TWENTY-THREE

Harn was setting as the party of riders crossed the highest ridge of the hills and came in sight of the sea. So unexpected was the sight that Jerry's breath caught in his throat. Memory came back to him of the first view of the city and the plateau seen from the Control Room of *The Hope of Man*, of the suggestion of a coastline beneath an orange-tinted screen of clouds. The dark, rippling plain that curved along the horizon, broken by crests that glinted in the white light of the sinking planet, seemed part of a different order of reality. A cold night wind blew from it, sighing through the valleys and passes, tugging at the creaking branches of gnarled, tenacious trees. Near him, Sechral woke momentarily and moaned softly. Jerry looked at the young Alanga, slumped against the solid bulk of his elder brother.

"How is he, now?"

Galdonn turned, slowly. His square, bearded face regarded the Earthman for several seconds, as if he were assessing the motive behind the query. Finally, he said gruffly: "The wound is less deep than it appears. He will be well again soon."

But Jerry read a different diagnosis in the unguarded flicker of Galdonn's eyes towards the injured man, even as he spoke. To hell with caution, he thought to himself, there's a man dying here. In a voice pitched to carry, he called: "I have medicines which may cure his wounds, if you will permit me to use them. But we must return to my vehicle to recover them."

Galdonn's features froze. Hostile glances were turned upon Jerry by the riders within earshot. Too weary and sore to care about possible consequences, he glared back at them with equal fierceness, silently cursing them for their superstitious conservatism. Riding at his right, Lae-Pinu's expression was unreadable in the dying light. Chailemm sat massively in his saddle, seemingly not to have heard Jerry's words. The rider Genli, whose shambri Jerry shared, murmured: "Speak not of the devices of science, stranger. If it is the will of Harn, the Speaker's son will recover."

Now the trail dipped down into a steep-walled valley filled with shadow. Coldness welled up from the hidden depths, lapping about them like a rising tide. Jerry clamped his tongue between his teeth to keep them from chattering as the chill seeped into his aching muscles. He was dismally certain that he would be unable to walk or sit for at least a week, when this spine-jolting ordeal was over. The impulse to turn up the heating unit of his suit was almost irresistible, but he fought it down, knowing the importance of keeping his captors in ignorance of the nature of the garments worn by the girl and himself. Soon the rocky hillsides had shut off their view of the sea, and the last pale sliver of Harn winked out. Through the intense blackness that followed, a glimmer of red began to emerge. It strengthened as they descended, and presently the smell of burning rose to Jerry's nostrils. At the same moment, a challenge rang out from the darkness.

"Who rides?"

Chailemm's voice boomed in reply. A robed figure, smudgily silhouetted by the distant fires, stepped into the trail. Bowing, the sentinel waved them onwards with a movement of the long spear which he carried.

The ground became mossy, the slope flattened out, and a short while later they were following the course of a stream that trickled lazily across the valley floor, towards a group of stone huts. Smoke drifted to them on the breeze, underlaid with the rich scents of flowering vegetation. Jerry, his senses sharpened despite his weariness by the need to absorb new information, suddenly experienced a thrill of pure, cold horror. Out of the night air overhead rushed a winged something that swooped across his line of sight, an arm's length or less before him. He jerked away from the apparition, bringing an explosive curse from Genli as his shoulder thudded into the Alanga's chin. The flying thing flared its wings, checked, and settled to the left arm of Chailemm. Lae-Pinu squeaked, throwing herself backwards so abruptly that only the Speaker's great strength and reach prevented her from pitching headlong to the trail.

"Steady, now... steady," Chailemm murmured. The girl, sitting as far from the new arrival as was possible, watched apprehensively as it extended downy forearms ending in tiny, almost vestigial hands, and clambered up the sleeve of the Speaker's robe to his shoulder. Seated there, it began to talk to him in a thin, piping voice. More of the creatures flew out of the darkness, settling to the arms of other riders. Only the one that came to Sechral did not alight, but flew continually about the shambri and its burden, emitting a keening whine that made Jerry's flesh creep.

"What are those things?" he asked of Genli.

"They are the chibba, the children of Harn," said the Alanga, ruefully rubbing his bearded jaw. "Once, long ago, they were mute, but Harn in his wisdom gave them the gift of speech. Now they guard our village at night, warning us of the approach of savage beasts."

People crowded into the firelight as the band approached. Some, who had been sleeping in the clearing, awoke and stretched and arose to greet their kin. It seemed to Jerry that the whole adult community — he saw no children — had abandoned their rest to be present when the riders returned. To see a stranger? he wondered. How long had they known of his presence *before* that encounter on the hillside?

They rode into the clearing. Women and slim girls with silver ornaments gleaming in their hair moved to greet their menfolk. Afterwards, their eyes turned in bold curiosity to the Earthman and the grey-clad figure of Lae-Pinu. A few elderly women tended cooking pots, a scattering of grey-bearded men squatted at the edge of the circle of warmth, looking on with sunken, indifferent faces. Through the crowd came a tall woman who walked with an athletic, yet wholly feminine, stride. She stood by Chailemm's shambri, surveying Lae-Pinu with bright blue eyes. The Speaker reached down and took her slim hands in his.

"Myrhial." The tone was formal, the clasp affectionate. With equal gravity, the woman replied: "Chailemm, my husband."

Her keen gaze passed now to Jerry, and something prompted him to make a courteous bow, or something as close to a bow as his situation allowed. But when he looked up again, she was staring at something beyond him and her face had gone quite blank. As he dismounted, leaning heavily upon Genli, Galdonn walked by bearing the limp body of Sechral. Together with Myrhial and two of the Alanga, he entered the largest of the stone buildings and closed the door. As the silent procession disappeared, Jerry's attention was caught by a movement just out of range of the firelight. He glanced, casually, and then for an instant his heart seemed to stop.

A girl with red hair walked toward the fires, her long robes trailing on the damp moss. She walked as if asleep, guided by some inner sense rather than by cognizance of the outer world. Jerry, without conscious thought, ran to meet her.

"Cathy!" His voice broke the hush that had fallen upon the crowd. "Cathy!"

Stumbling, slipping, hampered by his bound hands, he ran. Gasping, he halted before her, staring into the face that he knew better than any other in his personal universe. The familiar wide green eyes looked calmly back at him without sign of recognition.

"Cathy!" he cried, "My God, what have they done to you?"

CHAPTER TWENTY-FOUR

Panic reigned in the Hall of Judgment. Bathed in the yellow gloom of the Wall, the Elders of the city were motionless, paralyzed by a danger beyond their experience. On the floor of the vast room the ordinary citizens milled purposelessly, not knowing whether to flee or stay. The very air quivered to the crash and clang of beaten metal, waves of numbing sound that surged from the dim passageways converging upon the Hall. With each monstrous blow, fear mounted. In all the known history of the upper city of Beya-Sev, never had the gates and portals of the Sev-Kalan been so assailed. In all their lore, there existed no precedent for action in such a situation.

As if moving against some great pressure, Borud-Brahn, oldest of the Elders, took one lurching step towards the silent figure of Lae-Varka. The movement was contagious. As one man, his five colleagues rose to their feet. Spittle flecked Borud-Brahn's writhing lips. His outstretched hands clawed at Lae-Varka's throat, while unintelligible sounds of anger spilled from his mouth, thin and high against the brazen clangour from without. The Speaker for the Great Judge staggered under the attack, yet seemed unaware of what was happening. A concerted wail of dismay went up from the people below as they saw their leaders in disorder.

"Murderers! *Alabs!*" Screaming, a small, blonde-haired woman ran up the steps of the dais. She hurled herself upon the broad back of Borud-Brahn, clawing at the Elder's distorted face. The five others milled around the struggle, seeking to tear her away from their senior spokesman. She cried out again, in a paroxysm of rage and fear.

"Husband, husband! They will kill you! Fight! Fight!"

Lae-Varka woke suddenly from his trance. With a growl, he clamped thick fingers about Borud-Brahn's wrists, and heaved. The Elder reeled back and fell heavily against the table. Without pausing, the Speaker drove into the remaining councilmen with clumsy, powerful blows. They scattered in confusion. Breathing heavily, he stood, shoulders hunched and head lowered, heedless of the woman's chattering reassurances. Tentatively, one of the five approached Borud-Brahn, and stooped over his unmoving bulk. Then he backed hastily away, a sick look upon his thin face.

"He is dead!"

The words were scarcely audible, but the Elders needed no further telling. Skirting widely the glowering presence of the Speaker, they streamed down the steps into the dazed and bewildered audience. A wild medley of cries arose:

"What shall we do? How can we protect ourselves against the Sev-Alab?" And loudest of all: "Why does the Great Judge stay silent?"

Lae-Varka strode to the edge of the dais. His voice rang out over the clamour, stilling for a moment the aimless darting of the crowd. In fearful fascination they stared at the killer of Borud-Brahn.

"The Great Judge is silent because he has nothing more to say! The day of destruction has come upon Beya-Sev and the people must perish. Go, do whatever you wish, there is no-one to check or counsel you. Your leaders, your Elders, are weak, tired old men, devoid of hope or wisdom. Go!"

Without waiting to observe the effect of his words, he turned back to the Wall. His wife laid a hand upon his arm, but he shook her off.

"Go with the others. There is nothing more here for you."

She looked into his face as if it were the face of a stranger. His eyes watched her from another world, through a curtain of yellow mist. He said, again: "Go, woman. Save yourself if you can. If the Wall must cease, then there is no place for the Speaker, or need for sons."

Roughly, he pushed her towards the steps. As she falteringly retreated, there came a terrible screeching of torn metal that transcended all previous sounds from the embattled gateways. A man's voice yelled hysterically: "The barrier is broken! They are through!"

The crowd broke and fled, scurrying through arches and tunnels, scattering in a dozen directions. Alone with Borud-Brahn's corpse in the echoing vastness of the Hall, Lae-Varka walked unhurriedly to the console chair and seated himself.

CHAPTER TWENTY-FIVE

Tears blurred Jerry's vision. He reached out to cup Cathy's face in his bound hands, oblivious of the watching Alanga. His fingers, brushing aside a lock of auburn hair, touched a small, crooked scar, red against the fair skin at her temple. A flicker of pain broke the serenity of her gaze. And then, very slowly, awareness dawned. Her hands rose to touch his, warm on the numbed flesh.

"Je... rry?"

Scarcely breathing, he watched the transformation, saw the light brighten in her green eyes as memories linked to memories and the world became whole and coherent once more.

"Jerry!"

Standing amid the dismounted hunters, supported by Chailemm's solid bulk, Lae-Pinu saw the man and the girl embrace. Joy and bitterness filled her. She felt very small and cold and alone.

"The cure is complete." The Alanga Speaker's deep voice held an unexpected warmth. He laid one huge hand gently on Lae-Pinu's shoulder. "Come. You will need food, and a place by the fire."

Limping as circulation returned to her newly freed limbs, she allowed herself to be led to the central fire where it leaped and crackled within a circle of stone slabs. Liquid bubbled in a deep clay pot suspended above the flames. Strange, yet somehow appetizing, smells arose from it. She sat down upon a rug of shambri hair and let the heat and the hypnotic flicker of firelight lull her fears.

Presently, Cathy and Jerry walked into the clearing. To Lae-Pinu it seemed that his face had lost the tense, almost gaunt look that she had known. Beside him paced Cathy in her robe of brown, tall as the tallest of the Alanga women, her hair glowing a rich and coppery red. As they approached, Chailemm rose, towering over the assembly. Seeing Lae-Pinu seated nearby, Jerry gave her a broad, cheerful smile. To Cathy he said: "This is Lae-Pinu, who saved me from the biggest, gaudiest and most unpleasant computer ever built! I'll tell you all about it later!"

The English words were incomprehensible to the girl, but the tone of voice, and Cathy's warm greeting, brought an answering smile to her lips. With a faint feeling of envy she watched the Earthwoman pass on towards Chailemm with graceful, long-legged strides. Jerry said, as he halted before the Speaker: "It seems that I have a lot to thank you for, in spite of our manner of meeting. But why did you not tell me that Cathy was alive? You must have guessed that she was the woman I sought."

"Feelings are more truly revealed by actions, than by words," the Alanga replied. He drew a long knife from his belt, and gestured at Jerry's bonds. "I think we can trust you now! You were strangers, and your wife does not speak our language, and so we could not know your true intentions."

The keen blade shore through the ropes. Jerry flexed his wrists gratefully, feeling the tingle of increasing circulation in his veins.

"You are right, of course," he acknowledged. "Did your hunters meet us by accident, or have you been watching our movements ever since we left the city? And where did you find my wife?"

Chailemm laughed. "Too many questions after a long journey and with an empty stomach! Sit, Jericornelius and Cathy, and we will eat and talk."

Women brought wooden bowls of hot, savoury stew and set them before the Speaker and his guests. Jerry ate without qualms, knowing that Cathy had suffered no ill-effects during her time in the village.

Lae-Pinu, however, stared in consternation at the peculiar brown liquid in which pieces of a strange substance floated, mixed with what were obviously the chopped stems and leaves of plants. *People* did not eat *plants!* But people obviously did, she told herself, as the others ate with evident enjoyment. Hesitantly she spooned up a portion, and took a tiny sip, unaware that a great many pairs of eyes were covertly watching her reactions. The first sip was followed by the spoonful, and she settled down to serious eating. Chailemm re-opened the conversation.

"We have observed your movements from the day that your fire-car descended, Jericornelius. Had it not been for the necessities of the hunt, we might have been present when you met the flying device, and so prevented you from being lured within the city. Returning to your trail, we traced the marks of your vehicle, but were too late to intervene. We glimpsed the flyer as it entered the city wall, and realized what had happened."

Jerry translated this for Cathy's benefit. She smiled ruefully.

"Ill-missed by moonlight, to twist a phrase. But what I can't wait to know is — how did they get me out of the city? I can't remember the event very clearly, but it *must* have been the Alanga who saved me. There was —"

"The robot!" Jerry exclaimed, interrupting her. "Of course! That's who it was!"

Seeing her puzzled expression, he went on: "During the struggle with the Sev-Alab, the city savages, I glimpsed a tall figure in one of the corridors. It looked like the robot that admitted us to the city, but it must actually have been one of our friends here."

When this exchange had been explained to Chailemm, he seemed to debate inwardly for some moments. Finally, he said: "The ways into Beya-Sev are known only to the hunters, but I will tell you this much — the stream which flows from these hills becomes a river and disappears into the earth an hour's ride from the city walls. From this river, Beya-Sev draws its water, through many huge shafts. The people of the city have long forgotten the source of their water supply, and the fact that the shafts lead to the outer world."

"But the people who *left* the city," Jerry said, slowly. "Remembered, or rediscovered, those ways."

There was a longer pause. A certain tension had invaded the

conversation. At last, Chailemm continued in an altered tone.

"You are shrewd. I see that you did not waste the time that you spent in Beya-Sev. Yet truth can be a potent weapon —"

He broke off as a dark-robed man moved quietly into the firelight and murmured something that Jerry did not catch. The Speaker nodded. Rising, he said to the three guests: "I must leave you for a while. My people will see to your needs. Sleep well."

He strode away towards the hut where Sechral lay wounded. Cathy turned to Jerry.

"What happened? The atmosphere went distinctly frigid there, just before he left."

Jerry grimaced. "That was your husband putting his foot in his big mouth. I made a guess at the relationship between the Alanga and the city people — their languages are almost identical — and Chailemm obviously thought me too sharp to be healthy. Now I think his son must have recovered consciousness and they've called him in. I'll watch my words from now on."

"Speaking of words," Cathy said. "How have you become so fluent so suddenly in the native tongue? And how did you acquire this very pretty child who thinks you are the greatest thing since Neil Armstrong?"

"Can I help it if I'm the father-figure type?" He grinned at her, and then said soberly: "From Lae-Pinu's point of view, poor kid, that's too true to be funny. Let's tell our respective stories, and see what sort of a picture of the situation we can make from them."

They talked, with Jerry translating between Lae-Pinu and Cathy until the meal was over. The Alanga women and hunters spoke little to them, but were courteous enough. Afterwards, the women led Cathy and Jerry to an unoccupied hut that was clean and simply furnished, and took Lae-Pinu to share a room with the daughters of Genli. In the clearing the fires slowly dimmed.

Morning was brilliant, the sky a clear blue-green, the hills sharp and glistening with the pre-dawn rain. After a breakfast of fruit, the Terrestrials had climbed a winding flight of steps carved into the face of a steep slope, and stood now at the base of the most striking man-made object in the valley. Towering high above them, the rough-hewn stone figure of a robed man flung out its arms to the heavens. Craning his head to look at the sunlit torso and face, Jerry said: "It was pretty dark when I rode in last night, but I must have been really asleep in the saddle to have missed *that!*"

"Jerry." Cathy's voice was low but urgent. "Jerry, look at this bas-relief!"

He looked at the area she indicated, a circular depression in the grey-green, crumbling face of the pedestal. As if to convince himself of the reliability of his vision, his fingers traced the raised edges of the map carved there. Then he and Cathy stood staring at each other while the songs and cries of the villagers rose faintly on the morning breeze, until Jerry said, almost in a whisper: "It's all there, every curve and peninsula. My God, Cathy, that is a perfect, undeniable map of *Asia!*"

CHAPTER TWENTY-SIX

Speculation ran riot in Jerry's mind as he stood in the shadow of the huge Alanga statue, staring unseeingly at the sunlit hills and the distant green of the ocean. Near him, Cathy studied the enigmatic carving on the pedestal, moving from left to right as if a change in viewpoint might explain its uncanny resemblance to Earthly maps of Asia.

"It couldn't, perhaps, represent a land-mass on this planet?" she spoke tentatively, already aware of the answer.

Jerry shook his head.

"Not a chance, honey. We saw enough of the surface, as we orbited before landing, to be certain that there are no continents remotely like *that*." He drew a deep breath. "No, there's a beautifully simple explanation for the similarity. Except that it's weirder than anything we met in hyperspace —"

A girl's excited call cut across his words. Turning, he saw two young women in green robes, hurrying up the steep steps that led to the statue. There was something familiar about the appearance of the smaller of the pair.

"Why, it's Lae-Pinu!" Cathy exclaimed, laughing. "She seems to have picked up local colour as quickly as I did! What is she shouting?"

"The Sev-Kalan equivalent of 'Good morning!'" Jerry said. "But I guess she has more than that to tell us."

Holding up the trailing hem of her robe, Lae-Pinu ran across the rock platform toward them. Breathlessly, she gasped: "Cathee! Jeh-ree! I found her!"

"Steady, girl — take it easy! Who did you find?"

She reached for the hand of the taller girl, who had hung back. Pulling her forward, she said: "This is my sister Lae-Mura! She has become an Alanga! Isn't it fantastic?"

"Your older sister who was taken from Beya-Sev?" Jerry looked at Lae-Mura's yellow hair, at her huge dark eyes. "Yes, I can see the family good looks. She's remarkably healthy for a girl who was sacrificed to an all-devouring god!"

Lae-Mura looked faintly puzzled. Lae-Pinu rapidly explained Jerry's joke, while he summarized the situation for his wife's benefit. Smiling now, Lae-Mura said: "The legends that we were taught in Beya-Sev were tales to frighten children. The god of our people is Harn, the White One, who embraces all and in whom we are all one. Only under Harn is there life — the city is dead."

Jerry was reminded of Lae-Pinu's little sermon on the virtues of the food, in the prison in Beya-Sev. Cathy murmured: "Ask her about the map. She may be less tight-lipped than Chailemm."

"Good idea." He indicated the weathered bas-relief. "Lae-Mura, can you tell us what this carving represents? Is it some place known to the Alanga?"

She shook her head. "I do not know. Such things are not the business of women. Perhaps the Speaker and the wise men of our tribe could tell you."

"I might have guessed her answer, in this type of society," commented Cathy, when the translation was made. She looked squarely at Jerry. "You believe that it *is* Asia, don't you?"

"Yes. Incredible as it sounds, it seems even less probable to me that two completely distinct evolutionary processes could produce the degree of similarity that exists between ourselves and these people. I'm convinced that we've sprung from the same basic stock."

"Yet how could...?" Wonder shone in Cathy's green eyes. "Hindu mythology! If only I had had more time to listen to Hira on the subject. He was certain that there was a scientific basis underlying it all."

As she concluded, there came sudden, concerted cries from the girls. Simultaneously, he saw that they had all acquired a second shadow, a shadow that swept swiftly from north to south like the hand of some sinister clock. Wordlessly, he stared at the sky. Along the horizon, the straggling remnants of the rain-clouds had been caught up, boiled, steamed into nothingness in the wake of a vast, fiery mass that rushed across the vault of the heavens. While the incandescent track of its passage still burned on their retinas, the sea exploded. There came an intolerable sound, a thunderclap that drove them to their knees, a sound that crushed into inaudibility the whole compass of normal noise, an inverted silence. Ripped apart as if by a monstrous knife, the waters leapt skywards in two jagged walls, bursting at their crests into million-ton masses of spray. Literally, the water shattered, its basic structure torn apart by the terrible impact of the shock wave. The firebolt swooped below the northern hills, outrunning its own thunder, trailing its cone of devastation over the edge of the world.

Jerry, with blood streaming from his nose and mouth, staggered to his feet just as the shock wave struck the coastline. The rocks groaned and quivered. A thousand faults collapsed before the sudden pressure. Dust and fragments spurted as whole hillsides slid ponderously across their harder, deep-rooted foundations. Shielding his face with his arms, Jerry reeled blindly across the little plateau towards the huddled figure of his wife. Halfway to her, he collided with Lae-Pinu, who gripped his coveralls, yelling inaudibly. He swept her along with him in a tottering run to the base of the statue. Cathy, to his immense relief, sat up as they fell against the vibrating stone. Clinging desperately, each to the other, the three bowed their backs to the flying hail of rocks.

"Lae-Mura… Lae-Mura!" Lae-Pinu was screaming, but only now, at point-blank range, did her words reach Jerry. He cursed himself for forgetting the other girl. Raising his head, flinching at the scouring rasp of gritty particles across his face, he squinted into the storm. She was there, only yards away, crawling with infinite slowness across the plateau, the neck of her gown drawn over her head, protectively. He pushed away from the pedestal, ready to grab her. And then the sky fell. Or so his battered senses told him. A hurricane roared out of nowhere and in a split second the world vanished behind a cataract of salt rain. Lightning blazed and slashed through the downpour. The dust became mud, sliding from the hillsides in glutinous torrents.

A thunderous crack smote Jerry's ears. He looked upwards, one arm across his forehead, warding off the rain. In the eery green flare of the lightning, he saw the trunk and head of the statue topple slowly outwards, arms spread wide as if in a final benediction over the valley below. There was nothing he could do to help the others. He crouched in the rain, shaking. The statue crashed over the plateau's edge and disappeared in the murk.

CHAPTER TWENTY-SEVEN

The machines had broken through. The upper city, citadel of the Sev-Kalan, had fallen. Behind the grinding, clattering monsters that once had built the walls of Beya-Sev and maintained those walls for unreckoned centuries, the mindless hordes of the Sev-Alab poured in to ravage and destroy. Only the gigantic, brooding presence of the Great Judge struck some measure of fear into their cloudy, slow-moving minds, so that they still hesitated to approach the dais upon which a lone living man stood. The man was all but unaware of them. He had questions yet to ask. His thick fingers glided over the console.

Great Judge, why did you not warn your people of the arrival of the strangers in their fire-ship?

THE SOCIETY OF BEYA-SEV IS STAGNANT. IT SEEMED INTERESTING TO OBSERVE THE EFFECT OF NEW IDEAS AND TECHNOLOGY UPON ITS STRUCTURE. THE SURVIVAL POTENTIAL OF THE STRANGERS WAS ALSO OF INTEREST.

Then they are truly the cause of our overthrow! But why, Guardian of the City, have you abandoned your people to the beasts of the lower levels?

BECAUSE THE NEED FOR VIGILANCE IS GONE. MY PURPOSE IS FULFILLED. EVENTS HAVE MOVED BEYOND THE SCOPE OF THE POWERS GIVEN ME BY MY

CREATORS, YOUR ANCESTORS. BEYA-SEV MUST DIE. THE LONG SICKNESS HAS
BITTEN TOO DEEP.

The long sickness?

THERE IS LITTLE TIME FOR EXPLANATION. SUFFICE IT THAT THE AIRLESS
REGIONS BEYOND THIS WORLD ARE FILLED WITH FORCES INIMICAL TO LIFE.

Desperately, Lae-Varka pleaded: *The airless regions? Great Judge, I
do not understand. What has this to do with the Sev-Kalan?*

KNOW THIS, THAT THE SHIP OF THE STRANGERS WAS THE SECOND SHIP TO
LAND UPON BEYA.

Death came before his mind could grapple with the implications
of the Wall's final statement.

On a broad ledge overlooking the plain, Cathy and Jerry stood beside
the carrier, gazing at the smoking ruins of Beya-Sev. The light of a new
morning cast an orange tint upon the towering, billowing black clouds
that cast their gloom across plain and hill. At intervals, a white
brilliance would lance upwards from the tumbled stones, followed by
the crackle and rumble of unguessable energies breaking free of some
buried mechanism, the sound carrying clearly over the intervening
miles. The handful of Alanga riders assembled on the slopes above the
ledge muttered in awed tones and fought the restless stirrings of their
alarmed shambri. Jerry said bleakly: "When I first encountered
Chailemm, I spun him a story of coming disaster, because I thought it
might save my neck, and Lae-Pinu's. Well, it came true, and it's won
our release, but I don't feel proud of being a prophet."

"Don't talk as if it was your fault." Cathy turned her eyes from the
sombre spectacle to look at his troubled face. "Space is full of wandering
bodies, within planetary systems such as this one. Earth was struck time
and again in the past. The Alanga valley, I can see, must have caught
only the outer fringe of the shock wave. Beya-Sev was obviously on
the direct path of destruction."

"Yes, but was the fall of this planetoid a natural disaster — or was
it induced?" Jerry's voice was pitched low, as if the nearby watchers
might somehow grasp the meaning of his words despite their ignorance
of his language. "We've stirred up forces in this area of space, willingly

SAILING TO UTOPIA

or otherwise, that could have effects beyond our knowledge. And beyond our ability to put right."

"Darling, it's too late now to think like that. We are part of this world now, just as much as Chailemm or Lae-Pinu." Cathy glanced at the small, robed figure standing forlornly apart from the group, face turned to the ruins of her home. "What we must do now is to give the Alanga the help that we promised. This catastrophe has broken their old aversion to science by overwhelming their society with more demands for action than it can possibly meet. And there is no doubt, Jerry, that their community was dying, in the long view. Think of all those empty, decaying huts we saw, and the fact that there was actually another Alanga village, maybe more, somewhere in the hills, according to the tribal lore. All gone, now."

He sighed. "I know, Cathy, I know. We've learned more about Chailemm's people since the disaster than we might otherwise have learned in a lifetime. The fact, particularly, that after fleeing from Beya-Sev centuries ago, they were forced to make perilous trips into the city to carry off girls because the numbers of their tribe were declining year by year — that's a clear enough indication of racial decay, when added to my own observations within the Sev-Kalan community. But it doesn't make that mess out there any easier to take."

Chailemm's great voice boomed across the hillside, amid a chorus of fear and amazement from the riders.

"The fire-car returns! See, Jericornelius, where it falls!"

"It's true, Jerry, it's true!" Cathy fairly yelled, pointing at the northern sky. High, high above glittered a point of light that grew as it fell, sliding down an intangible wire to meet the ponderous mass of the spinning planet. Jerry, too, began to shout. He hugged Cathy to him, and in another moment they had swept up the startled Lae-Pinu and were hustling her into the seat of the carrier. Calling to the hunters to follow, he eased the vehicle into motion. But only the Speaker and Genli rode with him. The others remained, bunched on the hillside, an apprehensive group.

The Hope of Man made an impeccable touchdown not far from the stream that bordered the hills. Foam-jets spurted, laying the fires that sprang up around her stern, so that the wheels of the carrier made a gritty crunching as they braked within her shadow. The airlock was open, the silvery metal stairway extended itself to meet the travelers. And that was all.

"Where's Frank?" Cathy said tensely. "Jerry, do you think this is some sort of trap?"

Jerry stepped from the carrier.

"There's only one way to find out!"

He picked up the neurogun, gripped Cathy's hand briefly, and began to climb the stairway.

CHAPTER TWENTY-EIGHT

"So Minister Gavin stopped a slug," the *Guardian-Times* man observed brightly, over the breakfast table. Looking at him sourly, *Herald Tribune* growled, through a mouthful of toast: "Every damned thing around Gandhinagar City happens at four AM and you're always awake to see it!"

"Three AM," said *Pravda* and then went as pink as her leather leotards.

To cover her confusion, *Guardian-Times* held out his cigarette-case and murmured: "Have a Spinrad — the hay that makes the day!"

She smiled faintly at his burlesque of a current television commercial, but shook her head.

Spooning up yogurt, *Aftonbladet* enquired: "Do you think there is any substance to the Relativity people's claim that Hira had him assassinated?"

"Complete nonsense!" said *The Times of India* sharply. "The Marshal is a man of peace. He would never countenance such an action."

"Could be that removal of the Church of Relativity's head is the least bloody method of paralyzing the body," countered *Herald Tribune*. "Hira may reckon the death of one man a small price to pay for the preservation of peace. We all know that Gavin controlled the most effective force in opposition to the whole starship project. Maybe he's crazy, maybe not, but his organization is laser-razor."

"Is *what?*" asked *Aftonbladet*.

"Sharp," explained *Guardian-Times*. "And the tense is incorrect. Controls, not controlled. The Minister's death has yet to be confirmed. In the meantime, his capable wife will —"

Heavy footsteps interrupted him. Major Armstrong loomed in the doorway, his tanned, heavy-jawed face grim. A pistol hung at his hip. With a perfunctory nod of greeting, he said: "Until the present emergency is over, all flights have been canceled to avoid provoking hostile reactions from the crowds at the perimeter. There are no, repeat no, exceptions to this order. Anyone contravening it will be severely dealt with. The usual television communication facilities will be available until further notice."

Blast rattled the windows. White smoke boiled on the launching field, startlingly close. Major Armstrong wheeled about, strode swiftly from the room. The correspondents crowded to the windows, breakfast forgotten.

It was like coming home after a long absence, only to discover tiger tracks in the living room. Jerry prowled the corridors of *The Hope of Man*, neurogun at the ready, his senses almost painfully alert. Where was Frank Marek? A vivid mental picture presented itself of the stocky scientist crouching, laser pistol in hand, beyond the next corner. The thought was not pleasant. When he reached the first of the communication screens and activated it, he was surprised at the steadiness of his fingers.

The screen, connected to the Control Room, showed it to be empty. Good. From there, it would be possible to monitor every portion of the ship's interior. Jerry moved towards the central elevator, then paused. Supposing Marek knew where he was? Supposing he jammed the cage where he could pick Jerry off at his leisure? Steady on, son, he told himself, that sort of thinking fills graves. But he went away from the elevator and set himself to climb the vertical ladders.

On the plain, the city burned, intermittently spouting white fire and shattered stone in a manner that made any thought of a close approach futile. Cathy's attention jumped from city to ship and back again, until she could bear the tension no longer. Watched by a wondering Lae-Pinu, she searched for, and found, her laser pistol and tucked it into her belt. Then, with a reassuring smile to the now alarmed girl, she headed for the starship's airlock, thankful that she had discarded the Alanga robes for the freedom of her flexible, close-fitting coveralls. Chailemm and Genli watched her go, but whatever doubts may have passed through their minds, their bearded faces remained impassive.

"The computer room, Cathy. Come in — there's no danger."

She started as Jerry's voice boomed from a loudspeaker directly above her head. Then, realizing that he must have observed her entrance on the monitor screens, she relaxed with a sigh of relief. Ascending rapidly to the upper sector of the ship, she came to the open doorway of the computer room. Stepping through, she saw Frank Marek. Instantly her lingering fears melted into compassion.

"Catherine, m'dear..." The voice was a thin parody of his old sardonic rasp. He lay against the opposite wall, supported by Jerry, regarding her with bright, drugged eyes. Cathy's medical training told her, even then, that they could do little for him. Kneeling, she took one of his bruised, bloodied hands in hers. She said gently:

"Don't talk Frank. Just rest. We'll get you to your cabin and fix you up."

Marek gave a wheezing laugh. "I can die here... just as well as... in bed. Let me tell... you... what happened."

She glanced at Jerry. He gave an almost imperceptible nod.

"Go ahead, Frank. Take it slowly."

"Thank God you aren't... crying. Can't stand... sniveling..."

His voice dropped. For a moment his eyes seemed to lose focus. Then: "Didn't want to live... saw things in hyperspace that should have stayed... buried. Took ship up again to... throw her into hyperspace close to sun... destroy her and myself."

A trickle of blood ran down his chin. Cathy wiped it away. His flesh was icy against her fingers.

"Thanks..." His free hand began to work at a crease in his coveralls, back and forth, obsessively. "Hyperspace... threw us out at Phase One... distortion caused by presence of... stellar..."

There was a long pause. Marek rallied, went on.

THE DISTANT SUNS

"Asteroid on collision orbit with ship as we... emerged into normal space. Atomic screen... vaporized part of it, but too massive to be... completely destroyed. Ship had to decide... collide or take... evasive action. Made course change..."

He was fighting for breath. Cathy, unable to watch any longer without making some gesture of help, began to reach for the medical kit lying nearby, unsealed. Marek gasped: "Waste of time, girl... ship swung... I was in free fall... hit bulkhead..."

Jerry winced. Human flesh, floating weightless within the confines of *The Hope of Man*, driven suddenly like a slingshot against steel and plastic — he crushed the thought as Marek spoke again.

"Shook the kinks out of... my brain. Crawled here, cut off most functions of computer except those needed to... land ship. Watch computer, Jerry. All filled up with... crazy stuff I saw in hyper... hyper..."

He was dead. Jerry straightened, and they stared at each other across Marek's broken body. Finally, Jerry said: "It looks as if we have a lot of work ahead of us. Let's start now."

CHAPTER TWENTY-NINE

Lae-Pinu stood on the hillside, watching the shadow of *The Hope of Man* lengthen across the misty plateau. The light of the sinking sun turned the titanium hull to a pillar of fire, burning against the purple of the darkening sky. Close by the ship, dwarfed by her vast, baroque architecture, Cathy and Jerry Cornelius paused for a moment before leaving the soil of a once alien world. Shading her eyes against the orange glow, Cathy surveyed the marching hills patchworked with scrub and forest, the faint light in the air above them that hinted of the hidden sea.

"Strange," she said slowly. "I feel the sense of parting so much more strongly than when we left Earth."

"I feel that, too." Jerry's gaze followed hers to where the Alanga were gathered, a dark blur in the deepening dusk. One figure stood apart from the rest on the distant slope, "In the four weeks since the meteorite fell, we've become involved with the people of Beya in a way which has no real counterpart on Earth. At least, not for anyone in our sort of profession. God knows, we owed them all the help we could give. I'll never stop wondering if *The Hope of Man* deflected that meteorite *towards* Beya, or if it actually helped to soften an already inevitable collision by vaporizing part of the meteorite's mass."

"Yes…" A shadow crossed Cathy's face. "If my observations are correct, the Alanga and the Sev-Kalan were doomed from the beginning in a more insidious way. A war with unknown weapons, fought in some lost era of Asian history — a voyage across four light-years in a spaceship traveling at sub-light velocities… who knows? Exposure to radiation, at any rate, whether man-induced or present in space, setting up a slow decay, a long sickness…"

Jerry put one arm about her shoulders. "Come on, honey. Let's go, before we both break down! We're leaving one person, at least, happier than before."

Cathy smiled. "That's true. I have a feeling that the next ship reaching Beya will be met by the new Mrs Sechral!"

They gave a parting wave to the far-off watchers. Smoothly, the stairway folded itself into the hull as they entered the airlock. The airlock door slid shut.

Lae-Pinu waited until the last whisper of the spaceship's thunder faded across the plateau and the brilliant jet of nuclear fire merged with the appearing stars. Then, shivering, she began to climb the dark hillside to where the Alanga sat silently.

The cities of Earth were burning. In the bomb-scarred tower of Central Control, Marshal Hira studied the television screen's melancholy tally of death and destruction. New York had a million dead, Calcutta was a roaring pyre, London a battlefield… he blinked, angrily, as scenes and statistics merged and blurred before his weary eyes. How long since he had really slept? He couldn't remember. The world's hopes, the world's fears, had been wound too tightly, and restraint had snapped. If *The Hope of Man* did not return, would there ever be an end to the carnival of madness?

He straightened as the announcer said: "A bulletin from the Church of Relativity states that Minister Gavin, shot by an unidentified attacker several weeks ago, is still in a coma. His condition worsened last night, and —"

Hira switched off. Another day had begun. He left for the main conference room to map out another twenty-four hours' strategy. With luck, they would have that long.

Six levels lower down, *Herald Tribune* grunted in surprise as he trained a binocular viewer on a small helicopter hovering over the yellow dome of the Church of Relativity.

"Look at this! Kate Bell dropping in on her sister Sophie Gavin, with her husband at the controls!"

"That's Alex Bell, sure enough," said *Aftonbladet*. "I wonder what he and his wife are after?"

"Waiting for his ship to come in," answered *Guardian-Times*, appearing in the doorway in a scarlet dressing-gown. "Are there two cups of coffee left? Oh, good!"

Beyond the orbit of Pluto, in the outermost darkness of the Solar System, a space-station floated, its electronic senses turned always to the illimitable black gulfs between the stars. It had been built to respond to one signal only, the first that Man would send from interstellar space. It had waited a long time, but it was incapable of weariness or boredom. When the signal came, it began methodically to relay it to the worlds of men, close to the Sun.

"Proceed with landing," Hira said. "The field is clear. I repeat, the field is clear."

He couldn't stop shaking. It had seemed that nothing could be worse than the long weeks without news, while *The Hope of Man* voyaged to unknown regions and strange planets, but the period that had elapsed since the robot station signaled her return had been sheer hell. Without Kate Bell, who had persuaded her sister that the Church would suffer as grievously from the violence it sought to provoke as had its leader from a nameless gunman, the landing field would have been swamped by a sea of bodies. He rose now, unsteadily, and went to meet the descending ship.

The smell was overpowering. Cathy stood at the head of the stairway, averting her face from the breeze that blew over the field, carrying the stench of twenty million human beings and their refuse. Jerry sniffed.

"At times like this, I can appreciate Frank's point of view!"

"Poor Frank," Cathy said softly. "The first victim of hyperspace. With the knowledge we gained on the return trip, it should be possible to make things easier for the colonizing ships."

"Let's hope so." Jerry took her hand. "Here come Hira and the gentlemen of the Press. Well, we can tell them that there is a new Earth out there, a clean Earth."

Together they began to descend the stairway.

He added: "And may they make better use of it than we made of the old one!"

FLUX

For Christian von Baudissin

CHAPTER ONE

Max von Bek leaned forward, addressing an impatient question towards the driving compartment: "How long now before we get there?"

He had forgotten that this car had no driver. Usually, as Marshal-in-Chief of the European Defensive Nuclear Striking Force, he allowed himself the luxury of a chauffeur; but today his destination was secret and known not even to himself. The plan of his route lay safely locked away in the car's computer.

He settled back in his seat. It was useless to fret.

The car left the Main Way about half a mile before it met up with the central traffic circuit which flung vehicles and goods into the surrounding urban system like a gigantic whirling wheel. The car was making for the older parts of the city, nearest the ground. For this, von Bek was grateful, though he did not overtly admit it to himself. Above him, the horizon-wide drone and vibrating murmur of this engineer's paradise still went on, but at least it was more diffuse. The noise was just as great, but more chaotic and therefore more pleasing to von Bek's ear. Twice the car was forced to pause before dense streams of pedestrians issuing from public pressure-train stations, faces set and sweating as they battled their way to work.

Von Bek sat impassively through the delay, though already he was

SAILING TO UTOPIA

late for the meeting. What did it mean, he wondered, this Gargantua which sat proudly bellowing athwart the whole continent? It never slept; it never ceased to roar out its own power. And however benevolent it was towards its hundreds of millions of inhabitants, there was no denying that they were, every one, its slaves.

How had it arisen? What would become of it? It was already so overgrown internally that only with difficulty human beings found themselves room to live in it. If it were seen from out in space, he thought, no human beings would be visible; it would seem to be only a fast-moving machine of marvelous power but no purpose.

Von Bek did not have much faith in the European Community's ability to prolong its life infinitely. It had grown swiftly, but it had grown without the benefit of proper human design. Already, he thought, he could detect the seeds of inevitable collapse.

Patiently, the car eased forward through the crowd, found an unobstructed lane, and then continued on its complicated route. Eventually it made its way through a tangle of signs, directions and cross-overs, before stopping in front of a small ten-storey building bearing a grim but solid stamp of authority.

Guards at the entrance showed the gravity of the emergency. Von Bek was escorted to a suite on the fifth floor. Here, he was ushered into a windowless chamber with paneled wood walls and a steady, quiet illumination. At the oval table, the Government of the European Community had already convened and was waiting silently for his arrival. The ministers looked up as he entered.

They made an oddly serene and formal group, with their uniformly dark conservative dress and the white pads lying unmarked in neat squares before them. An air of careful constraint prevailed in the room. Most of the ministers gave von Bek only distant nods as he entered and then cast their eyes primly downward as before. Von Bek returned the nods. He was acquainted with them all, but not closely. For some reason they always tended to keep their distance from him, in spite of the high position he held — and for which he seemed to have been destined since childhood.

Only Prime Minister Strasser rose to welcome him.

"Please be seated, von Bek," he said. Von Bek shook the old man's proffered hand, then made his way to his place. Strasser began to speak at once, clearly intending to make the meeting brief and to the point.

"As we all know," he began, "the situation in Europe has reached the verge of civil war. However, most of us also know that we are not here today to discuss a course of action — I speak now for your benefit, von Bek. We are here to understand our position, and to propose a mission."

Strasser sat down and nodded perfunctorily to the man on his left. Standon, pale and bony, inclined his head towards von Bek and spoke:

"When we first sat down to deal with this problem, we thought it differed from no other crisis in history — that we would first consider the aims and intentions of the quarreling economic and political factions, decide which to back and which to oppose. It was not long before we discovered our error.

"First, we realized that Europe is only a political entity and not a national entity, obviating the most obvious basis for action. Then we tried to comprehend the entire system which we think of as Europe — and failed. As an industrial economy, Europe passes comprehension!"

He paused, and a strange emotion seemed to well just beneath the surface of his face. He moved his body uneasily, then continued in a stronger tone:

"We are the first government in history which is aware, and will admit, that it does not know how to control events. The continent in our charge has become the most massive, complex, high-pressured phenomenon ever to appear on the face of this planet. We know how to control it about as much as we know how to control the mechanism governing the growth of an actual living organism. Some of us are of the opinion that European industry has in fact become a living organism — but one without the sanity and certainty of proper development that a natural organism has. It began haphazardly, and then followed its own laws. There is one of us —" he indicated stern Brown-Gothe across the table — "who equates it with a cancer."

Von Bek mused on the similarity of the minister's conclusions to his own thoughts of only a few minutes before.

"Europe suffers from compression," Standon continued. "Everything is so pressurized, energies and processes abut so solidly on one another, that the whole system has massed together in a solid plenum. Politically speaking, there just isn't room to move around. Consequently, we are unable to apprehend the course of events either by computation or by common sense, and we are unable to say what will result from any given action. In short, we are in complete ignorance of the future, whether we participate in it or not."

Von Bek looked up and down the table. Most of the ministers still gazed passively at their notepads. One or two, with Strasser and Standon, were looking at him expectantly.

"I had been coming to the same conclusion myself," he said. "But you must have decided upon something."

"No," said Standon forcefully. "This is the essence of the matter. If things were that clear cut there would not be this problem — we should simply choose a side. But there are not two factions — there are three or four, with others in the background. The very idea of what is best loses meaning when we do not know what is going to happen. Logically, destruction of the community is the only criterion of what is undesirable, but even then, who knows? Perhaps we have grown so monstrous that there is no possibility of our further existence. There are no ideals to guide us. And in any case, there is no longer deliberate direction as far as Europe is concerned."

Standon took his eyes off von Bek and seemed to withdraw for a moment. "I might add," he said, "that after having had several weeks to think about it, we are of the opinion that this has always been the case in political affairs; only the fact that there was space to move around in gave the statesmen of the past the illusion that they were free to determine events. Now there is no empty space, the illusion has vanished, and we are aware of our helplessness. At the same time, everything is much more frightening."

He shrugged. "For instance, Europe, because of its massiveness, could absorb a large number of nuclear fusion explosions and still keep functioning. I need hardly add that at the present time such weapons are available to any large-scale corporation. There are even some small-yield bombs in the hands of minority groups."

Von Bek reflected as calmly as he could. Suddenly the crisis had slid over the edge of practical considerations into the realm of philosophy. It sounded absurd, but there was no denying the fact.

He appreciated the caution of these very self-composed men. Like them, he had a fear of tyranny, but history provided many warnings against hasty preventive measures. It was to avert tyranny that the conspirators murdered Caesar, yet within hours the consequences of their foolish deed had plunged the state into a reign of terror even worse than anything they had imagined. The ministers were right: there was no such thing as free will, and a state was manageable only if it was uncomplicated enough not to go off the rails in any case.

He said, "I presume everything has been done to try to analyze events?"

Standon gave him a tolerant smile. "Everything has been done! But the time element has foxed the computers."

As if this were a cue, a third man spoke. Appeltoft, whose special province was science and technology, was younger than the others and somewhat more emotional. He looked up to address von Bek.

"Our only hope lies in discovering how events are organized in time — this might sound highly speculative for such a serious and practical matter, but this is what things have come to. In order to take effective action in the present, we must first know the future. This is the mission we have in mind for you. The Research Complex at Geneva has found a way to deposit a man some years in the future and bring him back. You will be sent ten years forward to find out what will happen and how it will come about. You will then return, report your findings to us, and we will use this information to guide our actions, and also — scientifically — to analyze the laws governing the sequence of time. This is how we hope to formulate a method of human government for use by future ages, and, perhaps, remove the random element from human affairs."

Von Bek was impressed by the striking, unconventional method the Cabinet had adopted to resolve its dilemma.

"You leave immediately," Appeltoft told him, breaking in on his thoughts. "After this conference, you and I will fly to Geneva where the technicians have the apparatus in readiness." A hint of bitterness came into his voice. "I had wished to go myself, but..." He shrugged and made a vague, disgusted gesture which took in the rest of the Cabinet.

"That's a point," von Bek said. "Why have you chosen me?"

The ministers looked at one another shiftily. Strasser spoke up.

"The reason lies in your education, Max," he said diffidently. "The difficulties facing us now were beginning to show themselves over a generation ago. The government of the time decided to bring up a small number of children according to a new system of education. The idea was to develop people capable of comprehending in detail the massiveness of modern civilization, by means of forced learning in every subject. The experiment failed. All your schoolfellows lost their sanity. You survived, but did not turn into the product we had hoped for. To prevent any later derangement of your mind, a large part of the information which had been pressured into it was removed by hypnotic means. The result is yourself as you are — a super-dilettante, with an intense curiosity and a gift for management. We gave you the post you now hold and forgot about you. Now you are ideal for our purpose."

Inwardly, von Bek underwent a jolt — even more so because the account agreed well with his own suspicions concerning his origins. He pulled himself together before he could become introspective.

"Only I made it, eh? I wonder why."

Standon regarded von Bek steadily in the dim light. Again that strange layer of emotion seemed to stir in him, lying somewhere below his features but not affecting the muscles or skin.

"Because of your determination, von Bek. Because whatever happens, somehow, you have the capacity to find our particular Grail. Our remedy. Our way out."

Von Bek left the building even more involved in speculations than before. Appeltoft came with him. The car whined smoothly towards the nearest air centre.

He had a peg to hang his thoughts on now. The sequence of time... Yes, there was no doubt that the explanation of the titanic phenomena through which he was being driven lay in the sequence of time.

Looking around him, he saw how literally true were the statements just given him by the ministers.

After the formation of the Community, into which all the European countries were finally joined, the continent's capacity had accelerated fantastically. Economic development had soared so high that eventually it became necessary to buttress up the whole structure from underneath. Stage by stage, the buttresses had become more massive, until the super-centralized community was tied to the ground, a rigid unchangable monster, humming and roaring with energy.

Even the airy architectural promise of the previous century had not materialized. The constructions wheeling past the car had an appearance of Wagnerian heaviness, blocking out the sunlight.

He turned to Appeltoft. "So in an hour I'll be ten years in the future. Ridiculous statement!"

Appeltoft laughed, as though to show he appreciated the paradox.

"But tell me," von Bek continued, "are you really so ignorant about Time's nature, and yet you can effect travel in it?"

"We are not so ignorant about its nature, as about its structure and organization," Appeltoft told him. "The equations which enable us to transmit through Time give no clue to that — in fact they say that Time has no sequence at all, which can hardly be possible. It's why the computers can't help us."

Appeltoft paused. His manner towards von Bek gave the latter cause to think that the scientist still resented not being allowed to be the first time traveler, though he was trying to hide it. Von Bek didn't blame him. When a man has worked fanatically for something, it must be a blow to see a complete stranger take over the fruits of it.

"There are two theories extant," Appeltoft eventually went on. "The first, and the one I favour, is the common-sense view — past, present, future, proceeding in an unending line and each even having a definite position on the line. Unfortunately the idea has not lent itself to any useful mathematical formulation.

"The other idea, which some of my co-workers hold, goes like this: that Time isn't really a forward-moving flow at all. It exists as a constant: all things are actually happening at once, but human beings haven't got the built-in perceptions to see it as such. Imagine a circular stage with a sequence of events going on round it, representing, say, periods in one man's life. In that case they would be played by different actors, but in the actuality of Time the same man plays all parts. According to this, an alteration in one scene has an effect on all subsequent scenes all the way round back to the beginning."

"So that Time is in one sense cyclic — what you do in the future may influence your future past, as it were?"

"If the theory is correct. Some formulations have been derived, but they don't work very well. All we really know, is that we can deposit you into the future and probably bring you back."

"Probably! You've had failures?"

"Thirty-three per cent of our test animals don't return," Appeltoft said blithely.

Once they were at the air centre, it took them less than an hour to reach the Geneva Research Complex. From the air receptor on the roof, Appeltoft conducted him nearly half a mile down to the underground laboratories. Finally, he pulled an old-fashioned key chain from his pocket, attached to which was a little sonic key. As he pressed the stud a door swung open a few yards ahead.

They entered a blue-painted chamber whose walls were lined with information consoles. A number of white-robed technicians sat about, waiting.

Occupying the centre of the room was a chair, mounted on a pedestal. A swivel arm held a small box with instrument dials on the external surfaces; but the most notable feature was the three translucent rods which seemed to ray out from just behind the chair, one going straight up and the other two at right angles, one on either side.

The floor was covered with trestles supporting a network of helices and semi-conductor electron channels, radiating out from the chair like a spider's web. Von Bek found himself trying to interpret the set-up in the pseudoscientific jargon which was his way of understanding contemporary technology. Electrons... indeterminacy... what would the three rods be for?

"This is the time-transmission apparatus," Appeltoft told him without preamble. "The actual apparatus will remain here in the present time. Only that chair, with you sitting in it, will make the time transference itself."

"So you will control everything from here?"

"Not exactly. It will be a 'powered flight' so to speak, and you will carry the controls. But the power unit will remain here. We might be able to do something if the mission goes wrong — perhaps not. We probably won't even know.

"The three rods accompanying the chair represent the three spatial dimensions. As these rotate out of true space, time-motion will begin."

Stepping carefully across the trestles, they walked nearer to the chair. Appeltoft explained the controls and instruments. "They are semi-mechanical, for obvious reasons. This is your speed gauge —

you've no way of controlling that, it's all automatic. This switch here is 'Stop' and 'Start' — it's marked, you'll notice. And this one gives the point in time you occupy, in years, days, hours, and seconds. Everything else is programmed for you. As you see, it reads Nil now. When you arrive, it will read Ten Years."

"Point in time, eh?" von Bek mused. "That could have two meanings according to what you've just told me."

Appeltoft nodded. "You're astute. Pragmatically, my own view of straight-line time is closest to the operation of the time transmitter. It's the easiest to grasp, anyway."

Von Bek studied the apparatus for nearly a minute without speaking. The silence dragged on. Though he wasn't aware of it, strain was growing.

"Well, don't just stand there," Appeltoft snapped with sudden ferocity. "Get on the damned thing! We haven't got all day!"

Von Bek gave him a look of surprised reproof.

Appeltoft sagged. "Sorry. If you knew — how jealous I am of you. To be the first man with a chance to discover the secret of Time! It's the secret to the universe itself!"

CHAPTER TWO

Well, von Bek thought to himself, as he watched the young minister's lean, intense face, *if I had his determination I might have been a scientist and made discoveries for myself, instead of being a jacked-up dilettante.* "A dilettante," he muttered aloud.

"Eh?" Appeltoft said. "Well, come on, let's get it done."

Von Bek climbed into the seat built into the back of the chair. Camera lenses peered over his shoulders. "You know what to look for?" Appeltoft asked finally.

"As much as anybody. Besides — I want to go as much as you do."

"All right then. Capacity's built up. Press the switch to 'Start'. It will automatically revert to 'Stop' at the end of the journey."

Von Bek obeyed. At first, nothing happened. Then came the impression that the translucent rods, which he could see out of the corners of his eyes, were rotating clockwise, though they didn't change their positions. At the same time, the room appeared to spin in the opposite direction — again, it was movement without change of position.

The effect was entirely like druggedness and von Bek felt dizzy. He forced his eyes to the speed gauge. One minute per minute — marking time! One and a half, two...

With a weird flickering effect the laboratory vanished. He was in a neutral grey fog, left only with sensation.

The first sensation was that he was taking part in the rotating movement — being steadily canted to the left. As his angle to the vertical increased, the second sensation increased: a rushing momentum, a gathering speed towards a nameless destination.

000001.146.15.0073 — the numbers slipped into place, swiftly towards the right-hand side, slowly towards the left. 000002... 3... 4... 5... 6... 7...

Then the nausea returned, the feeling of being spun round — the other way, now. Light dazzled his eyes.

000010.000.00.0000.

When he grew used to it, the light was really dim. He was still in the laboratory, but it was deserted, illuminated by emergency lights glowing weakly in the ceiling. It was not in ruins, and there was no sign of violence, but the place had obviously been empty for some time.

Climbing down from the chair, he went to the door, used the sonic key which Appeltoft had given him, went through, and closed it behind him. He walked along the corridor and through the other departments.

The whole complex shouldn't be deserted after only ten years. Something drastic must have happened.

He frowned, annoyed at himself. Of course it had. That was why he was here.

The high-level streets of Geneva were equally deserted. He could see the tops of mountains in the distance, poking between metallic roadways. The drone of the city was missing. There was some noise to be heard, but it was muted and irregular.

As he mounted an interlevel ramp he saw one or two figures, mostly alone. He had never seen so few people. Perhaps the quickest way to find out what was going on would be to locate the library and read up some recent history. It might give a clue, anyway.

He reached the building which pushed up through several layers of deserted street. A huge black sign over the main entrance said:

MEN ONLY

Puzzled, von Bek entered the cool half-light and approached the wary young man at the Enquiry Desk.

"Excuse me," he said, and jumped as the man produced a squat gun from under the counter and leveled it at him.

"What do you want?"

"I've come to consult recent texts dealing with the development of Europe in the last ten years," von Bek said.

The young man grinned with his thin lips. The gun held steady, he said, "Development?"

"I'm a serious student — all I want to do is look up some information."

The young man put away the gun and with one hand pressed the buttons of an index system. He took two cards out and handed them to von Bek.

"Fifth floor, room 543. Here's the code. Destroy it and lock the door behind you. Last week a gang of women broke through the barricades and tried to burn us down. They like their meat pre-cooked, eh?"

Von Bek frowned at him but said nothing. He went to the elevator. The young man called, "For a student you don't know much about this library. That elevator hasn't worked for four years. The women control all the main power sources these days."

Still in a quandary, von Bek walked up to the fifth floor, found the room he wanted, unlocked the door, entered, locked it behind him and scratched the code.

Seating himself before the viewer, he used the appropriate panel and the references started to appear on the screen.

Hmmm... Let's see... Investigations of Dalmeny Foundation members. Paper VII: PARTIAL RESULTS OF THE BAVARIAN EXPERIMENT...

— Civil war imminent, the Council temporarily averted it by promising that thorough research would be made into every claim for a solution to the problems of over-compression. This, as we know now, was a stonewalling action since they later admitted they had been incapable of predicting the outcome of any trend. The faction, one of the most powerful headed by the late Stefan Untermeyer, demanded that they be allowed to conduct a controlled experiment.

— Unable to stall any longer, the Council reluctantly agreed, and a large part of Bavaria was set aside so that the plans of the Untermeyer faction could be implemented. This plan necessitated sexual segregation. Men and women were separated and each given an intensive chemo-psychoconditioning to hate the opposite sex. Next, acts were passed making contact with the opposite sex punishable by death. This act had to be enforced frequently, although not as frequently as originally had been thought. Ironically, Untermeyer was one of the first to be punished under the act.

— It is difficult these days, to make a clear assessment of the results of this experiment (which so quickly got out of hand and resulted in the literal war between the sexes, which now exists with cannibalism so prevalent, each sex regarding it as lawful to treat the other as edible meat) but it is obvious that measures for re-assimilation have so far met with little success and that, since this creed has now spread through Germany, Scandinavia and elsewhere, an incredible depletion of life in Northern Europe is likely. In the long run, of course, repopulation will result as the roving hordes from France and Spain press northwards. Europe, having collapsed, is ready for conquest, and when the squabblings of the USSA and the UEA are ended, either by bloodshed or peaceful negotiation, Europe's only salvation may be in coming under the sway of one of these powers. However, as we know, both these powers have similar problems to those of Europe in its last days of sanity.

Von Bek pursed his lips, consulted the index and pressed a fresh code.

Nobody could have predicted this. But by the look of it there's more to come. Let's see what this is... FINDINGS OF THE VINER COMMITTEE FOR THE INVESTIGATION OF SOCIAL DISINTEGRATION IN SOUTHERN EUROPE...

— The terms of reference of the Committee were as follows: To investigate the disintegration of the pre-experimental European society in Southern Europe and to suggest measures for reorganizing the society into an operating whole.

— Briefly, as is generally known, the European Council gave permission for the Population Phasing Group to conduct an experiment in Greece. This Group, using the principles of suspended animation discovered a few years earlier by Batchovski, instituted total birth-control and placed three-quarters of the population of Greece into suspended animation, the other quarter being thought sufficient to run public and social services and so on, reasoning, quite rationally it seemed, that in this way further population explosion would be averted, less overcrowding would result and the pace of our society could be relaxed. After a given time, the first quarter would go into suspended animation and be replaced by the next quarter and so on. This phasing process did seem to be the most reasonable solution to the Problem of Europe, as it was called.

— However, in ridding the population of claustrophobia, the system produced an effect of extreme agoraphobia. The people, being used to living close together, became restless, and the tension which had preceded the introduction of the PPG Experiment, was turned into new channels. Mobs, exhibiting signs of extreme neurosis, completely insensate and deaf to all reason, attacked what were called the SA Vaults and demanded the release of their relatives and friends. The authorities attempted to argue with them but, in the turmoil which followed, were either killed or forced to flee. Unable to operate the machines keeping the rest of the population in suspended animation, the mobs destroyed them, killing the people they had intended to re-awaken.

— When the Committee reached Southern Europe, they found a declining society. Little attempt had been made to retrieve the situation, people were living in the vast depopulated conurbations in little groups, fighting off the influx of roaming bands from France, Spain and Italy, where earlier a religious fanatic had, quite unexpectedly, started a jehad against the automated, but workable, society. This "back to nature" movement snowballed. Power installations were destroyed and millions of tons of earth were imported from Africa to spread over the ruins. In the chaos which ensued, people fought and squabbled over what little food could be grown in the unproductive earth where it had been imported and in the Holiday Spaces. Britain, already suffering from the effects of this breakdown and unable to obtain sufficient supplies to feed its own population properly, had begun sending aid but had been forced to give up this measure and look to its own problems — the sudden spread of an unknown disease which was found to have come from African refugees who had themselves suffered badly from the introduction of a synthetic food product which contained the germs. By the time we reached Southern Europe, the social services all over the continent had disintegrated and only the Dalmeny Foundation (which had commissioned us) and half a dozen less well-organized groups were managing to maintain any kind of academic activity...

As von Bek read on through the depressing texts, he felt the blood leave his face. At length he had checked and rechecked the documents; he sat back and contemplated.

The blundering nature of the experiments appalled him. Nothing could be a better confirmation of what he had been told at the Cabinet Meeting, and it made him doubt, now, that anything at all could be done to avert the calamity. If men were so blind and foolish, could even Appeltoft's incisive mind save them? Even supposing he succeeded in making a clear, workable analysis of the science of events from the information von Bek had obtained...

That part of it was out of his hands, he realized, and perhaps Appeltoft's confidence stood for something. Impatiently he rushed back to the laboratory, mounted the chair of the time machine, and pressed the switch to "Start". 000009.000.00.0003...

CHAPTER THREE

Soon there was a grey mist surrounding him as before. Rotation and momentum began to impress themselves on his senses.

Then his gauges jigged and danced, clicked and tumbled insanely. 009000.100.02.0000... 000175.000.03.0800... 630946.020 .44.1125 ...

Something had gone wrong. Desperately he tried to stop the machine and inspect the controls. Every dial registered noughts now.

But the laboratory was gone. He was surrounded by darkness.

He was in limbo.

000000.000.00.0000

Von Bek did not know how long he sped through the emptiness. Gradually, the mist began to return, then, after what seemed an interminable time, a flurry of impressions spun round his eyes.

At last, the time machine came to a halt, but he did not pause to see what was around him. He pressed the "Start" switch again.

Nothing happened. Von Bek inspected all the dials in turn, casting a long look at one which, as Appeltoft had told him, registered the machine's "time-potential" — that is, its capacity to travel through Time.

The hand was at zero. He was stranded.

Thirty-three per cent of our test animals don't return. Appeltoft's remark slipped sardonically into his memory.

The micro-cameras behind his shoulders were humming almost imperceptibly as they recorded the scene. Bleakly, von Bek lifted his head and took stock of his surroundings.

The sight was beautiful but alien. The landscape consisted of sullen orange dust, over which roamed purple masses of cloud, rolling and drifting upon the surface of the desert. On the horizon of this barren scene, the outlines of grotesque architecture were visible. Or were they just natural formations?

He glanced upwards. There were no clouds in the sky; evidently they were too dense to float in free air. A small sun hung low, red in a deep blue sky where stars were faintly visible.

His heart was beating rapidly; as he noticed this, he realized that he was breathing more deeply than usual, every third breath almost a gasp. Was he so far removed from his own time that even the atmosphere was different?"

Skrrak! The sound came with a brittle, frail quality over the thin air. Von Bek turned his head, startled.

A dozen bipeds were advancing, straggling on bony, delicate limbs through knee-deep strata of purple clouds which rolled in masses a few hundred yards away. They were humanoid, but skeletal, ugly, and clearly not human. The leader, who was over seven feet tall, was shouting and pointing at von Bek and the machine.

Another waved his hands: "*Sa Skrrak — dek svala yaal!*"

The group carried long slim spears, and their torsos and legs were covered with scrubby hair. Their triangular heads had huge ridges of bone over and under the eyes so that they seemed to be wearing helmets. Thin hair swirled around their heads as they came closer, proceeding cautiously as if in slow motion.

Von Bek saw that some of them carried curious riflelike weapons, and the leader bore a box-shaped instrument with a lens structure on one side, which he was pointing in his direction.

Von Bek felt the warmth of a pale green beam and tried to dodge it. But the alien creature skillfully kept it trained on him.

After a second or two, a buzzing set up in his brain; fantastic colours engulfed his mind, separating out into waves of white and gold. Then geometric patterns flared behind his eyes. Then words — at first in his brain and then in his ears.

"Strange one, what is your tribe?"

He was hearing the guttural language of the alien — and understanding it. The creature touched a switch on the top of the box, and the beam flicked off.

"I am from another time," von Bek said without emphasis.

The warriors shifted their weapons uneasily. The leader nodded, a stiff gesture, as if his bone structure did not permit easy movement. "That would be an explanation."

"Explanation?"

"I am conversant with all the tribes, and you do not correspond to any of them." The warrior shifted his great head to give the horizon a quick scrutiny. "We are the Yulk. Unless you intend to depart immediately, you had best come with us."

"But my machine…"

"That also we will take. You will not wish it to be destroyed by the Raxa, who do not permit the existence of any creature or artifact save themselves."

Von Bek debated for some moments. The chair and its three rods were easily portable, but was it wise to move them?

Idly, he moved the useless "Start" switch again. Damn! Since the machine no longer worked, what difference did it make if he moved it to the Moon? And yet to go off with these alien creatures when his only objective was to return to the Geneva Complex seemed the most obvious absurdity.

A sick feeling of failure came over him. He was beginning to realize that he was never going to get back to Geneva. The scientists had known that there was some fault in their time-transmission methods; now, he knew, the chair with its three rods had lost all touch with the equipment in the laboratory. It was, in fact, no longer a time machine, and that meant he was doomed to stay here for the rest of his life.

Helplessly he gave his consent. A quartet of warriors picked up the chair, and the party set off across the ochre desert, glancing warily about it as they traveled.

They skirted round the moving clouds wherever they could.

Sometimes the banks of purple vapour swept over them, borne by the wide movements of the breeze, and they stumbled through a vermilion fog. Von Bek noticed that the alien beings kept a tight hold on their weapons when this happened. What was it they feared? Even in this desolated and near-empty world, strife and dramas played themselves out.

An hour's journey brought them to a settlement of tents clustered on a low hillside. A carefully cultivated plot of some wretched vegetation grew over about half the hill, as though only just managing to maintain itself in the sterile desert. Tethered over the camp were five floating vessels, each about a hundred feet long, graceful machines with stubby, oblate sterns and tapered bows. A short open deck projected aft atop each vessel and the forward parts were laced with windows.

Von Bek's gaze lingered on these craft. They contrasted oddly with the plainly nomadic living quarters below, cured animal hides with weak fires flickering among them.

A meal had just been prepared. Von Bek's time machine was taken to an empty tent, and he was invited to eat with the chief. As he entered the largest tent of the settlement and saw the nobility of this small tribe gathered round a vegetable stewpot with their weapons beside them they reminded him of lizards.

They began to eat from glass bowls. It seemed these people knew how to work the silicates of the desert as well as build flying ships — if they had not stolen them.

In the course of the meal, von Bek also discovered that the machine the warrior had trained on him in the desert was one hundred per cent efficient. He had been completely re-educated to talk and think in another language, even though he could, if he chose, detach himself slightly, hear the strangeness of the sounds which came from both his mouth and those of the Yulk.

The chief's name was Gzerhtcak, an almost impossible sound to European ears. As they ate, he answered von Bek's questions in unemotional tones.

From what he was told, he imagined that this was an Earth in old age, an Earth perhaps billions of years ahead of his own time, and it was nearly all desert. There were about eight tribes living within a radius of a few hundred miles, and when they were not squabbling among themselves they were fighting a never-ending struggle for existence both with the ailing conditions of a dying world, and with the Raxa, creatures who were not organic life at all but consisted of mineral crystals conglomerated into geometrical forms, and, in some mysterious way, endowed both with sentience and the property of mobility.

"Fifty generations ago," the Yulk chief told him, "the Raxa had no existence in the world; then they began to grow. They are naturally reproducing intelligence modules. They thrive in the dead desert, which is all food for them, while we steadily die. There is nothing we can do, but fight."

Furthermore, the atmosphere of the Earth was becoming unbreathable. Little fresh oxygen was being produced, since there was no vegetation except at the plantations. Beside this, noxious vapours were being manufactured by a chemical-geological action in the ground, and by slow volcanic processes which drifted through the sand from far below. Only in a few places, such as this region where the tribes lived, was the atmosphere still suitable for respiration, and that only because of the relative stillness of the atmosphere, which discouraged the separate gases from mixing.

It was a despairing picture of courage and hopelessness which gradually unfolded to von Bek. Was this the final result of Man's inability to control events, or was the collapse of the European Community an insignificant happening which had been swallowed up by a vaster history? He tended to think that this was so; for he felt sure that the creatures who sat and ate with him were not even descended from human stock.

Lizards. The old order of the world of life had died away. Men had gone. Only these fragments remained — lizards evolved to a manlike state, attempting to retain a foothold in a world which had changed its mind. Probably the other tribes the Yulk spoke of were also humanoids who had evolved from various lower animals.

"Tomorrow is the great battle," the Yulk chief said. "We throw all our resources against the Raxa, who advance steadily to destroy the last plantations on which we depend. After tomorrow, we shall know in our hearts how long we have to live."

Max von Bek clenched his hands impotently. His fate was sealed.

Eventually he too would take his place alongside the Yulk warriors in the last stand against humanity's enemy.

CHAPTER FOUR

Appeltoft spread his hands impassively and looked at Strasser. He had done all he could.

"What happened?" said the Prime Minister.

"We tracked him ten years into the future. We got him on the start of his journey back, and then quite suddenly — gone. Nothing. I told you we lost thirty-three per cent of our experimental animals in the same way. I warned you of the risk."

"I know — but have you tried everything? You know what it will mean if he doesn't return…"

"We have been trying, of course. We are searching now, trying to pick him up, but outside the Earth's time-track all is chaotic to our instruments — some defect in our understanding of Time. We can probe out — but really, a needle in a haystack is nothing compared —"

"Well, keep trying. Because if you don't get him back soon we shall be forced to allow the Untermeyer people to go ahead in Bavaria, and we have no means of predicting the result."

Appeltoft sighed wearily and returned to his laboratory.

When he had left the chamber, Standon said, "Poor devil. And we sent…"

"There's a time and a place for sentimentality, Standon," Strasser said. "Also guilt."

CHAPTER FIVE

The Earth still rotated in the same period, and after a sleep of about eight hours, von Bek left his tent and stretched his limbs in the thin air, aroused by the sound of clinking metal. It was just after dawn, and the fighting males of the tribe were setting out to battle. The females and children, shivering, watched as their menfolk went off in procession into the desert. A few rode reptilelike horses, precious cosseted animals, all of whom had been harnessed for the battle. Twenty feet above their heads the five aircraft floated patiently, following the direction given by the chief below.

Max von Bek hung around the camp. He was apprehensive and edgy. About an hour after sunset, the remnants of the forces returned.

It was defeat. A third of the men had survived. None of the aircraft returned. Von Bek had learned the night before that, although the tribe retained the knowledge and skill to build more, it was an undertaking that strained their resources to the utmost, and the construction of another would almost certainly never begin.

Humanity's strength was depleted beyond revival point. The mineral intelligences would continue their implacable advance with little to stop them.

The Yulk chief was the last man in. Bruised, bleeding, and scorched by near misses from energy beams, he submitted to the medications of the women, and then called the nobles together as usual for their evening meal.

One by one, the wearied warriors took their leave and made their ways to their tents, until von Bek was left alone with Gzerhtcak.

He looked directly into the old man's eyes. "There is no hope," he said bluntly.

"I know. But you need not remain."

"I have no choice." He sighed. "My machine has broken down. I must throw in my lot with you."

"Perhaps we can repair your machine. But you will be plunging into the unknown…"

Von Bek made a gesture. "What could you possibly do to repair my machine?"

The chief rose and led the way to the tent where the machine lay. A brief command into the night produced a boy with a box of tools. The chief studied von Bek's machine, lifting a panel to see behind the instruments. Finally, he made adjustments, adding a device which took him about twenty minutes to make with glowing bits of wire. The time-potential meter began to lift above zero.

Von Bek stared in surprise.

"Our science is very ancient and very wise," the chief said, "though these days we know it only by rote. Still, I, as father of the tribe, know enough so that when a man like yourself tells me that he has stranded himself in Time, I know what the reason is."

Von Bek was astounded by the turn of events. "When I get home —" he began.

"*You will never get home.* Neither will your scientists ever analyze Time. Our ancient science has a maxim: No man understands Time. Your machine travels under its own power now. If you leave here, you simply escape this place and take your chance elsewhere."

"I must make the attempt," von Bek said. "I cannot remain here while there is a hope of getting back."

But still he lingered.

The chief seemed to guess his thoughts. "Do not fear that you desert us," he said. "Your position is clear, as is ours. There is no help for either of us."

SAILING TO UTOPIA

Von Bek nodded and stepped up to the chair of the machine. As he cleaned off the grime and dust with his shirt sleeves, it occurred to him to look at the date-register. He did not expect it to make sense, for it had too few digits to account for the present antiquity of the Earth.

But when he read the dial he received a shock. 000008.324.01.7954. Less than nine years after his departure from the Geneva Complex!

He seated himself on the time machine and pressed the switch.

Internal rotation clockwise... external rotation anti-clockwise... then the forward rushing. He plunged into the continuum of Time.

Minutes passed, and no sign came that he would emerge automatically from his journey. Taking a chance, he pressed the switch to "Stop".

With a residual turning of the translucent rods, the machine gave him normal space-time orientation. About him, the landscape was nightmarish.

Was it crystal? The final victory of the crystalline Raxa? For a moment the fantastic landscape, with its flashing, brilliant, mathematical overgrowth, deluded him into thinking it was so. But then he saw that it could not be — or if it was, the Raxa had evolved beyond their mineral heritage.

It was a world of geometrical form, but it was also a world of constant movement or, since the movement was instantaneous, of constant transformation. Flashing extensions and withdrawals, all on the vertical and horizontal planes, dazzled his eyes. When he looked closer, he saw that in fact *three-dimensional form was nowhere present*. Everything consisted of two-dimensional shapes, which came together transitorily to give the *illusion* of form.

The colours, too — they underwent transformations and graduations which bespoke the action of regular mathematical principles, like the prismatic separation into the ideal spectrum. But here the manifestations were infinitely more subtle and inventive, just as subtle, tenuous music, using fifty instruments, can be made out of the seven tones of the diatonic scale.

Von Bek looked at the date register. It told him he was now fifteen years away from Appeltoft, anxiously awaiting his return in the Geneva Complex.

He tried again.

CHAPTER SIX

A lush world of lustrous vegetation swayed and rustled in a hot breeze. A troupe of armadillolike animals the size of horses paraded through the clearing where von Bek's machine had come to rest. Without pausing, the leader swung its head to give him a docile, supercilious inspection, then turned to grunt something to the followers. They also gave him a cursory glance and then they had passed through a screen of wavy grass-trees. He heard their motions through the forest for some distance.

Again. He was filled with a barren misery.

Rock. The sky hung with traceries of dust clouds. The ground was clean of even the slightest trace of dust, but a strong cold wind blew. Presumably it swept the dust into the atmosphere and prevented it from precipitating, scouring the rock to a sparkling, ragged surface. He could hardly believe that this scrubbed shining landscape was actually the surface of a planet. It was like an exhibit.

Again.

Now he was in space, protected by some field the time machine seemed to create around itself. Something huge as Jupiter hung where Earth should have been.

Again.

Space again. A scarlet sun pouring bloody light over him. On his left, a tiny, vivid star, like a burning magnesium flare, lanced at his eyes. An impossible three-planet triune rotated majestically above him, with no more distance between them than from the Earth to the Moon.

He looked at the date register again. Twenty-odd years from departure.

Where was the sequence? Where was the progression he had come to find? How was Appeltoft to make sense out of this?

How was he going to find Appeltoft?

Desperately, he set the machine in motion again. His desperation seemed to have some effect: he picked up speed, rushing with insensate energy, and now he was not just in limbo but could see something of the universe through which he was passing.

After a while he got the impression that he was still, that it was the machine that was static while time and space were not. The universe poured around him, a disordered tumult of forces and energies, lacking direction, lacking purpose...

On he sped, hour after hour, as if he were trying to flee from some fact he could not face. But at last he could hide from it no longer. As he observed the chaos around him he *knew*.

Time *had* no sequence! It was *not* a continuous flowing. It had no positive direction. It went neither forwards, backwards, nor in a circle; neither did it stay still. *It was totally random.*

The universe was bereft of logic. It was nothing but chaos.

It had no purpose, no beginning, no end. It existed only as a random mass of gases, solids, liquids, fragmentary accidental patterns. Like a kaleidoscope, it occasionally formed itself into patterns, so that it *seemed* ordered, *seemed* to contain laws, *seemed* to have form and direction.

But, in fact, there was nothing but chaos, nothing but a constant state of flux — the only thing that was constant. There *were* no laws governing Time! Appeltoft's ambition was impossible!

The world from which he had come, or any other world for that matter, could dissipate into its component elements at any instant, *or could have come into being at any previous instant, complete with everybody's memories!* Who would be the wiser? The whole of the European Community might have existed only for the half-second which it had taken him to press the starting switch of the time machine. No wonder he couldn't find it!

Chaos, flux. All problems were without solution. As von Bek realized these facts he howled with the horror of it. He could not bring himself to stop. In proportion to his despair and fear, his speed increased, faster and faster, until he was pouring madly through turmoil.

Faster, farther…

The formless universe around him began to vanish as he went to an immense distance and beyond the limits of speed. Matter was breaking up, disappearing. Still he rushed on in terror, until the time machine fell away beneath him, and the matter of his body disintegrated and vanished.

He was a bodiless intelligence, hurtling through the void. Then his emotions began to vanish. His thoughts. His identity. The sensation of movement dropped away. Max von Bek was gone. Nothing to see, hear, feel, or know.

He hung there, nothing but consciousness. He did not think — he no longer had any apparatus to think with. He had no name. He had no memories. No qualities, attributes, or feelings. He was just *there*. Pure ego.

The same as nothing.

There was no Time. A split second was the same as a billion ages.

So it would not have been possible later for von Bek to assign any period to his interlude in unqualified void. He only became aware of anything when he began to emerge.

At first, there was a vague feeling, like something misty. Then more qualities began to attach themselves to him. Motion began. Chaotic matter became distantly perceptible — disorganized particles, flowing energies and wavy lines.

A name impinged on his consciousness: Max von Bek. Then: That's me.

Matter gradually congregated round him, and soon he had a body again and a complete set of memories. He could accept the existence of an unorganized universe now. He sighed. At the same moment the time machine formed underneath him.

All he could do now was to try to return to Geneva, however remote the possibility. How strange, to think that the whole of Europe, with all its seriously taken problems, was nothing more than a chance coming-together of random particles! But at least it was home — even if it only existed for a few seconds.

And if he could only rejoin those few seconds, he thought in agonized joyousness, he would be dissolved along with the rest of it and be released from this hideous extension of life he had escaped into.

And yet, he thought, how could he get back? Only by searching, only by searching...

He reckoned (though of course his calculations were liable to considerable error) that he spent several centuries searching through mindless turmoil. He grew no older; he felt no hunger or thirst; he did not breathe — how his heart kept beating without breath was a mystery to him, but it was on this, the centre of his sense of time, that he based his belief about the duration of the search. Occasionally he came upon other brief manifestations, other transient conglomerations of chaos. But now he was not interested in them, and he did not find Earth at the time of the E.C.

It was hopeless. He could search forever.

In despair, he began to withdraw again, to become a bodiless entity and find oblivion, escape from his torments in the living death. It was while he was about to dispense with the last vestige of identity that he discovered his unsuspected power.

He happened to direct his mind to a grouping of jostling particles some distance away. Under the impact of his will, it moved!

Interested, he halted his withdrawal, but did not try to emerge back into his proper self — he had the feeling that as Max von Bek he was impotent. As an almost unqualified ego, perhaps...

He allowed an image to form in his mind — it happened to be that of a cup — and directed it at the formless chaos. Instantly, against dark flux, lit by random flashes of light, a golden chalice was formed out of chaotic matter.

There was no doubt about it. It was not just an image. It was perfect. It was real.

Amazed, he automatically let go of the mental image and transmitted a cancellation. The chalice vanished, replaced by random particles and energies as before. The cloud lingered for a moment, then dispersed.

It was a newfound delight. He could make anything! For ages he experimented, creating everything he could think of. Once, a whole world formed beneath him, complete with civilizations, a tiny sun, and rocket-ships probing out.

He canceled it at once. It was enough to know that his every intention, even his vaguest and grandest thought, was translated into detail.

Now he had a means to return home — and now he could solve the government's problem for good and all.

For if he could not find Europe, could he not create it over again? Would that not be just as good? In fact, it was a point of philosophy whether it would not be in fact the same Europe. This was Nietzsche's belief, he remembered — his hope of personal immortality. Since, in the boundless universe, he was bound to recur — von Bek's discoveries had reinforced this view, anyhow — he would not die. Two identical objects shared the same existence.

And in this second Europe, why should he not solve the government's dilemma for them? He could create a community which did not contain the seeds of destruction! An economic community with the stability the prototype had lacked.

He began to grow excited. It would defeat Chaos's stand against the logic of the rest of the universe. A structure which would last. Otherwise, it would be the same in every detail…

He set to work, summoning up thoughts, memories and images, impinging them on the surrounding chaos. Matter began to form. He set the time machine in motion, traveling on to the world he was creating…

Suddenly he was in mist again. Rotating… rotation without change of position… rushing forward…

The numbers clicked off his dial: 000008… 7… 6… 5… 4…

Then everything steadied around him as the machine came to a stop. He was in Appeltoft's laboratory in Geneva. Technicians prowled the outskirts of the room, beyond the barriers of trestles. The time machine, its translucent rods pointing dramatically in three directions, rested on a rough wooden pedestal.

Max von Bek moved, still, aching and dusty, in the grimy seat. Appeltoft rushed forward, helping him down, anxious and delighted.

SAILING TO UTOPIA

"You're back on the dot, old man! As a test flight it was perfect —from our end." He flicked his finger over his shoulder. "Bring brandy for the man! You look done in, Max. Come and clean up; then you can tell us how it went…"

Von Bek nodded, smiling wordlessly. It was almost perfect… but he had not realized just how efficiently he had been taught a new language.

Appeltoft had spoken to him in the voice-torturing tongue of the Yulk.

Sailing to Utopia